Andrea Bolter has always been fascinated by matters of the heart. In fact, she's the one her girlfriends turn to for advice with their love-lives. A city mouse, she lives in Los Angeles with her husband and daughter. She loves travel, rock 'n' roll, sitting in cafés and watching romantic comedies she's already seen a hundred times. Say hi at andreabolter.com.

Award-winning author **Jennifer Faye** pens fun contemporary romances. Internationally published, with books translated into more than a dozen languages, she is a two-time winner of the *RT Book Reviews* Reviewers' Choice Award and winner of the CataRomance Reviewers' Choice Award. Now living her dream, she resides with her very patient husband and Writer Kitty. When she's not plotting out her next romance you can find her with a mug of tea and a book. Learn more at jenniferfaye.com.

CARIBBEAN NIGHTS WITH THE TYCOON

ANDREA BOLTER

FALLING FOR HER CONVENIENT GROOM

JENNIFER FAYE

MILLS & BOON

First Published in Great Britain 2021
by Mills & Boon, an imprint of HarperCollins*Publishers* Ltd,
1 London Bridge Street, London, SE1 9GF

www.harpercollins.co.uk

HarperCollins*Publishers*
1st Floor, Watermarque Building,
Ringsend Road, Dublin 4, Ireland

Caribbean Nights with the Tycoon © 2021 Harlequin Books S.A.

Special thanks and acknowledgement are given to Andrea Bolter
for her contribution to the Billion-Dollar Matches miniseries.

Falling for Her Convenient Groom © 2021 Jennifer F. Stroka

ISBN: 978-0-263-29988-5

08/21

MIX
Paper from
responsible sources
FSC™ C007454

This book is produced from independently certified FSC™ paper
to ensure responsible forest management.
For more information visit www.harpercollins.co.uk/green.

Printed and bound in Spain
by CPI, Barcelona

CARIBBEAN NIGHTS WITH THE TYCOON

ANDREA BOLTER

MILLS & BOON

For Ramona

CHAPTER ONE

"*BIENVENIDO*, SENORITA. WELCOME to Recurso Llave Dorada—the Golden Key Resort."

The mustached man in a yellow blazer offered Luna Price his greeting as soon as she stepped out of the limo. As she did, her eyes quickly darted left and right so she could be sure she wasn't being observed. Force of habit. Even though she was here through an arrangement with the exclusive M Dating Agency, all of whose clients were apparently rich and famous, Luna wanted to be certain that she wouldn't be recognized.

Without meticulously done hair, makeup and styling, she hoped she looked like a typical tourist. The hat, dark glasses, simple sundress and sandals she wore should serve as help. Even though she'd been out of the media's eye for quite a while, she'd never forget the unforgiving judgment the press gave a film star's appearance.

"I am Juan Carlos Ortiz, Dorada's manager," the gentleman Luna stood opposite continued. Embroidered above his jacket's pocket was the resort's logo of two palm trees, one leaning left and the other right, with a gold key across them. "Kindly follow me to a private reception area reserved exclusively for our M guests."

That was a good start in ensuring Luna's privacy. "Gracias."

While guests milled about in the area through the wide-open wooden doors, which allowed the check-in area to feel like an extension of the outdoors, Juan Carlos gestured for Luna to follow him to the right. "I trust everything about your journey to us was satisfactory?"

"It was." Indeed, Madison Morgan and her M Dating Agency had thought of every detail to make Luna's trip pleasant, despite her own apprehensions. A discreet SUV had picked her up from her parents' ranch outside of Louisville, Kentucky, as a limo would have drawn too much attention, and the chartered airplane that departed from a private terminal had every imaginable comfort.

As was Madison's design, Luna was to spend a secluded week with a man she'd never met and knew nothing about. And she hadn't been told until the plane was soaring through the air that she'd be doing it in the archipelago of Caribbean islands known as Puerto Rico. This was how M did business, arranging ultraprivate rendezvous for the elite around the globe. Although the entire prospect made Luna uneasy, the exotic destination had her interest piqued.

"This way, please." Juan Carlos held open a door on the side of the building and Luna stepped through. It was a salon-type room with two wooden desks beveled with designs of pineapples, a symbol of hospitality, and plush armchairs with yellow upholstered cushions. Large paintings of native flora and fauna decorated the walls. Open windows gave the space a light feel. She quickly observed that, with one exception, the few other people in this private reception area all wore yellow blazers, identifying them as resort staff. Juan Carlos gestured to a desk, then pulled out a chair and invited Luna to sit, which she would have done had she not been stopped dead in her tracks. Because when she caught sight of the tall man across the room wearing a business shirt and trousers—the one person not wearing the yellow blazer—she was unable to move.

It wasn't just that he was good-looking, which he certainly was—in Luna's line of work, attractiveness was an everyday commodity, and she'd learned the hard way that it had nothing to do with a person's character. There was something different about this man, though—he had a stature and commanding presence that had little to do with his physical gifts. It was as if the entire room was centered around him, as the employees fumbled over themselves to take the small travel bag he held, an offer he refused. "Thank you, no," he said in a low baritone. Another tried to hand him a drink, but he shook his head in rejection. "Thank you, no," he repeated, with a bit of impatience in his voice now.

Juan Carlos presented Luna with a large bouquet of tropical flowers. "Once again, welcome."

As she brought them to her nose to appreciate their fragrance, the tall man who was garnering all of the attention glanced to her. While she'd already noticed his close-cropped thick brown hair and long-limbed muscular build, once he focused his emerald-green eyes on her, something tugged at her heart. "Gracias for the flowers," she whispered.

Instantly, she hoped against that he was not the man she'd been matched up with for the week. No, he was too innately impressive, too statuesque. The last thing

Luna wanted was to feel pressure to be perfect for a powerful man, one with expectations and specifications. It was that very thing she needed to stay away from. She was not here to please someone, nor was she open to wanting to.

But two things occurred to her as the man's pointed stare became impossible to deny and their eyes met. One was the unconfirmed yet somehow undeniable knowledge that they were, in fact, each other's match for the week. The second was that while his exquisite face did rival that of a Greek god's, there was pain behind his eyes and in the set of his jaw. There was much simmering under his surface.

Juan Carlos, sensing the scrutiny his two guests were bestowing on each other, said, "We generally introduce M's guests to each other once they've reached their villa but you two seem to have met." *Met* wasn't exactly the right word. Luna had consented to M's conditions that she would not so much as see a photo or hear the name of the person with whom she'd be spending the week until they arrived at their destination. She trusted Madison's ability to unite people who were not only compatible, but also shared the same goals for the match. Which meant that he wasn't here to meet the love of his life, either. That was good. Luna had made it clear to Madison that she was seeking a week of easygoing companionship and that was it.

"Yes, we have." The words fell trancelike from the green-eyed man's mouth. He removed himself from the staff huddle and stepped toward Luna, where he presented his outstretched palm for a handshake. "Charlie."

"Luna." Managing the enormous bouquet with one

hand, she joined her other with his. The contact with his large, thick-skinned hand gave off more sparks than she wished. Not finding him appealing at all would have been ideal. The seven days were supposed to be a safe getaway for Luna. A segue back into casual dating. An escape where she could just be herself, not worry about her image or her appearance or anything other than short-term relaxation and enjoyment.

So she had hoped that she wouldn't even find her match attractive or intriguing. That would have been the easiest way to proceed. Now, faced with the reality of a magnetic man with hurt in his eyes standing before her, Luna had the impulse to run back to the limo and immediately return to the hidden safety of her parents' ranch, where she'd been for the better part of a year. She knew that she couldn't, though, that it was time to move forward. And, what's more, she was ready to do so. But now, with this man in front of her, she had the instant suspicion that the next week was going to be different than what she'd bargained for unless she kept her guard up.

"Senor and senorita, if you'll come with me, a golf cart will take you to your villa. The luggage has already been delivered." Luna looked to Juan Carlos, almost silently pleading for him to get her out of this situation. As many strangers as Luna had to meet in her line of work, this would be far more personal. And, therefore, terrifying. Their villa? Had she been crazy in letting Anush, her best friend and personal stylist, talk her into this agreement? It suddenly seemed so.

As they moved toward the waiting golf cart, Charlie absentmindedly placed his hand on her upper arm to guide her out of the salon. She bristled. It had been a long time since a man had touched her beyond a handshake, and it was still something she wasn't comfortable with. It hadn't even occurred to her that this week might put that to the test, as well—whether or not she was ready for physical contact with a man. In any case, the feel of his fingertips was both scary and thrilling, and wholly unwelcome. She moved away.

Juan Carlos made sure his guests were situated in the back seat of the cart before he took his place in the front beside the driver, and then off they went.

"Where did you fly in from?" Luna fumbled to make small talk. She hoped she hadn't offended him by rejecting his guiding hand, but she'd be establishing as many boundaries as she needed to.

"Heathrow. I live in Buckinghamshire," he answered with a polite chill in his voice that didn't match the warm skin she could feel sitting next to her. "A little over an hour's drive from London." It was only then that Luna clearly heard his British accent. Madison and the M Dating Agency's policy was that participants had to put their complete faith in her abilities, as they'd learn nothing about their matches ahead of time. So all she now knew was that Charlie was English, had big hands and a second golf cart's worth of emotional baggage. He was obviously wealthy or he wouldn't have been able to afford Madison's hefty fee. What more would she be discovering about him, and when?

"Yourself?" he asked as if it required effort.

"Kentucky," she answered without going into the details. It was her childhood home and the place where she'd spent the past twelve months.

"American. Have we met before?" He studied her. "You look familiar."

"Senor and senorita, may I present La Villa de Felicidad?"

"Wonderful," Luna murmured.

Juan Carlos gestured with a grand sweep of his hand once the golf cart came to a stop in front of the secluded structure at the end of the resort's property. Through a gate and far removed from any other buildings was its own sparkling cove, and no doubt a private beach. Charlie hadn't lost the headache that had joined him on his flight, although he couldn't fail to notice the spectacular setting where he was to spend the coming week.

The sky was a soft blue under which the gentle waves of the Caribbean glistened in the sunshine. "Oh, my…" Luna let the comment slip as they exited the golf cart, and Charlie had to agree. He'd been told accommodations would be at one of the Golden Key Concierges' luxury properties but hadn't known exactly what to expect. They followed Juan Carlos into the villa—*into* being a relative term as the enormous living space was completely open, with fresh air flowing through a secluded courtyard on one side and the beachfront on the other.

"Where are the walls?" Luna asked.

Juan Carlos quickly showed them to a wood cupboard near the entrance that contained an elaborate control panel and electronic devices. "Each wall, as well as portions of the ceiling, are fully retractable. They also provide shading options and climate control for the hotter parts of the day. Please utilize these choices however you wish. May I give you a demonstration?"

"Thank you, but I think I can figure it out." Charlie Matthews, CEO of his own biotech empire, AMgen, one of the largest in the UK and Europe, ought to be able to figure out how to retract a ceiling.

"*Bueno*. Would you like a tour of the villa or would you prefer to explore it yourself?"

"Let's have a quick look."

"The lounging and dining area." Juan Carlos pointed from right to left. "If it's acceptable, your personal chef and butlers will introduce themselves a bit later to obtain your preferences."

"Fine."

"Shall I assume you'd prefer dinner here in your villa rather than at one of our restaurants on the property?"

"Yes," Luna said quickly.

Juan Carlos led them farther inside. "And may I present the master bedroom."

"There's only one bed," Luna blurted out.

"Yes." Charlie looked around, estimating the villa's layout, and dreaded to ask, as he hoped the resort manager would intuit the situation. "Where are the other bedrooms?"

"Only this sumptuous master suite, senor. The villa was chosen specifically for you by Ms. Morgan."

"It won't do for us," Luna interjected.

"I'm sorry, senorita. Ms. Morgan has made all of the arrangements. Perhaps you'd like to speak with her."

"We will," Charlie replied shortly.

"Either way, I regret to inform you that none of the resort's other accommodations are even close in regard to the luxury and privacy of this villa and, in any case, we have no vacancies whatsoever."

So, Madison had kept this trick up her sleeve. Even though he, and presumably Luna, had clarified that they were not interested in using this week for a romantic tryst, the matchmaker had her own ideas.

"Wonderful," he quipped sarcastically.

The journey, the ride from the airport, the overeager staff and now the prospect of a week with a stranger and one bed was all crashing down on him. He was ready for Juan Carlos to take his leave. There was to be no tipping or money exchanged during this weeklong getaway, as all costs and gratuities had been taken care of previously, so their business was done.

"I'll bid you adios, then. I am at your disposal for anything you need. The golf cart will be left for your use and you'll find a video with Ms. Morgan's suggested activities for your stay. I hope you'll find the accommodations spacious enough to meet your needs and that your week with us at Dorada exceeds your expectations."

Much as he wanted him to depart, as soon as the manager left, Charlie's stomach lurched. This was really happening. It had been his right-hand man, and AMgen's COO, Tom Khatri, who had suggested that Charlie undertake this M Dating Agency excursion. But now that he was here, he wasn't sure how he'd get through it. A week with a woman he didn't even know? And why did she look so familiar? He was sure he'd met her before. The awkwardness of being alone with her was already uncomfortable.

Luna was still wearing her hat and sunglasses but he could see she was a willowy beauty, tall and very slim. Her floral cotton dress was hardly what he'd have expected a client of M's to be wearing, as the agency catered to a population that likely shopped at the world's most select boutiques. After they stood facing each other in a silence that became excruciating, he finally asked, "Did I notice that you speak Spanish?"

"Enough to get by, *más o menos*."

"When did you learn?"

"I studied it in school. Living in Los Angeles, where there are a lot of different languages spoken, gives me a chance to stay in practice."

"Los Angeles? Didn't you say you arrived here from Kentucky?" That seemed a bit suspect to him. He'd been to the States enough times to know that Kentucky was quite different from California.

"I, uh… My permanent home is Los Angeles. I've spent some prolonged time in Kentucky that's now come to an end." If that had been an attempt to clear up the confusion, her tone suggested the opposite.

She removed her hat and sunglasses, allowing him to see her in full for the first time. Sun-kissed blond locks cascaded past her shoulders in waves, framing her face. And such a pretty face it was, with big blue eyes, flawless skin and perfectly bowed lips. It looked as if she was without makeup, another thing that surprised him given M's reputation for attracting the polished crème de la crème from every corner of the globe. Charlie actually quite liked that she appeared so natural. It reminded him of a casual comfort he used to know, and something he missed so much the tears he thought had finally dried up threatened to reappear.

Now that he saw Luna's full face and hair, the sense that he knew her nagged at him again.

He realized he was staring when she broke in and asked, "Do you speak any Spanish yourself?"

"To order in a restaurant, maybe. I suppose I'll need your assistance this week."

"I'll do my best." She licked her lips in what seemed like a nervous response. It was quite inappropriate that he found the move sensual, but he wished she would do it again.

He looked out to the blue water and clean sand, which was visible from throughout the villa. "Well, these surroundings could hardly be lovelier."

"Yes. I don't know anything about Puerto Rico."

"It's interesting that Madison doesn't tell the participants where their destination will be."

"Yes, my friend and stylist, Anush, made all the arrangements. She knew about the agency." Ah, she had a stylist. That sounded more like M's clientele. Although she made a point of calling her a friend, too. That didn't seem like the behavior of any of the upper crust he'd ever known.

"Similarly, my COO, Tom, handled the details on my end." Blather seemed the only option. He was so out of practice in spending social time with a woman—with anyone really—that he didn't know what to talk about. And she wasn't helping any, giving short answers as her eyes glanced all around the villa. She wasn't going to make this easy on him. He wondered what criteria Madison used for her matchmaking. Did she look for people who were opposite types from each other, or ones that were more alike? Because something beyond the comely features of Luna's face told him that she might have as many demons to battle as he did. "Let me try to reach Madison and sort out this lodging situation."

"Yes, thank you."

He pulled his phone from his pocket but the call went to voice mail so he left a message and then sent a text.

"We'll have to wait for someone to get back to us." He opened his carry-on bag and took out his laptop.

"What sort of business are you in?"

"I have a biotech company."

"Would I have heard of it?"

"AMgen. We're mainly in the UK and Europe."

"AMgen. Well, of course, I've heard of it. Hasn't everyone? Charlie. Right. I think I read an article about you in a magazine. Charlie Matthews."

"Yes."

A magazine. Was that where he'd seen a photo of her, as well? Madison had mentioned that public figures needing the utmost discretion often used her service. Luna? Luna? It hit him like a ton of bricks. "Luna! Of course. You're Luna Price! I've seen some of your movies."

Juan Carlos must have taken the tropical breeze with him when he left because the air had gone still. Luna knew she was imagining it, as she could see the glorious palm trees swaying outside of the villa. It was just the finality that she, Charlie, this resort and Puerto Rico were going to be a unit for the next week. And now he'd recognized her. It was one thing to agree to this adventure in theory and quite another to be standing in the middle of it.

"While I understand that Madison works with a very select clientele, I somehow wasn't expecting a movie star." He said it as if he was aggravated.

"Sorry to disappoint." She shrugged snidely.

Now that he'd placed her, here it came. Once people knew she was Luna Price, film actress, everything seemed to change. They gushed all over her and stumbled over their words, and started treating her as if she was some kind of otherworldly creature who didn't bleed red or have the same ten fingers and ten toes they did. While, at the same time, they examined her as if she was a product that they had to decide if it was worth spending their money on or not. Luna was, of course, grateful for the life of privilege her fame had brought her, but deep inside it never got easier to be constantly measured and judged.

"I didn't mean it like that," Charlie retorted. "I'm just a bit shocked."

Although she'd been on dozens of film sets, where she'd had to meet cast and crew members for the first time, and had interacted with hundreds of fans, the ineptness she was feeling now was somehow different. Maybe because Charlie Matthews appeared to have a distant and absolute power. Since people usually fumbled all over her, the dynamic wasn't something she was used to.

"So we've established it then," she spat out. "I'm an actress and you're a tech genius."

"Genius. Yes." He snickered.

"And here we are." Ugh, Luna couldn't think of a time when she'd felt more off-kilter. She and tall, handsome, prickly Charlie Matthews were to spend seven nights alone together? She'd just like to get through the next five minutes. "I assume that Madison explained to you that I'm not using her services to find a long-term romantic match."

"Neither am I." She couldn't snap that out fast enough.

"I'm only seeking a sort of transitional week of rejuvenation."

"Exactly. Transitional." How were they going to begin

that promised relaxation? Luna's shoulders felt as tense as coils.

"Which is why it doesn't make sense that she booked us a place with only one bed."

"No insult intended but I'm not comfortable with that."

"I understand completely."

His eyes met hers but then ricocheted around the lounging area of the villa, as if he was trying to fix on something other than her.

She decided to break the stalemate. "I've never been to the Caribbean. Have you?"

"No. Do you travel a lot for your films?"

"A fair amount shoot right in LA. Others in Canada. And then for a few others I've gone on location."

"That must be exciting."

"It has its moments. I've been very lucky."

She wasn't ready to tell him yet that the first movie she was going to shoot after a year off was starting up right after this week in Puerto Rico. Or why that was so. Although she had a strange sensation that she and Charlie might get to know each other this week more than she had anticipated. There was something about him she couldn't put her finger on that made her feel she might want to genuinely talk to him, and listen. He had a sort of seriousness that she liked. She might need to keep reminding herself that this was no time to get caught up in someone. She was taking care of herself now and was nowhere near being willing to trust someone—she might never be. But each time his eyes shot away, her desire increased to have them back. There was a lot of story behind his green orbs—of that much she was certain.

"What sort of travel do you typically do?" she asked, continuing to chat, her breath easing. "Oh, and shall we have a cold drink?"

Juan Carlos had mentioned that the villa was fully stocked. They stepped over to a bar area that was done in rich woods with a bamboo ceiling fan overhead. Both of them were careful not to move too near to each other. Atop the marble counter were clear cylinders filled with juices that had slices of fresh fruit floating in them. Behind the bar was a coffee setup, with beans and teas from around the world. There was a wide array of rums. Luna recalled once reading that Puerto Rico was famous for its rum production. There were other spirits and liquors, too, from tequila to gin to aged scotch. All sorts of sodas and mixers were visible through the bar refrigerator's glass doors as were at least a half-dozen bottles of top-of-the-line champagne, along with a visible compartment that displayed gallons of ice cubes ready to help chill the hot August day.

Luna knew that she was nervous and, as such, took such a scrupulous inventory of the beverages. She resisted moving on to the open kitchen area, where gourmet and local food and snacks were bound to be overflowing. Being around a lot of food was potentially challenging for her, so she'd have to be diligent about the techniques she used to keep from reverting to old behaviors. She squelched the bubbling feeling in her stomach that served as a warning sign.

"Those juices look inviting," Charlie decided after glancing over the options.

"Yes, one is guava and the other is orangelo, a combination of orange and pomelo," Luna informed him as she read the scripted cards placed in front of each canister.

"Pomelo is similar to grapefruit. That sounds like a refreshing blend. Would you like some over ice?" He took the lead and selected two tall glasses that had the resort's logo etched on them.

"Gracias."

The corner of his mouth ticked up. When he had said he'd need her assistance this week because she spoke a bit of Spanish, a squiggle had crept up her spine. She'd been able to keep any expression from registering in her face, being an actress and all. But the idea of Charlie obliged to her in any way shocked her with possibility. Made her think of people who relied on each other, who finished each other. Who had the kind of real-life connection that Luna only knew how to act out in front of a camera.

Charlie Matthews was probably not beholden to anything or anyone. Luna noted to herself that she'd better not allow even a moment of fantasizing that this weeklong dip into the waters of dating was anything else. It already seemed that was going to be harder than it sounded with Charlie. His stoic posture, with that straight torso, was already making her think about being in his embrace. Her head against his no-doubt taut and solid chest. She even imagined what her lips might feel like against his. She was sure his would be firm yet alive. Shaking her head a bit, she snapped out of that thinking, almost ready to laugh at her own imagination. Wow, she hadn't been alone with a man in a long time.

"The chef is coming by to serve dinner at eight?" he asked, already knowing the answer because it was written on an information note left on the bar. "It's after five now. Shall we enjoy the juice while we familiarize ourselves with the villa and then perhaps have a rest? It's been a long day of travel."

Bartender Charlie moved behind the bar and filled each glass halfway with ice, then poured the orangelo drink. It was already delicious, and she hadn't even tasted it. The juice didn't look half-bad, either.

She moved closer to him, although with the bar between them, it was as if he was the server and she the customer. But when he handed her the drink and their fingers brushed, the playacting ended there. It brought her body to attention. The touch of Charlie's fingers as he handed her the ice-cold drink felt like a key to a door that she didn't know was locked.

CHAPTER TWO

JUICE IN HAND, Charlie gestured for Luna to follow him so that they could further explore the villa's features. He'd mentioned taking a rest afterward and as soon as he'd said it, the vibrations around them changed, as if they both realized the implications of sharing this space. Charlie hadn't spent time anywhere with anyone in a long while and had spooked even himself with the thought of them *resting* together under the same roof. As they strolled from the airy and opulent living and dining areas toward the gigantic master bedroom, the realization that the sleeping arrangements were still unresolved pounded between his ears.

"That has to be the biggest bed I've ever seen," Luna quipped. She followed with a quick sip of her drink, which she gripped tightly with both hands as if it was a security blanket. With the walls retracted in the bedroom and the warm wind flowing through, locks of her hair floated a little bit this way and that way. Charlie was sure they would be like spun silk to the touch. Low in his belly, a charge ignited, one that had been dormant for as long as he could remember. No, that wasn't true. He remembered exactly when that part of him had turned to ash.

The bed had four wooden posts and was made up with colorful bedding, some in a bright red floral fabric and others in a muted green-leaf design. Two low armchairs flanked a round table—it served as a sitting area and was positioned to view the private courtyard secluded by tall hedges. In the center of the courtyard, a table and chairs sat next to a Spanish fountain. Off to the side was a sparkling swimming pool, with everything fully enclosed for use by only the two of them. Charlie had stayed in deluxe accommodations all over the world but this had to be the most lavish.

"You'll sleep in here, of course." Given Juan Carlos's report that there were no other vacancies on the property, he felt the need to reassure Luna. "If we don't change to another setup."

"A romantic hideaway all to myself. How ironic."

"You might enjoy the amenities." This was no easier on him than it was on her.

"Yes, I will. Thank you. I just meant... I don't know what I meant." Her lips, glistening from the juice, took another sip. "Since Madison knew we weren't interested in being...physical, it's interesting that she chose this for us."

"I counted six overstuffed sofas throughout that immense living-room area. I'm sure any one of them will make a comfortable bed."

"So...you plan to sleep in the living room?"

"If need be. Surely we're not going to sleep in the same bed." That came out harsher than he'd intended. Luna's head leaned back, as if she was dodging the words. Ironic romantic getaway, indeed. He was busy telling one of the world's most beautiful actresses that, under no circumstances, was he going to lie down beside her.

They moved on to the expertly appointed master bathroom and then the kitchen, with its top-of-the-line appliances. After inspecting everything, Luna said, "Juan Carlos explained when I arrived that we'll have a personal chef bring our meals or prepare them here."

"Yes, that's why I had suggested that we both rest a bit and then dress for dinner. Although since we're eating alone, should it be casual attire?" Charlie was again reminded that he didn't know how to act around a woman in an informal setting, and the impending dinner was feeling like a challenge. He was so out of practice communicating with someone unless it was about work. In fact, there'd only ever been one woman he'd cared to behave properly around, and with her everything had been natural and easy. He was the boss to a large staff of employees, but knew how to keep himself at a distance. His entire inventory of social manners needed an overhaul.

"Casual sounds great," Luna replied.

A couple of hours later, Charlie sat up from where he was lying on the sofa when he heard a voice at the villa's entrance. "Senor, it's Chef Diego here, may I come in?" Charlie rubbed his face with his open palms. He hadn't been woken up by the chef's call, because Charlie didn't sleep...ever. But he'd surprised himself. With the mild afternoon and the sound of waves ebbing and flowing at the shore, he'd achieved a meditation that had transported him out of consciousness. As he stood, he began to tuck his shirt back into his trousers, but then, on impulse, decided not to.

"Yes, Chef. Come in."

Diego wheeled a cart into the villa, and was followed by another staffer with a second cart who left after his delivery.

Luna strode out of the bedroom. She must have heard that their visitor had arrived. "Ah, you're ahead of me," Charlie said, pointing to her change of clothes.

"The rainforest shower is just marvelous." Charlie would follow suit after the meeting with the chef and absolutely refused to imagine Luna naked in the shower in the meantime.

"You look beautiful." He hadn't really meant to do more than think that sentiment, but he hadn't been able to censor himself in time.

Luna was a sight for sore eyes. She wore a long, straight midnight blue dress, as simple as could be. It fell like a column down her tall narrow body. She looked even more stunning than she had earlier in her sundress earlier. She was very slim, with neither womanly hips or large breasts. With those shiny blond waves loose around her enchanting face, and barefoot, she was the picture of unaffected beauty. It was still hard to reckon that she was a glamorous movie star who wore designer gowns to awards shows and diamonds from the world's most famous jewelers. Here, in this private retreat, she was unrecognizable. Which was apparently how she wanted it.

"I didn't know how to pack for this trip to an unknown destination. So I brought a little of everything."

"Senor and senorita, it will be my pleasure to be your dining manager while you are with us at Dorada. It was indicated on your reservation that both of you are interested in sampling the flavors of Puerto Rico. Is that correct?"

They both nodded. Charlie felt like he'd been eating the same five dishes his housekeeper prepared for him for years now, with him not caring enough to speak to her about expanding her repertoire. Food had been simple fuel—one thing tasted the same as the next. When Tom convinced him to fly off to an unknown destination under the M Dating Agency's direction, the promise of unusual food had piqued his interest. He was glad that Luna had confirmed herself as game, too.

"I've brought some samplings I hope are to your liking. May I start you off with Puerto Rico's signature cocktail, the piña colada?"

Charlie had tasted that drink, rich with coconut milk and pineapple juice, before. While delicious, he thought it too sweet and heavy for dinner.

"Diego, perhaps tomorrow. Can you suggest a wine for tonight?"

"Of course, senor. I brought a couple of bottles."

"I'm so hungry," Luna chimed in. "I can't even talk about food without eating some. Do you have any snacks we can munch on?"

"Camarones al ajillo." Diego removed a tray that was being kept warm on a burner from his cart. Luna wasted no time in grabbing one of the succulent shrimp with her fingers and biting in.

"Que sabor," she said, signaling her approval. "The garlic. And goodness, I needed some protein."

"With our heritage deriving from Spanish, indigenous Taino and the African peoples, we have a rich culinary tradition," Diego explained. "If I may serve it, I've made for you tonight one of Puerto Rico's most beloved preparations, *arroz con gandules*, a dish of rice, pigeon peas and a *sofrito* of peppers, onions, aromatics and herbs. Along with a slow-roasted *pernil*—marinated pork shoulder. And for dessert, coconut pudding."

"Sounds great," she said.

"Might I suggest this pinot noir?" The chef presented a bottle. Charlie read the label and nodded.

Diego went about setting up the dining table in the courtyard, which was now bathed in the glow of moonlight. Charlie's phone rang. "It's Madison," he told Luna and stepped inside, away from the chef, wanting to keep the conversation private.

"Yes, we arrived safely. But we are dissatisfied with the sleeping arrangements. Luna assures me she made the same thing clear to you, as I did—that we are not her for a romantic liaison."

"Charlie, I always book my couples into a master suite. Anything can happen," Madison replied.

"Nothing is going to happen."

"Didn't you agree to leave things up to me?"

"Yes, but I would prefer not to be manipulated."

"I'm sure you'll find a way to be contented."

He supposed he could insist she find another resort. But the sofa would really suit him fine. "All right, Madison."

"Just relax, Charlie. Have an open mind. Give in to the island."

He returned, frustrated, to Luna and reported what Madison had said.

"I'm going to take a shower. I'll claim the other bathroom off the kitchen. I'll meet you at the fountain at eight?"

"Sounds charming," she giggled with an innocent blush.

"It wasn't supposed to be."

After the words fell from his mouth, he wished he could have taken them back.

"The candles and the moonlight provide perfect lighting," Luna said as she and Charlie sat at the wrought-iron table and chairs beside the courtyard fountain.

"Says the cinema professional."

She snickered a little. Charlie hadn't figured out Luna Price yet. She was nothing like he'd expect from a movie star. As she fidgeted with the voluminous shawl she'd thrown over her sleeveless blue dress, she seemed almost awkward. Not the confident beauty she projected onscreen. Illusion, he figured. Smoke and mirrors. He hadn't seen many of her movies so he wouldn't assume to know her public persona, let alone her private one. Which wasn't to say that her attractiveness was anything but undeniable. In fact, under the moon she was almost unbearably lovely.

"The *arroz con gandules* is delicious," she said.

"I'd never heard of pigeon peas before, so when Chef Diego explained the recipe, I was apprehensive."

"I thought I'd heard of a famous old-timey dish called pigeon under glass but then I remembered it was pheasant under glass."

He chuckled. "Neither sounds very appetizing."

"No. They don't." She turned her attention back to her food and took several bites, which she chewed slowly and with determination. "Pigeon peas are not that different to green peas. I like the peppers and herbs in this dish."

"Very flavorful."

Her shawl slipped down one arm again, revealing a velvety shoulder that looked even nicer in the flickering of the candles . She quickly righted the covering, though in a self-conscious way, as if she'd accidentally revealed a part of her body she didn't want seen. Rather strange for someone whose likeness was displayed on megascreens throughout the world.

After his shower, Charlie had slipped into khakis and a new white T-shirt, one of the many items his housekeeper had bought when he'd sent her to buy him a tourist's wardrobe, unsure what he'd need. He felt odd in his bare feet on the stone courtyard tiles, having taken Luna's cue in not putting on shoes. It seemed almost intimate, something only people who lived together did. Like he used to do. He wasn't the newfangled sort of tech billionaire who reported to his office in a hoodie and jeans. It was a suit and tie for him every day he went into town, which he did as infrequently as possible. He knew his formality was likely off-putting but it helped him keep his reserve, keep up the appearance of someone in control even though on the inside he was in tatters.

"I have to admit, I've only seen a few of your movies."

"Me, too."

"What do you mean?"

"I rarely watch my movies once I've shot them."

"Really? Why?"

"Because I'd only see flaws and things I wish I could do over again."

"I don't think anyone could accuse you of having flaws."

She giggled in that adorable way again. Luna had a

kind of wholesomeness that continued to surprise him.
"You have no idea how many of my imperfections the
press and the worldwide web have documented well."

"Nonsense. They're all idiots."

Spearing some of the unctuous tender pork from his
plate, he studied her some more. He hadn't had dinner alone with a woman in ages, in years. The figurative wounds that never healed reminded him of why.
They made sure that if Charlie was enjoying himself or
even just having a positive thought, the gashes would
open again. Reminding him of his loss. Recollecting
the tragedy.

For the first time, Charlie wished the cuts could be
at least bandaged over for a bit of respite. He knew
that they would never disappear. But maybe it would
be good for him if he didn't have to experience the radiating pain every moment of his life. He knew it was
he himself who scratched at the sores, kept them from
fading. That was his choice. It had become all he knew.
The ache was so agonizing that it demanded his full attention, all day, every day. As a matter of fact, it's what
had kept him inside his house for all these years. Night
after night, just him and his anguish. There was almost
a twisted comfort in it, because there was no risk. It was
something he could count on. It was his vigil.

But tonight, looking at Luna's sexy shoulders as she
continually fought with that shawl that didn't want her
to be covered up, Charlie wondered if he could find a
salve for his pain. Maybe Madison had a point. Maybe
there was a chance that the warm embrace of Puerto
Rico could ease him, even just a little.

"Tell me more about your flaws," Charlie said, but
the words had come out all wrong. What he wanted

to ask was about how she handled being in the public eye. He knew needed to start interacting again with the outside world. Not long ago, Tom had insisted Charlie come into London for a face-to-face heart-to-heart, and had told him—as both COO and friend—that AMgen's investors were losing confidence in the sorrowful and reclusive CEO who scarcely left his estate. That they want a visible face for the business. That the company's messaging as innovators and limitless thinkers was losing credibility when the leader existed in seclusion. Some even directly said that he should be seen dating women. That idea was utterly overwhelming. Yet Charlie did understand that if he was going to keep his company strong he needed to move forward.

"Famous faces really are illusions," Luna said, breaking into his thoughts. "It might not be obvious to you but if you looked at a publicity photo of me next to how I look tonight, you might not think you were seeing the same person. When you hear it referred to as the glamour factory, that's no joke. It takes a whole crew to deliver Luna Price."

"Sounds exhausting."

Luna went completely silent. Charlie could have kicked himself. What a ridiculous thing to say to a woman who'd had so much success in her chosen profession. Tom was so right that Charlie was out of practice interacting. Perhaps it wasn't that he needed to become more social and at ease with people. It could be just the opposite. That he needed to relearn how to be a proper English gentleman. One who kept his thoughts to himself.

He hadn't put his communication skills to the test for a while. Maybe what had happened during those interminable nights alone in agony and loss was that he'd become someone incapable of bull. Someone who cut to the truth. It was his bluntness that had become disconcerting, not his aloofness.

Or maybe it was her. Luna. Even though he'd just met her, his subconscious had detected in her a link. That glaze in her eyes. Something was going on with her under the radar. She lived in Kentucky, yet she lived in Los Angeles. None of that made sense. Not that it was any of his business. "Luna, I'm sorry. I shouldn't have said that."

Her words came slowly and with an exhale. "Oh, no, you're right. It *is* horrible sometimes. The stress can be overwhelming. It's what led me to my…" She noticeably collected her thoughts and pulled up her shawl again. "My need to get away for a while."

This was supposed to be both easy and easygoing. Time to press the reset button. "Amen to that. After dinner, let's watch the video of suggested activities."

"After all," she said, "we're supposed to be here to have fun."

"Right. Fun." Charlie thought he might need to consult a dictionary. He couldn't remember the meaning of the word.

Once the last of the creamy coconut pudding had been consumed, Charlie and Luna regarded each other across the table. Conversation during the meal had been a combination of strange and fascinating. He'd asked some personal questions and she thought she'd done a good job of skirting what she didn't want to answer, a necessary skill she'd honed over the years. Although something inside her actually did want to communicate with him candidly, she hadn't really told him anything about her past or present. What witchery did Madison Morgan have up her sleeve? She seemed to have paired Luna with someone who sincerely touched her inside with every stare those dazzling green eyes bestowed.

"Would you like coffee?" Charlie asked, pointing to the thermos left by Diego, whose meal had left them wanting for nothing.

"No. Thanks." It was Luna's turn now to do the inquiring. Curiosity propelled her. "What motivated you to contact Madison's agency?"

"It was all my trusted COO, Tom, who has been with me since AMgen's beginnings."

"Just a buddy looking out for a buddy?"

Charlie blinked a couple of times. "I haven't done much dating in the last ten years. In fact, I haven't done any."

"Ten years. That's a long time. I'd think as a leader of a successful empire, you'd have women clamoring to make your acquaintance."

"Some opportunists have tried, I suppose."

"I know all about that."

"I'm sure you do."

"Ten years. Hmm. Is it too personal to ask, were you in a relationship before that?"

His jaw ticked. She could tell he was making a decision about how to answer. "I was married. At a very young age."

"Oh, I see. And things didn't work out."

"Not exactly." His eyes dropped to his empty dessert bowl.

She didn't know what, or what not, to say. "So after ten years, why now?" Luna pivoted away from more direct questions about Charlie's marriage, which he clearly didn't want to be interrogated about.

"Frankly, it's a business move. The reclusive — what was it you called me earlier—tech genius rattling around in his mansion isn't acceptable to our newer investors. And if we're going to continue to grow the company the way I promised, I need the expansion and shareholder support."

"What did you promise?"

Charlie's brow furrowed. "Do you always ask such probing questions?"

"Actually, no. I have to make superficial *nice-nice* with lots of people, all the time. And answer ridiculous yet personal questions."

"I'm intrigued. Such as what?"

"About the image. As I was telling you before, no one cares about the real me. They want to know about Luna Price. What is her day like? Does she wake up before dawn to exercise with her trainer? What does she eat? What kind of shampoo does she use? What famous actor or director will she be seen out on the town with?"

"I don't know how you handle the scrutiny."

"I don't. That is to say, I had to take a break from all of it. That's why I've been in Kentucky."

"Ah, so I've been hiding in Buckinghamshire and you in Kentucky."

"I was attending to some personal business."

"I see." He leaned back in his chair, professional enough not to probe further.

"Tech billionaire. Married young, divorced young. You're an interesting case."

"I didn't divorce."

"Sorry?"

Did that mean he was still married? Luna was sure Madison would have verified his marriage status. Did she work with clients who were still legally married but long separated from their spouses? It didn't much matter to Luna, as she was not looking toward anything further than this week, but she hated to think about other M clients being paired with someone who was still in an unresolved relationship. What did he mean by *hiding*?

He bit out, "Perhaps we've had enough getting to know each other for the evening. Let's watch the video."

And so, the two people who obviously had a lot of skeletons in their closets moved from the courtyard to inside the villa. A group of sofas and armchairs was arranged in a cluster for the best vantage point of the enormous wall-mounted TV.

Luna sat at the end of one sofa, her feet under her bent knees. Charlie hesitated but then sat at the other end of the same sofa. Using the remote control, he quickly found the channel they'd be using for their stay, which offered options such as dining and housekeeping. It was apparent that anything they required would be quickly proffered.

"*Bienvenido.* Welcome to the Recurso Llave Dorada," the narrator of the video greeted. And thus began a montage of the leisure pursuits and sights that Madison suggested they might enjoy during their visit.

"Madison asked me what types of activities I like participating in. Did she ask you the same?" Luna looked over to watch Charlie in profile as he kept his eyes on the screen. My, but he was attractive. His gravity was born of intelligence—that much she could tell. But that chiseled jaw almost worked to his disadvantage because it was distracting in its appeal. She bit her lip in embarrassment as she secretly pictured kissing her way across his perfect bone structure. That wasn't one of the activities on the menu.

"I enjoy culture and music." Charlie clicked on that option and the video showed people at an outdoor concert dancing to the Afro-Caribbean music Puerto Rico was famous for. Would she and Charlie dance together this week? Suddenly, she desperately wanted to. Next was a video traveling through the streets and past various historic monuments in the city of Old San Juan.

"I'm looking forward to visiting there."

"Yes. I see Madison gathered our preferences and chose destinations accordingly."

"I said I enjoy water."

He gestured outside, where the ever-present sound of the waves lapping onto the shore was a simple serenade. "Our own private beach."

And he clicked on the water-sports option for a montage of every conceivable form. One could sail, use Jet Skis, snorkel, scuba dive and paddleboard, just to name a few. A happy couple embraced and kissed under a waterfall. At that image, Charlie stood and sneered, "It's getting late. It looks like we'll have plenty to keep us occupied while we're here."

Clearly, he'd had enough of her company. She'd have her hands full this week, learning the cues from this unusual man. She stood and said, "Okay. I guess that's it then. I'll just go into the bedroom as we discussed."

"Yes, I'll be perfectly fine out here and there's the extra bathroom so I won't disturb you." Somehow, she was already disturbed. It felt a bit sad to be so brusquely banished to the bedroom. Rejected.

She headed toward that extravagant master suite, where she'd be sleeping alone. Was she secretly wishing this was, in fact, a romantic rendezvous to be spent with the perfect match with whom she would fall in love? If she was, she'd better get that idea out of her head right away, because that was definitely not on either of their itineraries. Still, as she moved it felt like a slow march toward emptiness. Her rational side told her it wouldn't feel that way once she got used to him. This was a beautiful paradise where she could breathe and just be with a man, and not worry about what he thought of her. She'd never see him again after this. That was the point. She needed to appreciate it as such. "Good night, Charlie," she said as she began to round the corner.

"Luna," he called before she was gone.

"Yes." She turned around to face him.

"I'm not divorced. I'm a widower. Ten years ago, my wife and baby daughter died."

The breath in her throat stilled. "Oh, my gosh. What an unimaginable tragedy." Her heart cracked for him. Before she knew it, she started to move back into the room.

But he dismissed her instantly. "Good night."

CHAPTER THREE

"THERE'S COFFEE," CHARLIE announced when Luna emerged from the bedroom in the morning. He was perched on a stool at the granite-topped island in the kitchen with his tablet open to company business. Luna's tan bare legs caught his eye. They were long and graceful, and she moved barefoot across the floor like a gazelle.

"What is this?" She pointed to a black thermos and stone mugs sitting on a wicker tray.

"Café *con leche* Dorada. That was the server's description when he delivered it."

"Have you been up long?"

Charlie would have laughed at that question if the answer wasn't so pathetic. Of course, he'd been up long—he'd barely slept a wink. Which was no reflection on the comfort of the sumptuous sofas or the villa's open walls that brought a pleasant coolness in the wee hours. No, it was that he hadn't slept in a decade, not really. Oh, he dozed and sleep did overtake his always ticking mind on occasion. But he never slumbered heavily, never woke feeling refreshed and certainly never experienced the optimistic sentiment that a new dawn had arrived. That was his lot—to be wide-awake. On guard.

After his world changed forever on that snowy winter night so long ago.

"Yes. I called for breakfast and told the kitchen that unless we notified them further, they may choose our menus so that they include selections of traditional cuisine. I hope that's acceptable to you, otherwise we can certainly change it."

"No, that's great. My only request is that I eat at set meal times and have snacks available when I need them."

That struck Charlie as surprisingly rigid for an island holiday. He supposed that actresses both worried about their weight and were used to fitting in meals during film shoots. She was smart to have a routine. While Luna was very thin, he knew there was that old adage that the camera added weight. After she'd explained the glamour-factory standards she was held to, Charlie could hardly conceive of so many eyes on his appearance. Tom was the only one who had ever said anything to him about his, and that was just to suggest that Charlie dress down from the full suit and tie every time he went out. Which was why this morning he had chosen shorts and a loose linen shirt. He couldn't tell if the grey jersey T-shirt and shorts Luna wore were pajamas or morning loungewear. He did notice that she was not wearing a bra. A little twitch in his gut responded to that observation.

"There's fruit, eggs and *mallorca*, which are Puerto Rican sweet bread rolls. I can attest to their deliciousness."

She poured coffee and sipped from one of the mugs. "Oh, wow, I could get quite used to this."

Charlie's eyes widened. He knew Luna was only

referring to the unusual coffee, which was rich, just a bit sweet and frothy with steamed milk. But somehow, her words brought a special meaning to his mind and got him thinking about what it might be like to *get quite used* to greeting someone in the morning. It might make sleepless nights more bearable, knowing there was someone to rise with once morning arrived.

"Would you like to snorkel today?" He was ready to make a plan. That would give him less time to mull over what his life wasn't. He was here with Luna to relax and recharge, and that was it. They might as well try to have a pleasant time.

"Sounds good," she answered in between bites from the plate she'd served herself.

Charlie had already downloaded the app that they'd use this week to his devices. With a couple of taps, he booked a boat to take them to a snorkeling spot. After changing into swimsuits and cover-ups, they slid into the golf cart and he drove them to the dock. A small private boat, preloaded with equipment plus some other provisions like towels, snacks and cold drinks on ice, awaited them. The captain helped Luna onto the deck of the pristine white boat, Charlie following right behind. They took seats on a comfortable bench covered in turquoise-colored leather.

The sky was bright and the water shimmering. Once the boat had reached a steady pace Luna looked pointedly into his eyes and asked, "Do you want to talk about it?"

"What's that?"

"Last night. When you said good-night. You told me about your wife and child. I didn't get a chance to fully express my sympathies."

He couldn't maintain eye contact so his gaze drifted to the waves that the boat cut through. His late wife, Amelia, would like this, to see that he was out on the open water, in the sunny air, rather than cooped up in his mansion with the curtains drawn, head burrowed in work under artificial lighting. He forced—indeed, forced—himself to glance back to Luna, whose eyes he could feel on him.

"Thank you."

"Does that have something to do with why you're a client of M?"

"According to my trusted team, I've grieved for too long. Apparently I've become lost in my hermit lifestyle, and our investors and stockholders are nervous about the future of the company."

"Is the future of the company what's important to you?"

"Why wouldn't it be?" he barked.

"Sorry," she said, recoiling. "I didn't mean anything by that. Only that you lost your family. Some people might let their business fall to the wayside after something like that."

"AMgen has always been a promise I made to my wife," he retorted.

"I'm being too nosy."

"Shall we just talk about the weather?" he chortled to himself. He knew that Tom was right—it was time for him to either resurrect himself or truly be put in a grave beside his long-gone wife and baby. "Ten years were more than enough to spend in mourning."

"I can't imagine how you've functioned after the accident. I think I'd fold up into myself."

"That's exactly what I've done. Yet somehow I grew the company from my cemetery of a mansion, where I concentrated on my work day and night, and nothing else. I told Amelia I'd see my vision through. It's only that vow to her that has kept me going."

"I'm sure she'd be very proud of you."

He cocked his head. Proud. Yes, she probably would be. He owed his accomplishments to her. She inspired him. When they'd married at nineteen, he promised he'd give her a life filled with security and joy. And, indeed, that's what they'd had. Until fate stole it away from them.

Was it actually possible for him to start relating to people more? Maybe build something, someday, with a new woman? Nothing serious, but someone to help him see light where there was only darkness. Last night, or maybe it had already been morning, long after he'd heard any sounds coming from the bedroom suite, he had been lying on the sofa, staring at the ceiling. And he'd thought about what he'd said to Luna and what she'd shared with him. About the pressure of the public eye. About the never-ending scrutiny. Of course, she had a blessed life to have reached that level of success, but he could tell she was fighting her own inner battles. That made Charlie feel less alone. For the first time in ten years. It was somehow both a comfort and a shock to be with her.

The boat stopped once it reached the coral reef that was a renowned snorkeling spot. "I'm excited," she said as the captain came on deck to fit them with the masks, snorkels and fins they'd need. Once suited up, they lowered themselves into the water. As they submerged to see what worlds thrived under the sea, Charlie acknowledged that he hadn't done anything like this in an eternity. Couldn't he allow a little bit of adventure back into his life?

* * *

Under the water with an English tech billionaire. Luna could hardly believe the dichotomies in her life. Here she was after a year spent at her parents' ranch in Kentucky, with her daily therapy and coaching appointments, and Anush staying there with her for moral support. Soon she'd be returning to her life in Los Angeles, where her fame and fortune rested on the box-office count of her next movie release or latest magazine cover. And at the moment she was submerged in the Caribbean with this somber widower, who was as troubled as she was.

The undersea life surrounding them was magical. Brightly colored fish swam in schools, sometimes just a few in a group, yet other times what looked like hundreds of babies. Turtles waded by the alive reefs. It was wonderful to ponder their existence, which was far different from the lives of humans. This was good for her soul, Luna concluded.

Every so often, she and Charlie would turn to each other as if to comment on what they were seeing. His swath of dark hair swooshed as he swam. She couldn't help admiring the way the angular muscles of his back flexed as he moved through the water. He reached to pull her toward a display of boldly hued parrotfish. Holding hands with him under the water and watching the awe-inspiring show in front of them was a poignant experience she wouldn't soon forget.

"That was fantastic," she exclaimed when they popped their heads above water and removed their equipment.

"Incredible." He nodded. With the captain's help they returned to the boat deck. As they dried themselves with towels, the captain put out a spread of cold water and snacks. Luna whisked on her cover-up. Charlie slung a towel low around his hips and remained shirtless, the water droplets glinting on his golden skin, reminding Luna that she hadn't been physical with a man in ages. The recovery program she'd been going through demanded that she focus only on herself. But the dearth had been easy because she could no longer stand the type of men she'd been dating. Men she was sure would have little interest in her if she hadn't been a celebrity. Troy Lutt being the latest of that ilk. Most everyone in Luna's life was around to try to capitalize on what association with her would bring. Troy had taken that to a new low.

She most definitively wasn't planning to bring a man into her life. Though it was impossible for her to divert her mind from imagining touching Charlie's smooth-looking skin, and running her hands down the physique she'd watched so deftly glide through the water. She bit back a giggle at her private little thoughts, so opposite to her declared intention for the week. It was a sneaky yet harmless bit of amusement, though.

Once she and Charlie sat down on the boat's bench again, they both stretched out their arms and basked in the glow of the sun. After they were quiet for a bit, Luna couldn't help returning to the conversation they'd started earlier. Like he'd said, how much could they talk about the weather? Curiosity toward one another was natural. "Explain to me, what is your exact purpose for this week with the M Dating Agency?"

"Tom advised that I've become intolerable. Apparently a CEO who works night and day but rarely sees his staff in person, doesn't remarry or at least date, who attends shareholder dinners and meetings via video, is problematic."

"I suppose that makes sense. They want to know you're flesh and blood, and not a myth." For her, it was the other way around.

"Ghost is more like it."

He said that so matter-of-factly Luna winced. His loss was unfathomably sad. "That you've accomplished all you have is a testament to your devotion."

After he seemed to stifle the thoughts Luna wished he'd have voiced, he continued, "I agreed with Tom that I'd start leaving the house more."

"Which, naturally, begins with a week in the company of a stranger in a mysterious destination not of your choosing?"

He let out a belly laugh so robust it drowned out the sound of the boat's motor. It was a laugh that she hoped to hear from him again this week, selfishly, because she adored the sound of it. "In a roundabout way, yes. Since I met you yesterday, these are certainly the most words I've said to another human in probably a year's time. I need to work on my social skills."

"Ironic that the man who needs to talk more was paired with a woman who gets paid to speak."

"Yes. I've been wondering how Madison goes about making her matches."

They each opened a bottle of ice cold water and sipped. He was here to gear up to move forward. So was she, but forward to what? It was more like returning to something. To LA. To that life that had almost dragged her down to the bottom of the ocean, where she didn't think she'd ever breathe oxygen or see daylight again. Thank goodness she had gotten help in time.

The strangeness of this trip took hold of her, made her tense up. What on earth was she doing here with a man she'd just met? Was she ready? Yet maybe there was safety in this situation. Maybe she was to have this short interlude with Charlie, and then they'd go their separate ways, continents apart, and never encounter each other again.

She was so attracted to him. It was a giddy and alien sensation. She could imagine leaning over and kissing his full pale lips. Tucking herself into that outstretched arm and feeling the strength of his embrace. Further still, she envisioned sharing that sprawling bed at the villa with him, where they could be naked in the truest sense of the word, unbridled, uncensored, unselfconscious.

Charlie finally interrupted the silence. "What is it that you're here trying to *get over*?"

Even though she wanted to tell him everything, she chose to tell him nothing.

After the day on the water, Charlie and Luna returned to their villa and showered. They reconvened on the front patio, where cushy lounge chairs beckoned them to relax and watch the setting sun from their private beach.

"Chef Diego inquired whether we want him to bring dinner or if we'd enjoy cooking with him," Charlie said, reporting the message he'd received.

"That sounds nice, actually." She raked her fingers through her still-wet hair. The golden locks tumbled down from her scalp with bends and swirls. For the first time, it occurred to him why hair was described as wavy. Luna's mimicked the motion of the waves, which struck him as amazing. She looked so lovely stretched out on the lounger, with the long legs and pointed toes of a dancer. There was something profound about her organic beauty, a testament to the heavens. Charlie hadn't paid much attention to the attractiveness, or lack thereof, of the women around him. Because, frankly, there hadn't been many. An occasional AMgen employee who'd catch his eye, or someone from the mansion staff. But, overall, he'd been deadened to the charms of the female gender. He feared Luna had awoken a sleeping titan.

"Do you cook?" he asked, to get his mind off those shapely legs, which were on display given the short dress she'd put on.

"No."

"Never?"

"My mom has been cooking for me in Kentucky. In Los Angeles, I use a food delivery service. Three meals and two snacks arrive daily, all very organized."

"We mere mortals sometimes hear stories about the catering services on film sets overflowing with food and drinks all day and night during shoots."

"Oh, that's real. And the endless discussion and gossip about who ate what and how much. It's a badge of honor. The less you eat."

"The less you eat. There was a time in history when the more you ate was the status symbol."

"It's ridiculous. The press reporting on someone looking *relaxed* or *robust* or having a *new style*—all just thinly veiled code meaning they've gained weight."

"It must take special skills to have everyone's eyes on you all of the time."

"It messes with your mind. It did with mine, anyway."

"What an enormous amount of strain that must be."

"Senor and senorita, how was your day?" Chef Diego arrived in a golf cart and parked it next to the one Charlie had been driving. "Did you see many beautiful fish today?"

"It was spectacular, thank you," Luna replied with a smile as she swung her silky legs over the side of the lounger and rose. Charlie stood, as well. They watched as the chef unloaded his wheeled cart with the provisions he'd brought. They entered the villa, and Charlie was still surprised that he was staying in a structure without exterior walls. He'd felt no need to activate the glass enclosures, as the climate was delightful and, obviously, in their gated, private piece of paradise they didn't need to worry about intruders.

The three convened in the gourmet kitchen. "With your permission, tonight may I prepare for you Puerto Rico's official cocktail, the piña colada?"

Charlie and Luna looked at each other, her blue eyes twinkling. "Please," he answered.

They watched as the chef loaded pineapple juice, chunks of fresh pineapple, coconut cream, both dark and light rum and ice into a blender. "My personal touch," he explained as he squeezed in some lime. After whirling it into a thick, frosty emulsion, he poured it into shapely tall glasses, then garnished each with a triangle of pineapple and served them. *"Con gusto."*

"Deliciosa. The sweet and the cold are so good together," Luna exclaimed. "It's a vacation in a glass." Her tongue flicked the top of her lip to grab a drop, the movement not lost on Charlie. He stunned himself with his next thought. What it might be like to perform that lip-licking duty himself. And maybe to put a bit of the icy drink onto Luna's no-doubt warm skin, per-

haps behind her ear and drink it off as it melted. Was he going crazy? He never, ever, had thoughts like that. What was Puerto Rico doing to him?

"With your approval, tonight we will prepare one of the island's best-known dishes, *mofongo*."

"That's with *chicharrón* and green plantains?" Luna asked.

"Senorita, you've tasted it before?"

"No, I read about it in one of the magazines on the coffee table."

The three of them chuckled.

"Senor, I'll give you the honor of peeling the plantains and slicing them." The chef passed Charlie a cutting board and a knife. "These look like bananas, but the taste is much different," he said as he handed Charlie a bunch of the fruit. The skin was tough and thick. After peeling, Charlie began slicing them into disks.

"Senorita, if you'll heat the olive oil in the skillet."

Once they'd fried and drained the plantains, Chef Diego presented them with a mortar and pestle. "We call this a *pilón*. We will mash the plantains with the *chicharrón*, and garlic, and a little broth, as needed." The chef began placing chicken strips onto a sizzling grill. "*Chicharrón* are pork rinds that have been fried and seasoned."

Luna began the mashing, seeming to enjoy the task. "What's the history of this recipe?"

"Ah, good question. We believe it is an adaptation of the West African dish, *fufu*. Often you will see *mofongo* served in a rounded half-sphere shape. So we'll use these bowls as our mold." He showed them the glazed clay bowls.

"Why that shape?"

"As we tamp the *mofongo* into the bowl, we're going to scoop out the center and fill that with the grilled chicken. Then we will unmold it and surround it with hot broth, and as you eat you discover the chicken inside. Various fillings can be used."

Charlie was getting hungry from the descriptions and aromas. Once the *mofongo* was finished, the chef departed, and he and Luna took their plates to the courtyard again, as there could hardly be a lovelier place than under the twilight sky.

They also brought out the platter of fresh fruit that had been provided and the *arroz con dulce*, Puerto Rican rice pudding resplendent with raisins and spices.

As they ate, Luna regaled him with stories about other exotic destinations she'd been to. Charlie had traveled plenty himself for work, but chitchat didn't come as easily to him, so he appreciated her keeping the mood light while they ate. It was as if all of the years in his self-imposed isolation had caught up with him. There had been so much sorrow and anguish, so much grief and stabbing pain, that he'd forgotten there were other emotions. Being with Luna it registered how truly lonely he was.

CHAPTER FOUR

"Would you like to go for a swim?" Luna asked once they'd finished their dinner. Old habits forced her through a mental process before she made the suggestion. It was dark now in the courtyard by their private pool. Charlie might be able to make out the outline of her body, but no one was going to pass judgment on her figure.

Even though they'd been out on the water snorkeling earlier, she'd quickly shrugged off her cover-up before they'd dove in and, likewise, slipped it right back on when they were done. It was frustrating that her brain had drudged her through all of those calculations, but as she'd learned in therapy, they were merely floating thoughts. While she couldn't seem to stop them, they didn't have to have any power over her unless she let them.

"That would be...nice." Charlie sounded tentative. But it was too early to go to bed and they hadn't made any other plans for the evening.

They cleared the plates and put everything on the cart, which Charlie wheeled to outside of the villa entrance as arranged. That way none of the staff would come through during the night, and a new cart with breakfast would be magically delivered in the morning.

"I'll just go get changed," Luna said and headed for the bedroom. Luckily, she'd brought several swimsuits. All modest one-pieces, of course. No bikinis for her. She threw on one of the terry-cloth robes with the Dorada logo that had been provided and belted it around her. Back outside, there was a cabinet filled with fresh towels near the pool.

Charlie strode out in swim trunks and nothing else. While he talked about his social awkwardness and she'd noticed that conversation with him could be choppy, he didn't seem to have any physical inhibitions. Lucky him, she thought.

She tossed her robe onto a chair and they got quickly into the pool. He dipped under the water and came back up, his hair dripping. "Ah, good idea, senorita."

"Muchas gracias."

She swam to the far end of the pool and he met her there, and then together they swam back. It was so relaxing to take lazy strokes, one after the other, like a moving meditation. Anush had been right—this getaway was what she needed. An escape with nothing that needed her attention. Except for a developing problem. A six-foot, green-eyed problem that was moving through the water next to her. Because after a day on the snorkeling boat and then cooking and eating with him, she was enjoying Charlie's company far more than she ought to.

This week was meant to include as much pretending as one of the films she'd acted in. Part of Anush's impetus was to help Luna prepare to date again, but she'd sworn she wasn't going to waste her time on the losers and users she tended to meet. In any case, she'd have her hands full reestablishing herself in LA. Dating wasn't going to be in the picture anytime soon.

For Charlie, he'd be going home to his English estate, hopefully with the spirit he'd need to socialize
more, maybe date. This week was a sort of warm-up
for both of them. She needed to cancel out the already
developing feeling that it was going to be hard to say
goodbye to him.

They swam to a bench in the pool, where they sat
and looked up to the moon in the star-filled sky. "Did
you know Luna means moon in Spanish?" she asked
softly.

"Are you of Spanish descent?"

"No. My mom just heard it and thought it was pretty."

"Like you." The world deemed her pretty, too. If she
was wearing the right outfit and had the right makeup
and hair and so on. Somehow, though, Charlie saying
so touched her. A smile crept across her mouth.

"What were you doing in Kentucky for a year?" he
asked, not allowing for any meaningless blather.

"I—I got so far away from myself that I couldn't see
my way back."

His eyes met hers in a direct stare. Now it was him
who wanted to say something, but he seemed to be
having trouble getting it out. "Yes," he whispered, as if
he couldn't articulate more. His words echoed hers. "I
know the feeling of not being able to see my way back."

Their faces inched closer together as they sat on the
bench in the pool. Were they about to kiss? In an instant, she wanted to. More than anything in the world.
One inch closer still, and their eyes stayed joined in a
lifeline. The intensity was almost too much to bear. He
was hesitating. Maybe she should make the first move.
Tilting her head slightly, she leaned in.

She saw the arch in his shoulders as his back stiffened. His body language was clear. If she had thought the swell of yearning for each other was mutual, she'd been very wrong.

It was another long night of lying on the sofa, staring out of the villa at the night sky, but with sleep not coming. This time, Charlie had so much on his mind it was no wonder slumber eluded him. Luna had tried to kiss him in the swimming pool after dinner. What's more, he had most certainly wanted to kiss her back. To claim her tender lips and feel them move under his. To hear a catch of desire in her breath. The mere thought of that made his blood run scalding hot. It had been a decade. Ten long years, during which he'd scarcely even thought of intimacies with another woman, and never imagined that was something he'd ever have again. He assumed that was in the past for him. As if his hormonal system, his entire sexuality, had died along with his wife.

It was a subconscious reaction to lean away when it seemed a kiss with Luna was looming. Nothing like that was supposed to happen between them and he was glad he didn't act on the moment. It was too sudden, too shocking. But he couldn't stop ruminating over it. Welcome or not, Luna was digging up the mental and emotional grave he'd been buried in.

Quite early in the morning, Madison Morgan called, thankfully ending his restless night. "Charlie, I'm calling to inquire how things are going. Did the bed arrangement settle itself out?"

"We're sleeping separately, as intended."

"For now."

Charlie could only nod to himself at her single-mindedness. Sadly, he'd be proving her wrong but he was curious. "Can I ask you something? How do you go about matching people up?"

"That's my own secret formula, Charlie. As a mastermind, I'm sure you understand."

"Still, I wonder why you chose Luna and I as a pair?"

"Your question tells me you should leave your intellect in your luggage and just let things flow for the week."

"If you've done your work to know me at all, you'd know that's not in my character."

"Exactly, Charlie. Exactly." And with that, Madison ended the call. Charlie sank farther into the cocoon of the sofa where he'd spent the night replayed Madison's words.

"Hello," Luna called out softly when the sun had moved higher in the sky. Charlie rose and ran his fingers through his hair. She appeared in a long beach dress made of a golden fabric. With her hair as flowing as the garment, she was a mystical vision from the heavens. A throb in his loins made him feel like an animal. It was an exhilarating, virile sensation. He liked it.

"Let me get the cart with our breakfast," he said and hurried to the entrance, wanting to be the provider.

"Thank you," she replied ever so sweetly as he wheeled it in. A vase filled with flowers adorned the breakfast offerings.

After coffee, they dug in to the selections, and the ubiquitous and welcome tray of fresh-cut fruit. If she'd been upset by his unwillingness to kiss her last night, she didn't let it show. Then again, she was an actress, after all. "What would you like to do today?" He grabbed his tablet, ready to punch in their requirements.

"Another day on the water, perhaps? I'd like to try paddleboarding."

"Your wish is my command." With a couple of taps, he organized it so that someone would meet them at the shoreline with the equipment.

"And let's have the chef just deliver our dinner. Whatever he chooses. We had enough food decisions to make yesterday."

Soon enough they were at the waterfront. As they were both novices, a Dorada staff member named Martino, who was dressed in shorts and a polo shirt with the resort's insignia, gave them a few tips. He showed them how to use the paddles, and they practiced until they had the feel for it. Then they kneeled on their boards and headed away from the beach as Martino left.

"Do you want to try kneeling, sitting, lying prone, or standing?" Charlie said, keeping his board as near to Luna's as he could.

"I want to stand."

He did, too, but he also wanted to watch as Luna stood first. He felt better able to assist her if she needed it from where he was. As instructed, from her kneeling position she brought up one knee to her chest and flattened her foot on the board, then repeated the action with the other. With that stance, she was able to stand fully erect and stabilize herself. A huge smile spread across her face. "I did it!" Her enthusiasm was infectious, so Charlie repeated the same steps, until he stood tall on his own board. "Once you get the hang of keeping your balance you can just look out to the horizon while you paddle."

"It's marvelous." Charlie could hardly believe himself. From a mansion with dark heavy curtains he rarely drew open to walking on water with a gorgeous companion in the Caribbean. He couldn't be further from his norm. He was beginning to wonder which one was him, and who he wanted to be. Amelia wouldn't have liked what he'd become over the last decade. An outsider. A loner. Without excitement, without joy. He thought he owed his endless mourning to her and Lily, as a testament of his love for them. But walking in the memorial garden he'd planted for them on the estate's grounds was often the only time he saw sunlight. They deserved better than that from him.

They coasted quietly, both soaking in the sea and sun. Neither noticed an unexpected rough wave coming toward them. "Yikes!" Luna exclaimed and was promptly knocked off her board by its force. Her board skidded to one side, her paddle toward Charlie. He was able to squat and grab it.

Luna tumbled under the water, tossed by the undertow. Charlie kneeled to speed up his paddling, racing to get to her before the situation became perilous. The water wasn't terribly deep but he didn't want her to get hurt. He was able to reach his arm to her and sighed with relief when he felt her hand grab it and clutch on to him.

Anguish stabbed into him. The arm he gave Luna was the figurative arm he had never been able to extend to his wife and baby. Intellectually, Charlie knew there was nothing he could have done to prevent the accident that took away the world as he knew it. He hadn't even been there. But that didn't stop him from being haunted by the fact that he hadn't been able to save them.

He hoisted up Luna until she could get her knees

balanced on his board. "All you all right?" he asked right away to be sure.

"Oh, yeah." She laughed. "I guess we're beginners, after all. We should have seen that coming. Wait, are you okay?"

"Why wouldn't I be?"

"You're the one who looks white as a ghost."

"Thank you. That was very noble of you to react so quickly," Luna said to Charlie a bit later, as they were lying on a blanket atop the sand. She'd been surprised that Charlie looked so shaken after she'd taken the tumble off her paddleboard. "Thankfully, I'm a fairly competent swimmer."

Had he been afraid for her safety because he'd come to care about her in the short time they'd known each other? It was a charming notion, but she doubted it. Her potential peril tapped into something else in him, that much was obvious.

"I suppose in Los Angeles, you're in swimming pools and the Pacific Ocean quite a bit?"

"When I get the chance. I had been working a lot before my hiatus." Charlie handed her a cold bottle of tangerine soda from their picnic basket along with an assortment of seasoned nuts in a container. "Although *hiatus* is a polite word for what I did."

"You said Los Angeles had become too much for you."

"When I fled to Kentucky, I was two days from beginning a new film. I violated my contract and left a lot of people in the lurch."

"You said you were due to start another film after this week in Puerto Rico."

"Yes."

"So your reputation wasn't ruined to the point that people didn't want to work with you." She nodded her head, appreciating the support. Charlie Matthews might be a sad man, but he was a kind one at the same time.

She couldn't help recalling last night in the swimming pool. When she'd almost kissed him. It felt so right until, in the blink of an eye, it felt so wrong. And now those impulses were moving through her again. Pulling her toward him. She'd be lying if she didn't admit that his assist when she was swept off the paddleboard had been welcome, even if she didn't need it. No man had ever really cared for her well-being.

"True," she replied, agreeing with Charlie's assessment that her career hadn't been irrevocably damaged by her sudden departure, as the reason was purposely never explained to the parties involved. "I've done a great job of hiding my feelings for years."

"That's the spirit."

At that she chuckled, and Charlie did, as well.

"I suppose it'll be good to get back to work. This next one is an action blockbuster film. I play the love interest to the main superhero."

He shook his head back and forth. "This is terrible to admit to you, but I don't line up to see those big-event movies when they're released. I can report, though, that half of London does. They buy advance tickets and merchandise and create a frenzy. From a business standpoint, it's quite a phenomenon."

"And made me very wealthy. I'll tell you, though, someday I'd like to make more personal movies about ordinary women with real-life super powers."

"I'm sure you will." Another vote of confidence from him. Luna had better watch herself. A billionaire who had nothing to gain by sucking up to see what he could get from her could be a risky attraction. She didn't want to leave Puerto Rico with a broken heart.

Once the afternoon sun had lowered and they'd had their fill of mastering paddleboarding, they returned to the villa and showered. On a whim, Luna put on a slinky silver dress with spaghetti straps. She'd normally throw a scarf or light cardie over it, because every inch of her body she'd ever revealed ended up as someone else's concern, so she'd learned to cover up. Not that something as simple as a pashmina stopped the scrutiny, but at least they weren't discussing her skeleton. Tonight she was feeling comfortable enough around Charlie that she didn't feel the need to cover up.

The way those brilliant green eyes took her in when she emerged from the bedroom was all the validation she needed. Around him, she was the least self-conscious she'd ever been. She'd had only the briefest fleeting thoughts about her body when they were paddleboarding, which was huge progress for her. "You are, er, enchanting," he stuttered out, all the more adorable because he was awkward with the compliment. He looked awfully good himself in a black shirt not tucked into the jeans that were snug around his muscular legs.

They sat down in the dining room to eat the dinner Chef Diego had left them. *Pollo guisado* was a delicious spicy chicken stew. Dessert was a small chocolate cake in the shape of a heart, adorned with candied edible rose petals. The sight of the cake caused a catch in Luna's throat. That was a cake for lovers to share. The staff would have no way of knowing that she and

Charlie were here for what could only be described as self-improvement. In a way, for Luna it was the culmination of her treatment.

As she looked at the cake, she said, "I want to tell you about Kentucky." She needed to expose herself to him. To voice the words that she'd kept secret for so long. Doing so would cement her recovery. And he was the perfect person to talk to. A CEO with his own problems who lived half a world away from her. Someone she'd never see again after this brief interlude together.

"Okay."

"As I was expressing to you before, issues around appearance and perfection are common in my world. In order to compete, which is what it sometimes feels like, I had started to restrict the food I ate. Obsessing on it, really. It took me over."

His brow furrowed with concern. "It's unfortunate it went that far."

"Yes, it definitely snowballed when the paparazzi started to comment on how much weight I'd lost—positively of course, saying how enviably slim I was. In reality, though, my body weight had dropped so low that I hardly had the energy to get out of bed every day."

"Ugh," he growled, "disgusting that anyone would make *your* body *their* business at all."

"And then it reached a breaking point when I man I was dating, Troy Lutt, took some photos of me when I was at my lowest weight and sold them to the tabloids."

"I'd like to wring his neck."

"Yes, it taught me that people will sink to unimaginable levels for their own gain."

"Luna, I can't even fathom how horrible that must have been for you."

"I couldn't function. And yet the press ran those pictures as if I looked great. When I saw them, I knew I was looking at someone very ill, even though that's not what the world saw. I didn't want to put a name on my problem. I just wanted to consider it an occupational hazard that I'd be able to handle."

"Did you?"

"No. Thank goodness for my stylist, Anush, who, over the years, has become my best friend. The more she tried to point out that it had become an issue, the more I tried to push her away. I kept my family at a distance, too, but they knew. Anush kept on it, though, until I had to admit that I needed outside help."

"Thank you, Anush, whoever you are."

"She assisted me in arranging everything. A recovery program that wasn't far from my parents' ranch in Kentucky. My mom and dad were supportive and grateful that I was able to get professional support in time."

"And now?"

Luna took a breath before she answered. "I completed an intensive program for treatment of anorexia nervosa." There, she'd said the words out loud. The medical diagnosis. "I can now recognize triggers before they cause me to take regrettable actions. It's something I'll have to manage for the rest of my life but I know I can do it. We don't know each other but you'll have to believe me when I tell you that I wouldn't have been able to sit here and enjoy a meal a year ago."

"Thank you for sharing something so intimate with me, Luna."

It was incredibly liberating to tell the story to someone outside of her bubble. It had been a dark road she traversed, but she'd made it to the light. She felt bare but enormously relieved. Her adrenaline was running, giving her the courage to try again what she'd started last night in the pool. This time, when gravity brought their faces together, neither of them withdrew. Instead, they allowed their lips to meet, touching and then leaning away, touching and then leaning away. Her eyelashes fluttered uncontrollably. And then their lips parted and their tongues mingled, and Luna swooned under Charlie's kiss.

CHAPTER FIVE

"I NEED TO come up for air," Luna said as she removed her arms from around Charlie's neck after they'd been kissing for several minutes. Her move threw him into disorientation, so captivated had he been by her soft lips. She brushed her hair back off her face and swallowed hard. "I haven't kissed someone like that in a long time."

"I'll bet it's been longer for me than it has for you," he said as he brought the back of his hand across his mouth as if to wipe off what had just happened.

"You haven't been with anyone since your wife died?"

"Absolutely not." After the first year, old friends and colleagues had tried to fix him up with women they knew. Said it was healthy for him. He politely refused every time and they'd eventually given up. The loss of his beloved wife and child had left him not even curious about dating again. Amelia was the only woman for him. Now, at thirty-two, he was finally open to questioning his self-imposed exile. Charlie had even felt the spirit of Amelia come to him in the darkest hours of torturous nights and tell him that he needed more than what he'd whittled his life down to. "That was part of the impetus for this week with the M Agency. To remember how to socialize again."

"For me, too."

He had to admit to himself that he smarted with rejection when she'd broken the kiss. Before his brain had a chance to say no, he'd gotten lost in the pillowy sensation of her full lips on his, each of his hands on either side of her face. "I've forgotten what kissing like that felt like."

"So, what did it feel like?"

"Good. Dangerously good." He was grateful for the smile that admission brought, lightening the awkwardness of the moment. "Just for my education, did I kiss you or did you kiss me?"

"I believe it was mutual."

"I don't think it can be mutual. One person has to make that final move to initiate contact."

"I think it was you."

"No, I think it was you." Another welcome chuckle.

"Shall we agree to disagree?"

"And make a pact to be sure it doesn't happen again?" That fell out of Charlie's mouth as natural as day. Really, he was getting the sense he might like to do a lot more kissing of Luna's succulent mouth. And not just her mouth, either. Those inklings had been so suppressed in him, he could hardly believe that they were surfacing. Yet they were. Things were moving too fast. Maybe it was, in fact, time he opened to dating again. To sharing touch, physical intimacy. But it would be a slow process. This week was meant only to slip the key into the lock. He wasn't ready for the gates to open.

She'd probably experienced a tiny jolt of rebuff by his suggestion. That was okay. Better a little misunderstanding now than something much bigger later. "Of course," she murmured.

Revealing her eating disorder to him couldn't have been easy. He couldn't begin to understand what that agony must have been like for her. He hoped she wouldn't think that had anything to do with him suggesting that they didn't tempt fate with any more physical contact. "Not that I don't find you extremely attractive." He was hopeless, making a mess of his words.

"No, I understand. It was a moment. It's passed."

All squared away then. So why was Charlie at full-on war with his arms, which were fighting to wrap themselves around Luna's shoulders again? Eager to reinitiate the splendid meeting of their lips and tongues joined in that merging that made the world around him melt away. To bring his lips to her elegant neck, to the divot between her breasts that he bet smelled as fragrant as the flowers of the island. To take his mouth further still, into the secrets of her very being.

That he was in close company with a woman at all was hard to fathom. He'd so forgotten the pure charm of a woman, the fundamental differences that completed yin to yang, Adam to Eve. How Luna moved, with a limber slink that struck him as inherently feminine. How unspeakably soft her skin was. And what she was stirring inside of him—a primordial pull toward her, making him want to be both predator and protector at the same time. Was he ready for an awakening? Was it the right thing to do?

At last, he refocused enough to ask a question. "You've said your dating life has been under scrutiny as much as your appearance?"

"Oh." She cleared her throat. "Yes, the paparazzi

are almost as interested in who I'm seen with as they are with what I'm wearing. I go out with men who are in the entertainment industry that I've met on set, or sometimes my team matches me up with someone else who is single. Like Troy. My *publicist* fixed me up with him and then he embarrassed me publicly. There's irony for you."

Charlie wasn't able to understand what Luna's life was like. Evenings spent with men she didn't even know. Is that what he was supposed to be doing with new women? "Do you find that you get along with them?"

"I can pass an evening with someone. Invariably, they're looking to leverage being seen with me to further their own careers. The whole thing is riddled with insincerity."

"I'd imagine so." He studied her again, wondering if this rich and famous and troubled woman longed for basic things, like genuine love. Children. Like what he used to have. "Have you ever really cared about anyone you've dated?"

"To be honest, no. Very few people look at me and really see who I am inside. Like I told you, they see Luna Price. A thing. A commodity."

If he was with her, he thought, he'd show her every day that he cared about her. The woman, not the image. She deserved that much. What a strange predicament her life must be. No wonder she'd developed unhealthy behaviors.

In a natural sync, they brought the plates into the kitchen. He was still recounting the kisses they'd shared, and thought he might for the rest of his life. They'd been smart enough to recognize that they'd acted on impulse and wouldn't do it again. It was best not to confuse their intentions for the week. Still, he was reeling. It was more than just the possibility of opening up to a woman again, after he thought he never would, that had him in tumult. It was Luna specifically—she was reaching down into his soul with her own truth, which was terrifying in its starkness.

"It's nice to have this time with you, Charlie."

"Is it?"

She gave him a questioning look. Had he said the wrong thing again? "I'm going to bed. Good night."

"Good night, Luna."

Before she left the kitchen she lifted up on tiptoes to plant a silky peck on his cheek. As he watched her walk away, he bought up his hand to the exact spot that was radiating from where her sweet lips had touched it.

Charlie watched as Luna lean back and took a sip of her juice. It was another picture-perfect morning in their private courtyard. Equally scenic was his beautiful companion, in a gauzy dress that hid nothing of her lanky physique, all planes and angles. The unplanned kisses they'd shared last night hadn't lost their prominent place front and center in his mind.

"What does the company name AMgen represent?" She folded up one knee, pretzeling herself in the chair, and probably didn't realize how provocative that looked. The twitchy response in his center was proof.

"The AM is for Amelia. And gen, as in generation, innovation. I was a young man when I started the company."

"You married young, too."

"Amelia and I were schoolmates. We were together from the time we were teenagers. Married at nineteen, poor as dirt. We used the little bit of money we got as wedding gifts from relatives to start AMgen in a tiny office on Old Street in London. Amelia ran things and kept the books."

"And look at your company now."

"She grew up with nothing, raised by a single mother. I told her I'd give her everything she could ever dream of, and that our children wouldn't want for anything. That I'd be bold, take my ideas as far as they could go."

"The business grew quickly?"

"Yes. Every bit of money I made, I put back in. I was able to hire more employees and lease large office space. An unheard of ascension for someone my age, really. Then Amelia had a wobbly pregnancy so she stopped working in order to rest. When Lily was born, we were on cloud nine. We had it all."

He felt a veil of stone weigh down his face, even under Luna's compassionate watch. His had been an idyllic story to tell. Until the tragedy. Until the part that turned everything upside down. Until what was important was stolen away by a thief in the night.

"Charlie, I'm so sorry your happiness didn't last forever."

"It was a car accident at Christmastime. The roads were slick and icy. Amelia and the baby had been returning from a visit to her mother's house." He'd replayed the story endlessly, told it to countless psychologists and counselors in the beginning. It never got easier. "I was at home at the time. It was a trip she'd taken a hundred times, even in winter weather."

An exhale whooshed out of him. Would the gruesome details ever recede into the distance?

"Go on."

"The driver of the other car had an excessive amount of alcohol in her system. Slammed into Amelia's car at a high speed. My wife and baby were killed instan—" He couldn't finish the sentence. He didn't need to.

Luna got up from her chair and went to him. Such an unfamiliar gesture, yet he was grateful for an offer of affection. Still sitting, he wrapped his arms around her waist and pressed his face into the side of her hip. The loneliness he'd emotionally stifled for so many years beat within him. Sorrow overtook him. Perhaps the floodgates had opened a bit after last night, when Luna told him about her own deep struggles. She combed her fingers through his hair. Her pure and gentle consideration was a salve. Neither spoke for a long while.

"So, you see," he finally said when his breathing flowed clearly again, "I want to uphold my promise to my wife and child, to continue to grow, to challenge, to lead. I'll do whatever it takes. It's my way of keeping them alive. I'll never remarry or love again."

Luna sat propped up on pillows in the middle of the gigantic bed in the master suite. A beach-read novel lay on one side of her, the script for her next film on the other. She wanted to review her lines. Her phone and the TV remote controls were scattered on the bed, as well. The large flat-screen on the wall ran a sitcom without sound.

Earlier, in the courtyard, she'd witnessed a drama far more powerful than anything her profession could have produced. No movie, symphony, painting or any other art form could have expressed the gravity of raw emotion she'd seen when Charlie told her about the death of his wife and child. From the minute she'd met him, the suffering behind his green eyes was evident. Only now, she knew the exact specifics of why. As he recounted the early days of his marriage and the forming of his company, it was as if invisible bullets were shooting through him. He contracted here and there, jerked this way and that as he told the story with tiny, almost unperceivable movements that hadn't been unnoticed by her.

Afterward, she'd moved toward him on impulse, compelled by his pain to want to comfort him. Human to human, with no motive or forethought. It was the least she could do, the right thing to do. He'd clutched her tightly for a short moment, needing her as a pillar, as she'd guessed he might. Quickly enough, though, he finished and dropped his arms. Had he made himself too vulnerable? Or was it that the burden of grief he'd been carrying for ten years already knew only to rear itself in short bursts? Afterward, he said he was tired and wanted to rest a bit, a late-morning siesta. Alone in *his* portion of the villa, of course.

She imagined him stretched out on the luxurious sofa he'd claimed as his bed. *Hmm*, she thought with a wry smile, *did the sofa know how lucky it was to have him on top of it?* Those explosive kisses they'd *accidentally* shared still ricocheted through her. The power of his lips, coveting her, ushering her into a haze she didn't want to wake from. A yearning pulsed within her. Today, as he spoke of his undying love for his wife and baby, a longing she had never recognized began bouncing around in her.

Sprawling back on the pillows, Luna watched the ceiling fan swirl. The devotion he had described was nothing she'd ever known. Maybe she actually did hope for a man to love her, and whom she could love back. She was twenty-eight years old. It was time she made some decisions. What would it be like to have mutual admiration and respect with someone? To give and to receive. To hold one up when the other was down and vice versa. For someone else's best interests to be hers. That she'd been able to confide in Charlie about the anorexia felt like an enormous step. What would it be like to further share burdens with someone, along with joys?

CHAPTER SIX

LUNA'S PHONE BUZZED. "It's Madison Morgan. I'm checking in to see how things are going."

"It's unusual to be in such romantic surroundings
when neither of us are here looking for anything on-
going." She surely didn't need to tell the matchmaker
about the ups and downs and intimate forays that had
already occurred.

"And you're absolutely sure about that?"

"Yes." She answered definitively even though she
was no longer sure at all. "I'm here to reset on what's
important. And Charlie is here to get comfortable being
out there in the world."

"You know all about that, Luna. Help him out."

She didn't exactly understand what Madison was
talking about, but somehow Luna pictured her as a for-
tune-teller wearing a turban and staring into a crystal
ball.

Later that day, Luna decided to give Charlie a little
visual demonstration of her public skills. Maybe Madison was right—that was something she could help him
with.

"I'm Charlie Matthews. Who are you?" he joked
when she sashayed into the living room. Still lounging

on the sofa, he sat right up and rubbed his eyes with the heels of his hands.

"I told you. When I put *her* on, she's like a whole different person."

"You look positively…untouchable." When he paused, she'd thought he was going to pay her a compliment, but his tone was anything but complimentary.

"This is what the public and the press want to see. I'm larger than life," she exclaimed with a toss of her hair. "Supposedly some kind of aspiration."

"Uh-huh?"

She had given herself a head-to-toe Luna Price makeover before she exited the bedroom. "Let me take you on a tour from top to bottom." She sauntered to him with an exaggerated sway to her hips and zhooshed her hair with a widespread palm. "First, the hair is blown out with a handheld dryer. Next comes a straightening iron for sleekness. Then a curling iron for *unnatural* natural waves."

"But your hair is already wavy, isn't it? Or at least it has been for the last couple of days. Why would you straighten it to curl it?" Shirtless on the sofa with his own hair tousled, she had to get her focus off how sexy he looked in order to continue.

"Yes, but *actual* natural waves can't be relied upon, dah-ling. What if there was humidity in the air?" She picked up a lock and twirled it around her finger. "Or one curl was out of place? Disaster of epic proportions, don't you know?"

"I see." He smiled at her cheekiness.

Charlie's jaw had all but dropped open at her display. She wanted to cheer him up from the suffering he'd told her about over the last couple of days. Plus, if he was ready to date again, he'd probably be interacting with glamorous women befitting his billionaire status. Truth be told, she wanted to put herself to the test, as well. Had she really learned to put that self-awareness about her body in a proper place, where it wouldn't cause her so much pain? Was she ready to go back to stardom and the responsibilities that entailed? And was there a chance she could juggle that while relating honestly to a man?

Charlie fixed his gaze on her face, squinting to study the trickery she'd applied with a chemist's skill.

"Foundation makeup, administered so thoroughly that there isn't a spec of my face that hasn't been smoothed over until flawless."

"You're already flawless."

If she wasn't wearing so much makeup he might have seen her blush. "Eyeliner, several shades of eye shadow chosen from a complementary color palette, false eyelashes and a half gallon of mascara give my eyes that smoky look ready to attract anything they survey." She turned away from him, then snapped her neck sideways so she could shoot him a slit-eyed smoldering gaze over her shoulder. He fell backward onto the sofa as if he'd been shot. They both laughed.

She returned to her tutorial, gesturing to her face. "Brows have been enhanced. Bronzer added back the glow to my skin that the Puerto Rican sunshine had given me—"

"But the makeup had taken away," he interrupted.

"Wonderful. You're learning."

"Fascinating."

She mimed applying lipstick. "Lip liner followed by lipstick followed by lip gloss."

"So they'll be no kissing?" *Gulp.* There it was, mention again of that mind-bending kissing over the heart-shaped cake they never ate. The kisses that weren't supposed to have happened but that she couldn't stop replaying.

Back to the task at hand. "Certainly not. Mess up this work of art?"

"Of course, never."

She ran a hand down the length of her body. "Makeup applied everywhere the clothes don't cover. Not a freckle, mole or mark shall mar this perfection."

"It's—it's not the makeup that's perfection," he stuttered adorably.

"Luna Price devoted herself to reaching fame and fortune," she began, using a documentarian's narration, as if she was describing a herd of wildlife. "From as far back as she could remember, little Luna wanted to perform. Her mother used to sing to her, instilling in Luna a wish to express herself. Ruth Price had sung in school choirs and the high-school spring musicals, but lacked the confidence to pursue her interest professionally. Once young Luna had the same leanings, Ruth encouraged her to study acting and take seriously the talent she displayed."

"Hmm. How interesting."

"Next, what you don't see about the illusion." She continued her demonstration by grabbing a pinch of her dress and pulling it outward, just to let Charlie hear it snap back into place when she released it. "A secret undergarment from here—" she gestured under her bra line "—to here." She indicated above her knees. "That smooths and shapes me."

"What is that made of?"

"Something highly elasticized."

"Is that uncomfortable?"

"I can hardly breathe."

"Torture."

"But look." She curtsied. "No unsightly lumps or bulges."

"Aren't women intended to have lumps and bulges?"

"Not in Hollywood." It was fun not to take everything so seriously for a minute.

"Right."

"Luna's father, Jack, ran a small ranch. He was bemused by his daughter's playacting in the living room, and singing and dancing along to pop videos. Both Jack and Ruth only wanted their daughter to be happy, whatever road she chose."

"They sound like good people."

"Now, if you'll forgive me for being so personal, next comes a bra that basically begins pulling my skin upward from my knees in order to give me this—" she mimed cupping her own breasts "—cleavage. Inserted are silicone cutlets to add volume."

"So that's not all you?"

"Nope."

"Cutlets. What a term."

"And as you can plainly see, a simple black cocktail dress." She circled around to give him the full effect of the dress, which was skintight. Everywhere. "That costs more than some people make in a year."

"It's a little tube of black fabric."

"After earning a degree in drama from a state university," she went on, "Luna ventured to Los Angeles, like millions of other hopefuls, taking her shot at the limelight. She worked as a waitress, a delivery driver and at a cosmetics counter before she began to win small roles in films and television. With the help of a hardworking agent, scripts came her way and she was able to ascend to the top of her field."

"That's really remarkable. The odds must be one in a million."

His praise was different than what she heard from fans or read online; he acknowledged that she deserved everything that came to her. There was so much jealousy in LA. Yes, she'd had luck on her side but there had been many years of hard work.

"And finally—" she wiggled her fingers and then pointed downward "—constant manicures and pedicures. Deeming my feet worthy of stiletto sandals encrusted with Swarovski crystals."

"How can you walk in heels that high?"

"*Very* slowly. And on the arm of a beefy guy in a tuxedo for stability."

"I'm exhausted. How long does it take you to look like that?"

"A couple of hours. But worth it, no?"

"No."

She cocked her head in question.

"I mean, you're absolutely stunning," he explained. "No doubt about it. But…"

Oh. Was Charlie Matthews going to be just like the crowd in Los Angeles? Always looking to find flaws?

"I only meant that, to tell you the truth, I can't imagine you looking any more beautiful than you do coming out of the shower in one of your beach dresses with your hair blown by the sea breeze and no makeup concealing your creamy skin."

Tears blinked in Luna's eyes. No one had ever told her

that she looked beautiful without the Hollywood facade cloaking her every day. Since her career had taken off, she'd lived with that inch-by-inch examination of her from head to toe. That scrutiny had led her to a deadly relationship with nutrition, lest the naysayers find the imperfections they were looking for.

"Charlie," she said in a hushed tone with a bobble in her voice as she sat down beside him. "That's the nicest thing anyone has ever said to me."

Charlie didn't exactly understand why Luna looked like she was about to cry when he'd merely mentioned that she was prettier in her natural state before all of the piled-on enhancements she'd just demonstrated. He'd clearly pushed a sensitive button. "Well, you are fab-u-lous either way," he said, mimicking a glamorous voice to try to get her back into the jovial mood she came in with for her show and tell.

Dare he admit he was enjoying himself with her here on this weeklong adventure? They seemed to be able to quickly toggle from solemnity to silliness and then back again. To connect, really connect, with someone after so long was far more poignant than he expected it to be. Were he to return to England with the eventual goal of socializing with women, he wouldn't expect it to be a repeat of either the conviviality or the candor he was sharing with Luna. It was a fact that actually had him a bit worried.

While she did look glitzy in her movie-star makeup and dress, it was almost hard to reconcile her with the woman he'd been getting to know over the last few days. The Luna who was starting to mean something to him. Certainly Charlie had no intention of feeling for a woman ever again. Faded memories were all he'd held in his arms, and so it was to remain until he took his last breath. Perhaps this week was making him see that dinners and even physical intimacy might be possible again as long as they didn't touch his heart. Yet he was finding himself attached to Luna. Which could only bring him harm.

But the woman behind the lipstick was so alluring, he had an odd impulse to pull her onto his lap, wipe off all of the gunk and kiss her again like he had last night. To smell her fresh skin, not the perfume emanating off the makeup and hair products. To again burrow down into the authentic her, down to her soul. But these were more thoughts that were most definitely not part of the week's agenda.

A clench squeezed through his body at having her sitting beside him right now, he in only shorts that allowed the taut fabric of her fancy dress to brush against his bare leg. Having her in such close proximity was testing his will. He didn't like it and he liked it too much.

"All right. I just wanted to show you Luna Price in her full regalia. How about if I change back into something comfortable?"

He was curious how she'd even gotten into such an elaborate outfit all on her own. She was a pro, that's how. But he definitely found himself wondering about all of the undergarments she had described. Silicone cutlets to enhance her breasts? In the swimsuits and leisure wear she'd worn while in Puerto Rico, he'd had occasion, maybe more than once, to glance at the outline of her breasts. They were lovely and certainly needed no augmentation. Other than his hands holding them, that is.

Certainly, she should free herself from the confining garment she had explained. How did that work? he wondered. Did one simply step into it and roll it up on the body, then to emancipate from it, reverse the process? Why did it sound like a contraption that might be better off being battery-operated? What about remote-controlled, so that he could press a button and watch the piece roll off Luna and he could see her glorious body naked and uncontorted? He resisted a smile at his own imagination. Maybe he should get into complex women's undergarments as an AMgen expansion.

Next, he tried to picture the amount of products it might take to remove all of the heavy makeup she wore. Although those fire-engine-red lips were a classic symbol of female beauty, he longed to again see the dusty rose of her undressed mouth. He thought about washing her face himself, a soapy cloth lathering away all of the obstacles to her radiance. Standing behind her in front of the mirror, he'd lightly move the cloth in circles around her face, using special gentleness around her eye area. Then, pressing himself into her from behind, he'd bend her forward over the sink so that he could rinse her face over and over again with warm water. When all of the facade had been washed away, he'd grab a fluffy towel to pat her face dry. Then she'd be naked in every sense of the word.

Envisioning all of that was causing a throb in his loins. A wake-up call to that entire part of himself that he hadn't explored in so very long, he was convinced it was gone. He was as afraid of it as much as he welcomed it, alarming in its absolute power. Confused, annoyed even, he got up, strode right through the villa, out to the courtyard, and dove straight into the deep end of the swimming pool without saying a word.

By the time he got out of the pool, Luna had washed up and changed into a T-shirt and skirt, and had brought food out to the courtyard. She sat at the table spearing her grilled seafood with pasta, having started eating while he was still swimming. Charlie's mood had soured during the swim. He'd gone from having that pleasant eroticism he'd experienced thinking about ridding Luna of that costume she'd put on, which had led him to want to cool off in the water, to now being brought back to the dark cellar where he usually spent his days. He joined her and chomped listlessly on the food, knowing he wasn't being good company.

Once he'd begun wallowing in his grief again, aware of the blood having drained from his pallor, he neither had anything to say nor the voice to say it in. Sure, he could lose himself in the work of designing new technologies for medical advances. Alone with ideas in his extensively equipped home office, he could envision, create and problem-solve. But remaining emotionally consistent out in the world was a science he no longer had any aptitude for.

These last few days with Luna had been frightening. Because he'd vowed to never, ever rely on anyone again. Most definitely never risk a loss so great it would swallow him alive for a second time. And now investors and shareholders were involved in his personal business? Was it up to them to decide that he should date or remarry?

Most unexpectedly, Luna had pulled on his heartstrings. Her honesty, intelligence and humor had brought a light to his eyes that he thought had been extinguished forever. In the wee hours, when he imagined Amelia coming to console and advise him, he never told her phantom that he was too scared to let love back in. Because what if it was snatched away again, as she and their beautiful baby had been? There was too much uncertainty. He couldn't make the leap of faith.

He did understand that his solitude wasn't healthy for him. So he needed to get through this week with Luna and then perhaps he'd ask an attractive coworker to dinner in London. Not someone like Luna, though, who was summoning dangerous feelings—dangerous because they were real.

"You're sad," she said, as if she could sense his distance.

"I suppose."

"That's okay." How gracious she was. Far more than he was.

What he didn't want to say was that being honest was too hard. And, for that matter, too unfamiliar. He'd spent the better part of ten years in silence. Sure, there was the discussion with the housekeeper about the bedsheets. There were powwows with Tom and the other high-ranking staffers at AMgen. But it was always about the business at hand. Tom had long tried to reach out to him but Charlie had kept him at bay.

He'd seen the grief specialists after Amelia and Lily were killed. Whether they had done him any good he couldn't say. Tragedy was tragedy. There was no silver lining, no looking on the bright side. Time didn't heal the wounds. Every absurd clichéd phrase of comfort had meant absolutely zero to him. A shadow of a man, he'd marched forward nonetheless, one foot in front of the next. And now he had the next battle, to save himself from running AMgen into the ground.

He stared out to the hedge that enclosed the courtyard. The foliage reminded him of the memorial flower garden he'd planted on his estate. He'd installed a stone bench engraved with the names of his wife and daughter, to replace the white lawn chairs that had been there. With his gardener's guidance, Charlie had planted the flowers on his own. On hands and knees, he'd dug into the soil himself. Stayed at it for hours, day after day, until it was done. There had been some catharsis in that. The dirt under his fingernails at night was an exhibition of his grief. He'd chosen over a dozen varieties so that there would be blooms year-round.

It was a spot where Amelia had liked to sit. Even now, it was his favorite place on his grand, lonely property. He still went there to think. To read. Symbolically, it had become the place he felt loved. He suddenly wished he was within its safety right now. The vibrant colors of Puerto Rico, along with the equally vibrant woman before him, were too much to take. He may have made a mistake in agreeing to this week.

Although, he remembered, Madison's policy was to donate a large amount of the fee she charged for her services to charities that her clients had chosen. That was one of the reasons she ran the M Dating Agency. There was at least that to make the week worthwhile. He decided to make an effort at conversation. Luna had gone to so much trouble for him with her movie-star routine. And he'd become nothing but grumpy. He asked, "What charity did you choose to have Madison donate to?"

She opened her mouth to answer and he immediately cut her off. Told her all about the memorial garden he'd planted for his family. "And I thought that perhaps because that was meaningful for me, it might be for a lot of people, as well. To have a perpetual garden to embody the everlasting love they feel for their departed."

"That's lovely."

He took a couple of eager bites, noticing for the first time that he was hungry.

"But then I got to thinking," he went on, "that not everyone has a piece of land that they can plant on. So I had the idea to buy small plots here and there and turn them into community memorials. Where people from a lane or village could work together, kids and seniors alike. To collectively nurture their memories."

"How thoughtful."

He forked a few more bites of succulent fish and washed them down with ice-cold beer. "I felt it would be very special to me if Madison could make her donation to the project. Even though it was my money, some of the gardens could be in her name. And since this week is meant to be a step forward for me, that would resonate and be something I'd remember."

"What a wonderful idea."

"I'm sorry," he said, realizing he hadn't let her answer. "I asked about what charity *you* were supporting and then blathered on about mine. You make me want to share every thought that comes into my mind. You have a strange effect on me, Luna Price."

CHAPTER SEVEN

CHARLIE HELD LUNA'S hand as he led her to the ocean. It was the dark of night save for the stars and brilliant glow of the moon. Her feet padded through sand as she followed him down the beach.

"It's cool," she exclaimed once her toes made contact with the water, although it wasn't unpleasant as the easy waves gurgled over her ankles. "Feels good."

What also felt good was him holding her hand, and she hoped he wouldn't let go. His profile in the night caught her eye and then she wasn't able to tear her gaze away. Wading into the water and holding hands with this special man was like being on another planet, so far from the therapy sessions and doldrums the last months in Kentucky had become. It was time to move forward and as a manifestation of that she stepped farther into the water, still holding Charlie's hand as they immersed their legs up to their knees.

"The breeze across my chest with my feet in the water is a sublime combination," he remarked. "You had a good idea to come out for a night swim."

She was pleased that he was enjoying the activity. It had become obvious that Charlie was having a hard day and they'd postponed their plans to visit the city of Old San Juan until tomorrow. Luna had briefly considered booking an outing for herself and leaving him to rest and recuperate. Toying with a spa visit, another outdoor sport or maybe a shopping excursion to browse a local market, she instead decided to stay at the villa with him.

Earlier, she seemed to have had his full attention when she'd gussied up into movie-star garb and shown him a bit of how the Hollywood factory worked. It delighted her to no end that he didn't like all the fakery. She'd begun thinking that although it was nothing compared to the loss he had suffered, she'd known plenty of her own pain and that perhaps the heavens had sent Charlie to her as a balm, if not a cure. With it being her job to do the same for him.

Just like Charlie, part of Luna's objective in this M match was to broach the idea of dating again. She knew if she did, after everything she'd been through, it was not going to be the superficial, red-carpet appearance, where she was eye candy on the arm of eye candy. And she'd have to do a better job of guarding herself from piranhas like Troy Lutt, even if they were sent her way by well-meaning connections. If she was ever going to date again, other than necessary public appearances, it was going to be with someone noble. Someone like Charlie. She was so drawn to him, a man who walked with his pain in tow, who was only capable of being true to who he was. Flesh and blood. And tears.

"Let's go farther," he said as he tugged her hand and they plunged into the water up to their waists.

"Farther," she whispered to herself.

She knew that those one-time passionate kisses they'd shared had simply been on impulse—two people thrown together who had laid themselves bare to each other. But it was fleeting, and it meant nothing.

Which was fine. Better to know that right away, she thought, even as he held her hand firmly in his under the water. She didn't come to this M week with the intention of meeting her soul mate. They were here for a night swim, just to have some more relaxing entertainment, and that was it. She challenged, "Ready to go for it?"

"You mean in and under?"

"We're not just going to stay waist-deep, are we?"

"I'll go in farther if you will."

"Holding hands?"

"No, I think we'll need both our arms to swim."

He released his grip on her hand. She missed it instantly but knew it was necessary. "Let's try to stay beside each other."

"One. Two. Three. Go."

And with that, Luna swam into the ocean, allowing her head to dunk under as she stroked. The water was fairly calm so she wasn't afraid. Taking quick glances to the side, she saw Charlie's head bobbing as he swam, as well. Her heart began to pump with the exertion of swimming into the tide and she welcomed the extra oxygen intake with each breath.

When she reached the point where she couldn't dig her feet into the sand while keeping her head above water, she began to move to stay afloat. Charlie bridged the distance between them.

"The Pacific is too cold to swim in at night so this is a rare treat," she said.

"Thank you for sharing about your life in California. I can appreciate how stressful it must be, having how you look being intrinsic to your profession." He swam around her a bit.

"It's relentless. The paparazzi, or some sexist producer, is always there to mess up your confidence."

"Is it worth it?"

She snickered. "I've achieved my dreams. I've been very lucky and can't complain. But it cost me a lot, that's for sure."

"How long do you think you'll keep doing it?"

"As I'm sure you've heard, Hollywood isn't kind to women when they age. Sometimes the decision is made for you when you just don't get the roles anymore."

"What would you do instead?"

"I've always thought I might like to make smaller films about topics that are important to women. Maybe eventually as a producer."

"A glittering star with a conscience. Earlier, I'd been so busy telling you about the memorial gardens, I never got around to hearing which charity you designated for Madison's donation?"

Luna dipped her head under and whooshed up in a way that all her hair pulled backward away from her face, which made her feel clean and unfettered.

"There's a campaign that reaches out to teenagers to promote body positivity. If they need counseling and they're not able to afford it, this organization provides it."

"Ah, something very personal to you."

"Yes. I mean, I'm part of that illusion that could lead someone to feel that they don't measure up to a certain beauty standard. Heck, I feel that way every day—that I'm the one who doesn't measure up! It's very twisted."

Charlie got close. Only a few inches close, but as

her hands paddled to stay afloat, her leg touched his under the water and their arms brushed by mistake. "Do you not realize how beautiful you are, Luna? Inside and out."

"Hollywood is a very complex place. There are the most wonderful, creative people there, but there are also those whose sole purpose is to bring others down."

"I hope your time away from the limelight has shown you that it's only what you think of yourself that matters."

"Honestly, I hope so, too."

"I wish you could see yourself through my eyes."

He stopped swimming. Planted his feet. The waterline hit him at chest height. Once standing tall, he reached for her and pulled her to him. He placed his hands on both sides of her waist and lifted her up so that her face met his, their lips so near they were almost touching.

And then they were.

Was Charlie dreaming? Perhaps this was a strange doze of a nap taking him in and out of consciousness, as he kissed Luna in the ocean under the moon. But as his mouth pressed incessantly against the sublime plushness that was her lips, his nerve endings couldn't lie. He was very, very awake. When he craned his head back a little bit to gaze into her twinkling eyes, he had to believe the moment was actually happening. As soon as he did, his mouth returned to hers, eager, desperate to continue what was surely the most pleasant activity he'd experienced in as long as he could remember.

Nimble hands clasped around his neck and slim forearms encircled him, making him feel part of her. Beneath the water, it was a natural next move for her legs to wrap around his waist. It had been ten years since he'd felt a woman there, not to mention with the added sensation of the warm water they were immersed in.

In what was at first instinct until it became a decision, he submerged his arms to lift her tightly against him, one hand under each of her thighs until their centers pressed into each other save for the scraps of fabric between them. His core convulsed, raging with desire. They locked against each other, the ocean's current swaying around them.

"Is this wrong, Luna?" The question popped without forethought. They'd vowed not to have physical contact again. He hadn't come to Puerto Rico for romance or sex. "I wasn't expecting to feel the way I do about you."

He didn't give her a chance to answer before he had to take her mouth again with his. Swirling into a vortex of kisses, time under the stars stood still. All he could do was explore her. The tip of his tongue met hers in a slow dance that lasted forever, their lips sealed together. Her mouth was warm inside, charging him with internal excitement. He had a moment's wonder if even the ocean wouldn't be big enough to contain the surge of longing Luna had set free in him.

And surely she didn't object to his kisses as she returned each one, seemingly with the same gusto as he was giving. She confided, "I haven't been able to relax with somebody in a long time. If ever."

Amelia, who had been in the far recesses of his mind, made her way forward. Was kissing Luna a betrayal to her memory? That question, while standing in the middle of the ocean, with Luna's long legs gripped around him, demanded to be answered. Charlie already knew what Amelia would say. What she'd been saying for years. Yet he hadn't been able to listen.

Of course, she'd want him to be with someone else. If the situation had been reversed, he'd want the same for her. It went without saying that she wouldn't approve of what he'd become—an abandoned billionaire rattling around a dusty mansion with nothing to look forward to, no one to share anything with. She wouldn't have wanted her and Lily's deaths to become his, as had been the case. With every fiber of her being she would have hoped for his contentment. That he would know trust again. Find joy. Maybe even have more children. In any case, she'd have hated him for throwing his chance at happiness away because theirs had died. He wished that Amelia would send him a direct sign that she approved of his actions. But maybe she had and he wasn't able to see it.

He slowly ran his hands up Luna's spine and her passion seized his full attention. The way her back arched in response to his touch fueled the demand in his body, too. His arousal was growing to breaking point. When his hands slid up to her shoulders, he hooked his thumbs into each of the straps of her swimsuit. He slowly inched it downward, and gasped at seeing the first swell of her breasts. She gave him a smile, so that he was assured of her approval. The sight of that intimate skin glistening wet in the moonlight caused emotion to lodge in his throat. He was a sexual being again, a man with needs and wants and the vigor to pursue them!

He tugged her swimsuit done farther. With her legs still around him for leverage, his hands cupped her firm, tender breasts. His palms made wide circles, as he wanted to cover every inch, feel every graceful curve. Could there be a piece of art that was greater perfection than the slopes of her body? He thought not. When his fingertips rolled on her nipples, her head fell back in pleasure, encouraging him to continue.

Yearning demanded more as his hands went around to support her back. He kissed the center of her throat, his mouth trailing its elegant length down into the crook of her neck, then out to her shoulders and back again. Waves lapped around him, creating a world where liquid and solid were the same. He couldn't get enough. As soon as he found himself in one spot, he longed for the next. His mouth experienced ecstasy, as he kissed, licked, bit. She held his head to her, fingers moving through his wet hair as she moaned softly.

After an eternity like that, the roused man who had spent so many years in a lifeless state wanted even more. He peeled Luna's swimsuit down even more, his hands appreciating every inch of her sleek skin.

"Luna," he whispered as he kissed her ear, "if I take your swimsuit off, we may lose it to the Caribbean. Can I order you some new ones tomorrow?"

She laughed, a dulcet tone that melded with the percussion of the mild waves. "That's okay. I brought several others."

With all the permission he needed, he pulled the suit off her. He tossed it behind him and they heard a splash, both of them giggling as the garment sailed on its merry way to fates unknown.

Charlie's entire body pulsed at the thought, and sight, of Luna now naked in his arms, under no one's eyes but the moon's.

* * *

Left. Right. Behind. Underneath. Luna couldn't take her hands off formidable Charlie. A sweep along the side of his torso, rock-solid, entranced her so she indulged in it over and over, making mental notes of each toned muscle. The arousal in his eyes told her he appreciated the sensation as much as she did. This was new to both of them, but it was as if they were kindred spirits who had known each other for a lifetime. Merely returning home. Her fingertips tingled as she ran them along his chest, not learning but instead revisiting a place she hadn't been for far too long. She couldn't fathom how she'd become so attached to Charlie in such a short time, yet she had—her own caution, his rocky moods and the emotions only adding to the bond.

He brought her to him for another prolonged kiss, the taste of the ocean bracing his lips. She wrapped herself around him again, now naked, a creature of the sea, her hair cascading behind her like a mythological mermaid. Normally, Luna would be self-conscious. The famous actress whose likeness could be found not only on the big screen, but also on billboards and city buses. The world had had opportunity to study her and her body for years, a freakish reality that most people would never experience. They had indeed examined her. And had photographed, videoed, talked about, written, posted, tweeted and by every other method commented. She had been reduced to a product they were either going to buy or not buy, and if they did, would surely leave a user review for all to see. Those glaring eyes had driven Luna into an illness she had only recently come to understand.

Yet here, with Charlie, the sea and the sky the only

witnesses, she genuinely felt natural and beautiful. The water was exquisite and Charlie's height and long arms were a life raft that made her feel both liberated and shielded. Her hands continued exploring him everywhere they could reach. Until his swim trunks became an obstacle.

"Fair's fair, Charlie." She grinned. "I sacrificed a bathing suit. I think you'll have to, as well."

"Only if you can get it off me," he flirted, making her surge her with anticipation. Was this really all right? she asked herself. To have enough faith in him to not use her? This accomplished man didn't want anything from her, didn't need her for personal leverage. It was okay to just have a good time with him tonight, wasn't it? So what if soon they'd part and become nothing but each other's pleasant holiday recollection. Tomorrow's worries could wait, couldn't they?

Opening her eyes wide to his challenge, she swooped one leg and then the other away from him and thrust her hands underwater. Trying to find a hold to yank on his trunks, she bobbed so much in the water that he broke away. And chuckled.

"You're. Laughing. At. Me?"

"I told you, you have to pull them off." He lifted his arms as if to make it easier for her, but when she was able to latch on to the fabric again, he managed to twist away. "Come get me, movie star."

She scrunched her nose in pretend frustration. "I'm after you, CEO." And, with that, Luna lunged at him. He broke loose again, but not before she managed to get a good hold on the elastic waistband against the small of his back. He tried to swim away, but this time the trunks didn't go with him. A jerk on her side, a twirl on his and, finally, triumph was hers. She held the suit high in one hand like a victory flag and then flung it adrift. Both of them exploded into laughter.

He brought her to him. There was nothing funny about the smoothness of his hips, which she could now splay her hands against, without barrier. And then to his sturdy haunches. His arousal pressed against her and she reached for it, velvety in the water but rigid and throbbing underneath the skin. She stroked in a manner that must have been pleasurable to him because he shut his eyes. His face was magnificent in the night. The straight nose and long eyelashes. Shadows accentuated his prominent jaw, which she kissed her way along, still maneuvering her hand under the water. Her mouth rode leisurely down the center of his chest, the wet skin somehow tasting like sunshine. Her titillation grew to an unexpected urgency.

"Let's go," she said, just as she did *let go* of him, which produced just the result she was after: an agonized moan from his sexy mouth.

"Argh, what are you doing to me?"

"Race you to shore." She didn't wait for a response and boldly took off with confident strokes. He followed.

When they reached the dry land in front of their villa, Luna quickly said, "I'll be right back." She dashed into the master bathroom, where she'd seen condoms in the lavish basket of toiletries provided. Grabbing them with a salacious smile no one saw, she rushed back out. Only to be immediately tackled by Charlie, who pulled her down atop the towels he'd laid out on the beach.

The sand was easy under her back as Charlie caressed both of her arms, from her shoulders all the way down to her fingertips. He came back via her torso, slowly up her rib cage. She had a moment's wince of insecurity about her body. Eating disorders could bring confusion. Sometimes she thought she was too thin, other times overweight. On hiatus from everything including men, part of her therapy was to reckon with herself as a sexual being, as desirable, regardless of what her disease was telling her.

Charlie wasn't judging her. Measuring her. Calculating how to take advantage of her. His moves were an expression of pure truth, of male hunger, of a need they both had. She knew she was strong enough now to quell those voices in her head that caused her to doubt her beauty.

Remembering one of the mantras learned in therapy, she chanted it inside her head. *You are perfect just as you are.*

As the late-night winds wisped over her naked body, his mouth covered hers...until it started to travel once again. The inside of her wrist. The side of her leg. He kissed her breasts. Her stomach. Anywhere he went, she welcomed it. He lifted his head and whispered, "You are more luminous than the Caribbean moon that watches over us."

"You're beautiful, too, Charlie."

With that, he put on the condom and moved back up so that he could kiss her mouth as their bodies joined completely, undulating together in the sand, mimicking the perfect rhythm of the tide's ebb and flow.

CHAPTER EIGHT

"'The colonial architecture is indicative of the Spanish influence in Puerto Rico,'" Luna said, reading from the touring app she'd downloaded to her phone as she and Charlie roamed the picturesque city streets. "*Viejo*—that means old. San Juan is known for its colorful buildings and cobblestone streets."

"Does it say anything about why the cobblestones are blue?"

"They're called *adoquines*, and they're a waste product of iron smelting that was brought from Spain."

The sky was unclouded, the air was clean and Luna Price was the most enchanting being in the universe. In her cotton coral-colored dress and flat brown sandals, she looked like a carefree tourist, blending right in, not attracting notice except perhaps for her simple loveliness. That Charlie had just spent a mind-altering night of lovemaking with a famous actress, no less, seemed utterly surreal in the noonday sun.

"Shall we look in that shop?" he asked as he presented his arm to help her navigate across the stones and their uneven surface. A bell attached to the front door chimed when they entered.

"Pretty," Luna said as she admired the jewelry on

display. "I saw a description on the app. These are Taino pieces, the jewelry of the native people in Puerto Rico."

"*Te gusta?*" asked the shopkeeper, an older woman with a friendly grin.

"*Si.* Very unique. What are they made from?"

"Clay, wood and leather."

"I like those earrings." She gestured to a pair that were long and dangly, with beads that seemed to be made out of dried clay.

"Each has a sun pendant on the bottom," the woman pointed out.

"Hold them up to your face," Charlie suggested. The shopkeeper handed Luna a mirror. She brought one of the earrings to her delicate lobe. Charlie was struck with the impulse to take said earlobe between his teeth as he had last night, but he knew this was not the time or place. In fact, it would be smart if he never took Luna's earlobe, or any other part of her, into his mouth ever again. Although that sounded to him like an unimaginable fate.

Oh, how luscious last night had been, the feeling of his bareness in the sea, an organism in the biotic world, in the wild. And, to boot, in the company of the most vital and sensual woman he had ever known. Together they had intermingled in an aquatic dance of kisses and limbs. Then they took their voyage to shore, to the tender sands where they brought each other to ecstasy again and again as the waves provided music for their journey.

But where was he now? Charlie tried to understand as he watched Luna admire the jewelry. He hadn't agreed to the M Agency agreement for this, to be totally entranced by a woman who had come here to help with her rehabilitation, just as he had. He wasn't ready for the *real thing* with anyone...was he?

"May I buy those for you, Luna?"

She giggled a bit before answering. "I have my own money, you know." Which actually was funny, as she possessed, no doubt, a substantial fortune.

"I know, but it would mean a lot to me to give them to you." Words were falling out of his mouth with him not even sure where they were coming from. But he did want to buy the earrings.

"That would be very kind, Charlie. Thank you."

Outside of the shop, Luna took the earrings from the tissue they'd been wrapped in. "I think I'd like to wear these today. Can you help me put them on?"

Eager, he held the delicacy of Luna's ear in what felt like the most important job in the world. The earrings looked perfect with her outfit as they resumed their touring.

They visited Viejo San Juan's best-known landmark. El Morro or, properly, Castillo San Felipe del Morro, the fortress and military outpost. Construction on the massive structure began in 1539 by Spanish settlers and it was in use until 1961, when the US Army retired it to establish a museum. They walked through the recreations of the barracks and kitchens, which showed how the soldiers there might have lived. From the outdoor top levels, they could see the Atlantic Ocean. Charlie's gut panged when he envisioned a few days from now, when the week would end and he'd depart for the UK, and she would go in the opposite direction, to LA. The distances of land and sea had never seemed greater to him.

He surprised himself with the thought that Luna mattered to him now, something he'd never have imagined when he'd first arrived in Puerto Rico. They strolled the vast front lawn of the fortress. He blinked twice to make sure he was seeing clearly and not hallucinating. Dozens of people were flying colorful kites.

"It's a local tradition to fly kites on this lawn, according to my travel guide," Luna said, reading from her app. The kites sailed through the air, held aloft by everyone from squealing schoolchildren to seniors to tour groups in matching T-shirts. "Is something wrong?"

He hadn't realized that his emotions had registered on his face. His Amelia had loved kite flying. He could remember many occasions, now parading through his mind, when the weather was optimal and she'd drag him along with her to do so. Selecting one of the half-dozen kites she owned, she'd pile a picnic basket into the car and off they'd go. He always enjoyed himself so much because of *her* enjoyment of the activity.

"I can't wait until we share this pleasure with our children," she'd said one happy day early in her pregnancy, smiling and caressing her burgeoning baby bump, her kite high. Charlie's throat tightened as he kept his now glassy eyes fixed on the vibrant display, unable to articulate the aching in his chest.

But afterward, sitting on a bench in one of the charming town squares of Viejo San Juan, his temperament lightened. His outstretched arm made its way around Luna's shoulder and they sat watching the pedestrians promenade this way and that. She hadn't pursued an explanation as to what had bothered him while watching the kites fly. He sensed she knew that in that moment he was being torn down by the past. It was as if she understood. His ease around her was presenting a new world. One that was confusing. One that he certainly didn't have a map for.

"Shall we eat?" he suggested after noticing that the sun was moving. It was important for Luna to eat at consistent intervals. "I found a recommendation from the resort's list."

They turned onto a street with the most vividly painted buildings Charlie had ever seen. From mint-green to petal-pink to lavender to pale yellow, with all of the windowsills and trim done in white. Wrought-iron balconies displayed flower boxes. The café had a patio shaded by red umbrellas. He pulled out a white chair for Luna to sit in, then positioned his next to hers rather than across. That way he could be next to her and they could both gaze out to the narrow lane.

"Everything looks good," Luna said as she perused the menu. "I've read the starter dish of sweet eggplant is really special."

"And for the main course, let's try the steak Fortaleza."

"Which means fort."

"Beer to drink."

When the waiter arrived, Charlie ordered, pleased with his pronunciations.

"Thank you again for these," she said as she fingered an earring. They had been priced comparably to the beer he'd just ordered, yet he felt on top of the world that she liked them. He had to remind himself that he was the CEO of a billion-pound corporation. Not a barefoot boy infatuated with a pretty girl on a sunny island.

The food was delectable. The grilled eggplant drizzled with locally produced honey tasted like gold. The steak was sliced open and stuffed inside with ham, cheese, onions and peppers, and served with a creamy mushroom sauce on top. It was exquisite. As was his companion.

"Buena noches," the catamaran driver welcomed Charlie and Luna as they boarded for their short cruise to Vieques Island after they'd eaten.

"Buena noches." Luna greeted the middle-aged man with bulky muscles straining against his white T-shirt and shorts.

"Have you been enjoying your stay in Puerto Rico?"

"Si, the food is delicious and today we toured the city."

"You are in for a very special night."

As they left shore, the speed at which they channeled through the water had the wind whipping through Luna's hair and against her skin. It felt extreme and adventurous. As it did having Charlie beside her. He had made such impassioned love to her the night before it still reverberated through her. Yes, he was a man who had endured the most unspeakable agonies, which still overtook him and attacked without warning—as she'd witnessed this afternoon, under the pleasant skies as the two of them had watched the kite flyers—but perhaps because of his pain, rather than in spite of it, the fervor that they shared in the sand last night had shot to her core. He was a realist, he didn't pretend like everything was perfect, didn't live in fantasyland. Popularity and approval had no meaning to him. She respected him. And he had made her start to believe in something that she'd never dared to before.

As they arrived on the small island, she looked forward to seeing a famed Puerto Rican attraction, the

brightest bioluminescent bay in the world. At the shoreline, the kayaks and wet suits they'd reserved were waiting. Once ready, under the starry sky, they paddled with
oars into the center of Mosquito Bay. Like many visitors
to Puerto Rico, they'd come to see one of nature's most
unusual displays. Millions, maybe billions, of tiny mi-
croorganisms lived in the water of the bay. And when
the water was disturbed by the oars of a kayak, or even
by a hand through the waves, the organisms lit up, creating a light show. It was an environmental phenomenon, and the sheer brilliance was hard to believe. Luna
gasped at the sight.

"How stunning," Charlie called out, turning back toward Luna from his position in the front of the kayak.
With other people in kayaks or boats all around them,
the explosions of light came from every direction, ra-
diant bright blue erupting from the still black water.

"How can this be?"

"The natural world is humbling."

Temporarily holding his oar in only one hand, Charlie reached his other hand behind him to grab hold of
one of Luna's so that they could be joined while experiencing this marvel. After they took it all in for a few
minutes, he lowered their clasped hands into the water
beside the kayak and splashed, so that they could pro-
voke the light with their own hands. They sprayed light
toward each other, laughing at the miracle of it.

Oh, Charlie, she thought. How was she ever going to
forget this week? To move on as planned, and go back
to California and the pressures that had done so much
damage to her? She'd been unprofessional in her exit
a year ago. Desperate, she'd left that set even though
production had almost begun. She'd inconvenienced

the rest of the cast, the crew, her agent and all of her
team, and cost the studio a lot of money. Even if the
year she'd spent in recovery made her question whether
she still wanted to stay within the Hollywood machine
anymore, she had to at least return to make good on
the contract she'd signed. The dreams she'd sometimes
had about making her own movies, expressing her art
in way that she was in control of, seemed out of reach
until she cleaned up the mess she'd left. Maybe she
was ready to leave the industry entirely. Go back to
Kentucky, perhaps? Help her parents with the ranch
as they grew older? Invest in a business? Whatever
the case, she had to return to LA first and see everything through.

As planned, she'd leave Dorada and all that had happened there behind. Leave Charlie behind. A man who
she was beginning to think she might like to stay near,
and not just in Puerto Rico... In his own awkward way
he'd made her feel completely accepted. Made her imagine a lifestyle she had never dared to consider.

Last night, after they'd brought each other pleasure
upon pleasure with their bodies and, she had to admit,
their souls, they'd stretched out in the sand and looked
up to the sky. He'd reached for a beach blanket to cover
them and they rested, spent and hazy. She got lost in
thought about different roads her life could have taken
and sensed Charlie's mind had gone to a similar place.
It was comfortable to be beside him.

After a while, though, it had gotten cold, and she
was sleepy so they went back into the villa. She hoped
he'd join her in the bedroom, where they could sleep
in a lover's embrace. But he'd said he wasn't tired and
wanted to check on some work. They shared a sensu-

ous kiss good-night, yet she retreated to the master suite alone with a ring of sadness through her bones.

In the center of the plush bed, surrounded by pillows and bedding, she'd convinced herself it was for the best. Someone who pretended for a living should surely know not to get sucked into the charade. This week with Charlie was simply what it was intended to be. Thinking of it otherwise could only lead to disappointment and pain. Even if she was willing to reconsider her own oath, his was to never love a woman again. She doubted he'd go back on his word to the memory of his family.

"That was just extraordinary," Charlie said when they got back to the villa after the bioluminescent bay. "I think I'd like to return to Puerto Rico someday."

"Soon it will be time to go home."

"For you, the word *home* must have two separate meanings."

"Home is Los Angeles," she affirmed. "I really do have a gorgeous house in the hills. Panoramic views, lots of light. I'm very fortunate."

"Why doesn't that sound convincing?"

"I'm apprehensive about going back. I hope I'm strong enough for all of it this time."

"It seems like you'll be returning with your eyes wide open."

He made her feel so reassured. What would it be like to have someone on her side, by her side, all the time? While her team was loyal, she'd never let anyone in that close. She'd never dared because there had never been anyone who wasn't affiliated with Luna Price, the commodity, rather than just plain Luna Price, the woman. That she'd begun to think Charlie was that one elusive person—the exception to the rule—was a hazardous game. Even if she was ready to let someone in, Charlie wore his tragedy as a barrier. He wasn't going to let go of what had come to define him. And he was entitled to that, if that was what he wanted.

But tonight was different than last night's parting. Tonight it came as a shock when they were standing between the living room and the bedroom and he backed Luna against the doorway and pressed himself into her. Trapping her with an arm on either side of her head, he kissed her with a verve that made her knees tremble. Forcing his whole body against hers, she felt his arousal in full strength. He ground into her with force. "Luna," he rasped in her ear. "Luna."

The unadulterated eroticism ran purple through her veins. To be so desired stirred her profoundly and her body yielded to his. Their lips met, tongues desperate for more. Then, all at once, he lifted her into his arms and carried her to the previously unchartered kingdom of the master bed.

When Charlie felt the glow of sunlight on his eyelids, they clicked open. His surroundings were strange. He'd become accustomed to the grooves of the sofa cushions, where he'd been laying his bones at night, and the play of light and shadow from that vantage point. He knew he was still in the villa, with the wafting scent of the courtyard flowers and the sounds of morning waves just steps away. The silky warmth next to him made his head turn in that direction. Luna, curled toward him, eyes closed, was a sight to behold.

He realized that of all the extraordinary things that had taken place since he'd come to Puerto Rico, what happened last night beat them all. Not the surreal show of nature's lights on Vieques Island. Not even the sizzling lovemaking that he and Luna had engaged in. No, the most surprising turn of events was that Charlie had slept. Slept! All night!

He'd forgotten what a rested body felt like. With each breath, oxygen traveled to the far reaches of his bloodstream, which hadn't received any in a decade. The pervasive tightness across his forehead was gone. The little niggles of aches that he'd sometimes spent the night distracted by were imperceptible. His muscles were relaxed but invigorated. His mouth ticked up in approval.

"Good morning," Luna cooed as her eyes opened and she stretched her arms above her head.

A quick check of Charlie's phone confirmed what he'd already suspected. "*Buenas tardes.* It's afternoon already." Yes, he'd slept not just through the dark hours, but well past the first light of dawn.

"Hmmm," she sang, a tiny murmur that reminded him of some of the sounds of pleasure that had come from her throat last night. Sounds he most definitely wouldn't mind hearing more of.

He brushed away errant golden strands in front of her face and his fingers lingered in her luxurious hair, intertwining the locks in his fingers. It was something he thought could occupy him for hours. "What do you want to do today?"

"According to our itinerary, tonight we're going to a rum tasting. And to hear live music and have dancing lessons."

"Dancing lessons?"

"Yes. Apparently we both told Madison that we enjoyed music so she's set up an evening where we're going to learn the traditional bomba style of Puerto Rican dance."

His brow crinkled. "I don't know about that." Although really, why not? What did he have to lose? Charlie Matthews was finally aroused and flourishing again. What would be better than dancing the night away with this amazing creature on their island paradise?

"So how shall we spend a few hours until then?" she asked.

Instead of answering, he showed her. With every fiber in his being.

As the sun moved through the afternoon, they laid with their limbs in a tangle after having brought each other to bliss once again. He wheeled the food cart into the bedroom and fed her a meaty grilled sandwich and juicy fruits. They lolled in a half daze for who knew how long, adjusting now and then to reach for a different part of each other. Something that he was certain he could happily do for an endless amount of time.

Endless. His own words repeated over and over and over in his head. He thought of yesterday. Of visiting the fort and how seeing those kites in the sky had reminded him that he'd never be granted for a second time the conjugal peace and security that he had with Amelia. That had been a once-in-a-lifetime love, snatched from him along with the expression of that love, their baby girl, her sweet orange ringlet curls like those of her pretty mother's.

The kites at the fort were little demons in the sky, sent in a swarm to encircle and torment him lest he begin to have too much sincere companionship and enjoyment with this new woman, who had brought optimism back to a heart that had decided against it. Lest he feel slightly less alone and lonely. That was how his life had worked since Amelia and Lily died and he assumed it would always be that way. The gravity of the universe saw to it that Charlie stayed casting downward. And if, even for a second, his neck tilted backward so that his eyes could look ahead, forces knocked him to the ground. Showed him a sign.

Wait a minute. A sign! Hadn't he begged Amelia to send him a signal? Did the holy spirit, the ancient qi, the essence of his young wife that stayed tucked inside him, communicate as he'd begged her to? To let him know that she wished for him to be complete again, to inhale with all of the power in his lungs. To smile and laugh and stumble and share his days and nights with another woman. He'd directly asked Amelia if it was okay to love again.

Was her vibration within him calling out to be heard? Had it actually been her handiwork that Charlie had taken this trip to Puerto Rico? Did Amelia put Luna in his path because she'd chosen her for him? And decided that they would visit that fort to make him see that there were still blue skies and August breezes to be had? And that, yes, she wanted him to find delight and fulfillment with someone new?

CHAPTER NINE

"Salud!" CHARLIE TIPPED his rum glass to touch Luna's and then they both sipped.

"This is the amber?" With six glasses in front of them, each with a small pour of translucent liquid of varying hues, she wanted to make sure.

"Yes, that one is considered to have a rich, full body."

Luna knew to only take small sips of the offering as she didn't want to become sleepy. They still had plans to go dancing, which she was greatly looking forward to.

He read aloud from the laminated card that had arrived with their tasting flight in the secluded high-backed booth at the dark bar. "There are eighty types of rum. And it's Puerto Rico's chief export. It's been produced here since the fifteenth century as a by-product of the sugarcane industry."

"Its base is molasses, right?"

"Yes, it's then mixed with water and fermented." As they talked, Charlie ran his finger under the thin strap of the red tank top Luna wore. Uncharacteristically for her, she was baring a lot of skin in the wisp of a covering that seemed right for working up a sweat on a hot summer night. Although he needed to behave himself with that delicate tug on the thin fabric's strap, she mused, because his touch was so distracting she might forget about the dancing plan after all.

"The darker varieties are aged in charred barrels. That's why they have a stronger flavor." He teased her by continuing to both lightly tap his fingers on her shoulder and read from the information card.

"Let's try the one called silver."

He picked up the glass of one of the clear tastes and brought it to her lips. She sipped and then he made sure to bring his mouth to the exact spot where hers had touched the glass to take his own sip, the move not lost on her. "That one is so much lighter. It would be nice in a mixed cocktail."

"Mmm," he answered, but seemed more focused on running one finger up and over that strap of her top and into the crook of her neck, a sensation so exquisite it made her back arch.

As suggested, she'd dressed traditionally for their bomba lesson later. The Dorada staff had provided her with a long skirt of many ruffles and a tremendous amount of volume, the type that would open to a full circle if laid on the ground. The outer fabric was white with beautifully applied red fabric flowers. And the underside of the skirt was a dense floral pattern of many colors. When she danced, she would lift them up with her hands, so the detail was important to both sides of the construction of the skirt. Included in her delivery to the villa was one perfect hibiscus, the national flower, along with hairpins for her to wear it behind one ear. Choosing her own red tank top to match, the outfit gave her a sexy, potent feel.

Charlie wore his own white jeans and untucked white shirt, the color men typically dressed in for the dance.

His eyes were like iridescent emeralds, and she tingled at the memories of his commanding mouth covering every inch of her during the lazy sensual afternoon they'd spent in bed.

"Now the spiced rum." She lifted a taste of another one.

"Golden color with spices and caramel sometimes added."

"Yes, I taste that." It was the flavor of him she was tasting, though. He pervaded all of her senses and she could only drink, hear and breathe him. Her thoughts shocked her. She'd assumed, accepted even, that a true and meaningful relationship wasn't on her horizon, especially after years of being taken advantage of and basically used as a human ladder for other people's ascension. She'd considered that weasel Troy Lutt the last time she'd even try. Maybe she could find some decent guys, not in the entertainment industry, to occasionally date. That would have to be enough.

When they got to the dance club, it was as lively and invigorating a scene as the mind could imagine. People were dancing both inside and outside on the patio, which gave way to a public plaza, and all the way around the fountain that anchored the cobblestone space. At the designated spot, they met up with the teacher, named Julia, and the small group of other students. Dressed in a purple-and-yellow dancing costume, Julia gave them a brief background on the cultural traditions. "Bomba is both the dance and the name of the musical instruments," she said while pointing to a row of seated men, each with drums that they beat in steady rhythms. "It originates from the heritage of the African slaves who were brought here to work on the sugar plantations. It is not just a dance, it is a part of our culture."

Luna's hips were already beginning to sway to the seductive percussion. She followed as Julia instructed the women to lift their skirts and to swish and sway them in aggressive expressions and with passion. She continued, "Tell a story with your skirts and your movements. The dancer leads the music rather than the other way around."

Charlie moved to the tempo, as well, although seemed unsure of what to do quite yet. He smiled watching Luna take to the dance and wave her skirt to and fro while shimmying her shoulders.

"Senors," Julia called out to the gentlemen, "you make strong, jerky and sudden movements that originate in your belly." At first, Charlie followed the moves of some of the experienced men in the crowd with a little inhibition, but then he started to move more assuredly. He gyrated, letting the dance emerge from him organically. The grind of his hips made Luna forget how to swallow air.

Together, they abandoned themselves to the rhythm, to the plaza full of people, all engrossed in a near-spiritual experience as they danced and danced and danced. All grooving together, locals and tourists, young and old, faces of every creed and color, the drumbeats taking them higher and higher. People smiled at each other. Flirted. Watched the children with delight. There was one pronounced feeling that swept through the air so distinctly you could almost see it. Love.

As the beats mesmerized their minds while their bodies moved with openness, it was a moment of profound connectedness to everything around her that

Luna had never felt before. That reassured her she
was finally mentally and physically on a healthy road
after a dark year. The past hadn't defeated her. In fact,
she was mighty. Luna Price was back. Because of the
bomba. Because of the skirt she wore that encouraged
her to write her own narrative, and be nothing more or
less than who she was. Because of the balmy winds of
Puerto Rico, which she would never forget. But most of
all because of this unforgettable man in white dancing
in front of her. A man to whom she didn't know how
she was going to bid adios.

The next day, as Charlie reached down for Luna's hand
to help pull her up a steep incline, he thought about how
Puerto Rico had seeped into his bloodstream. Today,
deep into the misty El Yunque rain forest, the scent was
so fresh he wished never to smell anything else. Countless species of plant life surrounded them and only the
rustle of nature filled their ears. He pointed to a flock
of birds. "Look at them."

Soaring, the winged creatures were the embodiment
of liberty. He wished he could somehow join them, taking Luna along, of course. But the end was near, and
they would not fly away together. Charlie was to return home tomorrow to England, to his artifact of a
mansion. A changed man, just as was the plan, but the
gains somehow seemed hollow in the face of having to
part from Luna.

After a long hike in which they saw wildlife, including
the famous coqui frogs, which were endemic to Puerto
Rico, they visited the Yokahú observation tower, with

its stunning views of the vast green mountains and the ocean.

"It's been an amazing week here, hasn't it?" he said from the top of the tower, where they were standing, holding hands, taking it all in.

"I can't believe it's coming to an end."

"What if we didn't leave just yet?" he offered, slightly less than halfway serious. "Just because we agreed to a week with the M Dating Agency doesn't mean we have to vacate. I'll just book us in for another week." He hardly recognized his own voice but the thought of letting Luna go tomorrow was too much to endure. Last night, when they had danced with reckless abandon among the crowd in Viejo San Juan, Charlie had been ready to pull up roots and buy them a villa here that they could call their own forever.

"That's a lovely thought," Luna said with a squeeze to his hand. "In fact, you even suggesting it touches my heart." He still didn't know if he was talking realistically, but with her, he had come to start thinking out loud. "But I have to get back to LA. I really screwed up there. I have to make this film. Set wrongs to right."

Of course. Thank goodness she was the voice of reason. He was surprised he'd even had that idea. It had been crystal clear that he'd come to Puerto Rico only so that he could return to the living a little. Mission accomplished. The cobwebs had been dusted off. He was energized. But there was no point in prolonging the inevitable. His life wasn't here. Or with Luna...despite what Amelia's voice was telling him. This time, he might know better than her what he was, and wasn't, capable of.

Maybe life wasn't in the stuffy manor of Buckinghamshire anymore, either. Maybe it was time to sell that stone reminder of death, that gigantic gravestone that he had been taking cover behind. Should he buy a deluxe flat in London with all the cutting-edge bells and whistles befitting a tech billionaire? Where he could bring home beautiful women at night that he'd usher straight out the door in the morning? One thing was certain. This week had changed him forever.

He and Luna took lots of photos and selfies from the observation tower that he knew he'd look at and cherish for the rest of his life. Once back down to the ground, they were hot and sweaty, so they located one of the natural pools that El Yunque was known for. Prepared, with swimsuits under their clothes, they tossed their outer layers and jumped in. They swam to a waterfall, its rush producing a powerful roar. Charlie pulled Luna to him and wrapped first one, then the other, of her arms around his neck. His circled her waist.

"Let's come back some day." He didn't phrase it as a question.

"Yes."

"Yes."

He brought his lips to hers and kissed her as the waterfall gushed down on them. His eyes closed—he was lost in the moment. Another freeze frame that he would have and hold until his dying day. Because he didn't believe they would ever really return to the paradise of this week. That wasn't what was meant to be.

"Charlie. I have another idea," she said after an urgent round of kisses. "What if you came to LA with me? I'll be on set during the day but you could sightsee or work. We could be together in the evenings."

Go to California with her? "I can't do that."

"I know. It was just a fleeting thought," she said hastily and then took his face in her hands and kissed him again, although this time it felt a bit like goodbye.

Much as he could envision spending every day with Luna, whether ordinary or eventful, that wasn't their destiny. They both got what they'd come to Puerto Rico for. Now their kites were meant to fly off in different directions.

"Have you had breakfast?" Charlie asked as he entered the master suite, where Luna had all of her belongings and open suitcases laid out on the bed. Where last night they'd shared their bodies with each another one last time. There had been a different mood in the air, though. No longer was it a lair filled with sensuality and courage and exploration and candor. Last night the structure housed one long nonverbal farewell followed by a brief sleep. Everything that had been discovered, unleashed and enacted this week would be packed up in separate luggage and flown to separate destinations, never to comingle again.

Luna had been holding the tears back in her eyes ever since they had woken up and Charlie excused himself to the living room, where the closet and armoire there had been his base camp, as was originally agreed upon, until the week had taken such an unlikely turn. And now the tide had reversed again, returning the universe to the configuration that was originally intended. Melancholy shaded Luna, darkening a morning that could have been cheerful in another circumstance.

"No, did you wheel the cart in?" Luna answered his inquiry without looking up. She made busywork of folding her bathing suits into a neat pile. Her vocal cords wanted to sing out for the red swimsuit lost to the Caribbean during their first glorious joining, which now felt like a lifetime ago. Since then their bodies and souls had come together so many times that the state of being apart had become the more unnatural one. She'd been reflecting on how much she'd miss him when he'd merely gone into the other room to pack. She had no idea how she was going to weather being separated by continents.

"Yes, it's in the kitchen."

"Thanks, I'll get something in a minute." Luna would need to grab a plate to munch from while she arranged her carry-on bag. She couldn't possibly sit down opposite Charlie's eyes and exchange pleasantries about their stay at the resort. In fact, she'd be lucky if she could bundle up the pieces of her heart that had already broken off before they shattered into a million grains and scattered onto the warm sand that grounded their villa. This week had meant more to her than she could ever put into language, and she had the sense that any more said was only going to make the inevitable moment even worse.

With her back still to him as she wound the charging cords for her electronics into manageable spirals, she heard him begin talking. "Well, it's official. I haven't a thing to wear. I read we'll be having a heat spell, even hotter than here, so you'll need to take me shopping for desert-weight clothes."

The collection of words that came out of his mouth dispersed from each other and floated in space, trying to rearrange themselves into a comprehensible sentence. But Luna wasn't able to grasp hold of them. She rotated her head around, although only slightly, as she didn't feel strong enough to meet his handsome visage. "Sorry?"

"I've got the beachwear my housekeeper bought me for this trip, and a couple of English woolen suits. I don't think that'll be quite right for the west coast, will it?"

"Wha…at?" Again, Luna admonished herself not to draw any conclusions from the reference to the word *west*. Mustering courage from the tips of her toes, hoisting it up through her hips, chest and, finally, her head, she slowly turned all the way around.

There was no way she could have known about the wide grin that had been waiting for her to pivot.

"I may be a little slow on the uptake but I'm surely not a fool," he said as he stepped toward her. "Which is what I'd be if I let you fly out of my life."

"You mean…"

"Los Angeles, here we come." He closed the distance between them. He kissed her forehead, her eyebrows, cheeks, lips and chin. The breath in her chest pumped through her so fast she thought she could hear it. Not having let in just how much it was destroying her to have to part with him, the reversal switched on an adrenaline release. She felt like jumping up and down.

"What? You changed your mind? When did this happen?" she asked, throwing her arms around him with a force that bent him to the side. His chuckle against her face was delightful. "Last night, we fell asleep in each other's arms, knowing it would be our final night together."

"You'd fallen asleep, Luna. I didn't sleep a wink. I couldn't bear to miss even a second of being able to hold you."

A gulp trickled in her throat. "Charlie."

"I don't know what I'm doing. I've only known my life with Amelia and my life without her yet still tethered to her. I'm terrified but I'm willing to try, if you are."

"I am, too." Still, joy was sparking out of her. No matter what happened, at least it didn't have to end here and now. He was right—what did they possibly have to lose?

Although it was that sobering thought that robbed the smile from her face. Because there would be a lot at stake if they tried to turn this week into something more than a gateway to greener pastures, and then failed. He couldn't take any more loss, and could she withstand the disappointment? What did she know about trustworthy relationships? They both had so much to learn. Perhaps it wasn't a good idea for him to come to LA, where all her terrors lived, waiting to attack her in the night. Maybe she'd be best to return alone, to tackle those old foes first.

But looking into his eyes, it seemed anything would be worth it not to have to leave him. She deserved companionship that made her feel good inside. Without having to actively do anything but be by her side, perhaps Charlie would be a buffer between her and the jackals determined to bring her down, as per their manifesto. And he wasn't talking about relocating to California, was he? It was too early for a decision like that.

"I don't know how long I can stay," he said, beginning to provide answers to the inquiries marching across her mind like a strip of ticker tape. "As you know, I have in-person business in London I have to start attending to. But I can extend my leave for a bit. As a matter of fact, I have offices in Silicon Valley that I haven't visited for years. It would be beneficial for me to pay a visit. See people face-to-face." The high-tech bastion of Silicon Valley was just a short hour-long plane trip north from LA.

"So while I was sound asleep last night, you were concocting this whole plan?"

"That and more. I texted with an assistant to arrange for my private jet to take us to LA." She loved that he'd drafted everything out, thought to tease and tickle her with his change of plans.

After they'd packed and double-checked that they hadn't accidentally left anything behind, Luna sensed that Charlie was having the same thoughts as she was, as they took one last look throughout the villa. The secluded courtyard where they'd shared meals and secrets. The swimming pool where moods had been processed, fears laid wide. The ocean beyond where they'd played in the water and first merged bodies in the unplanned union they'd found with each other. Inside, the living room where Charlie kept his distance until there was no longer need for that. And the master bed where they'd shown each other beauty that surpassed the bright flowers and pink sunrises they'd witnessed. La Villa de Felicidad. Where two lonely souls met and had been changed for all of eternity.

"Ready?" Charlie asked and reached for her hand, the multiple meanings of his one-word question gonging through her head.

CHAPTER TEN

LUNA WAS NERVOUS while she watched her idyllic week in Puerto Rico get further and further from view as Charlie's jet soared them high into the sky. She was elated to have him unexpectedly beside her, but not knowing what the future would bring for them worried her. And she had a lot to face when she got back to LA. A year away was a very long time. But a sense of fun won over her busy mind as they chatted during the flight.

"Is there anything you haven't done in LA that you'd like to?" she asked, momentarily forgetting that there were few places she could go without being recognized. While she'd been able to hide under sundresses and dark glasses in Viejo San Juan, the paparazzi in Tinseltown had a way of finding anyone and everyone, regardless of how hard they tried to be avoided.

"I've been to Los Angeles many times but I've never visited those really touristy places, like the stars on the sidewalk of Hollywood Boulevard."

"The Walk of Fame. That's a funny thing to think about seeing with me since one of those stars is mine!" She remembered the dress-up game she'd played for him at the beginning of the week, showing him how she could slide in and out of her movie-star persona. Would she be able to slip it on and off so easily once she got back to the town that only saw one of her dimensions?

"I want to see it. Will you take a photo of me with your star?"

They chuckled. Surely no one would identify her gawking at her own star, especially if she went far in the other direction by wearing baggy clothes and one of the wigs she kept at home for just such an occasion. She thought of Anush, who was on her way back to LA, as well. She'd texted with her a few times from Puerto Rico but hadn't shared any details about Charlie because none of it seemed real. It was Anush who had taught Luna how to disguise herself so that she could go out in public, as long as she was careful not to look anyone in the eye or linger anywhere too long, as the paparazzi always seemed to spot her if she wasn't ultracareful. She hoped the brutality of Los Angeles, *her* Los Angeles, wouldn't be unbearable to Charlie.

As they landed at LAX, he'd taken it upon himself to book a limo. He wouldn't have known that she usually traveled back and forth from the airport in a smaller town car. The driver of the stretch limo had to take extra caution to navigate the winding canyon roads that led to Luna's house in the hills. The white wooden security gates swung open only after Luna punched an access code into her phone.

"Luna, this is marvelous," Charlie said upon first glance of her sprawling home. She'd flown back a couple of times during her treatment in Kentucky, but she really hadn't lived here for the better part of a year. A mixture of emotions ratcheted through her—she was glad to be back but somehow dreaded it at the same time. The limo driver unloaded their bags. With more key codes, she opened the main door.

"Let me show you around." She gestured for him to follow her into the living room with its overstuffed furniture and wide-open space. Windows everywhere showcased views of LA, from the skyscrapers of downtown to the east, to the Pacific Ocean to the west.

"I don't suppose it's too difficult to wake up to a sight like that."

"I've been very fortunate."

Luna's mind spun. She was showing herself the house as much as she was to Charlie. Her home, if LA even was home anymore. It was hard to take in at the moment. The quiet day-to-day of Kentucky, with its big sky, under which she'd uncovered, aired and then stomped out a terrible chapter of her life. Then there was tropical Puerto Rico with the spicy food, spicy music and this man who'd somehow landed in the living room of what was either her palace or her prison.

Charlie was in tow for the moment, but she knew better than to believe anything permanent would grow between them. He'd clearly said as much. His unexpected presence in her life had clearly been sent to her from the gods to be the final component of her transition and healing. Which she was certainly grateful for and she needed to keep a firm hold on that outlook. On top of the strangeness of being back in the house and with Charlie, far from their secret island bliss, was the fact that she was due on set tomorrow after her long absence.

She knew what to expect. There'd be staring and assessing and gossiping. She didn't particularly like the director of this film, finding him arrogant and sexist in the telemeetings they'd had. Not to mention that she was bored with the big films she was cast in, always as the love interest or sidekick to a man, and never a powerful woman. *Too fragile-looking.* That had been the latest explanation a casting director had given when she'd missed out on a role she'd wanted. *You could blow her over with a slight breeze.* Luna knew that wasn't who she was. But she also knew that filmmaking relied on archetypes and her place in the mythology wasn't going to change. That's why she'd thought about making her own movies, telling her own stories. But after a year away from this industry town, she had to play by the rules first, step back into the high-heeled stilettos she used to wear.

"What a kitchen," Charlie remarked, entering the large red, white and chrome room. Memories twisted in Luna's gut, though, as they stood in the center of the open-plan layout. Because when her eating disorder had held her in its tight grip, the kitchen had become a frightening torture chamber in the hills, a circus-funhouse mirror of distortion. A place where what, when and if to eat, or not eat, occupied hours, days—it had been an agony that would seem petty or privileged to someone who didn't understand the hold of the disease. For a long time now, an organized eating schedule and all of the therapy she'd undergone had helped her exist without being in battle with herself and with food, but recollections of the chaos came flooding back to her nonetheless.

"I'm sure the kitchen at your mansion isn't exactly a hob and a hearth," she said quickly, hoping the sound of her own voice would drown out the unwelcome thoughts.

"It's enormous, actually. Several ovens, refrigerators

and dishwashers. Easily able to cater parties for a hundred. Of course, it's absurd that it's only for me. Even when Amelia and Lily were there..." His words trailed away while his jaw ticked in the interim. Then he continued, "In any case, it's strictly the domain of the staff. I never step foot in it. I wouldn't have a clue where anything was kept."

"Maybe while you're here we should try to cook the mofongo like we did when Chef Diego gave us our lesson." Dorada was thousands of miles away now, both literally and figuratively.

"I'd love that."

Next, she showed him her bedroom. While she had plenty of other spaces where a guest could stay, even a detached cottage by the pool, she assumed they would share a bed during his time here. Remembering that he didn't sleep well and had set up his own private domain within the open walls of the villa, she pointed to the sequestered alcove in the room that had a desk and chaise lounge that she used to use as an office. "Feel free to make that area yours."

As his eyes scanned the room, she could tell he was as full of apprehension as she was. It had been one thing to talk about him coming to LA and being incorporated into her life, if only for a limited amount of time, but it was quite another to actually do it. They were as awkward as if they'd just met, not acting like two people who'd bared both their souls and their bodies to each other for almost a week. His suit of armor was back on, whereas she felt like one long open wound that hurt to touch. What a pair.

Luna glanced at the bed that the housekeeper had freshly made up for her return. She and Charlie could make love right now. Perhaps that would bring back the ease they'd begun to feel with each other at the villa. Somehow, though, that didn't seem right. She had an idea. "Do you want to go out for a drive?"

They were meandering down a Los Angeles canyon road driven by actress Luna Price in her electric-powered sports car. Had Charlie's famous insomnia played a trick on him yet again? Was he actually hallucinating? From the heat of August in England to the Caribbean steam of Puerto Rico to the arid scorch of the west. His world had been tipped upside down.

"Do you usually drive yourself around town?" he wondered, as she'd spoken so often about the unrelenting attraction of the press to shiny objects such as her. "Surely the tinted windows of a bodyguard's vehicle is more in keeping with the life of a glitterati."

She turned down the rock music she'd been blaring ever since they'd gotten into the car in her covered garage. Explaining that the housekeeper had maintained her cars in her absence, she chose the smaller of the two, the other was an SUV, for their jaunt. Neither were superflashy but he'd still been surprised she kept cars at all. "It's just too unbearable not being able to just hop into a car sometimes and get away. That was an autonomy I wasn't willing to sell. Believe me, the studio will send a car first thing in the morning tomorrow."

He had to admit that Luna looked incredibly sexy as she competently maneuvered the sharp twists and treacherous cliffs of a drive she obviously knew well. With the windows down, her golden waves flew through the air and her unmadeup face glowed. His mouth tipped a private smile at the fun they'd had *dressing her down* for their outing. The exact opposite of when she'd put on her glamazon gear at the resort.

"What do you think?" she'd asked him, emerging from her bedroom closet when they'd decided to go out. In athletic shorts made of a synthetic material, blue with yellow stripes down the sides, coupled with a loose grey T_shirt and sneakers, Luna Price surely did know how to take it down as well as she did to amp it up. In fact, she looked like a skinny young college student in the getup.

"Decidedly less than glamorous, if that's what you were going for," he'd answered with a nod. "And now what, a baseball hat?"

"Mmm, that's a tricky one. The paps are usually on to women in baseball hats. Pick me a wig." She'd pointed to her dressing area, where a shelf held half a dozen wigs on pedestal stands. One was a short, brunette hairstyle. Another, shoulder-length and curly. Another still was long but very dark and stick-straight, unlike her own glorious blond waves.

"How about this one?"

"Grab it. I'll put in on when we get out of the car. And a hat, too." She'd pointed to a rack that held an assortment of styles. He'd chosen a black bucket hat. Then she'd pointed to the door and said, *"Vámanos,"* reminding him that even though she spoke Spanish, no words in any language had been needed when it came to the brazen thrust of his body against hers during those erotic nights at the villa. Charlie still didn't know how he'd let himself end up in Los Angeles. But just as Luna found benefit in time away from an environment that had become unhealthy for her, maybe it was the same for him.

When they arrived onto flat ground at the bottom of the canyon and then drove to the tourist section of Hollywood Boulevard, Charlie guessed where they were going. "I get to see the famous Luna Price's star on the Walk of Fame?"

"You and the ten million who visit annually," she said, stopped at a red light while a countless throng crossed the busy boulevard. She put her arm over her face to block it. Then she turned onto a side street and parked, obviously knowing exactly where her particular star was located.

Once she cut the engine, she looked all around to make sure no one was watching. With the coast clear, she deftly twisted her own hair into a tight spiral and affixed the dark wig to her head. Tilting the rearview mirror toward her, she adjusted and tucked until not one strand of her own lustrous hair was visible. She then topped the wig with the bucket hat Charlie had selected for her. Already wearing sunglasses, her camouflage was complete. Indeed, she didn't look much different than many of the other people strolling down the street. They got out of the car and she tapped her key fob to hear the ping that the doors had been locked.

He was confused by all the quick changes. The movie-star act she had put on at the villa. Now the camouflage just to walk down the street. What about the other her, the flesh and blood of the woman he'd been making love to with all of his might? He couldn't get a footing.

As they walked up to Hollywood Boulevard, she offered some historical perspective on the sidewalk stars. "The first ones were placed on the ground in 1958. Now there are more than two thousand six hundred of them, stretching the length of about a mile."

While Charlie had held meetings in deluxe offices in Century City, browsed the designer shops of Rodeo Drive and eaten cutting-edge tasting menus in the restaurants of celebrity chefs, he'd never just been a tourist on Hollywood Boulevard. Luna rounded the corner, passing businesses peddling everything from pizza to souvenirs. There was even an oddities museum.

"Bus tours to the stars' homes! Bus tours to the stars' homes!" a hawker yelled out, trying to book seats for his next departure. He called over to Luna, "Would you like to see where the movie stars live, miss?"

"Not this time," she answered politely then snickered to herself.

"Do those people know where you live?" Charlie asked when they were out of earshot.

"Thank heavens, no. It's mostly a scam. Maybe a house where someone stayed a long time ago or where some older star from the Golden Age once lived."

"Feeding in to the Dream Factory."

"Smoke and mirrors, honey." Even though she said it in a mock glam tone, it jarred him that she called him *honey*. Was she just being flippant or was she implying something sincere?

Or maybe he still hadn't met the real Luna yet. And maybe he never would. What if the woman in Puerto Rico was another persona she projected as a way to escape the star label that attracted eyes to her every move? Whereas he thought she was being earnest, it could have been quite the opposite. Perhaps she herself didn't even know what was real. Regret flashed through him, and he questioned if he shouldn't have come here to further unravel her and make things even more complicated for himself.

In front of a taco shop, among other five-pointed stars spaced an equal distance apart all up and down the boulevard's sidewalk, was Luna's.

"Look at that," Charlie said, shaking his head at how surreal the moment was. "Luna Price. Do they all have the emblem of a movie camera under the name?"

"No. That's for people in movies. There are others with television receivers, radio microphones and so on."

"What are they made of?"

"I happen to know! They're constructed from coral-colored terrazzo, which is chipped marble. And the rim, name and emblem are brass."

"Don't they do a big unveiling ceremony when they put in a new one?"

"That was a very special day," she said wistfully. "Before Hollywood started to eat me alive."

"Well, it's an amazing accomplishment."

She smiled as if truly proud. "Thank you. It is."

He handed her his phone. "Take my photo with it." She complied and then they took selfies with the both of them and the star. The silliness of it all relaxed them and they made funny faces and giggled until their sides ached.

A tour group walked by, distinguishable because they all wore matching laminated cards on red lanyards around their necks. Some diligently checked every star on the walk, perhaps looking for someone in particular.

In front of hers they overheard an exchange. "Luna Price. What ever happened to her? She hasn't worked in a long time."

"I never liked her, anyway."

It was a laugh-or-cry moment. Fortunately, Luna chose the former. They both burst into hysterics and Charlie tugged her down the block.

"Ms. Price." A knock was heard at Luna's trailer door. "We need you in five."

"Thank you," Anush Vardanyan called out as she opened the door a crack. Charlie had met Luna's best friend and employee a couple of hours earlier, when the two women reunited after last being together in Kentucky. He knew it was Anush who'd made the reservation with the M Dating Agency, taking it upon herself to decide the week's transition before going back to work would be just what Luna needed. Charlie wanted to hug the dark-haired young woman dressed all in black for her foresight, as meeting Luna was one of the most important things that had ever happened to him. Anush had also been instrumental in getting her into treatment for her eating disorder in the first place.

"Ms. Price, can you turn your head this way for me?" a makeup artist asked while he added the finishing touches to Luna's heavily painted and powdered face as she sat in the styling chair. She complied.

"Ms. Price, can I get you a little more to the left?" asked the hairdresser, who was working on her locks at the same time, and whose request required Luna to move in the opposite direction the makeup artist had asked for.

"Ms. Price, may I apply one more gloss coat to your nails?" the manicurist chimed in, which forced Luna to extend her hands while her hair and eyelids were being attended to. Now Charlie couldn't see her face from the angle he was sitting at on one of the sofas in her lavishly appointed trailer. But he could see from her reflection in the mirror that all of the primping was taking its toll as her eyebrows were raised and her lips were a straight line. They'd been at it for well over an hour. A protective instinct in him wanted them to stop.

Inside the trailer was a bathroom with a shower, a dining table and chairs in a kitchen area, a high-tech office nook, two sofas facing each other and a huge mounted television monitor. Luna's dressing area held racks of costumes. The makeup chair was in front of mirrors that adjusted to present different angles, and various lighting options.

"Charlie," she said, managing to call out among the tangle of hands on her, "have you ever been to a film set before?"

"No, I haven't."

"Be prepared to be bored. We do things over and over again. There are a lot of people to please."

"I'm sure I'll find it fascinating. Don't forget, I spend my days in front of a computer screen."

During moments of this whirlwind adventure with Luna, Charlie had here and there momentarily forgotten that he ran a huge tech empire in a land called England far, far away, so enthralled had he become with all things Luna.

The lump of coal that he carried in his chest would forever remind him of the past, of the losses that could never be replaced. The sounds that called to him in the night, even here in LA, the pierce of a screaming baby even though Charlie wasn't with his young Lily when the accident took her life. Those voices, he could never run away from. He was checking in with Tom first thing every morning and there were no burning fires and so his mind hadn't really been on business, which was a first in ten years. Was it actually okay for him to take a little more time to rejuvenate? He couldn't convince himself that it wasn't.

When Luna stood up after the ministrations were complete, it was quite the presentation. The movie industry was serious business, and these were professionals at the top of their game. Luna looked…quite simply flawless. Not a hair out of place. Her skin as smooth as a slate of marble. Almost otherworldly. Almost bloodless. Not at all like the animated face that he had laughed so much with that he thought his sides would split on the way home from their jaunt to Hollywood Boulevard yesterday. He still couldn't tell who was really who in this town of artifice.

When they'd gotten back to her house yesterday, Luna had warned him that she needed to get to bed early because she'd be up at dawn. He'd assumed she meant slumber. After a quick dinner they fell into her big comfortable bed to delight in each other, so that she still got to sleep on time, something else they chuckled about.

He'd lain awake and watched over her as she rested, learning the lights and shadows of her bedroom, wondering to himself how long he should stay and what coming here at all might mean. To her. To him. It was all so unexpected, finding in Puerto Rico a bond that seemed like one in a million.

Oh, Amelia, were those kites on that sunny lawn of El Morro really a sign?

"Here we go," Luna said to him now, with a gesture toward the trailer's exit. Anush swung the door open and a muscular handler was there to accompany Luna to set. Charlie, Anush and the glam team followed behind. Charlie was fascinated at the entourage he had become part of. They walked a short distance to the soundstage, a cavernous structure as big and tall as a barn. But once inside, Charlie could see that a set of an office had been constructed.

"Films are shot out of sequence," Anush told him as they entered the stage. "Today, Luna, playing Alice Stephens, is going to be kidnapped by the evil Gaseous Goblin."

"Oh, no, no, no," a booming voice called out. The film's director, Kitt Kormen, a compact man in his thirties who wore a cap backwards on his head, charged over to Luna and her group. "She looks horrible in that dress. Is she hot, or is she a potato sack?"

A costumer rushed over. "Kitt, we approved this in meetings. Do you want to see it with a belt?" Charlie noticed a few members of the crew who were mulling about stopped to watch Kitt's tirade and whispered among themselves.

"I want to see a dress that doesn't make her look like a stone pillar. Can we get something with shape? Is that too much to ask?"

If first impressions were right, Charlie could see why Luna didn't like Kitt. A gentleman might have welcomed a movie star back onto a set after her time away from the cameras. Charlie could see the stress wash over Luna's face, even under all the makeup she wore. She'd told him about this kind of scrutiny regarding her looks. That it was part of the job. A part that she wasn't well able to cope with, and had led her to dysmorphic ideas about her body. A body that Charlie adored touching and tasting and wrapping himself around. A body that was perfect.

While everyone waited for some new dresses to be considered, Luna and the team filed back to the trailer. Anush went to her car and returned with a stack of men's clothes in her arms. "Charlie," she said as she entered the trailer, "Luna said you needed some clothes for your time in LA. We guessed at your size. Do you want to try these on?"

Charlie looked at Luna, who had sat carefully in a chair so as not to muss her hair and makeup. "Oh, so now I'm the one who has to model outfits for approval?"

"Ha," she jeered. "Misery loves company." And they laughed again.

CHAPTER ELEVEN

"So, what is actually going on with you and Charlie?" Anush asked a few days later after entering Luna's trailer. "You didn't tell me you were bringing him back to LA." She set the two iced lattes she'd picked up for them on a table. Luna had been rehearsing some lines before being called to set and was ready for a break. She picked up her drink and with a well-practiced maneuver she was able to get the straw between her teeth so that she could enjoy it without marring her perfectly applied lipstick. They were alone because the beauty squad was out at lunch.

"Puerto Rico wasn't what I was expecting, that's for sure."

"Great."

"You rascal. You were hoping this would happen when you booked the M Dating Agency trip, weren't you?"

"Guilty as charged. I thought the whole thing would do you good, but what's wrong with letting a man get to know you and not *her*?" Anush emphasized the last word as she swept out her arm, indicating the racks of costume and surfaces strewn with photos of Luna. "That's what resulted, isn't it?"

"Oh," Luna said on a whoosh of breath. "I don't know. It's complicated. He lost his wife and child. He'll never get over his heartache. It's all fun and fine now, but what about the long run?"

"Anybody could say that about any relationship. You can't predict the future."

"It's just that when I was in therapy, there was a lot of talk about me taking care of me. And keeping the focus on that."

"What are you afraid of?"

Luna took another sip of her drink. "I feel like I'm falling in love with him." She let the words settle all around her to decide if they were true. Which they were. She absolutely adored having Charlie here at the studio and with her at night. She could have never guessed at the security that would make her feel. He'd flown up to Silicon Valley today and she was looking forward to his return. He was going to accompany her to a film premiere tonight. She was in such a better mental state that even Kitt's tantrums were easy to keep in perspective. Charlie was the unforeseen element that Luna hadn't known was missing.

But she was afraid of a crash. She was afraid of counting on anyone. Afraid that she didn't know how to trust. What if she ruined it by being too needy? Or not needy enough? Afraid of the words he'd said, that he'd never love again, plain and simple, for fear he couldn't withstand any more heartbreak.

"Why is falling in love a bad thing?" Anush persisted. "I want to fall in love. Doesn't everybody?"

"I don't think he'll be able to do it again." Especially if he stayed in LA much longer. He was not part of this artificial world that was her stock and trade. He was a quiet man and even though that was something she felt so calm and comfortable around, the reality was that she had a loud life.

"So you'll take it one step at a time."

"Stop being so optimistic," Luna teased.

"Isn't that why you keep me around?" Anush smiled back. "So, what are you wearing tonight?"

And suddenly, as one of the most glamorous women in the world, she was reduced to a giggly teenager who wanted to look cute for her prom date.

Judging from Charlie's response, she succeeded. Anush had helped her pick out a slinky green dress that Luna secretly favored over the others because it matched the color of Charlie's eyes. It was sleeveless and with a neckline that made a *V* so low it almost reached her waist. In fact, Anush employed the Hollywood magic of double-sided tape to keep it from becoming scandalous when Luna moved.

In his slim-cut black suit, no doubt bespoke from the finest tailor London had to offer, Charlie was knee-bucklingly handsome. Which was good, because he could have no idea of the inspection that was about to take place. When the driver brought him to the studio, where Luna had dressed after wrapping the shoot for the day, the look on Charlie's face was classic. Like a cartoon rabbit whose eyes popped from their sockets and bounced outward on springs. His lascivious glance started at her exposed throat and made its way slowly, ever so slowly, at that, down the open expanse of her chest until his eyes settled where the fabric finally came together just above her waist. Even though he'd told her many times that he liked her naked and natural better than in any of the other guises she wore, she had to admit that she liked looking sexy when she was about to introduce him to the world as her man.

Even though the studios, and her team, had often paired her up with someone for public appearances, it had never felt like an organic date. Yes, on occasion she'd spent the night with one of them at a hotel afterward, but dawn had always brought out selfish ambitions or opportunistic efforts that she saw right through. Like when she'd been tricked by Troy Lutt, who was out to make a buck off her mistake in being with him. Being driven home up the hill, alone, on those mornings after had been the most hollow and lonely Luna had ever felt, and often led to those horrible internal battles about her body and food.

So for the first time, she was going to arrive at a big Hollywood event on the arm of a man she cared about. A tiny worry about being drained dry again by the bloodthirsty press percolated within her, though, and she didn't know how Charlie would respond to the limelight. After all, he'd come to Puerto Rico to get ready to put on his own public face after so many years in isolation. But Hollywood was no place for a slow start; it was straight into the frying pan.

Still, part of her was excited to reclaim her place as one of the queens of Tinseltown. She deserved a comeback with all of the fanfare. After the driver pulled to the curb where the red carpet began, he came around to open the door for them. Charlie stepped out first and turned to extend his arm to help Luna out. As soon as she emerged, the screams of her name began. She took Charlie's arm and they turned to face the crowd side by side. But he didn't manage the proud and privileged smile she needed him to beam to the camera. Instead, the massive barrage of flashing camera lights were so bright that Charlie quickly jerked his arm up to cover his eyes from their blinding burn.

Luna's New Man! The world's best-known celebrity-watching site graphics were big and bold on the screen across a photo of Luna and Charlie from the night before. Over early morning orange juice and peanut butter on toast at her white breakfast table, Charlie was reading out loud to her from his tablet. Switching to another site, he read . "'Luna Price's return to Hollywood after an unexplained absence included the first viewing of what looks to be a romantic liaison. Sources identified the mystery man as Charlie Matthews, British billionaire who founded the wildly successful biotech firm AMgen at the tender age of nineteen. Hats off to the jolly chap who captured Luna's heart.'"

"Jolly chap?" Luna looked up from the script she was half studying. "They think they're being cutely British with that? That's cheap, even for them."

"Ugh, how can you bear this crap?" Charlie paused for a swig of his juice, then tapped on another article. "'Matthews could star in his own drama, which would be a weeper, as ten years ago his young wife and child were killed in a car accident.'"

His hands dropped from the keyboard. His face turned ashen. It was as though a still thickness had fogged the air.

"Oh, Charlie," Luna murmured, barely above a whisper. "I'm so sorry. These gossipmongers are completely soulless. They'd sell their own mother for a story." This was exactly what she'd feared. That the brutality of the world she inhabited would cause him harm. She'd chosen this—the bad with the good was a trade-off. But he didn't belong, and there was no benefit to him being stripped of his privacy and dignity.

"Apparently," he mumbled back. Before he could go further, she asked to see his tablet. For two reasons. One, he didn't need to read anything else that might make mention of the personal trauma that had defined his adult life. And secondly, she figured she'd take her pain straight up and get it over with. She punched in the addresses for the fashion sites that would have been at the premiere last night in droves.

It didn't take her long to find what she knew she would.

"'Luna, trying hard to reestablish her big place in the film industry with an unfortunately small swath of a dress.'

"'Looking like a four-leaf clover, Luna might be lucky in love but will win no pot of gold for her neon-green dress better suited to a teen pop star.'

"'Only someone like Luna, who has no curves, could pull off the engineering feat required to keep that dress up.'"

Her gut began to bubble.

Is she hot, or is she a potato sack? Kitt's comment from her first day on set replayed in her head.

Only someone like Luna, who has no curves...

And then she found yet another site that had caught a photo of them that first day, unbeknownst to her, on Hollywood Boulevard. "'What is Luna hiding under those baggy clothes and wig? Did visiting her own star give her a needed ego boost?'"

There it all was, just as she had left it a year ago.

The press's unending cravings. It didn't even seem to matter if it was true information or not. They wanted to assume, insinuate, guess. All the old feelings gurgled back. That her success hadn't really been earned, but it had been granted. She could be a glittery enough object that held fascination, but only if she was constantly vigilant. Being perfect all the time was the only formula, yet perfection was subjective. How could she please everybody all the time? Therapy had taught her that she couldn't. But something was stuck between her intellect and her emotions. Which is what had led her to make mistakes and keep secrets. Secrets she held tightly, silently, in the dark rooms of her mind until they almost killed her.

And now she'd brought Charlie into the wreckage. How foolish she'd been, in the throes of seduction, underneath a magical waterfall on a faraway island, to ask him to come into this zombie feeding frenzy of her life. This was a side of the real her that nobody would want to be around. She pushed away her plate of toast, no longer hungry.

"My car will be here soon," she said softly. "Do you want to come to the studio with me today?"

Expecting him to say no, she was relieved when he agreed.

"Yes. I've got some work to attend to, but I can do it there." His eyes were dull, but he bravely stood to get ready.

Kitt and the screenwriters decided to make a couple of dialogue changes, so Luna spent a lot of the day waiting. She sent Anush home and banished the squad from her trailer until needed. Had she or Charlie been in a better mood, they could have played a card game or something to pass the time. But the morning's headlines still resonated through her, and she suspected Charlie was second-guessing everything, as well.

"The phone call came at eleven fifty-six in the evening," he said, eyes fixed on the painting of a tree above the table.

"What call?"

"The police. To tell me that an accident had occurred. They told me there was no point in me coming to the scene as they'd be rushing the victims to the hospital. I have almost no recollection of running through the house to get to the car, only of myself driving in the dead of an icy night." Luna looked around her trailer. The shoes that cost thousands of dollars. The styling chair where a half-dozen people made their livelihood by servicing an industry of make-believe. Nothing mattered at all in the face of Charlie's tragedy. "It was Lily's six-month birthday. That would indeed make for a tear-jerker of a film, wouldn't it?"

Tears rolled down Luna's cheeks. She didn't care if her makeup artist was going to have to start his work over again today. Her heart shattered for Charlie. She reached for his hand, which was next to hers on the sofa. He accepted it, but distractedly. With her other hand, she stroked his forearm up and down, down and up, hoping to soothe him in some way. A small crook of his lip told her he had noticed.

When she was finally called for a quick reshoot, Charlie followed along, perhaps just for the activity. The sun had already gone down and a fair amount of the crew had been dismissed. So, unusually, a handler wasn't sent to accompany Luna the short distance to set.

As soon as they stepped out of the trailer, she heard it. *Click, click, click, click.* Rapid-fire, like bullets from a machine gun. Someone with a long-lensed camera was in the vicinity. *Click, click, click.* The sound would be forever etched in her brain. On and on it went. Whoever the photographer was would take hundreds of shots, hoping for the one good one that would make a sale to the tabloids. Charlie, with tension in his eyes after reliving the night that altered him forever, heard it, too. He whipped his head around and located the camera being focused on them. The glower he pierced the photographer with could have curdled blood.

The next morning, he checked his phone and showed it to her. Sure enough, there was a photo of Charlie seething, with Luna by his side, the reason for his scowl misconstrued. The caption read, Luna Price's new love affair—already on the rocks?

Charlie walked Luna out her front door and waved her off as the driver took her to the studio. He'd had enough of being trapped in her trailer, which seemed even more of a fortress now that he'd witnessed the relentless paparazzi, who perched like vultures everywhere she went, planning their attack, always ready. That Luna could withstand their constant presence was hard to believe. In a way he felt proud of her, proud that she ultimately must have a very strong character to stand up to all of that limelight. He knew it had gotten to her, which is why she'd taken the year off. He hoped, for her sake, that her recovery tools would be enough to keep her from sliding back into danger.

She'd suggested he take one of her cars and go out to the beach while she worked, promising that they'd meet tonight for a low-key dinner at home. Sensible advice, and perhaps a drive to the ocean would do him good. He still couldn't shake the bloodthirsty face of that photographer yesterday, the vicious glee he took in snapping shots when he shouldn't have. Not long after Luna left, Charlie got into her car and flipped the ignition. Swooshing down the canyon was exhilarating and he cranked up the rock 'n' roll Luna had programmed.

The Pacific Ocean was as fierce as he remembered it, with tall waves exploding onto the shoreline. The waters surrounding sweet Puerto Rico were so much milder by comparison. He parked the car and walked down the path leading to the beach. It was still morning and the beachcombers were just beginning to stake their claims in the sand with blankets, picnics, toys and towels. A windy morning, at that, which is why he watched a few people struggle to anchor the poles of their umbrellas.

He took off his shoes, rolled up his pants and went as far as ankle-deep into the bracingly cold water, where he began his stroll. He thought of Luna's luminous face under the tender moon of Puerto Rico.

Luna, Luna. With her, he'd begun to think that energy could whoosh through his veins again. She'd re-awakened him sexually, made him virile and potent once more, able to howl into those sultry Caribbean midnights. Together they'd looked into the mirror and been willing to face what they saw. For a brief moment in time, Charlie thought he could change that reflection from a man whose heart and soul and spirit had already been used up into someone whose well was full again. Who had hope.

But his central nervous system told him otherwise. He'd put a tiny crack in that hard shell, certain that he'd now be able to manage a dinner date or attend a party under the guise of civilized society. Puerto Rico let in just a sliver of light so that he could appease his employees and his investors. Progress had been made. That was enough.

He couldn't survive at Luna's level of interaction with the human race. She deserved someone who could. Someone who could even rise above it to put boundaries around the invasion. Charlie had built a wall around himself, but the space was only large enough for him. In Puerto Rico, he'd thought for a minute he might be able to tear down the barriers and truly live out in the open, in trust, in faith. The last few days in LA had shown him how wrong he'd been.

He kicked the sand and shook his head. A family playing on the beach caught his eye. The woman and the littlest ones filled colorful plastic containers with sand. An older girl, probably about ten, the same age Lily would have been if she was still alive, and her father were trying to fly kites. Amelia and her kites. The vivid displays of kites at the El Morro in Viejo San Juan. Charlie had convinced himself that they were a sign from Amelia, assuring him that not only could he smile again, but also that he could love once more.

In this morning's swirling wind, the girl and her father couldn't get the kites into the air. They floundered, flopping over and over in the sand, the lines tangling into a mess. That was the real sign, Charlie thought to himself. Not being able to fly the kite. Not even getting it off the ground.

CHAPTER TWELVE

"LUNA, SIT UP STRAIGHTER!" Kitt yelled over as he and his cinematographer, Hans, viewed her through several camera lenses.

"The shoulders are still off."

"And I don't like the shadow under the chin."

"You're slouching, Luna. Can you *please* sit up straighter?"

"I can blend out some of the width here and here." Hans gestured something to Kitt.

Luna could feel the simmer within her. It always began as little bubbles in her gut, like a fountain just beginning to gurgle. Making her feel restless, uncomfortable in her own skin. Listening to the two men talk about *the shoulders* and *the chin*, as if she was a collection of inanimate parts, the bubbles were multiplying. They made her want to sink down into the spring so that their words couldn't reach her. It was starting again. She knew it as sure as she'd know night from day.

She and Charlie had spent the day apart. He texted that he'd gone to the beach. Things weren't right between them—they could both feel it in their bones. They were a million miles from the carefree shores of Puerto Rico. Him being in LA wasn't working out.

* * *

That night, Luna was detained on set for so long that by the time she got home, she'd missed the dinner they were planning. She found Charlie asleep on one of the living room sofas, the golden glow from a lamp obscuring half of his face. Knowing that sleep didn't come easy for him, she wasn't about to disturb him, so she covered him with a blanket and turned off the light.

She'd already had both the assistant director and her manager tell Kitt that she needed to keep reasonable hours if she was going to do her best work. Last time she'd approached Kitt herself, he'd reminded her that after she'd disappeared last year, throwing off the production schedule for the film and costing the studio millions of dollars, she might want to be less demanding. She remembered in therapy discussing how to circumvent people who pressed her buttons. Wisely, she'd decided not to have any conversations directly with Kitt anymore. But it had been a trying day. She forced herself to eat a sandwich and then got into her own bed, alone.

In the morning, she promised Charlie a rain check on dinner. And so indeed, before the moon had risen too high in the sky that night, she and Charlie sat at her kitchen table for a home-cooked meal, albeit one prepared by her housekeeper.

"You haven't touched your food," he observed.

The bubbles began to percolate inside her again. She hated people noticing or commenting on what she ate. Pausing, she realized that he was only trying to help.

She picked up her fork and knife, then sliced into the roast chicken with a seasoning rub she'd asked her housekeeper to prepare. Bringing the bite to her mouth, the spices reminded her of lovemaking in the sand and of Charlie's smile, which she hadn't seen in days.

She followed one bite with another. As they'd talked about in therapy, if she took the right actions then the right thinking would follow.

"It doesn't seem as if things are going well on the film."

"Perhaps I came back to a movie set too soon," she replied, voicing what she'd been thinking. "This week is triggering me. I thought I was further along in my recovery."

"I know what you mean. What we shared at Dorada made me think for the first time since my family's death that I might be able to start again with someone new," he said, eyes cast down on his dinner plate and not on her. But then he lifted them. "Not with *someone*. With you."

"But?"

"I can't smile for the cameras. I can't put makeup over the wounds that still burn me until I'm red and chapped every single night. Yes, I'll rise up enough to do what I need to do to keep AMgen growing and thriving, even if I'm not. But I think that's all I'll ever be able to manage."

"I don't know if I can smile for the cameras anymore, either. Even though I used to be a master at disguising who I really was inside. I was more of an actress in my personal life than I ever was on the silver screen. I'm not sure it's worth it anymore. I have some more soul-searching to do."

They finished eating in silence. Was he thinking what she was? About what might have been? The American movie star and the British tech billionaire. Two damaged people finding each other in the darkness and hanging on for dear life was the stuff fantasies were made of. Because kindred spirits don't come around every day. Because the safety, comfort and chances they found in each other's arms was too rare and precious a gift to let go of.

But that wasn't their script.

"It's time for me to go home to England."

Sorrow manifested in one tear that made a slow slide down Luna's face. "I know."

Charlie had never hated a flight more. As his jet rocketed him through the clouds, he squeezed his eyes shut for a minute. It was as if the week in Puerto Rico and this second one in California had happened in a trance. Like a vision, from which he was supposed to emerge from and then forget, getting on with his life, until the details faded away like the vast county of Los Angeles, with its endless suburbs and swimming pools that looked like little dots of turquoise viewed from the sky.

When his regular driver picked him up at Heathrow in London, his familiar face confirmed that Charlie was indeed home. The route to his estate was one he'd traveled many times, although his driver's voice sounded tinny and distant.

The entrance hall looked like a mausoleum today. Which, in essence, it was. For ten years Charlie had considered it a cemetery, one he'd refused to leave. As if staying in the house kept Amelia and Lily nearer to him, and he was watching over his family, even though their remains were in the ground miles away. Images of Luna's skirt as she danced the bomba and all that had transpired between them paraded in front of him, a vision from another lifetime. The tombstones were the only things that were real.

While he sifted through the mail on his desk, he could only think of Luna. First viscerally, of her silken skin and lush lips and sweet smell, like sugar in the sun. The unbridled eroticism they shared was shocking. His hunger, his sovereignty, his want for her breathed a charge back into him. But it was more than that. Even though he and Amelia had enjoyed fulfilling lovemaking, he'd been just a young adult then. Not yet in touch with his own physical prowess. Not even knowing he was capable of a savage fervor that scorched the earth he and Luna traversed. What they'd unlocked within each other was life-changing. He'd never be the same man. As he brought his luggage into the foyer for his housekeeper to unpack tomorrow, an empty thud of finality beat in his chest.

He and Luna had also knocked into a stunning candor with each other. Perhaps it was the nature of the setup through the M Dating Agency. They were both people who needed a passageway to whatever was next. Even though Charlie might never be able to exorcise the haunts of this house, he felt different indeed, although perhaps not in the ways he'd have expected. Would Luna defeat her own enemies? For a brief moment he thought they might be able to trudge on their paths side by side. But no, he'd have to walk alone. The pain of a fresh solitude needled up his spine.

There was that something between them that couldn't be put into words. Lying on top of her, their bodies speaking in the most intimate way possible, their solar plexuses met, as well. The auras that emanated from each of them into the ether had become one. There was no separation of his spirit from hers. It was a tie he'd never known anything of, not even with Amelia. He was only able to receive it after earning the maturity he held now. Unfortunately, he dared not trust it. Because if he was wrong, if their synthesis was only born of circumstance and loneliness, it could easily betray him or evaporate. He couldn't withstand any more defeat.

Had he hurt Luna by deciding to leave LA? It was with a flat resignation that they both agreed the M encounter, as planned, and the unplanned week in LA were all they would have together. Clearly, her year away from the spotlight hadn't sorted all of her issues. She needed to get right within herself. But a voice within him screamed that they could have helped each other conquer it all. He hated himself for not being able to try. She was where the light shone. Without her, everything was dim. His palms flattened against the cold walls of his stone corridor as he made his way to his empty bed.

"Good to see you." Tom greeted Charlie with a firm handshake at the shareholders' meeting the next day.

"I can't promise I'm a changed man in every respect, but I understand what I have to do." He'd been dutifully shaking hands with guests for an hour. It was exhausting.

"Not changed 'in every respect.' What does that mean? What happened? Charlie, I have to say that I was hopeful when you decided to extend the trip and go to LA."

"Hopeful about what?"

"That in Luna you'd unexpectedly met someone you might create a future with."

"Perhaps I bit off more than I could chew there."

"Did you find out that you and Luna weren't compatible, despite M's careful matchmaking skills?"

"Quite the opposite."

"Then what are you waiting for? Amelia and Lily have been gone ten years. Are you going to mourn for your entire life?"

"Believe me, I ask myself the same question all the time."

"Tell me about her."

"Luna? She's marvelous. Vibrant and smart and thoughtful. I'll cherish our time together for the rest of my life. Thank you for setting that up," he said wistfully. He honestly didn't know if he wanted to thank Tom or hate him. For showing him what he could have had if he'd been able to reach out and grab it. That was like taunting a hungry man with food but not letting him eat.

"I read something philosophical not long ago that said something to the effect of when you're lying on your deathbed, it's nothing you did—like eating that chocolate mousse, or taking that impulsive trip to Prague, or telling someone you loved them—that you'll have remorse over. It's the things you didn't do for which you'll have regret."

That night, he sat on his oxblood leather chair sipping a brandy in front of his unlit fireplace like an old man. Was he at the end of his life? That wasn't fair to him. That wasn't fair to his memories or to Luna. He had to tear down the stone walls. Earlier, Tom had inferred what Charlie already knew. That he loved Luna. Dearly. Urgently. Wholeheartedly. LA had cast doubt in him about who Luna was. Was she the humble rancher's daughter or the Hollywood star millions admired? The fragile creature that crumbled under pressure or the warrior who put herself back together? But he'd realized that she was all of those things. And more. He wanted to hold dear every precious facet of her. Embrace it all. Forever.

"Wake up, sleepyhead." Anush's voice came through Luna's phone once she'd swiped it open after hearing the ringtone of Puerto Rican drumbeats.

"I'm not due on set to..." She stopped herself, remembering that she wasn't shooting with Kitt. She had a TV appearance today. A film that was finished a year and a half ago was finally being released and she had a press interview to promote it. "Oh, right. I have to be *her* again this morning."

A flicker of anxiety pinged through her. Would she look good enough? Would the camera operator be one who flattered or was careless? She mentally reviewed her talking points.

"I've got the tan-colored suit for you with the midnight blue blouse if you're still feeling good about that," Anush offered.

"Which shoes?"

"The brown slingbacks."

"Okay." Luna moaned and stretched like a cat. She didn't want to get out of bed and face the morning, but she had to.

"Why don't you bring Charlie along? That ought to make the day sweeter." Silence. "I'm winking even though you can't see it."

Silence again.

"Luna?" Anush coaxed.

"Charlie went back to England."

"Why?"

"There was no point in him staying."

The night before last, they'd agreed that they weren't going to be able to turn the magic they'd found at Dorada into something long-lasting. Luna had been due early on set again yesterday, so she'd gone to bed. She'd sensed Charlie all night on the chaise in the alcove she'd assigned as his space. His rustling told her that he hadn't slept much, either. In the morning, they were like professionals who had completed a deal. They thanked each other for the time they'd shared. He gave her a matter-of-fact kiss on the cheek before slipping into the back seat of the car he'd arranged to take him the airport. Luna, barefoot and in a thin pink robe, had stood outside and watched the car take the curves in the road away from her house before she let her tears fall.

"Luna, you're one of the most glittering stars on the planet. Men find you beautiful. Women want to be you. What is it *you* want?"

Charlie. She wanted Charlie. Nothing had ever felt as good as being with him in Puerto Rico had. There, she felt safe. Accepted. Looked after but respected at the same time. Heard.

She hadn't been able to keep that fire kindled once they got back to LA. The pressure was too much. It was understandable. She'd just returned from a year away, when she'd learned to manage her shadows. How to see them for what they were. To circumvent negative thoughts before they turned into destructive behaviors. She was a work in progress but she'd made leaps and bounds from where she was a year ago, when she'd hidden in that dark place of denial, alone, keeping secrets.

Of course, she could see in hindsight that it had been too much to bring Charlie into that complex fold before she'd even had a chance to sort it out. Yet they couldn't haved said goodbye at Dorada. What they'd shared there was too special, they'd come to mean too much to each other. It was an honest mistake of hers to invite him here, but a mistake nonetheless.

Maybe someday she would have enough distance from the phony priorities that had brought her down and she could think about finding a man who didn't care when the public inevitably moved on to the next pretty face. Perhaps after her star had faded she could find someone to live out a companionable existence with. Although she'd always know that she let *the one* slip away because she'd convinced herself she wasn't ready for him. Anguish overtook her until she could barely breathe. Logic didn't make sense. There was only her heart aching to put her hand in his and trudge the road as one. Was someone ever ready for love?

Love.

She was in love with Charlie. The words bounced from left to right, front to back in her mind. In love. In. Love. It was an active state, present tense. In. Love. The most amazing thing that had ever happened to her. And yet he was over five thousand miles away and out of her life.

The crew at the taping studio where Luna was to do her interview had her sit every which way while they adjusted lights and sound. The interviewer, Blick Jenson, host of a widely watched entertainment news program, was known for pushing outside of the agreed-upon topics. As it was, her emotions were raw, so she was apprehensive, and would remain on guard until the segment was over. Once they began, as an actress she easily spoke with enthusiasm about the role that had actually bored her to tears. She had only complimentary things to say about yet another director who had made her feel like a plastic doll under his command.

True to form, Blick began probing. "Luna, we haven't seen you in a year. Will you share with us where you've been and why you took a break from Hollywood?"

Definitely not a subject on the approved list. She bristled, resentful at him for not following the rules of respect, for putting her on the spot. Luna's management team had decided that absolutely nothing would be said about her absence. She'd simply pick up where she left off and the public's curiosity would die down soon enough. Movies were released on all sorts of odd schedules relative to when they were shot, and she'd swiftly make up for lost time.

Yet as she was about to pivot his question to something safer, that bubbling fountain in her belly began to fizz. Only this time it wasn't because her eating disorder was possessing her body, about to make her undo all of the hard work she'd done in Kentucky. No, it was quite the opposite. Those bubbles had become her power. Her truth.

Charlie. How much she'd learned from him! He was incapable of pretending, whereas Luna was a master at pretend. He was who he was while Luna had made a fortune being anyone except herself. But no longer.

"I haven't shared this before," she told Blick, whose eyes widened as he leaned forward from his chair opposite her with interest. Of course, he was as bloodthirsty as the rest, eager for an exclusive scoop. "I was in treatment…for an eating disorder."

The crew, from electrician to lighting tech to makeup artist, froze in their tracks. A pin dropping would have sounded like thunder.

But the words had already fallen out of Luna's mouth. There was no stopping now. Nor did she want to. This would be the next phase of her healing. No longer in the shadows. She continued, "Those of us in front of the cameras are very blessed to be in our professions. When people think of celebrities, they often imagine us as having perfect lives, and looking perfect while having them. Moviemakers deliver to the public a fantasy, a getaway from real life and human problems. Representing that escape took its toll on me. I became sick with anorexia nervosa. Once I realized how bad it had gotten and how much I needed help, I went into a recovery program."

As the hush continued to permeate the set, Blick asked more and more questions until Luna had told him, and the entire world, everything there was to tell. It was absolutely cathartic. Her lungs expanded, her vision sharpened. It was one of the crowning moments of her life, especially when she considered that her confession might be able to help others who were struggling with eating disorders to come out from the dark. If she'd been able to hold a torch for even one person's path, her entire position of fame was worthwhile. She wouldn't let the world judge her for who she was anymore and a feeling of freedom swept over her like a bird in the wind of a limitless sky.

It was almost peace. But there was something essential missing. Something that she'd never find true tranquility or inner wellness without. Something that was six feet tall with nakedly green eyes, and whose embrace gave her those wings. That was another truth that had become clear on this day of candor. She was entitled to a pure and healthy relationship. One where she could love and be loved with complete sincerity. That's what she wanted. She wasn't going to let her fame, or her eating disorder, take that from her. She'd never experienced anything even close to the joy and honesty she'd had with Charlie. She didn't have to live without it and she wasn't going to.

CHAPTER THIRTEEN

"Meet me back at the villa," Charlie demanded. It was dawn in Buckinghamshire, which meant late at night in Los Angeles. But he hadn't been able to wait even one day to place the call that his gut had been fighting for.

"Charlie?"

"When can you take a few days off from filming?"

Standing out on the stone terrace outside of his bedroom, he surveyed the gardens and grounds of his property. The estate had come back to life all of a sudden, even though that wasn't literally possible. It was he who had reignited his own light inside and that made everything look brighter. His grass was the greenest green and the marble was a reflection of his inner gleam. The trees had never been taller, the pond was shimmering, the ducks stately. This home that he had bought to raise a family in had waited for him. During all the grey years, when he'd shuffled like an automaton up and down the polished halls, the house never gave up. Now, all the curtains were drawn back again. Sunshine filled the rooms, and soon the leaves would fall, followed by the winter snow, before spring would bloom anew once again. Charlie wasn't going to be in a daze for even one moment of it. Every leaf would have his full attention. Because he was in love again.

"Let's talk about it at the café in Viejo San Juan, where we ate the grilled eggplant with honey." He thought of how sultry Luna was in those Taino earrings he'd bought and how he couldn't take his hands off her. What he hadn't realized then was that she held his heart in her hand. And always would.

"I'm glad you called. I had this interview and—"

"Yes, I saw it!" Which was why he couldn't wait another minute to talk to her. He'd been all but bursting open with pride. "I want to hear every detail about it. In person. Tell that pipsqueak of a director that you have a personal matter that needs immediate attention. I'll send my plane tomorrow."

"As it happens, during the next few days Kitt is shooting some action sequences that, of course, I'm not in."

"Oh, I could kiss that little weasel after all. I'll arrange all of your transportation. See you at the villa." He tapped off the call with his skin tingling.

When Luna stepped onto the plane at the private hangar at LAX, her jaw dropped open. "Charlie! What are doing here? I thought I was meeting you at Dorada."

"I thought so, too. Until I realized that meant I'd have to wait seven extra hours to see you. So I decided to come get you myself." Charlie had been standing just inside the entrance door so that Luna wouldn't see him until she boarded the plane.

His flight crew milled about but smiled at the prank. They must have sensed his excitement and the sea change within him. Though he'd never been an ogre, he was probably unpleasant to be around as he traversed the globe when AMgen business demanded it, but never with any gusto for travel. Never any gusto for anything.

Once Luna stepped all the way into the cabin, the crew backed away and Charlie threw his arms around her waist, lifted her off the ground and twirled her in a circle. "By the way, I love you," he said into her ear, having forced himself to wait until they were in person to utter those three crucial words.

She leaned back her head and stared at him with those clear blue eyes. "You do?"

Talking to himself in the moment, he fought not to feel rejected by her lack of *I love you, too*. His exuberance was probably not what she expected, and she hadn't known all of the conclusions that had become clear to him once he'd returned to England. It would be all right, he counseled himself. Once they got back to the villa everything would fall into place.

After the flight took off, the attendants brought out an extravagant meal of lobster to start, followed by a creamy pasta, but as they flew across the US, he could tell Luna was regarding him with caution. Like she was deciding something. He didn't like it. He'd become so confident and sure of his feelings for her. It would have been so much easier if she'd been able to do the same. But he could wait, he kept reassuring himself. He'd been getting ready for her for ten years, he just hadn't realized it. What were a few more days, or even weeks?

While they watched a movie to pass the time, Luna dozed off. Then after using the plane's grandly appointed bathroom, she emerged freshened up. He stared deep into her eyes, hoping the love that was overflowing within him would radiate around them and flow inside her. Instead of the smile he'd hoped to receive, though, her mouth flattened into a straight line as she sat down next to him.

"What's wrong?"

"I just don't know if I can have someone look at me the way you do."

"Why?"

"Because what if you stop? What happens when you see a side of me you don't like? When I'm too boring for you? I don't want to get accustomed to someone showering me with care like that."

"Well, you'd better get used to it. Because I'm going to be doing it for the rest of our lives."

Her brow furrowed.

It was okay. He'd show her. He'd have to.

"Welcome back to Recurso Llave Dorada," the manager, Juan Carlos, exclaimed as he ushered Luna and Charlie into the golf cart. Motoring along the familiar path that led to La Villa de Felicidad, Luna flushed with striking memories of the private fantasy world she and Charlie had created. She closed her eyes. The resort did have a particular smell like nowhere else, of fragrant plants native to the area, and Charlie's warm arm pressed against her was divine. The sea air running through her hair made her feel at one with the island.

Once Juan Carlos departed after unloading their luggage, Charlie wrapped an arm around Luna's waist and brought her to him for a homecoming kiss that pulled her up on her toes. While they'd kissed on the plane, they hadn't been alone. Now the privacy of the villa was theirs once more. Her arms wound around his neck before she'd asked them to, so instinctive was her draw to him. Birds chirped in the background as they kissed and then kissed some more.

In fact, it was the most natural thing in the world when he picked her up into his arms and carried her to the master bedroom, where they had given themselves to one another in every way. Clothes flew off and the plush bedding was tossed back. Luna didn't know where her hands and mouth wanted to go first, she longed for him so. Running the tip of her tongue down the length of his neck, the familiar taste of his skin was spicy and salty and sweet all at once. The moan coming from his vocal cords vibrated against her lips. His sound excited her further, thrumming in her core, driving her. They brought each other to the clouds before collapsing, breathless for the moment. After a while Charlie dozed off, giving Luna immense satisfaction that his body and mind were resting.

Lying in his arms, though, trepidation was a cruel overseer, making sure Luna didn't completely relax. This was now the third go-round with Charlie in only three weeks' time. In LA, after the interview, she'd been secure that she was ready to keep Charlie as hers forever. Once she boarded his plane, however, she wasn't so sure. It hit her that they'd somehow met both the best and the worst of each other but nothing in the middle. What would the realities of the day-in-and-day-out pain he'd always carry look like and how would she manage a lifetime commitment to keep the monster that lived inside of her caged? What if they gave one another their all, but they couldn't make their partnership work? Both stood the chance of total destruction. Now she was filled with uncertainty. She stared at the ceiling, chewing on her lip.

* * *

That night, they had a late dinner in the courtyard. Charlie was barefoot, in a loose linen shirt and pants that swayed a bit with the breeze—he looked like the picture of easygoing handsomeness. Not only liberated from the suits and ties his prominence and power dictated, but also shorn of the hipster clothes he'd worn in LA to blend into her world. Which version was the real him, after a fortnight had rocked their old selves to the ground?

"You haven't told me how your interview was received," Charlie said and then reached across the table to take one of her hands in his.

"Kitt was livid, of course. Why should the focus be on my well-being while he was shooting a blockbuster I didn't even mention? Likewise, I was supposed to be promoting a film I shot ages ago, not talking about my personal transformation."

"Why am I not surprised?"

"My team was in shock, too, that I talked about it so openly after we'd had several meetings to discuss the strategy and I had agreed with the decision not to mention my eating disorder at all."

"What changed your mind?"

She paused. Had a sip of the sparkling water that had been poured into a stemmed glass. The answer she was going to give was complete and accurate. "You."

Charlie's mouth hitched into a grin. "Me?"

"You showed me that it's okay to be who I am. You make me feel like I don't owe anyone anything except my authentic self."

"And how did the public react to that?" Reassuringly,

he stroked the top of her hand back and forth with the pad of his thumb.

"Social media went crazy. It was one of the top trending topics."

"Positive or negative?"

"Both. One contingent appreciating that I shed light on an important subject that affects hundreds of thousands of people. Once I calmed my publicist down, I got her to post eating-disorder helplines and links for people reading who might be in need."

"That's wonderful. How could there be anything but praise for your courage?"

"Are you kidding me?"

"What do you mean?"

She picked up her phone and scrolled.

Luna Price, who has made a fortune on her enviably svelte physique, now tells Hollywood that it's put too much pressure on her. Talk about biting the hand that doesn't feed you.

It's somehow someone else's fault that Luna Price can't live up to her own image. The typical self-obsession that makes movie stars into clichés.

Why didn't she try eating a pizza, gaining five pounds and noticing that no one cares?

"Oh, my love. We'll file lawsuits."

She chuckled. "You can't sue people on social media for writing insulting things."

"It's defamation of character."

"You want to hear the strangest thing? I don't even care about the response to what I said."

"You don't?"

"I really don't. I've spent so many years trying to please everyone and racing to stay on top. Like everything is some mountain you have to claw your way to the top of." He brought her hand to his mouth and kissed the top of it. "I'm just done."

"What does that mean?"

Good question. She thought out loud. "I'm done being perfect. Done caring what other people think." And done coming up with reasons why she couldn't have what most people dream of. "And I'm done with a life you're not in. I love you, Charlie."

Without letting go of her hand, he stood, bringing her up with him so they could embrace under the moon. "And I'll tell you something else," she continued, fired up. "A year wasn't long enough away from Hollywood for me to really get my health back. Might you have a spare room at your mansion?" Their lips met in a joining that Luna now knew was her home.

Charlie swung his hips with the abandon he remembered from when they were here last time. The groove got under Luna's skin, too, and she flitted the ruffles of her skirt while she fixed a seductive gaze on him until he thought he'd melt like hot candle wax. He wanted nothing more than to dance this night away with her in Viejo San Juan. No, that wasn't true. What he wanted was to dance with her every night.

"You haven't told me what you think about my idea," she said after they cooled down with *piraguas*—shaved ice with flavored syrups. "I can base myself in the UK, at least for a while."

"What I think is that you'll like my estate in Buckinghamshire. It's serene and private." While for all these years it had felt gloomy and isolating, with Luna inhabiting the property it would be as alive as the dancing was in this plaza. He'd never believed that he'd fling open his doors again. The entry to his home. And to his heart. But now he couldn't wait.

He added, "And, if you're not comfortable there, we'll get a place in London."

"I've never been in a real relationship."

"I know. We'll figure it out."

"I don't even know if I want to be in show business anymore."

"We'll figure that out, too. You and I. We'll be able to face anything as long as we're together."

Their joyous dancing lasted until the wee hours, then they fell asleep on the beach on a blanket in the sand in front of the villa. Charlie slept soundly, waking surprised when slumber had come so easily again with her in his arms.

Over morning coffee, Luna checked her phone and had a message from Paris. She excused herself to return the call inside the villa. He wondered whom she knew in Paris and realized he had much to learn about the woman he planned to spend the rest of his life with.

"Well, well," she said as she returned to the front patio after quite a while. "The universe must be tuned in to our master plan."

"What do you mean?" He gestured for her to sit beside him on a lounger on the sand and have some spicy café con leche.

"That was Bernice Dubois."

"The film director?" One of France's best-known directors, she had been consistently wowing at film festivals and winning awards lately.

"Yes. She saw my interview with Blick Jenson. She's struggled with an eating disorder herself."

"Interesting."

"She's written a script about a woman whose life is almost ruined by it until she's able to get the proper treatment. She just offered me the role."

Joy swelled in him. "You've said you wanted to start making films that were important to you. What did you tell her?"

"That I had to read the script first, of course. But that I was very interested." As the news set in, she added, "Oh, my gosh. Do you know what this could mean for me?"

"I'm so happy for you."

"She asked if I thought my schedule would allow me to spend some time in Paris once I finish the shoot I'm on."

"I love Paris. Which, by the way, is a very short distance from Buckinghamshire," he said with a wily smile.

"I owe so much of it to you. If it hadn't been for you, I wouldn't have had the courage to open up in that interview. You've become a new mirror to see myself in."

"I could say the same about you." He leaned over and cupped her velvety cheek with his hand, brought his lips to hers, both of them giddy with anticipation about the future. "You pulled me out of the darkness. I never expected to shine in the light again. You made my life worth living again. You are simply magical, my love."

"No one has ever loved me just for me. I don't have to prove myself to you. You have no idea how much you've changed my whole being in the blink of an eye. You've given me myself back."

"And I always will, my Luna, my beloved."

They held hands and looked outward, watching the morning sparkle over the Caribbean.

"I'm going to miss Puerto Rico," she said wistfully.

"We'll come back," he said as he went down on one knee in the sand and pulled a small velvet box from his pocket, opening it to reveal a sun-glinted diamond ring. "On our honeymoon. Will you marry me?"

Luna's smile told him everything he needed to know. "I will, Charlie. I will."

EPILOGUE

FRIENDS AND WORK colleagues congregated in the garden until they were told to take their seats because the ceremony was to begin. Luna's family and her Hollywood team were there. Anush was a lovely maid of honor in her pewter-colored dress. And Charlie's COO, Tom, made a dignified best man in his grey suit. Bernice Dubois and Luna's new French friends were in attendance, as well. In the back row, Madison Morgan of the M Dating Agency looked on, the results of her handiwork earning her a well-deserved smile of pride.

Charlie waited at the altar as he watched his future father-in-law walk his magnificent bride down the aisle. She approached in her slinky champagne-colored dress holding a bouquet of flowers she'd requested be picked from this very garden—from the monument that Charlie had planted in his mourning so many years ago.

The memorial garden had become a happy place, where Charlie and Luna came to walk and talk frequently. So much had happened in the months since Luna accepted the acting role with Bernice. The two women had already formed a production company to make films about women's issues and several projects were underway, with others planned. Luna was easily able to base herself in Buckinghamshire. In fact, she had nothing short of a corporate office set up in an unused wing of the mansion. Charlie was delighted that those floors were being used for something important.

As the officiant pronounced them husband and wife, Charlie could not have been more in love with the woman who was now his wife. Their kiss was met with cheers and applause. They had the good wishes of everyone in attendance, most of them knowing what challenging paths Charlie and Luna had had to follow in order to get to this moment.

The sun was out, the flowers were vibrant and the bees were buzzing. Looking up to the light blue sky, he could hardly believe what he saw. A rainbow-striped kite soared up toward the clouds. Where on earth could it have come from? A neighboring property, perhaps? A child at a party having accidentally let go of the line?

A strong feeling of warmth filled Charlie on the inside. He knew what the kite meant. *Thank you, Amelia*, he mouthed.

At the luncheon following the ceremony Charlie and Luna made the rounds, visiting guests at every table. One of his employees asked, "Where are you going on your honeymoon?"

The bride and groom beamed enormous smiles to each other, then answered in unison, "Puerto Rico, of course."

* * * * *

FALLING FOR HER CONVENIENT GROOM

JENNIFER FAYE

MILLS & BOON

PROLOGUE

Verona, Italy

SHE WAS IN CHARGE.

It hadn't been her goal. She had been satisfied with working in the background.

Still, Carla Falco now sat in the CEO's chair, and it was time to sign off on the payroll for the Falco Fresco Ristorante empire. Her gaze moved down over the sizable disbursement requisition, making sure everything looked in order—

The office door burst open. She glanced up to see her father stride into the room with a frown on his face. For a man who'd had two heart attacks in less than a year with the most recent one barely two weeks ago, he certainly didn't look feeble. In fact, he reminded her of a charging bull with steam emanating from his nostrils.

He wasn't supposed to be here. He was supposed to be at home, following the doctor's orders of modest exercise and a lean, wholesome diet. More importantly, he was supposed to be relaxing instead of stressing over the family business. That was her job now.

"How could you do it?" His voice boomed through the large office.

She stood and moved to the door. She caught her assistant, Rosa's, surprised look and sent her a reassuring smile before closing the door so they could have this conversation in private instead of having the whole office hear them. Then she turned to him. "I suppose you're referring to halting the expansion into Sicily."

"Yes! We talked about this. I told you I wanted to build there."

"And after looking at the numbers, as well as consulting with department heads, I have to disagree with you. We need to focus on our current properties. Many are now older and in need of updating."

His face filled with color. He was so worked up he couldn't speak. She'd known he wouldn't be happy about the decision, but she was hoping he wouldn't hear about it for a while. In fact, she'd gone to great lengths to keep this information under wraps, but it appeared her father had a mole in the company. Why didn't that surprise her?

She moved to his side and then gestured to one of the two black leather armchairs facing her desk. "Sit down."

He didn't say anything for a moment. Then he moved to the other side of the desk and sat down in her chair. "I think sitting down is exactly what I should do."

"Papa, what are you doing?"

"I'm taking over my position as CEO once more. Your services are no longer needed."

Her mouth gaped as her mind struggled to make sense of what had just happened. "You're firing me?"

His gaze narrowed in on her. "I'm giving you time to concentrate on your life."

"This is my life."

"No. This is my life. You need to go find your own." His voice was firm.

"But you're in no condition to return to work. You should be at home resting."

"I've rested. All I do is rest. I'm done resting."

His definition of rest and hers were two different things. He showed up at the office every day, looking over her shoulder and questioning everything. If she didn't do something quickly to change things, she would never win the respect of the employees now reporting to her. She would be ineffectual as the CEO, and her father's beloved company would flounder.

Not to mention that every time her father visited the office, he got worked up over something. These were the details he didn't need to concern himself with at the moment. His focus should be on his precarious health and how to strengthen his body.

Her mind raced for a way to fix the situation. She knew what her father wanted more than anything— for her to marry. It was an idea she'd been toying with lately. Maybe she could make a deal of sorts.

"What would you say if I was willing to make you a deal?" She knew her father thrived on wheeling and dealing—the higher the stakes, the more he enjoyed it.

He paused for a moment as though he was trying to figure out her angle. Then, in a more normal tone of voice, he asked, "What sort of deal?"

"What if I agree to get married?"

His eyes lit up with interest. "I'd say it was about time. Who is it? Fernando from dinner last night?" He rubbed his chin. "Or perhaps it is Edwardo that caught your eye."

"You're rushing ahead." She had him on the hook. Now she just had to keep him there.

His gaze narrowed. "I know that look in your eyes. You're up to something."

"I'm just being a businesswoman."

He grunted. "Leave the business up to me. You have other matters to worry about."

"Ah, yes, marriage. What are you willing to sacrifice in order to see me married?"

"Sacrifice?" His shocked tone reverberated off the tall walls with their floor-to-ceiling windows and various watercolor paintings of Italian life. "What is it you want in exchange?"

"I want you to hand over the reins of the company for—" she rushed to think of an appropriate length of time "—a year."

He didn't move. He didn't even blink. He just stared at her. Though she knew him well enough to know the wheels in his mind were turning. He was trying to figure out how to work this in his favor—how he could get everything he wanted. But it wouldn't work. Not this time.

He shook his head. "Not a year. A month."

She pressed her hands to her hips. She could be just as stubborn as him. "A month isn't enough time to rearrange the furniture in this office."

His silver brows rose high on his forehead. "You're going to change the office? But I love it the way it is—"

"No, I'm not." She sighed. "That was just a figure of speech. But you know exactly what I mean. I need more than a month. You need more time to recuperate."

He shook his head. "When you get married, you're

supposed to concentrate on your husband. Not spend all your time in the office."

"You let me worry about my marriage and my office hours. But since you aren't interested in negotiating, let's forget it. I have work to do in my office. It's time you went home." She turned for the door, all the while hoping he would stop her. "After all, the doctor hasn't released you for work."

She took slow, measured steps to the door. She thought of stopping and speaking to him, but she knew her father was a shrewd poker player. He would see a bluff from a long way off if she wasn't careful. And it wasn't truly a bluff. If he went for this deal, she would be getting married. The thought sent dread skittering down her spine. But she would deal with that if or when the time came.

"Okay." The resigned tone of his voice said that she had won. "Three months."

She didn't immediately turn; she hesitated just for a second or two, just like any good negotiator would do. Because he might be her father, but he was a businessman first, last and always.

She needed time to implement her plan to modernize the restaurant chain. She'd already been in talks with various department heads. But it was going to take a long time to give hundreds of restaurants makeovers.

When she faced him, she said, "Six months." It would give her enough time to firm up a plan and start the renovations on a couple of restaurants—enough to show her father what a difference it would make to their patrons and eventually their bottom line. When he went to negotiate further, she cut him off. "Six months, not a day less, or the deal is null and void. And I want this in writing."

And then her father smiled. "You do have your father in you. Nicely played. Now who is the man you've chosen to marry?"

"All in due time. First, we have a contract to draw up. The rest will follow."

It was only then that she let the reality of this deal sink in. She was getting married. She was about to marry someone she didn't love. She was in so much trouble.

CHAPTER ONE

Two weeks later

"MARRY ME."

Seated in a little out-of-the-way café on the outskirts of Verona, Franco Marchello wordlessly opened his mouth. He immediately forgot what he'd been about to say. Surely he hadn't heard correctly. Because there was absolutely no way Carla Falco had proposed to him.

Still, he'd seen her glossy red lips move. The words she'd spoken, he must have gotten them mixed up. That was it. His mind raced to come up with an alternative: Carry me? Bury me? None of the alternatives made a bit of sense.

Franco swallowed hard. "Excuse me, what did you say?"

Carla didn't smile. In fact, she looked quite serious, the way he imagined seeing her at the head of the table in a boardroom. "I asked you to marry me."

That's what he thought she'd said. And yet he had no idea why she'd propose to him.

Sure, they might have had a good time at his brother's wedding two weeks ago at Lake Como. She had been the maid of honor and he'd been the best man, but that had been one evening of laughter and dancing. Maybe he hadn't wanted the evening to end so soon, but Carla had avoided his attempts to turn the evening into something more intimate. So what had changed her mind?

The following week, he'd invited her to dinner. She'd been hesitant until he assured her that it would be a proper business dinner. After all, she'd rebuffed him once. He wasn't about to subject himself to being rejected twice—no matter how beautiful he found her or how her glossy lips tempted him. He made it abundantly clear that the only thing on his mind was a mutually beneficial business arrangement.

Even though it'd been dinner for two, as promised, he'd kept it all aboveboard. He'd pitched her the reason she should consider putting Marchello Spices back in all her family's restaurants. She'd told him she didn't have the authority to make it happen. Her father was still controlling every aspect of the company. But she had been curious enough to agree to review the projections. He knew if she saw the same potential that he'd seen in those numbers, she wouldn't be able to ignore them. At last, he had an in with her father, who'd refused numerous times to meet with him—all because of an old grudge between him and Franco's grandfather.

And that's where things had ended—on the sidewalk outside the café. Had there been something in his drink that evening? Had he blacked out and totally forgotten about some torrid romantic night together—anything to explain this most unexpected proposal?

Because he didn't do marriage—no way. He was a Marchello. Marchellos were notoriously bad at marriage. At least his parents had been.

But then again, his younger brother had just gotten

married. That was what had initially led Franco directly into Carla's orbit. And they'd been running into each other ever since. Now it seemed as though the entire world had completely and utterly rotated off its axis.

He struggled to swallow. His brain raced to find the right words. "Why do you want to get married?"

He purposely failed to include himself in that question. Maybe she just wanted to get married to anyone and he just happened to be standing in the wrong place at the wrong time.

She glanced away. "Perhaps I jumped a bit ahead."

"You think?" When his words caused her to frown, he quieted down. Now that the shock had worn off a bit, he was anxious to hear what this was all about.

She toyed with the spoon resting on the saucer next to her teacup. "My father isn't well."

"I heard about his heart attack the night of my brother's wedding. How's he doing?"

"The doctors have warned him that if he doesn't slow down and watch his diet, the prognosis isn't good."

"I'm sorry to hear that." Now he understood the impromptu proposal. "And you want to get married to make him happy, in case something happens?"

"No. I want to get married so nothing happens to him."

He had absolutely no idea what any of this had to do with him. As far as he knew, her father hated not just him but his whole family. "But surely you have a boyfriend to marry."

"If I did, do you really think I'd propose to you?"

Okay, so he was still missing something. "Our families hate each other." He shook his head. "This is a very bad idea."

The story went that his grandfather and Carla's father used to be good friends. They would play cards at their private club. But Carla's father started drinking a lot and his gambling got out of control—so much so that he risked his restaurant empire. Desperate not to lose everything, Carlo Falco cheated at cards. And the two men haven't spoken since.

Carla crossed her arms. "If your grandfather hadn't lied about my father—"

"He didn't." Franco stopped himself just in time, because if he'd said more, he knew it would hurt Carla, and she didn't deserve it.

She blindly loved her father, oblivious to his faults. Who was he to steal that from her? Franco knew what it was to live without a father's love. He didn't want to be the one to drive a wedge between Carla and her father.

She arched a brow at him. "Stands to reason you'd be on your grandfather's side."

Anything he said about the ill feelings between their families was just going to make matters worse. And it wasn't helping him understand Carla's sudden proposal.

"I'm confused. Why you think we should get married?" He gazed at her until she glanced away.

"My father refuses to let me run the company as I see fit, even though I have a business degree that is doing nothing more than collecting dust. He's more intent on having me plan his social functions while he works on finding me the appropriate husband—someone who can step in and run his company."

"And you think I can run his company on top of managing my own family business?"

A frown pulled at her beautiful face as her gaze met his once more. "Certainly not."

"Then I still don't understand."

She sighed and glanced out the window at the bustling piazza. "My father is resistant to hand over the reins of the company to me, even though he's had a massive heart attack." She failed to mention the most recent heart attack as she'd promised her father to keep it quiet. "Instead he spends all his time parading men in front of me, hoping I'll choose one to marry."

"So I was right." He'd warned her about her father's matchmaking at his brother's wedding to her cousin.

"Yes. I confronted him, and the rumors are true." She didn't sound happy about it. "He started this matchmaking before he'd had his heart attack, but now he's gone into overdrive. So in order for me to be able to pick my own husband and also to prove to my father that I'm quite capable of running the business, I've negotiated a deal with him. According to our agreement, I have until the end of the year to marry. If I don't marry by then, the deal is null and void. But I don't intend to waste any time with the formalities. Once I'm married, I can run the company any way I see fit for the following six months."

"You arranged a marriage contract?" He didn't know if he should be awed by her or worried about her.

"In a manner of speaking. All with the best of intentions." Then her big brown eyes turned to him. "So, will you do it? Will you marry me?"

Her insides were knotted up with nervous energy.

Carla couldn't believe she'd been pushed into this unbelievably awkward position. She'd never imagined she'd be marrying for business, not love. But if she didn't do something drastic, she feared her father would work himself to death, quite literally. Just the thought made her heart clench.

And though she was marrying someone that her father would be totally opposed to, she knew if her father gave Franco a chance, he would see what she'd seen—that Franco was a good guy. If he wasn't someone she could reasonably trust and respect, she wouldn't have made this totally outrageous proposition.

Buzz. Buzz.

Her gaze moved to her phone that was quietly resting on the table. Even though it was the same ringtone, it was Franco's phone going off. She glanced across the table as Franco sat there like a statue, staring unblinkingly out the window. His phone buzzed again.

When he didn't move this time, she said, "Franco, it's your phone."

That startled him out of his deep thoughts. As he reached for his phone, she studied him. From his short dark curls on the top of his head to his clean-shaven face to those intense, dark eyes that felt as though they could totally see through her, to his aristocratic nose and finally to those very kissable lips—not that she'd had the luxury of feeling his mouth pressed to hers.

While he rapidly sent some text messages, she continued her leisurely view of the man that she'd just proposed to. He had broad, strong shoulders and a muscular chest. And then there were his hands, with his long, lean fingers. Her mother would have said that he had the hands of a concert pianist—as her mother had been a concert pianist until she'd married. But if Carla were a betting person, she'd say that Franco didn't know the C key from the A.

Franco slipped his phone in his pocket. His gaze met hers. "Sorry. It was business."

She nodded in understanding. "No problem. I know your family business is as important to you as mine is to me."

His eyes lit up. "We do have that in common. But you've obviously misinterpreted our time together—"

"I didn't." Heat rushed to her face as she realized he thought she was in love with him—nothing could be further from the truth. "I have no illusions about what a marriage between us would be like."

His gaze narrowed in on her. "So you're not in love with me?"

She couldn't hold back the laughter that bubbled up inside her. Sure, he was drop-dead gorgeous, but he had one big fault—he was like her father, always thinking about business. And she had no desire to marry anyone. "Of course not. Is that what you thought?"

He shrugged. "Well, that's usually why people get married."

"But we're not usual people, are we?"

"Even so, I'm not getting married—not to you or anyone else." His tone was firm and unbending.

She wasn't giving up now. "Listen, I know this marriage idea is a bit of a surprise—okay, it's a big shocker—but don't dismiss the idea so quickly. It could be beneficial to both of us."

He didn't say anything for a moment as he continued to stare at her—as though he were trying to break through her barriers and read her most intimate thoughts. Not that she'd let him get that close.

She'd already been hurt enough by her college sweetheart. Matteo had been Mr. Popularity, and she'd been the socialite with all the right connections.

Matteo had been eager to get into politics, and though she saw herself as being more than a politician's wife, she'd agreed to marry him. Her parents had been delighted. And so after graduation, they'd delayed the wedding and instead thrown themselves into Matteo's first campaign.

It had been a grueling year of public events, dinners and interviews. She felt as though the layers of her life had been peeled back for all the world to see.

It wasn't just her life the press had delved into. And that's when they'd exposed Matteo's duplicity. The story of him conducting an affair with his campaign manager was front-page news, complete with a picture of them wrapped up in each other's arms kissing.

Just the memory made her shudder inwardly. She'd barely dodged that disaster. She never wanted to let herself be that vulnerable again.

She gave herself a mental shake, chasing away the troublesome thoughts from the past. She was no longer that doe-eyed girl who thought love would win out. Her heart had been hardened. She was much more practical now.

While Franco might be the most handsome man she'd ever met, she had absolutely no intention of acting upon that chemistry. This would be a business arrangement, nothing more.

His gaze narrowed. "Beneficial how?"

"Should I marry, I assume full control of the company for six months, during which time my father can't override any of my decisions."

A flicker of interest ignited in his dark eyes. "And what's in it for me?"

"I know you want your products once more on all the tables in the Falco chain. That's a lot of tables—many more than there were back when our families were doing business together."

"And you will have the power to make that happen."

She nodded. "My signed, sealed and official agreement gives me all the power, once I marry."

Franco's brows rose. Her totally outlandish scheme had caught and held his attention. She suppressed a smile that threatened to lift her lips. Now wasn't the time for gloating over a plan that would not only benefit the two of them, but more importantly it'd help her father—even if he was too stubborn to see it.

CHAPTER TWO

Marriage was out of the question.

It was tantamount to self-destruction.

And yet this proposal was most tempting.

Franco couldn't believe he was not only entertaining the thought of marrying Carla but also very tempted to say yes.

With his appetite long forgotten, he glanced across the table. Carla's unfinished meal had been pushed off to the side. It appeared neither of them were that hungry. He paid the check, and then they headed outside. He had no particular destination in mind.

When he'd accepted her request for this dinner, he figured it would be to turn down his latest business proposal to place his spices back in the Falco Fresco Ristorantes. Carla's family's company was the largest restaurant chain in all of Italy. It spanned from the northern fringes of the country down to the warm shores of Naples. It'd taken decades for the chain to be the most well-known name in Italy, but they'd succeeded. And Franco liked to think his family had something to do with it, seeing as his family's spices were what they'd used in the restaurant until more recent years.

But why did the success of both of their businesses have to hinge on marriage?

He raked his fingers through his hair as he tried to figure out another solution, one that was amenable to both of them. He stopped walking. He turned to Carla and gazed into her beautiful brown eyes. For a moment, he forgot what he was going to say. Her beauty, well, it was unique, and it didn't come from makeup.

It started with her heart-shaped face, her warm brown eyes and long lashes. She had high cheekbones, a pert nose and lush lips. She was stunning. But he refused to let himself get distracted. This was too important.

He swallowed hard. "Does your agreement with your father state that you have to marry me in order for it to be valid?"

"Of course not. My father hates your family."

He refrained from stating that his grandfather felt the same way about her father. Though he did recall his grandfather's warning that he couldn't trust a Falco. So did Carla have something else in mind besides a business arrangement?

"I propose you marry someone else," he said, though the idea of Carla pledging her heart to someone else didn't appeal to him—not at all. "And then you'll be free to do business with my company."

"I've considered the idea." She hesitated.

"And?"

When her gaze met his, her eyes were shuttered, blocking him out. "And I can't trust anyone else to do this."

"And you think you can trust me? Maybe you should talk to your father about that." He was certain her father would talk her out of this crazy idea.

She stepped up to him. "I can trust you because I know you're totally opposed to marriage."

"And what does that have to do with this?"

"It means that when it comes time to dissolve this partnership, you won't give me a hard time. You won't have developed any illusions that there was something more to this arrangement than what we agree to now."

There was certainly more to Carla than he'd ever imagined. This cool and calculating businesswoman was a side of her that he'd never seen before, and he wasn't quite sure how to react. Part of him respected the fact that she took her family's business so seriously that she'd be willing to go this far to look after it. Luckily he hadn't had to go that far—well, not yet.

He'd worked like crazy over the past several months, meeting with smaller restaurant chains and grocers, but no satisfactory deals had been reached. His grandfather had made sure to point out his failures. The comments still stung. But Franco was determined to prove to his grandfather that he was a skillful businessman. And now Carla was offering him a prime opportunity to do exactly that, but could he afford her price?

He couldn't believe he was asking this, but stranger things were known to happen. "How long would the marriage have to last?"

"Six months."

Six months. Twenty-six weeks. One hundred and eighty-two days. A lifetime.

As they resumed walking, he forked his fingers through his hair again. The last thing he was worried about at this moment was appearances. He was more worried about breaking the promise he'd made himself when his mother had dumped him and his brother on their grandparents' doorstep—he would never let himself be vulnerable again. And that included marriage—most especially marriage.

But this wasn't a typical marriage. Right?

His sideways glance met Carla's expectant look once more. "And do you promise that if we do this—if we marry—you won't expect anything from me?"

She averted her gaze. "There might be some stipulations."

He knew it! He knew when it came to marriage no one could be trusted. "Forget it." He shook his head. "We aren't doing this."

"Don't you even want to hear the stipulations before you write off my offer?"

Did he have to hear them? She probably wanted weekends together, family gatherings and all the other stuff that people did when they were trying to show the world their marriage wasn't a complete and utter sham. He wasn't doing it.

"No. Forget it."

"Well," she said, "you might not want to hear them, but I'm going to tell you. There will be no stepping out on the marriage. So you'll have to say goodbye to any girlfriends for the length of our marriage. I won't be made a laughingstock."

Hmm...that wasn't so bad. It wasn't like he had a serious girlfriend. Unlike his brother used to do, he did maintain girlfriends for longer than two weeks. But he made it perfectly clear from the beginning that the relationship wouldn't go anywhere. It was all for fun—nothing more.

But the last woman he'd casually dated had been a little scary. So he'd been avoiding dating for the past couple of months. He didn't see how Carla's stipulation would be an issue, especially with a wife like Carla. His gaze lingered on her. They could definitely have some fun together.

"And we will not be consummating the marriage." It was as though she'd read his mind. Was he that obvious about his attraction to her?

"Are you sure that part isn't negotiable?" He sent her a teasing smile.

She glowered at him. Okay, so she was taking this all very seriously. He supposed he should, too, though he didn't want to. No matter the outcome, there was still an integral part of him that was utterly opposed to this arrangement.

He cleared his throat. "Sorry. I guess I'm just really having a hard time taking this seriously."

"Don't I look serious enough for you?" Her unwavering gaze met his.

"It's not that. You definitely act as though you're negotiating the most important deal of your life."

"Then what's the problem? I thought this deal would give you exactly what you wanted."

He rubbed the back of his neck. "It's the marriage part that I'm having problems with. Couldn't we just fake the marriage like my brother and your cousin did with their engagement?"

"It has to be a real marriage, otherwise I won't assume control of the company and I won't be able to hammer out a mutually beneficial arrangement to put your products back in my family's restaurants. But this time around, I'm foreseeing a much bigger tie-in and promotion."

She certainly knew how to sweet-talk him. But still,

he'd promised himself not to marry—not to make the same mistakes as his parents. He knew a secret about their marriage—a secret that his brother didn't know—a secret he wasn't supposed to know.

His conception had been a mistake. That's how his father had put it in an argument with his mother. He was the mistake that kept them married longer than they'd wanted. If it wasn't for his presence, his parents would have gone their separate ways without destroying the childhoods of both him and his brother.

And though the logical part of his brain said that none of it was his fault, the other part of him felt bad that his mere existence had caused his brother so much harm, from their father walking out on them to their broken home to their mother abandoning them on their grandparents' doorstep.

But if he didn't do this—if he didn't agree to marry Carla—how much more damage would be done? Because those products that were in danger of being pulled out of production weren't just from the company's past. They were the future of the company.

The company's sales had slumped over the years. Younger buyers weren't recognizing the Marchello name. They weren't rushing to the grocers to buy their product, so it was just a matter of time until their company became extinct. Did he really have a choice in the matter?

"Wait." Carla's voice drew him from his intense thoughts. They paused along a quiet stretch of sidewalk. When his gaze focused on her, he saw her withdraw folded papers from her purse. "This should explain the details of the agreement."

He was a little dumbfounded that she would have a

legal agreement already drawn up. Surely he'd misunderstood. But when he wordlessly took the papers from her, he saw her name at the top followed by his.

He was shocked that she would think he would just readily agree to such an outlandish idea. After all, he wasn't an author, like his younger brother, and eager to live out a fictional life.

But he was also impressed with Carla's get-it-done attitude. It said a lot about her. It also told him that they had a lot in common. Was it something they could build upon? Not as in building a real marriage, but a real business relationship. Something told him that this deal, though it went against everything he'd ever promised himself, was too good to pass up.

And besides, it would be a marriage on paper only. Soon it would be over—though not soon enough.

He glanced down over the top sheet, catching the important details: their names; the length of marriage; the agreement to display, use and serve Marchello spices in all Falco Fresco Ristorantes.

"Okay." He folded the papers. "I'll have my attorney go over these. Then we can sign the papers and set a date for the—well, you know."

"The wedding. I had a thought about that, too."

Why was he not surprised? It appeared she had thought about everything. He wondered if this was a sign of how things would go with their m...arrangement.

He cleared his throat. "And what would that be?"

"I think we need to get moving on this. We can get married at the same time we sign the papers."

"That soon?" His throat grew tight, and it was getting hard to breathe.

"Is there a reason we should put things off?"

Other than to give him more time to get used to the idea—which was never, ever going to happen—nothing stood in their way.

When his gaze met hers, he saw the worry reflected in her eyes. It was now, as the initial shock subsided, that he noticed the shadows beneath her eyes and the lines bracketing her mouth. Though she might be proposing this plan, it didn't appear it had been by choice but rather one of self-preservation.

"If you aren't interested in the deal, I'll find someone else."

She didn't say it, but he filled in the blank—she could easily find another willing participant. And if she were to do that, he was certain the door would be firmly closed on ever getting his products back in the Falcos' restaurants.

"I'll do it." Once the words passed his lips, he felt as though he'd just shackled himself to Carla.

He gave her a quick glance, from her long dark hair to her warm brown eyes down to her pouty lips that were just begging to be kissed. Okay, so there were much worse people to be chained to.

"Good." She glanced around as though trying to determine where their meandering had led them. "Perhaps we should turn around." When he nodded in compliance, she said, "Have your attorney look over the contract, and we'll set the date to finalize everything."

"Don't you mean set our wedding date?" He couldn't resist pointing out the obvious.

Color flared in her cheeks. "Yes, that, too."

So she wasn't any more eager than he was to exchange wedding vows. But it wasn't going to be that easy.

"I have some demands, too," he said.

Carla's eyes momentarily widened with surprise before she returned to her neutral expression. In a practically monotone voice she asked, "What would those be?"

"We need to move immediately on getting Marchello Spices back in the restaurants."

She nodded. "I knew you'd expect nothing less. It'll be our first order of business."

"I have other ideas—"

"I'm sure you do, but don't get ahead of yourself."

"But I won't sign unless it's in writing about Marchello Spices being returned to tables immediately."

As they continued their stroll, Carla didn't say anything at first. In her beautiful eyes, he could see the wheels of her mind turning. Surely she had to see the merits of this plan. It would breathe new life into the restaurant chain. It would benefit both of their companies.

"Have your attorneys write up an addendum to the current agreement and I'll have my people go over it."

He stopped next to her small yellow sports car. "I'll do that."

"Remember, time is of the essence."

"This will be my top priority." He opened the car door for her. "Are you really sure you want to do this? This agreement is quite unprecedented."

Her unwavering gaze met his. "Sometimes sacrifices have to be made. It is a marriage in name only. And it is only six months. But it has to look convincing. My father has to believe this is a real, traditional marriage. Anything less and he'll have us tied up in litigation."

He sighed. "Agreed."

"So how do we get him to the wedding without him

knowing that he's going to our wedding? Because he'll need to see it with his own eyes if he's to believe it." She paused as though giving the dilemma some serious thought.

Franco gave it some thought. "I know. We'll invite everyone to a special event—a special announcement."

Her eyes lit up with interest. "I like the way you think."

"Just remember, this was all your idea."

"How could I forget? But it'll be worth it in the end. Everyone will get what they want or need."

He nodded in understanding. It wasn't until he was seated in his own car that he realized he'd been holding his breath. Perhaps because he'd been holding back an argument—this was too much of a sacrifice for business.

Wait. Had he just thought that? He was the one who was all business, all the time. But this marriage contract felt over-the-top even for him.

What if Carla changed her mind about what she wanted from this marriage? Then he recalled her cold and businesslike demeanor during their dinner. She was no longer the fun and vivacious young woman that he'd met at his sister-in-law's villa not so long ago. Something had changed in her—something he couldn't identify.

And when it came down to it, her offer was just too good to pass up.

But could he really utter the words *I do*?

CHAPTER THREE

THERE WAS A diamond ring in his pocket.

It felt as though it were burning a hole through his slacks.

Franco thought back to when his grandmother had given him the ring, the same evening she'd given his brother an heirloom ring to properly propose to his now wife, Gianna. His grandmother had told Franco that she was giving him the ring, even though he wasn't involved with anyone, because he was the type to play things close to his chest. And she doubted when the time came to propose that he'd come to her for the ring.

He'd tried vehemently to refuse it, but what can you do when your grandmother gives you that look? You know, the one where her face turns serious, a brow is arched over the rim of her glasses and the look in her eyes says *if you don't do what I say, you're going to live to regret it*? Yeah, that one. Well, that's exactly what she'd done to him. And the last thing he'd wanted to do was have his grandmother upset with him. Because he loved his grandmother dearly—she was the only true mother figure in his life. She never wavered—never shrank away. She was calm and she was steady.

So when Carla sounded frantic about making time for

her father, attending to business at the office and preparing for the quarterly board meeting, he'd offered to have his assistant send out invitations to a private party where a big announcement was to be made as well as throw together an intimate wedding. Carla had sounded so relieved when she'd accepted his offer. And that was why he had a diamond ring readily available when his assistant had asked about Carla's engagement ring. It was the one detail he needed to take care of personally.

Still, this wedding was so much more involved than he'd been prepared for when he'd first agreed to the marriage contract. He'd thought they'd exchange empty vows and then coexist for six months. Instead, they needed a real wedding with select guests and a photographer. He'd had no idea their arrangement would go to these lengths in order to sell it to her father. But Franco didn't want to leave anything up to chance.

Today was their wedding day. Franco's gut was tied in a knot. He hadn't eaten a thing since yesterday. Not even coffee appealed to him. He wondered if all grooms felt this anxious.

He pulled to a stop in a no-parking zone, right in front of Carla's apartment building. He couldn't back out now. He just had to get through the day the best he could.

Franco exited the car at the same time she stepped onto the sidewalk. She rushed up to him with her overnight bag in hand. Her face was pale, but that was the only clue she was nervous.

"Are you ready for this?"

"As ready as I'm ever going to be. My father wasn't happy about the mysterious party, but I talked him into going. What about your grandparents?"

"They're out of the country."

"Oh."

He didn't like her disapproving tone. "What's the matter?"

She shook her head. "Nothing."

When she moved to walk past him, he stepped in her way. "If we're going to marry, you have to learn to talk to me."

She glanced away. "I just wondered if getting married without your grandparents—well, if it would bother you."

"If this was a real wedding, yes, it would. But since this is a business arrangement, I can live with it. In fact, it'll be easier this way. Besides, it's probably best my grandfather and your father aren't in close proximity."

She nodded in agreement.

He took her bag and stowed it in the boot of the car before they set off on their journey. The fact of the matter was he had a surprise in store for Carla. He hoped she'd like it.

"Where are we going?" she asked as they headed away from the center of Verona. "I thought we'd have a quick wedding in the city."

"You'll soon see."

She turned to him. Her expression was very serious. "We don't have time for distractions. We have to get the papers signed and then we have to get straight to work. I have to let my key people know that we're shifting gears and focusing full-time on our collaboration."

"That can wait for a day."

"No, it can't—"

"Yes, it can." He could hardly believe he was saying these words. And all this time his family had accused him of being a workaholic. Obviously they didn't know Carla very well, or they might realize that she definitely outdid him.

"Franco, if we're going to make this all work out in time, we can't waste a moment."

"But for any of it to work, we must marry—"

"Quickly and without fuss—"

"Aw…but you forget that your father needs to believe in this marriage—a marriage to a Marchello. You know as well as I do that he's going to fight this marriage. If we aren't careful, he'll prove us frauds, and then our agreement will be null and void."

Her mouth opened. No words came out. Then she pressed her lips together with a deep sigh. "Fine. What do you have in mind?"

"You'll see. Trust me."

"That's the problem," she said. "I don't trust you."

He let out a laugh. The truth was that he didn't trust her, either. It definitely wasn't the correct way to start a marriage. But then again, this was a business partnership. And when it came to business agreements, there was always a bit of distrust. So the way he saw it, they were okay with this. But as they headed out of the city, he realized there was one other thing they needed to deal with sooner rather than later.

He swallowed hard. "There's something else we need to do to seal the deal."

Carla turned to him with concern reflected in her eyes. "Do I even want to ask what you're referring to? Because if this is about consummating our marriage—"

"It's not, I assure you." Though that's one part of the day that might be quite enjoyable. As soon as the thought came to him, he dismissed it. Blurring lines between business and pleasure was never a good idea.

He pulled off to the side of the road. He reached in his pocket and pulled out the ring. There was a distinct gasp from Carla. He glanced at her, but she wasn't looking at him. Her full attention was focused on the ring in his hand.

"If we are going to do this right—" his voice wobbled, at least to his ears "—we need to be properly engaged. So... Carla Falco, will you marry me?"

Her gaze flickered to meet his. He could see the wheels of her mind spinning. He hadn't thought this would catch her so off guard. Didn't all women look forward to receiving a diamond ring? Her gaze moved back to the ring, but she didn't reach for it.

"Go ahead. Take it." He moved it closer to her. "It won't bite you. I promise." When she still didn't reach for it, he said, "You know you have to play the part, just like I do."

At last she took the ring from him and slipped it on her finger. "I guess you're right." She held up her hand, letting the light twinkle off the diamond. "It's very pretty."

"It was my great-grandmother's ring."

"Oh." She quickly pulled it off and handed it back to him. "I can't accept this, even on a temporary basis."

"I want you to wear it." And then realizing how that might sound, he clarified himself. "I mean my grandmother expects my wife to wear the ring. If you don't, everyone will wonder why you don't have it on. Do you really want to answer those questions?"

"No. I suppose not." She placed the ring back on her

finger. "But it's going to make me very nervous. What if I damage it?"

"You won't."

"But I might."

"It'll be okay because I have no intention of using the ring for a real marriage, so no one will know."

"I'll know."

They continued to ride on quietly, each lost in their own thoughts. What had sounded like a good idea at one point—a means to an end—was now sounding so much more involved with so many entanglements. He couldn't help but wonder what details he'd forgotten about for this big day. He'd just have to hope they wouldn't be big enough to be noticed by anyone—including their families.

It had been a week of negotiations.

A week of hammering out the details of their future.

If Carla had any doubts about proposing a marriage between herself and Franco, those doubts were quickly quelled. Nothing about this upcoming marriage felt personal in the least. Her gaze strayed to the heirloom diamond ring on her finger. Okay, maybe it was a little personal.

The thought that her father's reckless disregard for his own health had pushed her to this drastic decision hadn't gone unnoticed. Though she was very upset with him, her concern about his teetering health trumped everything. And so she would go through with this crazy plan.

She leaned back against the buttery-soft black leather of the chauffeured sedan. She glanced over to Franco.

A large gap yawned between them. She took comfort in knowing that he wasn't any more anxious for this union.

And though when they'd first met she'd thought he was attracted to her, she now realized it must have all been in her imagination. Because ever since she'd proposed to him, he'd kept a respectable distance from her.

This was going to work out just the way she'd planned. Still, the thought of a loveless marriage left her saddened. Call it the romantic in her or maybe she'd read one too many romance novels, but she'd been under the illusion that marriage was supposed to be about love. Nothing could be further from the truth where they were concerned.

But without emotional entanglements, she'd be able to focus her full attention on the family business. That was what she wanted after all. She just had to keep that in mind.

Carla turned her attention back to the passing scenery. "Where are we going?"

"You'll like this. Just relax," Franco said.

Carla sighed. The truth was she couldn't relax. She'd barely slept a wink the night before. She'd watched infomercials, thinking they'd bore her to sleep. No such luck. She'd tried chamomile tea. Nothing. At last, she'd lain in the dark, tossing and turning. Sometime in the middle of the night, she'd nodded off. She wondered if all brides were this nervous.

Not that this was a real wedding. It wasn't like she had feelings for Franco. Though he was gorgeous. He was so serious most of the time.

She chanced a glance at Franco. He was staring out the window. And then he consulted his Rolex. He was probably wondering how soon this wedding would be over so he could get on with his business.

But what would he be like if he were marrying for love? Would his sole focus be on his bride? Would he be able to think of anything else but spending every waking moment with his beloved? An uneasy feeling churned in the pit of her stomach.

She let out a soft sigh and turned away. It wasn't like she wanted him to look at her that way. She knew how fleeting love could be. And when things fell apart, it was messy and painful. She refused to set herself up to be hurt again.

Just outside the small village of Gemma, where her cousin lived, the car slowed and turned into a short drive. It led them up to a stately house that sat right on the edge of Lake Como. The house appeared to be three stories with tall windows. She didn't recognize it.

She turned to Franco. "What are we doing here?"

"I thought it'd be a good place to have a wedding."

As the car pulled around to the front of the villa, she caught a quick glimpse of the lush garden bordering the lake. Her attention turned to the impressive villa. It had floor-to-ceiling windows, allowing a picturesque view of the lake.

Whoever owned this villa was most fortunate. She couldn't even imagine how much a house in this stunning setting would cost. Though she'd always thought her father had the most beautiful house in the Lake Como region, she had to admit that this house definitely rivaled it. No, it surpassed it in size, location and sheer beauty. What a place for a wedding.

"Who owns this place?" Carla asked.

"I do. Now that my brother lives here, I wanted to have a place close by."

"It's beautiful."

Standing off to the side of the driveway was a stylish young woman with a digital notepad clutched in her arm. A smile lit up her face as she looked expectantly at Carla. Who was she? Carla glanced over at Franco, waiting for some sort of explanation.

"Go ahead," he said. "Everything is waiting for you."

"Everything?" She didn't know what to expect.

He lowered his voice so as not to be overheard. "We both know this has to look real or else your father isn't going to believe it."

She opened her mouth to argue but then wordlessly closed it. As much as she hated it, Franco was right.

"I've seen to all the details, including a few guests as well as my brother and your cousin."

"You invited them, too?" she whispered. "But why? Couldn't you have just invited people from your office?"

"You do want people to believe this marriage is real, right? Isn't that the only way your agreement with your father will be ironclad?"

"Yes, but…" Her frantic thoughts were fragmented. "This…it feels wrong. We invited everyone under false pretenses."

"You don't think they'll be excited by the surprise wedding?"

She frowned at him. "That's not what I mean. They'll assume that you and I…that we're…"

"In love? I know." His hushed tone was matter-of-fact.

"And it doesn't bother you?"

He shrugged. "I guess I'm just used to people making assumptions about me."

This stirred her interest. "What sort of assumptions?"

This time he glanced away. "All sorts of things. That I'm a bloodthirsty businessman. That I ran off my father so I could assume the CEO position."

"But that's ridiculous. He left when you were just a little kid." When Franco's surprised gaze turned her way, she realized she'd overstepped. "I'm sorry. My cousin told me a little of Dario's background, which is also your background."

Understanding flashed in his eyes. "Anyway, people are going to think what they want, but in the end, I think our families will understand that we did what we thought was best for everyone."

She had her doubts. "I really hope you're right."

He reached out and gave her hand a quick squeeze. "It's going to be okay."

She wanted to believe him. This was her one chance to get her stubborn father to do the right thing—hand over the reins to the company so he could get his strength back. And whether she wanted to admit it or not, it was the right thing for her, too.

Her gaze searched his. She'd had no idea Franco would go to these lengths. But why shouldn't he? He had a lot riding on this wedding. The entire future of his company was on the line.

"I don't know if I can do this," she whispered.

"Sure, you can. Everything is in motion. All you have to do is act like the loving fiancée."

"Everyone thinks we're in love?" When he nodded, she asked, "Even your assistant?"

"Most especially her."

"Why?"

"Because she is our front person. She has to legitimately be able to sell our whirlwind love story to the guests."

"You mean my father?"

He nodded once more. "I don't think your father is going to be happy about you marrying a Marchello."

"No, he won't. He wasn't happy when my cousin married your brother. He'll be furious about our marriage."

"But your agreement with him didn't say whom you had to marry, so we're good." His gaze searched hers. "Do you think you'll be able to pull this off?"

Part of her said that it was too much, but the other part of her—the business part of her—said she could do this if it meant saving her father from himself.

"Yes." Her answer was soft but firm, even if all the while her stomach roiled with nerves.

"Relax. It's all been arranged. I'll see you shortly." And with that he walked away with an older woman who wore a dark skirt suit with her dark hair pulled up in a bun.

Carla wasn't sure what to expect. When she'd initially broached the subject of marriage, she'd expected something quick, efficient and businesslike. But this lakeside villa was so far from anything she'd had in mind. This was the setting for a real wedding. Not what they were about to do.

Still, as the young woman continued to stare at her with that plastered-on smile, Carla had no choice but to step out of the car and find out what Franco had in store for her.

Carla approached the young woman. "Hello. I'm Carla Falco."

"Oh, I know who you are. I've seen your photo on the

internet. It's an honor to meet you." The young woman's face filled with color. "I can't believe I got to plan your wedding. We better hurry inside before the guests begin to arrive." The young woman set off down the stone walk toward the large double doors of the villa.

It was true. Carla was in the news quite often, as she sat on many charity boards. And lately, her father's health scare had propelled them into the headlines. The public had a vested interest in the welfare of Falco's Fresco Ristorantes.

What in the world had Franco planned? It really seemed like a lot of trouble for a fake wedding. Well, it would be real on paper, but still, it wasn't like they were in love or anything. But she had to admit that her curiosity was piqued, and so she followed along.

CHAPTER FOUR

"WHAT ARE YOU DOING?"

It was the same question Franco had been asking himself ever since he'd agreed to Carla's absolutely off-the-wall idea. And what made him think a brief marriage—a marriage based on a mutually beneficial business arrangement—would end any better than his parents' painful and disastrous divorce?

His gaze focused on his younger brother, Dario. There was expectation on his face. If he couldn't get his brother to believe in this marriage, what chance did he have of convincing anyone else? Still, he had to do his best.

Franco raked his fingers through his hair. "I'm getting married."

Dario moved to stand in front of him. His gaze searched his face. "You don't look like a man anxious to walk down the aisle."

Franco attempted a reassuring smile, but catching his reflection in the mirror, he realized his smile ended up as some distorted look that was more a frown than a look of happiness. He glanced away. "It...it's complicated."

"She's pregnant, too?" Dario's eyes widened.

"No!" Franco's voice thundered through the room.

He swallowed hard and then lowered his voice. "Wait. You said *too.*" It took him a second to string his thoughts together. "Are you saying Gianna is pregnant?"

Dario smiled and seemed to stand a bit taller. "She is."

"Congrats!" Franco hugged his younger brother and clapped him on the back. "That's awesome."

"Thanks. It is pretty great." Dario wore a big, happy grin. But then he sobered up. "But we're talking about you and Carla. Are you sure—"

"I'm sure she's not pregnant. You know I wouldn't let that happen."

Relief reflected in Dario's eyes. "I should have known after what you went through with Rose that you would be extra cautious. But sometimes things happen."

Franco tried to block Rose from his thoughts, because every time he thought of her, he once again grew angry at her deception. Rose had lied to him about being pregnant, knowing he could never turn his back on a child of his own. In the end, it'd all been a ploy to get him to marry her. And after a fake pregnancy test, she'd almost snared him into a loveless marriage. But when he'd insisted on a second test with his doctor, the truth came tumbling out.

"Carla is nothing at all like Rose," he ground out.

"I didn't mean to imply that she was."

"Good." Franco began to pace the floor, feeling like a caged animal.

"I'm no expert on marriage, even if I am married. But I'm just going to put this out there—marrying the woman you love shouldn't be complicated. It should be all about you and her and being anxious to share your life with her."

Franco's head snapped back around to look at his brother. "I can't believe you said that. I thought you were the one who was totally opposed to marriage."

Dario shrugged. "What can I say? Gianna changed my mind."

"Apparently. But what you two have, well, it isn't the same with Carla and me."

Dario's dark brows furrowed together. "How is it, then?"

Franco hesitated. It was on the tip of his tongue to tell his brother everything. But then he recalled promising Carla that he'd keep this all to himself. It was the only way this was going to work.

"It's just nerves." Franco's tone was firm.

Dario reached out and gripped Franco's shoulders. "Listen, if you aren't sure, back out now. It'll be best for the both of you—"

"No. This is what's best." He pulled free from his brother's hold. He turned away from Dario's concerned look. It's what was best for his family's future. It's what was best for Carla's very stubborn father. It's what was best for their respective businesses. "Trust me."

Silence filled the room, and for a moment all Franco could hear was the pounding of his heart echoing in his ears. In all his life, he never imagined that he'd be standing in this position. Today was his wedding day—a wedding to a woman he didn't love and who didn't love him.

And then that last thought struck him. He was worked up over nothing. If they weren't emotionally invested in this union, there's no way they could get hurt. There was nothing to worry about. Nothing at all—

"This isn't right," Dario said. "You need to take more time to think this marriage over."

"This from the man who faked his own engagement." Now when he spoke his voice was calmer, more certain.

"That was different."

"Was it?" This time it was Franco nailing his little brother with an inquisitive stare. "As I recall, you came up with your fake engagement spontaneously."

Dario's gaze narrowed. "I had to do it. You and the family wouldn't have left me alone to finish the book otherwise, and…and Gianna had her own reasons to go along with it."

"Yet it all worked out in the end." He was truly happy for his brother. And though Dario had found his own true love, that didn't mean Franco would find his.

"But that is different," Dario said. "Gianna and I had time to get to know each other really well before we said *I do*. How much do you know about Carla?"

He hadn't been expecting a pop quiz. "I know that when she smiles, the whole world lights up." That was no lie. "I know she's had a lot on her shoulders with her father's failing health." He paused as he drew on his memories. "I know that she prefers capellini to spaghetti. I know she loves wine but not scotch." His gaze searched his brothers. "What else do you want to know? How she likes to be kissed?"

Dario's face scrunched up in a look of disgust. "Ugh! No. You can keep those details to yourself."

"Good." A smug smile came over Franco's face at his ability to quiet his brother.

The truth of the matter was that Franco had yet to figure out how he could kiss her and not mess up their very delicate working relationship. But that didn't mean he hadn't been curious about how her full, luscious lips would feel beneath his.

"You're sure about this?" Dario asked one last time.

"I am. I know exactly what I'm getting myself into."

And now that he realized not loving his wife meant that he was protected from any pain when the marriage ended, he just had to keep up the barrier between them.

As for the kiss that he'd been wondering about, well, he would just have to go on wondering. Because he knew that a single kiss with Carla wouldn't just be a single kiss. It would lead to another kiss and another one until things totally spiraled out of control. And where would that leave them?

He gave himself a mental shake. It would be best just to avoid the whole thing. No kissing. No spiraling out of control. And definitely no falling for beautiful, enticing Carla.

This all felt so unreal.

Today was her wedding day.

Carla didn't care how many deep slow breaths she breathed in and blew out or how many times she assured herself that this was only a business arrangement, she couldn't settle her wildly beating heart. She'd negotiated million-dollar deals—deals that could have crippled her company—and she'd been able to handle them calmly and coolly. Why couldn't she do that now?

As she followed Franco's assistant, Mia, through the entrance of the stately villa, she felt as though this whole day was some sort of out-of-body experience. She frantically went over all her options—they were few. In the end, she came back to the same conclusion that she'd come to when she'd masterminded this totally outrageous plan.

They made their way up a set of sweeping steps to the second story. At the end of a very short hallway was a dark wooden door. Mia opened it and stood aside for Carla to enter. When she stepped into the spacious and warmly decorated room, she found she wasn't alone. Her cousin Gianna was standing out on the small balcony.

Gianna turned and rushed inside. "We need to talk."

"What's wrong?" Was it her father? Her heart raced. Had something happened to him?

Gianna smiled. "Relax. It's good news. But I can't wait any longer to tell you."

"Well, tell me."

"I'm pregnant." Gianna's whole face glowed with happiness.

"That's wonderful!" Carla hugged her cousin. When she pulled back, she said, "Congratulations. I'm going to be, what? A second cousin? Or is it first cousin once removed? That always confuses me."

"I don't know about that, but as soon as we get you married, you'll be the baby's aunt." Gianna continued to smile at her like the wedding was the best thing in the world.

Carla swallowed hard as she forced a smile to her face. If only her cousin knew the truth about the wedding, she wouldn't be so happy. "This is a day for lots of celebrating." Carla turned to Mia. "Thank you so much for everything. But we've got it from here."

Mia nodded. "But before I go, I wanted to show you what Franco ordered for you."

"Ordered for me?"

Mia smiled and nodded. And then she showed both women the rack of wedding gowns and maid of honor dresses. There were accessories to choose from. And there were even flowers in her favorite color—plum.

After they thanked Mia for all her help, Franco's assistant left them alone to go check on the groom. Carla wanted to dislike the woman, who was Franco's right hand, but she couldn't. Mia was one of those people who was genuinely nice.

And though Mia spoke highly of her boss, she was also engaged to a man who made her eyes twinkle with love when she mentioned him. Besides, it wasn't like Carla had any hold over Franco. Sure, they were going to be married, and yes, they'd agreed to be faithful to each other, but that didn't mean they would have a traditional marriage—a marriage like her parents'.

Immediately, her eyes blurred with unshed tears. In that moment, she realized what was really bothering her—her mother wasn't here to share this day with her. She'd always thought as a young girl that her beloved mother would be next to her as she reached the major milestones in her life.

Her mother's absence left a gaping hole in her heart that time hadn't sufficiently healed. As her gaze moved across the rack of stunning dresses, she realized she'd always thought she'd be trying them on with her mother looking on, helping to choose the right one.

Now she was about to marry a man she didn't love in order to protect her father from an early grave. And her mother wasn't there to calm her rising nerves. Nothing about this was right.

Tears dropped onto her cheeks.

"Are you all right?" Gianna moved to her side.

Carla swiped away the tears. "I'm fine. It's just a lot. And…and I wish my mother was here to share this day with me."

Gianna hugged her. "She's here. She wouldn't miss it."

Carla pulled back and nodded. "I know. It's just not the same."

And if she was looking on, would she understand her daughter's choices? Would she understand how her abrupt absence had made Carla desperate to keep her father in her life as long as possible?

Gianna turned to Carla. "And you have me. I'll always be there for you. But why didn't you tell me?"

At first, Carla thought her cousin knew about the marriage contract, and then she realized that was impossible. Other than the army of attorneys, who weren't allowed to speak of it, only three people knew of the marriage contract: her father, Franco and herself. And she was quite certain none of them would speak of it. She knew her father was too proud a man to tell people that he'd been cornered into an agreement to hand over the reins of his company to his daughter in order to get her to marry.

"You mean about the marriage?" Carla moved to the rack of hangers with white garment bags hanging from it.

"Of course the marriage." Gianna looked at her with an I-can't-believe-you look. "It…it's all so sudden."

"Once we knew what we wanted, we didn't want to wait."

Gianna nodded in understanding. "Does your father know you're marrying a Marchello?"

"Not exactly." Carla lowered her gaze. "You know

how he feels about the Marchellos. If he knew ahead of time, he'd do whatever he could to stop it."

"I'm so sorry. But he'll learn to like Franco. He's a good guy, just like his brother." Gianna held out her hand. "Let me see the ring."

Carla turned and held out her hand with a ring that was quite unlike the style of ring she would have expected from Franco. Somehow she'd expected something big and flashy from him. Instead this ring was smaller and modest. It was exactly what she would have selected for herself.

The fact that it was an heirloom piece she still found surprising. Why would he give her something so meaningful? You only gave rings that had been handed down through the family to people you loved. And they did not love each other. Of that she was certain.

Gianna oohed and aahed over it, making Carla feel increasingly uncomfortable.

"Gianna, there's something I need to tell you—"

"I know. We have to get a move on. We don't want the bride late for the wedding."

At that moment, she recalled her agreement with Franco to keep the real reason for the marriage to themselves. It was the only chance their marriage contract would hold up under her father's scrutiny. And she wasn't kidding herself into believing that her father wouldn't fight this marriage. But he had no grounds to win, because they were truly going to be husband and wife. The acknowledgment swept the breath from her lungs.

"Carla, are you all right?" Gianna stared at her with worry reflected in her eyes. "You suddenly look pale."

"I, uh—" She struggled to string two words together. "I just need some water. It's a bit warm in here."

Gianna hesitated as though she were going to press the point, but then she kindly moved away to retrieve a glass of water.

Carla knew she had to get a grip on her nerves. This marriage was in the best interests of everyone, including her stubborn father—most especially her father. If it wasn't for him and his risky behavior, she wouldn't even be considering getting married at this stage in her life.

She told herself that everything was going to be all right. She just had to get through today and then life would return to normal. With the marriage behind them, she'd be able to focus on business instead of constantly worrying that her father was overdoing it.

Yes, that's what she'd focus on as she looked through the selection of wedding dresses. This was just a job. Nothing more. She just had to stay focused on the end result—her father would be able to retire and feel reassured that his beloved company was in her safe hands.

CHAPTER FIVE

IT WASN'T TOO LATE.

There was still time to escape.

Franco wore a crisp white shirt and black tie with his tux as he stood by the lakeside, waiting for his bride. *His bride.* The words echoed in his mind as his palms grew damp and his stomach churned. His gaze strayed to the car sitting off to the side of the villa. All he had to do was jump inside and head for freedom. But his feet felt as though they'd been cast in cement.

Part of his mind said that this was the price he'd have to pay to prove to his grandfather and everyone else at the company that he was capable and willing to fully step into the CEO role. He couldn't let a marriage certificate chase him away from fulfilling his dream because he had heard his grandfather mutter something about selling the company.

Running Marchello Spices had been all he could think of since he was young. Perhaps it was a goal that distracted him from the fact that he rarely saw his mother, who was always off with a new husband spending time at the beach in some far-flung country. Or the fact that his father was never around. It was so much easier to focus on something that was more in his control.

And so as a child he'd accompanied his grandfather to the office as often as he would allow him. Franco recalled what it was like being able to go into the CEO's office. And then when he'd been able to sit in his grandfather's seat, he thought he was such big stuff.

He'd wanted to be just like his grandfather when he grew up. He wanted to run the family business and make his grandfather proud of him. And now it was all at his fingertips.

He just had to get through these next few minutes. He'd swear his knees were shaking. He'd glance down and check, but he was frozen in place. He'd never been more nervous in his life. He couldn't imagine what he'd be like if this was a real wedding with real expectations of abiding love for now and forever.

Cold fingertips of apprehension worked their way down his spine. His heart began to beat wildly. His breathing came in one shallow gasp after the other. Was he having a heart attack? Yes, that must be it. He tugged at his too-tight shirt collar. He was certain of it.

He shouldn't do this.

He *couldn't* do this.

"Ladies and gentlemen, gather round," Dario said. "You've all been invited here for a surprise wedding."

There was a round of oohs and aahs.

And then the wedding music began to play. This was his last moment to escape a marriage that would cause nothing but pain to both of them. Or stand here and solidify his company. His mind told him to leave—quickly. There had to be another way—a better way—to keep the business intact and not to lose his seat as CEO.

And then Carla stepped onto the patio. In slow, measured steps, she headed toward him. Her steady gaze met and held his. The longer he stared into her eyes, the calmer he felt. His breathing slowed, and his heartbeat resumed its normal rhythm.

Carlo Falco stepped in front of his daughter, impeding her progress. Oh boy, what was going to happen next? The breath stilled in Franco's lungs as he watched.

"You aren't going to marry *him*." Carlo gave the word *him* an offensive sound.

"I am." Carla's voice was firm.

Franco inwardly cheered her on.

Still, Carlo didn't move as father and daughter continued to glare at each other.

Franco loudly cleared his throat, hoping to distract them from the inevitable argument. It appeared to work when Carla stepped around her father.

Her gaze reconnected with Franco's as she approached him. He wanted to tell her how proud he was of her for standing up to her father. He knew it couldn't have been easy for her.

Franco sent her a reassuring smile, because suddenly this wasn't all about him and what he was risking. It was about helping Carla break free of the hold her father appeared to have over her.

And as long as Carla was by his side, he could get through this—they'd do it together. Finally, he was able to think clearly. He took a moment to really look at his bride. She stole his breath. She wore a long lacy gown that gave a peek at her crystal-studded heels. The gown gathered around her slender waist.

The fitted bodice was decorated with crystals that sparkled in the sunlight. It was held up by two thin straps. Her hair had been pulled up and studded with little white flowers.

But it was the smile on her beautiful face that pulled it all together. She was smiling directly at him. It filled his chest with warmth and a feeling he'd never experienced before.

She couldn't believe she was still walking.

Her knees felt like gelatin, and her ankles were wobbly.

Carla's heart had launched into her throat when her father had stepped in front of her. Anger had flashed in his eyes. She'd thought for sure he was going to make a scene, but then someone had cleared their throat as though reminding them that they had an avid audience. Her father may have refrained from making a public scene, but she knew it wasn't over.

She pushed thoughts of her father to the back of her mind as she continued marching toward her destiny. This really felt like a genuine wedding. It definitely wasn't the simple legal arrangement she'd envisioned. Franco had arranged for a truly authentic wedding including a white lace wedding gown. Oh, and let's not forget the flowers. They were gorgeous plum and blush peonies with greenery to accent the bouquet.

With all the attention to detail that had been put into the day, she was beginning to think there was a whole other side to her soon-to-be husband than she'd originally imagined. The next several months might not be the utter drudgery she'd been imagining.

When she neared her intended groom, she noticed that he cleaned up quite well. He wore a black tux with a black necktie and a crisp white shirt. It looked very sharp on him. He'd shaved, and his hair was still damp from a shower.

She could scarcely believe this was really happening—a wedding born out of desperation for the two things she loved most—her beloved father and the restaurants where she'd spent so much of her childhood. Because if she didn't make this big sacrifice today, there was a great possibility she'd lose both of them. And that couldn't happen—she wouldn't let it happen.

The longer she stared into Franco's dark, mesmerizing eyes, the more solid her steps became. This was going to work out. She'd picked the right partner. Franco wanted this business deal to succeed as much as she did.

As for that rap-a-tapping of her heart, well, that was just nerves. Pure and simple. Because there was no way the best man from her cousin's wedding had gotten past the carefully laid wall around her tattered heart.

She'd already let one man get close, only to find that she couldn't trust him, and he'd shattered more than just her heart—he'd stolen away her trust, not only in men but in her own judgment. But she wouldn't have that problem with Franco. Her heart wouldn't be on the line.

She continued toward him. She was almost there. She could feel his unease with this whole arrangement. She could totally sympathize.

Just a little longer. Soon it will be over.

And then she stopped in front of him. Could he hear the pounding of her heart?

"Join hands," the minister said.

Before she could utter a word, Franco took her hands in his own. It was only once his steady grip held her fingers that she noticed the slight tremor in her hands. Okay, so she was a little more nervous than she'd been willing to admit.

And then the minister started a traditional service. There was way too much reference to love going on— way too much. She felt like a total fraud. She needed to do something—say something. If the minister kept talking about how their lives would forever be intertwined, she was never going to make it through the wedding.

Before she could utter a word, Franco leaned over and whispered to the minister, "Could we just skip to the important part?"

The minister sent him a knowing smile, as though this wasn't the first time a couple had been anxious to rush to vows. Only Carla was certain the other couples' haste hadn't been because the mention of love and forever while marrying someone they weren't romantically linked with made them uncomfortable.

"Do you, Franco Giuseppe Marchello, take Carla Elana Falco to be your wife?"

There was a pause. Carla's gaze rose to meet his. She immediately saw his indecision. *No. No. We've come too far for you to back out now.*

"Franco," prompted the minister.

Her gaze flickered to the minister, whose attention was fully focused on her intended. She turned back to Franco. His gaze was downcast. What was he doing? Wasn't it too late to reconsider this marriage?

She squeezed his hand, hoping to jar him back to reality. His head immediately lifted. When his gaze met hers, she looked at him expectedly.

"I do." His response was faint.

The minister smiled and nodded. He turned to her. In a calm, steady voice, the minister said, "Do you, Carla Elana Falco, take Franco Giuseppe Marchello to be your husband?"

Her tongue stuck to the roof of her mouth. This was it. This was the final part. All she had to do was utter two little words. It'd seemed so simple when Franco had to do it. But now that it was her turn and all eyes were on her, she suddenly realized the enormity of saying *I do* and how it would have an enormous impact on her life—every single aspect of her life was about to change.

Franco squeezed her hand just as she had done for him. Her eyes rose to meet his. And in his intent gaze was the expectation that she would follow his lead and seal the deal. After all, this had been her idea in the first place.

She swallowed hard and couldn't help but wonder if this was going to be the biggest mistake of her life. And then she uttered in a strangled voice, "I do."

Relief reflected in Franco's dark eyes. Apparently he didn't want to be left standing at the altar. They turned to the minister, who said a few words and then declared them husband and wife.

"You may kiss the bride." The minister beamed at them.

Oh no! How could she have forgotten about this part? Because there was no way that they were going to seal this business deal with a kiss. That was simply above and beyond their agreement. Surely Franco would agree. After all, it wasn't like he was into her.

She turned to Franco to tell him that they could skip this part. Her gaze flickered to his. She could read the look in his eyes. It was one of desire. He was going to kiss her. Her pulse raced with anticipation. This shouldn't happen, but there was a part of her that had always wondered what it'd be like to be kissed by him.

His hands spanned her waist. As he drew her nearer, it was only natural for her to reach out to him, placing her hands on his broad shoulders to maintain her balance. Because there was no way she would voluntarily reach out to him—wanting to feel his powerful muscles beneath her fingertips.

And then, as though there was a magnetic force drawing them together, she felt her body lean toward his. She felt helpless to resist the attraction. Her heart pitter-pattered faster, harder. It echoed in her ears.

As though time were suspended, everything moved in slow motion. Her husband was about to kiss her. She was married. *Married.* The word echoed in her mind.

In the next millisecond, she pressed against his hard, muscular chest. *Oh my!* The air stilled in her lungs. The initial protest evaporated.

The touch of his lips to hers settled her frantic thoughts, allowing her to focus on him and her—on this dizzying, delicious kiss. His touch was warm and firm. His lips moved slowly over hers. A moan swelled in her throat. No first kiss was supposed to be this good—this addictive.

She gave herself up to the moment. She leaned fully into his embrace, giving herself to him. Her lips began to move beneath his. Because she wasn't going to turn away from this most amazing experience. She never wanted this wondrous sensation to end—

Someone cleared their throat.

Carla was immediately jerked out of the trancelike state she'd been in. Her feet came crashing back down to earth. She jumped back. Heat rushed up her neck and set her cheeks aflame. Well, if she'd wanted to convince her father that this marriage was real, that should have done it.

She didn't dare look at her new husband. She didn't want him to see how his kiss had warmed her cheeks and shaken her to the core. Because none of this was real. The marriage wasn't real. This wedding wasn't real. And that kiss hadn't been real.

Sure, it had all happened, but it was all a show. She just couldn't get caught up in their playacting. And it was all her father's fault. If he wasn't such a stubborn man. If he wasn't willing to risk his life to keep working—keep making sure their company was ever expanding at an alarming pace—she wouldn't officially be Mrs. Franco Marchello. That acknowledgment made her heart leap into her throat.

Mrs. Franco Marchello. Oh my!

Wedding guests rushed forward to congratulate them, but she couldn't focus on anything but this insurmountable mistake she'd made. She went through the motions as her mind struggled with the reality of what they'd just done.

The one thing she knew was that there would be no more kissing Franco. No way. Because it was dangerous. She couldn't think straight when he was so close to her. And when his lips were touching hers, all she could think was how much she wanted more of him—so much more.

That had gone totally wrong.

He'd only meant to give her a brief, passive kiss.

Franco inwardly groaned as he realized the kiss had been anything but brief or passive. There had been sparks that he hadn't seen coming. Those sparks had ignited a flame. And now he couldn't get Carla out of his system.

And that shouldn't have happened. It was a total miscalculation on his part. Because Carla was the last person on the planet he should be kissing. It wasn't that he didn't find her attractive. He thought Carla was the most beautiful woman he'd ever known. Any man with an active pulse couldn't deny her beauty.

The problem was the fact that she was Carlo Falco's daughter. And he had been duly warned by his grandfather not to trust a Falco. That's why Franco had had his team of attorneys go over the marriage contract twice. It was ironclad. This knowledge still didn't help him breathe easier.

"You really outdid yourself." Carla smiled at him, as they stood off to the side of the party. She lowered her voice so as not to be overheard. "I thought it would just be a small, forgettable exchange of vows, but you made this whole experience a lot more enjoyable and less businesslike. Not that I've forgotten this is all business, but still it was nice. Thank you."

Her words shocked him—in a good way. He swallowed hard. "You're welcome. I'm glad you liked it."

"I did." And then she leaned in close. "I almost believed it was real."

"But it was real. And now we have a show to put on for our guests." As the music played in the background, he held his hand out to her. "Shall we, Mrs. Marchello?"

She placed her hand in his and they started toward the dance floor—

"Not so fast." Carlo Falco stepped in front of them. His face was full of color as his brows were drawn together in a formidable line. "We need to talk."

Franco gave Carla's hand a reassuring squeeze. "Let's step over there."

"Not you." Her father's deep voice rumbled with barely restrained anger.

Franco wasn't going to let Carla take the brunt of her father's anger alone. They'd agreed to this plan together, and they'd see it through together. "We're married now. If you have something to say about that, you can say it to both of us."

Carlo's gaze moved to his daughter. "Is that how it's going to be from now on? A Marchello is going to do all the talking for you?"

"Papa, calm down. There's no need to get so worked up."

Her father's gaze narrowed. "So does he speak for you?"

"No. I can speak for myself. But in this case, I agree with my husband—"

"Husband, ha! This sham of a marriage is never going to last. You only agreed to marry him to spite me. When you're ready to admit this was a mistake, you know where to find me."

"But Papa, wait—"

Carlo stormed off. His pace didn't so much as slow down as she continued to call out to him. Nor did he give her a backward glance. Franco supposed that was something else Carlo had in common with his grandfather— a short temper and the feeling that they knew what was best for those around them. It was a quite an assumption on their parts. Franco's muscles tensed with anger. Carla wiggled her fingers, letting him know he was squeezing her hand too tightly.

When he glanced at her, he noticed how her eyes

shimmered with unshed tears. "It'll be okay." He wasn't certain of it, but those were the first comforting words that came to mind. "He just needs a little time to get used to the idea."

"I knew he'd be upset—" her voice wavered with emotion "—but I've never seen him that upset."

"You can't do anything about it now. Let it go for the moment. You being miserable all evening won't change anything."

"But I should go talk to him."

"And tell him what? That you're going to cave in and dissolve our marriage? Remember why you did this."

She drew in an unsteady breath. "You're right. He needs to cool off. I'll reason with him tomorrow."

"It sounds like a plan." He sent her an encouraging smile. "Now, would you like to dance?"

It was then that she glanced around at all the people trying not to stare at them and failing miserably.

"I suppose we'd better." She didn't waste any time as she led him to the dance floor.

Once on the dance floor, she placed her hand in his. He pulled her close. As they moved around the temporary dance floor, his heart pounded. He told himself it was from the physical activity, but secretly he knew it was from holding his beautiful bride so close—so temptingly close.

Carla laid her head on his shoulder as the photographer took their photo. It was then that Franco smelled the peachy-floral scent of her hair. He inhaled deeper. Maybe this marriage thing wasn't going to be so bad after all.

Just then Carla's heel came down on his foot. He bit back a yelp of pain. He was suddenly jarred from his fantasy. He couldn't help but wonder if her misstep had been accidental or intentional. Because her movements had been smooth and graceful up until that point. Was it possible she'd read the direction of his thoughts?

With that in mind, he loosened his hold on her waist, allowing some more space between them. Maybe then he would cool down and his imagination wouldn't keep tiptoeing into forbidden territory.

CHAPTER SIX

FOR THE MOST PART, it had been an amazing evening.

She could have danced all night long.

With Franco's attentive assistance, Carla was finally able to shove the scene with her father to the back of her mind. She found herself smiling. Why not? The worst was over. They were married now. There was nothing to contemplate. The deed had been done.

Still, it was hard not to be utterly and totally distracted by her dashing husband. *Husband*. That was going to take some getting used to.

She had to admit that Franco and his assistant had planned a pretty awesome party. And she noticed him smiling throughout the evening filled with delicious food and endless dancing. Though he entertained the guests, he was still an attentive husband. What happened after this evening, well, she wasn't going to let her mind go there. At least not yet.

Franco stepped up to her. He held out a flute of champagne. It wasn't her first or second glass that evening. At first, she'd been hesitant to drink any, but as the festive mood of the evening swept over her, she found herself letting her guard down and enjoying the evening. After all, she couldn't spend the next six months at odds with her husband.

But the evening was winding down, and guests were departing. And secretly she didn't want to see it end. She wasn't ready to go back to reality with its endless meetings and arduous negotiations.

"Did you enjoy yourself?" Franco asked.

"I had a delightful time." She sipped the sweet, bubbly champagne.

He arched a brow. "Truthfully?"

She took her finger and made an X over her chest. "Cross my heart."

Gianna approached them. She leaned forward and gave Carla a hug. "I'm so happy for you. And best of all, we're sisters-in-law. Isn't that awesome?"

Carla hadn't thought of that before. "Yes, it is."

She glanced over as the two brothers shook hands and then clapped each other on the back. Franco looked more relaxed now than she'd ever seen him. Maybe it was just the relief of this day being over. If so, she had to agree with him. It had been surprisingly fun, but now she was exhausted.

After a glowing Gianna and her clearly besotted husband left, Carla turned and was surprised to find some people still on the dance floor.

Franco held his hand out to her. "May I have this dance?"

"Haven't you had enough dancing?"

He smiled. "Not with my beautiful bride."

Heat rushed to her cheeks. Even though she knew he was still playing a part, she couldn't help getting caught up in the moment. And it was impossible for her to deny the way his words made her heart pitter-patter, even if she only admitted it to herself.

What would it hurt to let the charade continue just a little longer? After all, it was too late now to visit her father. And it was too late to do any business. So for the moment, she was all Franco's—so to speak.

Carla finished her glass of sparkling blue champagne. Her favorite. Then she placed her hand in his and they made their way to the dance floor. A slow ballad started to play as Franco pulled her into his arms. She didn't hesitate as he drew her in close. She told herself it was the effect of the bubbly that had her giving up on keeping a modest distance between them.

The softness of her curves pressed up against the hard planes of his muscled chest. The breath caught in her lungs as every nerve ending in her body tingled with desire. She closed her eyes and rested her head against his shoulder. After all, he was now legally her husband— why not enjoy the advantages of the situation?

They danced one slow song after the next. With her head turned in toward his neck, she inhaled the scent of soap combined with a spiciness. It was utterly addictive and totally intoxicating. She was even tempted to press her lips to his neck. She wondered how he'd react. She should do it. She'd thrown all other caution to the wind today.

At the last moment, she restrained her impish impulses. That would be taking their charade too far, right? She couldn't possibly have Franco brush off her advances. If so, how would she ever live with him for the next six months? Therefore, she had to tamp down these unexpected and unwanted desires. But that was easier said than done, because her body refused to abide.

Instead of stepping back and allowing space between them, she stayed right there pressed up against him.

All the while their bodies brushed together and an undeniable flame of desire was building into a massive inferno that threatened to consume her. What was Franco thinking? Did he desire her as much as she wanted him?

She thought of lifting her head to look into his eyes and ask him, but she didn't have the nerve to do it. Because while she was looking for signs of desire in his eyes, he'd be able to see her own growing desire for him. It was best to stay where she was. Because when he held her so close, there was no way he could read anything in her expression. As for body language, well, that was a totally different subject.

Franco stopped moving. Disappointment swelled up within her. With great regret, she lifted her head. "You don't want to dance any longer?"

He smiled at her. "The music has stopped, *amore*."

She tried to listen over the pounding of her heart. It was then that she realized the music had indeed stopped. And when she glanced around, she found they were alone on the dance floor.

"Where did everyone go?"

"Home, I imagine."

The only others were the band and some servers who were clearing the last of the glasses. A sense of disappointment came over her when she realized the celebration was over. She understood the absurdity of such a thought, because in the beginning she'd been the one dreading this wedding. And yet Franco had gone out of his way to make it a very enjoyable evening.

As a cool breeze off the lake brushed over her bare

skin, she found herself rubbing her arms. With autumn not far off, the evenings were growing much cooler. Funny that she hadn't noticed the dip in the temperature at all when she'd been wrapped in Franco's arms.

"Shall we go inside?" Franco asked.

"We're staying here tonight?"

"Yes. Is that a problem?"

She thought about it for a moment. It wasn't like she had anyone waiting for her at home. She had her own apartment and didn't so much as have a pet. So there was no one to miss her. And she'd already made arrangements with her father's live-in companion to keep an extra close eye on Carlo this evening.

"It's no problem at all. Tomorrow will be soon enough to adjust to the reality of our new situation."

He once more offered his arm to her. Who would have thought that Franco Marchello was such a gentleman? She smiled as she slipped her hand into the crook of his arm. They strolled into the villa that had obviously just been renovated. Everything inside was shiny and new.

They kicked off their shoes by the door. It was only then that Carla realized how sore her feet were from dancing in heels all evening. But she'd been so caught up in the festivities that she hadn't noticed until now.

Franco slipped off his tux jacket. He removed the black tie and then he unbuttoned the collar. He undid his cuff links and rolled up his sleeves. Though it was a much more casual look, it made him look even more attractive—like a real-life James Bond.

While Franco set to work building a fire in the living room's stone fireplace, she poured them some more bubbly. In her nervousness, she filled the glasses a bit too much. Oh well, it was a night for celebrating. She held out a glass to him.

When Franco resisted taking the glass, she said, "Go ahead. We have a lot to celebrate."

"We do?"

She nodded. "Our plan is underway. Tomorrow you and I will start figuring out the best way to advance both of our companies. I see a beautiful future for both of us."

He clinked his glass against hers. "I'm looking forward to it. But business will come soon enough. Let's just focus on the here and now." They settled on the couch and sipped the sparkling wine. "Did you enjoy the day?"

"Other than the scene with my father, it was a wonderful wedding."

His gaze flickered to hers and then moved back to the fire. "If you're having regrets, it's not too late to back out."

She shook her head. The truth was she'd never considered getting married against her father's wishes. "If this had been a real wedding, yes, it would have been unbearable. It's hard enough not having my mother in my life. I miss her every day—every time I need some advice. With my father being my only living parent, I just can't imagine having him angry at me if this were a real wedding, but luckily it's not." Then realizing how that might sound, she said, "You know what I mean."

Franco nodded. "He loves you a lot. That much is very obvious."

"I don't know if he loves me a lot. People that love you don't normally push you into a marriage you don't want or block you from taking over the business when it's for their own welfare. And then get furious when you finally marry like they wanted."

"That's not exactly fair. You know how he feels about my family. You knew he wouldn't take it well."

"I just wish he trusted me to know what's right for me and would stop trying to push me into what he thinks I should do."

"I think he's done all of it because he's worried something might happen to him and he doesn't want you to end up alone."

It wasn't like she was a child. She could pick out her own husband—just like she'd done. Not that Franco was really her husband—well, legally he was, but not in her heart.

She decided it was best to skip over the marriage and husband part; instead she asked, "Then why doesn't he trust me with what he loves most in this world—the restaurants?"

Franco paused as though giving her question due consideration. Then he rubbed the back of his neck. "I wish I could give you an answer, but I have no idea. You're very smart, well-educated and full of energy. I think he's foolish for wanting someone else to fill in for him."

His spontaneous compliments warmed a spot in her chest. "You really think I'm that well suited for the position?"

His gaze once more met hers. "I do. You'd be my first pick."

"Thank you." She smiled at him. She had no idea that he thought so highly of her. It was like he'd bestowed yet another wedding gift upon her—one that meant so much more than the designer wedding dress or the glittering diamond wedding band.

Her gaze lowered and she lifted her hand ever so slightly, letting the firelight play over the arrangement of diamonds encompassing her finger. He certainly hadn't withheld anything for this marriage—even if it was only a temporary one.

She wondered what his extravagance meant. Did he wish there was more to this marriage than there was? Her heart fluttered at the thought. Or was this just his generous way?

It was at this point that she realized just how much she didn't know about her extremely handsome and mysterious husband. And since they'd already talked about her complicated relationship with her father, it was time she learned a bit more about the man she was married to.

"And what about you?" she asked. "What was it like to get married without not only your grandparents but your mother and father as well?"

He sighed and leaned his head back against the couch. As he moved, he slid a little closer to her, making her heart pitter-pat faster. "If this was a real wedding, I couldn't have done it without inviting my grandparents. For better or worse, they've always been there for me—even when my grandfather vehemently disagreed with me."

"I'm glad you have them. But what about your parents? I've noticed you never mention them."

"What's to mention? My father is like some distant uncle that stops by once in a blue moon when he's in town and is gone again before any meaningful connection can be established. And my mother, well, she's around for the important events, but her focus is always on her ever-revolving romances."

"I'm sorry." Carla didn't know what else to say.

Her mother had always been there for her—right up until she died. Even hiding the truth of her illness from her so she wouldn't have to worry. Though Carla would have much rather known about the severity of her mother's illness. She might have done things differently. Might have stopped what she was doing to spend those last days with her mother. But this conversation wasn't about her.

"It's okay." The anguished tone of his voice said it was anything but okay.

Her heart ached for that little boy who'd been tossed aside and forgotten. How could someone do that to their child? It was unimaginable.

She swallowed her rising emotions. "That must have been so hard for a young boy not to have either of his parents around."

"I figure they had their reasons to keep their distance. After all, my grandfather isn't an easy man to deal with."

"You think that's the reason they left."

He shrugged. "I think it's my father's reason, but not my mother's. She doesn't listen to anyone but herself. But my father, well, I think he couldn't do anything right in my grandfather's eyes, and he got tired of trying."

"But why would they leave you and your brother?"

"I'm not sure. I wouldn't put it past my grandfather to threaten to fight for custody of us. After all, we are the heirs to the Marchello estate. And without my father around, we were even more important to him."

Sympathy welled up in her for the little boy Franco had once been, who didn't understand why both of his parents had disappeared from his life. How could his parents just abandon him and his brother? Who did such a thing?

She turned to Franco to tell him how sorry she felt for him, but when his gaze met hers, she immediately forgot what she'd been about to say. The longer they gazed into each other's eyes, the faster her heart beat.

Had he moved closer to her? Because their shoulders were now touching. Or was it possible that she had leaned over toward him? There was this undeniable desire drawing them together. Her entire body tingled with an excited awareness.

When it came to husbands, she'd definitely come up with a winning one. There was no denying that he was handsome, but even more than that he was thoughtful. What kind of man went to all this trouble for a wife in name only?

She couldn't even fathom the extremes he would go to for a woman he loved. And she didn't want to imagine it. Not now. Not in this moment.

Because no matter their reason for exchanging wedding vows, the truth of the matter was that they were legally husband and wife. And though she wanted to tell herself that it was all a business arrangement, she couldn't deny that there had been a definite shift in the ground beneath her feet when she'd said *I do*.

And now when she stared at her newly minted husband, she wondered if that kiss they'd shared when the minister had pronounced them husband and wife had been real. Because she'd swear her feet had been floating above the ground. It was that good—that heart-poundingly amazing.

A loud pop of wood in the fireplace made her jump. The champagne sloshed over the sides of her glass and dripped down over her fingers. When she glanced down at the sticky mess, she realized that it had spilled onto Franco's white dress shirt.

"Oh no. I'm so sorry."

"No big deal."

She was horrified. "I'll get something to dry it." She spotted some napkins placed next to trays of finger foods left for them by the catering staff. She grabbed a napkin and then turned to Franco.

As she knelt on the couch next to him, she pressed the napkin to his abdomen. Being left-handed, she had no choice but to place her other hand on his chest to keep herself from falling into him.

She ran the white cloth up his side, all the while feeling the steely strength of his muscles. Her mouth grew dry. She didn't dare meet his gaze. He'd know where her thoughts had strayed.

"If you were trying to cool things off between us," he said in a deep, gravelly voice, "it isn't working." And then he moved to unbutton his shirt.

Carla's mouth grew dry as she watched him undo one button and then the next. "What...what are you doing?"

A little smile lifted the corners of his mouth. "Taking off my wet shirt so you won't worry about it any longer."

She sat back on her heels as he pulled his shirt free. She shouldn't be sitting there openly staring at him, but she was helpless to stop. His chest was so toned, it was though he spent every day at the gym. His tanned

skin was smooth, and his chest had a smattering of
dark curls. Wow!

Her fingers tingled to reach out and work their way
up his torso. She resisted the urge. She wasn't quite sure
how that was possible. Maybe it was the fact that at this
moment her mind was overwhelmed with everything
that had happened today.

She finally dragged her gaze up to meet his. She
didn't know what she expected to find, but it sure wasn't
the desire flickering in his eyes, mirroring her own rising needs.

One moment, she was sitting there looking at him,
and in the next his lips were pressing to hers. If she
thought their first kiss as husband and wife had been
something, it was nothing compared to this passionate embrace.

Without an audience, there was no need to hold back.
And he most certainly didn't as he wrapped his arms
around her, deepening the kiss. Then, using those muscles she'd been admiring, he swept her into his arms and
repositioned them so she was lying back on the couch.
He settled on top of her—the full, lean length of him.
And they were still kissing—oh, were they kissing.

And right now, Carla had absolutely no desire to stop
this delicious moment. After all, what was to stop them?
For the next six months, he was her husband. And yes,
maybe they had made some initial ground rules about
what was expected from the marriage, but as his mouth
moved over hers and her fingers trailed over his bare
shoulders, she couldn't quite recall what those ground
rules had been.

CHAPTER SEVEN

LAST NIGHT HAD been a mistake.

A complete and total mistake.

Franco couldn't believe he'd let himself spend the entire night with his new bride. It had been the most amazing evening—one he wasn't soon to forget. Oh, who was he kidding? He was never going to forget it. Carla was the type of woman who left her mark upon your life.

He raked his fingers through his hair as he paced back and forth in the living room. He hadn't even been married for twenty-four hours before he'd broken their agreement to keep things uncomplicated and totally platonic.

Luckily for him, Carla had still been asleep when he'd awoken that morning. But he knew she'd be up soon, and then what would he say to her? How would he explain how he'd let things get totally and absolutely out of control?

As his mind rolled back over the highlights of their evening together, a smile pulled at the corners of his mouth. So maybe it wasn't all bad. In fact, it had been quite good—

"Morning."

At the sound of Carla's voice, the smile slipped from his face. Hesitantly, he turned. Carla wasn't smiling but she wasn't frowning, either. His body tensed as he waited for her to start yelling at him about how he'd broken all the rules when he'd slipped off his shirt and then proceeded to kiss her.

He could blame it on the alcohol, but that wasn't the truth. The fact was he'd been fantasizing about kissing again her ever since they'd been pronounced—he hesitated, still not at all comfortable with their new marital status—since they'd formalized their agreement. It was in that moment—with the memory of them taking a vow of forever, in sickness and in health—that he came back to reality. The excitement of the evening wore off and he could finally think straight once more.

He cleared his throat. "Morning. There's coffee in the kitchen."

"Thank you." When she smiled, he felt his heart beat faster.

He struggled not to return the smile. It was better to cool things off now before either of them got in too deep and ended up getting hurt in the end. And there would be an end. He didn't believe in marriage—in forever. And this was just a business arrangement, nothing more.

When Carla turned toward the kitchen, he followed her. "I was thinking we should get back to the city as soon as you're ready."

She poured herself a cup of coffee. "I'm sorry I slept so late." She yawned. "I'm just really tired."

Her back was to him, so he wasn't able to read the look on her face. He shifted his weight from one foot to the other. "About last night—it was a mistake."

Carla spun around. Her gaze narrowed on him. For

a moment, she didn't say anything. This just made him all the more uncomfortable. He couldn't help but wonder if that had been her intent.

Still, the longer the silence lingered, the more awkward the moment became. So he said, "I don't want to hurt you. And if I let you think this is the beginning of something, it'd be a lie—"

"Good. I was hoping you didn't get the wrong idea, either." Her voice was calm and restrained.

It wasn't the reaction he'd been anticipating. Most women he'd been involved with always wanted more than he could offer. And some got very angry when he set them straight.

She took a big gulp of coffee before turning to him. "I just have to run upstairs and grab my stuff. Then we can go." When her dismissal of their lovemaking left him speechless, she asked, "Is there something else?"

"Um, no. So we're all right?"

"Sure." Her voice was light and upbeat. "Why wouldn't we be?"

And with that she sailed out of the kitchen with her coffee cup in hand. He was left standing there with his mouth hanging open. Had that just happened? Was his lovemaking that unremarkable?

Disappointment assailed him. He didn't know what he'd been expecting from her, but it hadn't been a complete dismissal of their passionate night. He should be happy. This gave them a chance for a do-over—a chance to keep things purely platonic.

But he knew any attempt to forget what they'd shared the night before was going to be difficult. No. It was going to be a downright impossible feat. There was no forgetting Carla.

* * *

She had to get away.

Her bare feet moved up the steps silently.

Carla tripped at the top of staircase in her haste to get away from Franco. Her free hand reached out, grabbing the banister. Luckily she'd drunk enough of the coffee that it hadn't splashed over the side.

She didn't tarry on the landing. The last thing she wanted was to face Franco again so soon. She didn't want him to know how his words in the kitchen had cut her deeply. And she had a sinking feeling that her disappointment and pain were written all over her face. How she'd kept it all together in front of him had been her best acting job ever.

She rushed inside the bedroom she'd shared with Franco. With the door shut, she leaned back against it. Her vision blurred. Tears threatened to spill onto her cheeks.

She grew angry with herself for getting worked up. But when he'd so easily dismissed their lovemaking— a night that felt like it was the beginning of something real between them—she'd felt as though she'd been cut to the quick. She didn't readily open herself to someone like she had with Franco.

Maybe it was the wedding vows—to love, honor and cherish. Or maybe it was the litany of romantic ballads they'd danced to all evening. Or maybe it was a bit too much champagne. Or perhaps it was a lethal combination of all those things that had had her letting down her guard last night. Franco had gotten closer to her than any other man had ever done, including her loser ex-fiancé.

And worse yet was she'd let herself fall into a false

sense of security with Franco's soul-stirring kisses, his gentle caresses and his endearing words. Ugh! What was wrong with her? He was probably that way with all his women—

She halted her thoughts right there. She just couldn't deal with the thought of him being so loving and attentive with anyone else. Maybe it had been a one-night sort of thing, but she wanted to believe that it was special. She wanted to think their night together had been unique for both of them. Even if it wasn't going to happen ever again.

Because whether she liked it or not, Franco was right. They'd agreed not to let things get messy for a reason. It was best not to get caught up in some fantasy, because in the end she'd get hurt. Because Franco didn't do relationships, unless they were of the business variety.

They only had six months in which to make their plan a reality. And if they were so wrapped up in—well, whatever happened last night—they wouldn't put all their energy into making this venture a huge success.

She quickly grabbed her things—including her wedding dress—and headed for the door. It was time they got back to reality. She was certain once she was home that they would be able to keep the lines in their relationship straight. There would be no more confusion— no more kisses or anything else.

CHAPTER EIGHT

THE RIDE BACK to Verona seemed to go on forever.

Carla couldn't wait to step in her apartment. She just wanted a few minutes to herself before she faced her father. Being back among her things would make her feel grounded—make her feel more like herself—not like Mrs. Marchello.

But when they reached the city, Franco didn't make the turn toward her place. "Wait. You missed the turn."

"No, I didn't."

Of course he did. "My place is the other way."

"And my place is this way."

"But I don't want to go to your place. I have to go see my father."

As Franco maneuvered the car along the sparsely filled road, he chanced a quick glance at her. "You do realize that you're going to have to move into my place, don't you?"

"What? No. No. That isn't going to happen." She crossed her arms.

In a gentle, nonaggressive voice, he said, "Don't you think it's going to look strange to people if we live apart?"

She inwardly groaned. Why did everything that had to do with Franco have to be so complicated? Maybe in her haste to figure out all the legal ramifications and rushing to make sure her father was sufficiently looked after, she might have missed some of the complications of this plan.

She wanted to argue with Franco. She wanted to tell him that it would be totally fine if they lived separately, but she knew that none of that was true. Drat him for being so logical.

"Fine," she said, "You can move into my place."

"I don't think so."

She turned to him. "Why not? It has two bedrooms."

"I've been to your place to drop off papers, and I've seen how small it is compared to my penthouse. Trust me. We'll be much more comfortable at my place."

Trust him? The echo of her father's warning rang in her ears. She'd trusted Franco last night by letting him see a vulnerable side of her, and look where that had gotten her. He'd brushed her off in the light of day, leaving her pride sporting a painful bruise.

She'd trusted her ex and he'd cheated on her, all the while boldly lying to her face about the reason for delaying their wedding. And then there was her father, who'd taught her that trust was supposed to go both ways. And yet he staunchly refused to trust that she was making the right choices for the right reasons.

So no, she wasn't ready to trust Franco so easily. And she wasn't ready to give in on their living arrangements just because he said so. "But my place is closer to the office."

"Your office. Not mine. My place is between them both."

That much was true. She was running out of reasons why they should stay at her place instead of his. And quite honestly, she just didn't have the gumption to keep fighting him over this. As it was, she had to deal with her father in the near future. She was going to need all her energy to deal with him and make sure her marriage to Franco didn't cause him to have a medical setback.

"Okay," she said softly.

"Excuse me, did you just agree to stay at my place?"

"Yes! Yes, I did. But don't push it."

He was quiet for a moment as he negotiated a busy intersection. "Do you want to move your things now?"

"No. I need to go to my place, change clothes and go see my father. It's time he knows that I intend to take over control of the company. Immediately."

"Agreed. I'll go with you."

"Absolutely not!"

Franco slowed the car as he pulled off into a parking spot. "Why not? I'm your husband."

She shook her head. "It'll be too much for him with you there."

"What do you mean, too much?"

There was quite a bit she'd failed to tell Franco about the true reason behind her move to take over the company. Because when all was said and done, she was willing to give up the company. However, she wasn't ready to lose her father.

"Just trust me." She pleaded with him with her eyes, hoping he'd let the subject rest.

The truth of the matter was that she hadn't wanted to dig into the painful details. She would do whatever it took to see that her father was well taken care of since that stubborn man wouldn't do it himself. And no, she didn't want Franco to see her vulnerable again.

Franco's dark gaze probed her. "If we're going to trust each other, we have to start talking to each other."

He was right. Maybe if they'd slowed down long enough to talk last night, they'd have reminded each other of the rules of their marriage, but instead they'd let their desires take over and everything had spiraled out of control. It was a lesson learned.

She glanced down at her clasped hands in her lap. Memories flashed in her mind of seeing her father in a hospital bed. Not once. But twice. She wrung her hands together.

And the last time he was in the hospital, with all the wires connected to his chest and the IV in his arm, his complexion had been the same pale shade as his white sheets. Her tattered heart had tumbled down to her heels.

Carla closed her eyes, willing away the troubling images. She couldn't go through that again. She couldn't lose him already. Because if she did—if she lost him— she'd be all alone in this world. And she wasn't ready for that, either.

Sure, there was Gianna, but she was happily married now and expecting her first baby. She wouldn't have the time to spend with Carla like they'd done in the past. And though she was immensely happy for her cousin, she knew that things would never be the same again.

But how did she explain any of this to Franco without him seeing her as weak? Because when it came down to it, they were now business partners. And there would be a lot of negotiating in the future of how to handle this venture between her national restaurant chain and his expansive line of spices. It would be quite an endeavor—one where she needed to hold a strong edge so as not to be bulldozed by him and his narrowed pursuits.

"It's my father." She hesitated, trying to tamp down her rising emotions.

"I know he isn't happy about our marriage, but there's no way he can break the contract as long as we're married. My attorneys went over everything. They said it was as ironclad as they'd ever seen."

She shook her head. "It's not about the contract."

"Then what is it?" His voice was soft and coaxing.

What would it hurt to tell him? Sure, she'd promised her father not to disclose information about his second heart attack because he'd been worried that his business associates would view him as weak. Her father was the strongest, proudest man she'd ever known.

And telling Franco now when her father was out of the hospital and doing well, according to his physicians, wouldn't be a big deal. After all, Franco was now her husband. And maybe if he understood why their combined effort to put his spices in her restaurants was so important to her, he'd be more of an ally than an advisory. Secretly she longed for Franco to be on her side. Otherwise these next six months were going to drag on forever.

"You know that my father had a heart attack the night of Gianna's wedding, but what you don't know is that just recently he'd had a second heart attack, and this time they had to do bypass surgery."

Sympathy reflected in Franco's eyes. "I'm so sorry."

"He doesn't want anyone to know."

"Why not?"

"He's afraid people in the business world will treat

him differently. But while he's worried about getting back to work, the doctors are worried that with the amount of damage to his heart, running a business of that size will be too much for him." Her voice wobbled with emotion. "And I just can't lose him. Not yet."

Franco reached out and pulled her close so her head rested on his shoulder. "He'll be all right."

She wanted to believe him. "So you see why you can't come with me today. I just can't risk getting him too upset."

"I understand."

One man in her life understood her decisions, but would the other one be as understanding? She had her doubts.

Everything was changing so quickly.

Carla hadn't lingered at her place. She'd quickly packed the essentials and then headed to her father's house. She told herself that she was in a rush to get back to work—not to see her husband again, even if he was so easy on the eyes.

But first, she had to speak with her father. She found him in his home office. "Hello, Papa."

He glanced up from the paper he was reading. He slid off his reading glasses. "What are you doing here?"

"Hello to you, too." She sensed his bad mood hadn't faded like she'd hoped. She nervously spun her wedding rings around her finger. "What have you been up to?"

He sat forward, resting his arms on the desk. "The real question is why have you married a Marchello?"

The sight of his pale complexion and gaunt cheeks

had tears stinging the backs of Carla's eyes and silenced the rebuttal in the back of her throat. Not so long ago, he'd been the strongest man she'd ever known. But not one but two heart attacks had taken their toll on him. He was different now. He constantly hovered over her as though he didn't trust her judgment where business was concerned or even her personal life. She'd endured it because she didn't want to do anything to get him worked up. But things couldn't continue that way.

"Tell me you came to your senses and backed out of that marriage." Her father's voice was still deep and vibrant. His sharp gaze needled her.

She swallowed hard. "No. Franco is a good guy." She truly believed that or she wouldn't have gone through with this plan. "You just need to give him a chance."

Her father shook his head in disapproval. "Don't trust him. The Marchellos cannot be trusted."

"Why?"

Her father grunted. "The details don't matter. Just heed my warning."

"This grudge or whatever it is, is it the reason you no longer carry their products in our restaurants?"

"It is. Trust me, it's for the best." And then he quirked a brow at her. "How did you know?" Before she could answer, he said, "You've been talking to Franco."

"I have. He's my husband."

"You can tell him that as long as I live, his family's products won't be in any of our establishments. Ever."

"Even if it's good business?"

"Doing business with a Marchello is never good business."

"I won't waste my time trying to convince you otherwise. Just know now that I'm married, I'll be assuming full control of the company while you recuperate. And you might as well know that I'll be reintroducing the Marchello Spices in the restaurants."

Her father's bushy brows rose. "You can't do that!"

"But I can. Remember the deal we signed?"

He pointed at her. "You tricked me."

"No, I didn't. I simply did what you wanted—I got married."

"You were supposed to marry a good and honest man." His hands waved through the air as he talked.

"I did. If you would just give him a chance—"

"I won't. I refuse." He crossed his arms over his chest.

She wasn't going to push the subject. "Have you been monitoring your blood pressure and writing it down like they told you at the hospital?"

"Yes."

"And taking all your meds?"

"I can take care of myself. Now go."

"But Papa—"

"I said go." His voice boomed in the office.

She didn't want to leave him like this, but she didn't see where she had much of a choice. With her being there, he was just getting more worked up. And it wasn't like he lived alone. Since his first heart attack, she'd hired him a live-in companion.

She turned and headed for the door. She hesitated in the doorway and then turned back. "I'm happy. I just thought you'd want to know."

Her father's gaze met hers, but he didn't say anything.

She walked off to find Aldo and let him know that her father was still agitated, so he should keep a close

eye on him that evening. She'd gotten married and assumed control of the company with her father's best
interest in mind. He'd see that when he calmed down.
She hoped.

CHAPTER NINE

CARLA HAD GONE directly from her father's house to the office. Still upset with both of the men in her life, she immersed herself in her work. Thankfully there was a lot of it.

Not in the mood to speak to anyone, she silenced her phone and let the calls go to voice mail. Of course, she kept an eye on the caller ID just in case it was anything about her father.

There was one call from Gianna. Two from business associates and an amazing four calls from her—erm, from Franco. But considering how easily he'd dismissed their night of lovemaking, she didn't feel compelled to stop what she was doing to take his call.

Even though she'd only been out of the office a day and a half, her email was overflowing. By the time she'd sorted through them, it was past dinnertime.

Part of her felt guilty for not telling Franco that she wouldn't be around for dinner, but the other part said they were roommates at best and she didn't owe him updates on her schedule. The truth was that she had no idea how to act toward her husband who wasn't really her husband. It was so confusing.

When she arrived at the penthouse, it was getting

late. She felt weird about being there. She let herself inside with the key Franco had given her. This was only her second time there. The first time had been to go over some items in the marriage contract.

"Franco?" She paused inside the door with two bags slung over each shoulder and a big suitcase with wheels.

The lighting in the apartment was dim. And she didn't hear anything. Was he even home? She recalled his phone calls. Maybe she should have answered. Did he leave her a voice mail? She fumbled with her purse to retrieve her phone—

"Carla, you're here." Franco stepped into the spacious foyer. He looked relaxed, with his hair a bit scattered, the top buttons on his shirt undone, and he was walking around in his bare feet. "I wasn't sure what time you'd be home. I tried to call you."

"Sorry I missed your call. I was buried in work." Heat warmed her cheeks. "You know how it is when you've been out of the office for a while."

"Here." He stepped up to her. "Let me take those for you." When she relinquished her load, he said, "I'll put these in your room."

"Thank you."

"You can make yourself comfortable in the living room. I just had a pizza delivered. Help yourself to it." And then he set off with her luggage.

Guilt assailed her. Here he was being all nice and thoughtful while she'd been ducking his calls. She placed her purse and phone on the large square coffee table where she noticed Franco's phone and a fat manila folder. It appeared he'd been working at home.

Remembering her way to the guest bathroom, she freshened up. When she returned to the living room, she found Franco sitting there. He served up a slice of pizza for each of them. For a moment they ate in silence. With her stomach knotted up most of the day, she hadn't eaten much. As she kicked off her heels and curled up on the large couch, she found her hunger had returned. She devoured her slice of pizza.

Carla served them each another slice. "I'm really sorry about turning off my ringer."

"It's okay. I've been known to do that a time or two." He sent her a reassuring smile. "How did things go with your father?"

She found herself opening up about the whole awful affair. It all came tumbling out, and it felt good to get it out there.

Sympathy reflected in Franco's eyes. "I'm really sorry—"

"You have nothing to be sorry about. This whole marriage thing was my idea. I knew it wouldn't go over well, but I didn't think he'd be this mad."

"Do you want me to speak to him?"

"No." She shook her head. "Thank you, but I think that would just make everything worse."

"I'm sure he'll come around. Just give him a little time."

She nodded. "I'm sure you're right."

While they finished the rest of their pizza in silence, Franco turned on the television to a police drama. She got drawn into it, but her eyelids grew heavy. She leaned back on the couch. She just needed to close her eyes for a moment. Just a moment.

"Carla?"

She heard her name being called, but she wasn't ready to move. She was so warm and comfortable. And she'd been dreaming that she was wrapped in Franco's arms as he led her around the dance floor. She didn't want it to end, because by the look in his eyes, she was certain he was about to kiss her—

"Carla?" Someone jostled her.

Still in a sleepy fog, she leaned forward, pressing her lips to his. His touch was warm and gentle. Her lips moved over his. Her fingers reached out, stroking the stubble on his cheek. In her mind they were standing in the middle of a grand dance floor with white glitter lights all around them. She was wearing a flowing white wedding dress, and Franco looked dashing in his black tux. And she pulled back to tell him that she loved him. He spoke her name. Was he going to say *I love you* first?

"Carla? Carla, wake up."

Her eyes flew open. It took her a moment to gain her bearings. And then with horror, she realized she'd dozed off with her head on Franco's shoulder.

She sat straight up. "I'm sorry. I must have been more tired than I thought." Heat warmed her face as she fumbled to grab her phone and purse. "I should go to bed."

"Do you want me to show you to your room?"

She shook her head, still not looking at him. "I've got it. Um…good night."

And then she set off in the direction she'd seen Franco take her luggage. The bedroom was done up in tans and blues. A big sleigh bed dominated the room, but there was no sign of her luggage.

She moved to the other side of the hallway. This bedroom was done up in peaches and cream. When she spotted her luggage, she knew she was in the right place. She stepped inside the room and closed the door.

She pressed her back against the door and closed her eyes. What must Franco think of her? How had she ended up draped against him? Just the thought brought the heat back to her face. At least she hadn't talked in her sleep—had she?

With a groan, she moved away from the door. She glanced around the modern bedroom with its minimalist decor. She tried to decide if this was Franco's taste in decorating or if he just hadn't bothered to take the time or effort to add some personality to the apartment. She shrugged and turned to the bags Franco had insisted on carrying for her. They were now spread out over the king-size four-poster bed.

She pushed the memory of that vivid dream to the back of her mind. Even before it, she hadn't been sure how to act around him. Maybe they just had to figure out this new development in their relationship. And they'd have plenty of time now that they were not only living in his penthouse but also working together.

The only thing she did know was that her father was wrong about Franco. Maybe his grandfather was a liar, but not Franco. If her father would just give him a chance, he would realize what a kind and upstanding guy he was—a man they could conduct a successful business deal with.

Carla set to work, unpacking her things and placing them in the empty walk-in closet. She decided to look upon this temporary move as an adventure. And in the end, they would all get what they wanted.

Most of her clothes were hung up when her phone rang. She rushed over to the bed. The caller ID displayed the name of her assistant, Rosa. It was strange for her to call her so late, but since Carla had been out of the office for the wedding, things had piled up. Maybe she'd missed something urgent when she'd been at the office earlier.

She immediately pressed the phone to her ear. "Rosa, what's wrong?"

"This isn't Rosa, it's Rose. And why are you answering my boyfriend's phone?" The high-pitched voice hit the wrong chord in Carla.

Was it possible she'd grabbed Franco's phone instead of her own? "Who's your boyfriend?"

"Franco Marchello. Now put him on the phone."

So it was true. She was holding Franco's phone. Her grip tightened. He'd told her that he wasn't seeing anyone. Had he lied to her?

In her mind, she heard her father saying, "*I told you so. You can't trust a Marchello.*" Immediately anger pulsed through her veins. She refused to be made a fool of.

"Franco can't come to the phone." Carla wasn't sure how she kept her voice so calm and level, because she was anything but that on the inside.

"Who is this? Is this his assistant?"

"No. This is his wife. And I'd appreciate it if you wouldn't call my husband again." And then she disconnected the call.

She rushed out of her room, hoping to find Franco in the living room. He wasn't there. She checked the kitchen, but the lights were out. She turned to look at the door just off the kitchen—Franco's bedroom door.

She was pretty certain if he'd gone out that he would have let her know. That meant he must be in there. It was the last place she wanted to speak with him, but this wasn't going to wait. She needed her phone back.

She marched to the other side of the apartment and rapped her knuckles on the door.

"Hang on," he called out.

She didn't want to wait. She didn't want to see him. How dare he make a fool of her? With each passing second, her temper rose. She seesawed between telling him exactly what she thought of him and keeping her emotions to herself, not letting him see that it got to her.

When the door swung open, Franco stood there shirtless, showing off his muscular chest with broad shoulders. A pair of navy boxers hugged his trim waist. "Hi. Did you need something? More towels?"

"Uh…no." She struggled to drag her gaze back to his face.

He smiled as amusement twinkled in his eyes. He propped himself against the door. "I'm not a mind reader, so you'll have to tell me what has brought you to my door." And then his eyes widened as though he'd figured out what she wanted—him. He opened the door wider. "You can come in."

Heat swirled in her chest and rushed to her cheeks. How dare he think she was going to sleep with him again? If he thought he could have her and a girlfriend on the side, he was very wrong.

"I trusted you to keep your word," she said, trying to keep her emotions at bay. "I knew going into this arrangement that it would be hard—it would definitely have its challenges. But I thought you and I were adult enough to handle it."

He raked his fingers through his hair, scattering the short dark strands. "What are you talking about?"

She glared at him. He was playing with her and seeing what she knew. What if there was more that she didn't know—more women she didn't know about? An uneasy feeling churned in the pit of her stomach. She refused to acknowledge that the feeling eating at her felt a lot like jealousy. She was not jealous. Not. At. All.

She refused to play into his game. "Like you don't know what you've been up to and with whom."

"I don't or I wouldn't have asked you."

"Either adhere to our legal agreement or I'll sue you for breach of contract." She held out his phone. "Our phones got mixed up. I'd like mine back."

His eyes widened as his lips formed an O. He retreated to the table next to his great big bed, and she couldn't help but wonder how many times Rose had been in this room. Carla immediately stopped the thought. She wasn't going there. What he did before their marriage was none of her business. He just had to follow their agreement while he was her husband. It wasn't too much to expect.

He returned to the doorway where she'd remained. "Listen, I don't know what you think is going on, but I can assure you that there's been a misunderstanding."

Her unwavering gaze met his. "I didn't misunderstand anything. But you might want to have that conversation with your girlfriend."

She grabbed her phone from his hand and then returned his phone. Not waiting for him to say anything further, she turned and headed back across the hallway. It wasn't until she was inside her room with the door shut that she expelled a pent-up breath.

Did he really think she didn't know what he was up to? She wouldn't stand for him sneaking around behind her back. She told herself it was all about them adhering to the deal and it had absolutely nothing to do with not being able to stand the thought of Franco holding another woman in his arms and kissing her the way he'd kissed Carla. None at all.

What in the world had gotten her so worked up?

And why did she suddenly think he had a girlfriend? A wife was plenty for him. There was no way he'd want to please two women at once. That would be a very dangerous proposition. He shook his head, chasing away the troubling images.

But if Carla was truly his wife in every sense of the word, did she really think another woman could tempt him away? Definitely not.

It didn't take Franco long to realize that a woman he'd briefly seen before he'd met Carla had phoned. He inwardly groaned. The woman was trouble. The last he knew, she'd been called away for a lengthy business arrangement in the United Arab Emirates.

He didn't want to call Rose. In fact, it was the very last thing he wanted to do, but with Carla having a total fit, he had to know what Rose had said to her so he could try and undo it. Because while he didn't care what Rose thought about him, he cared very much what Carla thought.

The conversation with Rose was mostly one-sided as she regaled him with all her business triumphs in the United Arab Emirates. Every time he interrupted her in order to cut to the chase, she started over and the conversation just went on and on.

Sometime around midnight, they finally got around to the part he'd been waiting for—Rose's conversation with Carla—the one where she'd introduced herself as his girlfriend. Franco had inwardly groaned. She wanted to know if it was true that he was now married. He'd told her he was and happily so. Rose was furious. She accused him of leading her on and that she would never forgive him. She hung up on him, which was fine by him. And then he blocked her number, which was something he should have done long ago.

His immediate thought was to go to Carla, but at this late hour, he suspected she'd be sleeping. The last thing he wanted to do was wake her up. She was already upset with him. He didn't want to make it worse.

As it was, he barely slept that night. It only took one phone call to destroy the trust that he'd built up with Carla. He wanted to believe it was their working relationship he was worried about, but he wasn't that good of a liar. He liked Carla a lot. She was easy to be around. And he could talk to her like no one he'd ever known. She listened to him and didn't try to force him to do this or that. Quite frankly, he'd really miss her if she were to disappear from his life.

He halted his thoughts. Had he really just admitted that? Even if it was just to himself, it was wrong. He couldn't let himself get attached to Carla. He refused to let her or anyone get that close, because he knew what it felt like when the people in his life walked away.

He'd intended to clear things up with her first thing in the morning, but she'd slipped out the door while he was in the shower. This couldn't wait, so he headed straight to her office. He needed her to understand that he took this arrangement as seriously as she did.

He arrived at Carla's office just after nine. He didn't wait for Carla's assistant to announce him. "I have to speak with my wife."

He opened the door and barged into Carla's office, not caring who was in there.

Carla's widened gaze met his, and then her eyes narrowed. "What are you doing here?"

He closed the door behind him. "We have to talk."

"No, we don't. You just need to make sure your girlfriend knows to stay away from you."

In that moment, he realized what was going on. Carla wasn't particularly worried about how Rose might affect their business arrangement. No, this was much more personal. Carla was jealous. A warm spot started in his chest and then spread outward. A smile tugged at the corners of his mouth at the thought of his wife being jealous over him.

Then it dawned on him how dangerous this all could be. Because if Carla took this marriage too seriously, it would mean she would be hurt when it ended. And it would end. He just didn't want her getting hurt.

"Rose has never been my girlfriend. The only one who thought that was her."

Carla's mouth gaped slightly. She promptly pressed her lips together. "She must have had a reason to think those things."

He vehemently shook his head. "Not from me." He didn't want to get into all this, but Carla had right to know since she was his, um...wife. And so he told her how Rose had claimed to be pregnant so he would marry her.

"That's awful. Who does such a thing?"

He rubbed the back of his neck. "I don't know. But I never want to go through something like that again."

"I don't blame you. No one should ever lie about something so important."

"Not only that, but I'm not planning on having kids."

Her gaze searched his. "Do you mean now? Or ever?"

"Never."

Carla stood and moved around her desk, pausing just in front of it. There was quite a length between them. "So where has Rose been all this time?"

Franco approached her, stopping just in front of her. His gaze searched hers, willing her to believe him. "She's been out of the country for work. She just got back. But don't worry, I told her I was happily married."

A warmth returned to her eyes. "You did?"

"I did. Isn't that part of our agreement? Putting on a happy front for everyone?" He needed to remind both of them that this marriage wasn't real.

Carla blinked, and it was though a wall had gone up between them. "Yes. Yes, it is."

And suddenly he regretted his words. He slid his hands around her waist. "But it doesn't mean we can't have some fun. I'm getting used to being your pretend husband. It has a lot of benefits."

And then he leaned in and pressed his lips to hers. It had been a spontaneous action. He should have thought it through. He was just about to pull away when her hands slid over his shoulders. They wrapped around his neck as she deepened the kiss. It would appear he was back in her good graces—her very good graces.

He'd always heard his married friends say that the fun of fighting with their wife was the making up. He never really understood what they'd meant until now. But this was definitely worth a restless night, because kissing Carla had never been better—

She jerked back and frowned at him. "What are you doing?"

"What am I doing? What are you doing? Because that kiss went both ways."

She stared at him, but he wasn't able to read her thoughts.

Knock. Knock.

"Come in," Carla called out.

"Excuse me." Rosa's tentative gaze moved between them. I thought you'd want to know that your nine thirty appointment is on their way up."

"Oh, yes. Thank you." Then Carla, looking like a no-nonsense professional, turned to him. "This is important."

He was being dismissed. He was a Marchello. People didn't dismiss him. But as his wife turned her back to him, he realized she wasn't like other people. So be it.

He turned and stormed out the door without another word. He'd thought she'd wanted him, but obviously he'd been wrong. He'd be sure to keep his distance going forward.

But once he was outside in the fresh air, he cooled down. She'd stung his pride, nothing more. Because in the end, she was right. It's better to keep things professional between them. He was foolish to think he could enjoy the benefits of their arrangement without emotional entanglements. After all, sex with Carla was never purely physical for him. It was so much more.

CHAPTER TEN

THEIR FIRST MEETING.

Their first official meeting as Mr. and Mrs. Marchello.

During the week following their wedding, they'd worked hard to bring their respective staffs on board with their ambitious plans for this venture. And to Carla's relief, the news was mostly met with enthusiasm. There were some of the old guard that were not enthused, as they'd been swayed by her father's derogatory comments about the Marchellos. But she was working hard to convince them to embrace this mutually beneficial partnership.

When she looked across the conference room table at Franco, she tried to see him purely as a business associate, but that was impossible as their steamy wedding night and the subsequent kisses were always at the edge of her thoughts. And that was making it really hard to focus on the task at hand—breathing new life into the Falco restaurants.

At one time her family's restaurants had been the place to be. Lines of people would form out the door as they waited for a table. Now business was steady, but it wasn't impressive. People didn't stand out on the sidewalks for an hour wait because they just couldn't live without a bowl of Falco pasta or their signature salads with house dressing or their fresh-baked bread with the flaky crust.

Her father had been so focused on expanding the chain that he hadn't slowed down to refresh the menu or update the original restaurants. She'd strongly urged him to reinvest in their current properties, but he was always talking about expanding the business.

Now at last she had a chance to implement her own plans. And her new husband was a part of that plan. She glanced over at him as he spread out his papers and set up his laptop.

"I've given your spices some thought," she said.

"I'm thinking that some special blends should be placed in the middle of the table in a caddy."

"How many spices were you thinking would be Marchello brand?"

"All of them."

"No." She shook her head. "I said we'd work together, but I didn't say you were taking over."

For a while they haggled back and forth. She remembered her father's warning about not trusting a Marchello. She'd made that mistake on their wedding night, thinking that possibly there could be something more to their arrangement than business, but she had obviously been mistaken. But it wasn't the first time she'd been wrong about a man. Her thoughts strayed back to her two-timing ex-fiancé, Matteo.

Her back teeth ground together. She shoved the troubling memories to the back of her mind. She had to stay focused on their business arrangement.

Franco wasn't interested in her. He'd made that abundantly clear on the car ride home...erm, to his place.

But then there had been that kiss in her office. What was up with that?

She didn't know the answer. He confused her, and that was another reason not to get too comfortable in this new living arrangement. Everything was only temporary, except for the business. And she had to be extra careful that Franco didn't take over.

Franco expelled a frustrated sigh, crossed his arms and leaned back in his chair. "I don't know what you want from me. You keep rejecting my suggestions."

"Because they are—" She hesitated as she searched for the right word. She wanted something less bold but maybe she just needed to be up front about it all. "Well, it's boring."

"Boring?" When she nodded, he said, "I don't hear you coming up with any better ideas."

"I've been giving it some thought."

"And the only way for patrons to become familiar with our spices is to have them in front of them and to try them on their food."

"I think that's one way." Her phone buzzed with a new message from her assistant, wanting to know if she should order them lunch in. Carla responded that it was good idea.

"Okay. Keep going. What else do you have in mind?"

She thought he was agitated with her, but when she glanced up, she noticed interest reflected in his eyes. "I've done some brainstorming."

He leaned forward. "Let me see what you have come up with."

She closed her laptop. "I don't think so."

He frowned at her. "I thought this was a partnership, one where we shared everything including the good and the bad."

"But this is just some brainstorming. A list of ideas."

"Good." He reached for her laptop. "Maybe something on your list will help us."

She slid the laptop out of his reach. "I don't think you understand. This is a stream-of-consciousness technique that I've learned to do. It's just whatever popped into my mind at the moment." And she would feel too exposed if he were to read it.

He sighed and then he leaned toward her, resting his elbows on the table. "If we're going to work together, we have to be able to trust each other."

Her gaze met his. "I've been told to be wary of Marchellos."

"And yet you married one."

She opened her mouth and then promptly closed it without uttering a word. He was right. She just had to put her father's negativity and predictions of doom and gloom out her mind. He didn't know Franco like she knew him. He was an honorable man, who cared about his family and his family's business. Franco might not have any allegiance to her, but if he wanted his business to succeed, he needed her business to succeed.

With a resigned sigh, Carla opened her laptop and slid it across the table to him.

"Are you sure?" His gaze searched hers.

When she nodded, he pulled the laptop closer and his gaze perused her ideas—some were totally outlandish, others were too basic but hopefully there would be something in there that they could build upon, because time was ticking.

"I like this one," Franco said.

Since she couldn't see what he was pointing at, she asked, "Which one?"

He glanced up at her and gave her a sheepish grin that made her stomach dip. "Sorry. I forgot that you aren't looking at the screen with me. Why don't you move over here next to me?"

She wasn't so sure that switching her seat was such a good idea. There was something reassuring about having a big wood table between them. There was little chance of their fingers touching or their bodies brushing up against each other. It kept the match of desire from being struck and passion from flaming up and destroying this productive business relationship that they were struggling to form.

But it wasn't like they were conducting some heated affair. Sure, their wedding night was nice, but it wasn't anything spectacular—oh, who was she kidding? No one had ever kissed her quite the way Franco had done. When she was in his arms, she felt as though she were the only woman in the world.

Still, if she didn't move next to him, it was like admitting that his nearness got to her—that he had some sort of power over her. She glanced over at him as he continued to study her list. Her pulse raced as she took in his handsome face with his dark eyes, smooth skin and strong jawline. She was kidding herself, because nothing could be further from the truth. He did get to her. She just had to learn to ignore her body's heady response to him.

Against her better judgment, she stood. She moved around to the other side of the table and sat down next to him. She made sure to leave a respectable distance between them.

Franco pointed to the screen. "I think the first two are a bit out of our reach, and we don't really have the time to do something so involved."

"I... I agree."

"But this third one about incorporating the spices into your menu is a great idea."

"You like it?" The words slipped past her lips before she could stop them.

"Actually, I have our kitchen working on some new recipes that I was planning to use for promotional purposes, but if you'd like to use them in your kitchens, I think we could work something out."

She shook her head. "I don't know. We provide very traditional fare."

"I understand. Not all the recipes would work, but I think others could be modified so they would fit in with what your restaurants offer." He turned to her. "Would you be willing to give it a try?"

This would be the first thing they agreed on. She rolled the idea around in her mind. Besides the fresh paint, new decor and all new linens, perhaps the menu could use a bit of a facelift.

But she wasn't ready to let Franco see just how much the idea appealed to her. "I'll consider it, but I'd like to sample what you have in mind before I allow our kitchens to start working together."

He smiled and nodded. "I expected nothing less."

"Instead of just plain, solitary spices, what if we make some blends specifically for the restaurants?"

He nodded. "I like the idea."

She struggled not to show the surprise about him freely admitting that he liked her idea. Maybe this partnership didn't have to be so constrained. Maybe it would be all right to let her guard down a little with him.

The thought brought a smile to her lips. She had a feeling they could do great things together. And in the end, it would benefit both of them—um, their businesses, of course.

"With all the work we've already done independently, we're really ahead of the game," she said as her gaze scrolled down over her checklist.

"I agree," Franco said. "That's why I'd like to propose we roll out this promotion in stages."

"Stages?"

He nodded. "I know we have six months in which to make this plan a reality, but wouldn't it be more impressive to reveal our plans ahead of time and grow the anticipation?"

Carla leaned back in her chair while twirling a pen. What Franco was suggesting was so ambitious. They'd have to push themselves and their staff harder than they'd ever worked before. But was it possible?

"What exactly do you have in mind?"

Franco reached into a black leather-bound binder and pulled out a stapled set of papers. He placed them in front of her. "I propose we launch this venture in six weeks' time—"

"Six weeks?" She shook her head. "I'll never get everything done in time. I'm giving all our original restaurants a facelift. This timeline isn't possible in that short amount of time."

"Okay. But what if you were to complete one facelift—say, the flagship restaurant? Would that be doable?"

She gave it some thought. "I think so."

"Good. We can send in some photographers to document the facelift. It can be used in the campaign. Maybe something like…'we're spicing things up with Marchello Spices and a new look, but we're keeping the same dishes you've come to love generation after generation.'"

Carla grabbed her pen and immediately began writing.

"What are you doing?"

"Writing it down before I forget. It's really good. Maybe you're in the wrong line of work. If you ever want a second career, you might want to consider advertising."

Franco let out a deep laugh. He was so handsome normally, but when the worry lines smoothed, he was the dreamiest. And he was so close—close enough to lean over and kiss.

His phone rang and he answered it before she could put her thoughts into action. She told herself that it was for the best—but it didn't feel like it.

CHAPTER ELEVEN

THEIR PLAN WAS coming together.

Two weeks into their venture, and the basic structure of their PR campaign was in place. Part of Carla was exhilarated that her first major endeavor as the CEO of Falco Fresco Ristorantes was moving along so smoothly. But the other part of her knew that the sooner this deal came to its conclusion, the sooner Franco would disappear from her life.

The truth was she'd enjoyed this time with Franco. He brought out her creative side. He coaxed her to think outside the box...in more than one way.

Their lives had taken on a certain routine. Monday had become their day for collaboration, and the rest of the week they split up to work with their own staffs. When the weekend rolled around, she spent Saturday with her father, who refused to speak of her husband. Carla was all right with avoiding the subject of Franco, as her feelings for him were too confusing to explain.

But when Sunday came, they were expected at Franco's grandparents for dinner. At first, it had been awkward with Franco not putting off the wedding until they'd been back in the country. Franco insisted that he just couldn't wait another day to make her his wife.

He was so charismatic that she almost believed him. His grandmother grudgingly forgave him while his grandfather didn't give any hint of his feelings toward their marriage.

With the circumstances of their marriage sorted, his grandmother welcomed Carla with open arms. His grandfather, on the other hand, wasn't as friendly, but he at least acknowledged her presence, which was more than her father was willing to do for Franco. With each passing week, she'd grown more comfortable attending Sunday dinner—almost as though she belonged there.

However, this sunny Monday morning, she glanced across the desk anticipating Franco's reaction as he examined the mockup of their new menu. It had a colorful center insert introducing the new Marchello Spices. Her gaze took in his dark eyes to his smooth cheeks and strong jaw. And then there was his mouth. Oh, the delicious things he could do with it.

The longer her gaze lingered on him, the faster her heart beat. She should be focusing on these important decisions, but she found herself utterly distracted. What would it be like if they were a real couple?

Would Franco still be so willing to help her with the business? Or would he be angry that she was more focused on things at the office instead of spending time at home with him? Would he understand her devotion to her father and her need to do whatever it took to care for him?

She'd like to think that Franco would be understanding about all of it. After all, he was a workaholic just like her. And if he understood her career drive, then would he understand her other needs—needs that had nothing to do with spreadsheets and profit margins. Would he be more than willing to satisfy them?

It wasn't like they didn't have chemistry—they had that in spades. In fact, their problem was keeping all those sparks from erupting into a flame—

"Carla?" Franco's voice drew her from her fantasy.

"Um, what?"

"I said this looks really good."

"Really? You like it?" She'd been unsure if she'd chosen the right color combinations.

"Yes, I do. You did great." He smiled at her, making her heart flutter. "We make a great team."

Carla stood and moved to his side of the desk. "Yes, we do. Just sign here." She pointed to the form that required both of their signatures. "And then we can get these off to the printers."

When she offered him a pen, their fingers touched. Every cell in her body tingled. Her gaze caught and held his a moment longer than necessary. Her heart tumbled in her chest.

In that moment, she had to wonder why she'd insisted on a platonic relationship. He took the pen and scrolled his name on the appropriate line. And then he turned to her, but she was standing a little too close and his shoulder brushed against her. She should step back, but her feet refused to comply.

"Shall we celebrate?" Her voice came out in a breathy tone.

Desire flared in his eyes. "What did you have in mind? Maybe an early dinner?"

"No. I don't want to wait that long."

He reached out, gripping her waist. "I like the way you think."

His mouth pressed to hers, making time stand still. And yet her heart beat wildly. It didn't matter how many times he kissed her, it always had the same intoxicating effects as the first one.

As he drew her to him, she willingly followed his lead. Her arms wrapped around his neck, allowing her fingertips to comb through his thick, dark hair. As she gave herself over to the moment, a moan of pleasure swelled in the back of her throat.

She was kissing her husband. Those last two words played over and over in her mind. It was so strange to know they had a piece of paper that said this display of affection was all right and encouraged. Not that she needed any encouragement.

She took over the lead and intensified the kiss. It was impossible for her to get enough of him. She pushed him back against the edge of the desk, ignoring the sound of pens and papers falling to the floor. Reality had no room in this moment. Her fingers moved to his tie, pulling it loose so she could get to the shirt buttons beneath—

"What is going on here?" The boom of her father's disapproving voice immediately chilled her blood.

She jumped back. Her heart stilled as she groaned inwardly. She couldn't believe she'd been caught making out with her husband by her father, of all people. Where was her assistant? Why hadn't Rosa headed him off? She knew Carla didn't like to be surprised by her father.

Carla smoothed her hands down over her clothes, making sure nothing was out of place. And then, with heat warming her whole face, she turned to him. It didn't seem to matter how old she got, her father had that effect over her. Why was she acting like she was a teenager again, getting caught making out on the couch with her boyfriend?

She swallowed hard. "Papa, what are you doing here?"

His gray brows furrowed together. "This is a business office. I didn't think I had to explain my presence. So am I to presume this so-called marriage is real?"

Carla chanced a glance at Franco. She sent him an apologetic look as he straightened his tie. She'd never meant for this to happen. Of all the times for them to lose their focus on work and let the passion between them flare up and consume them.

With his tie straightened, Franco draped an arm around Carla's waist and drew her near. "Yes, it's a real marriage."

Franco's unwavering stare met her father's. It appeared there was to be a battle of wills. *Oh no! This is not good, not good at all.*

Carla pulled away from Franco's hold. She stepped closer to her father. "Papa, what did you need?"

Her father's gaze turned to her. "He's lying to you and you don't even know it."

"Lying? Lying about what?"

"Everything. This marriage. This business deal. When it's all over—when he gets what he wants—he'll leave you with nothing but a broken heart. He's a liar just like his grandfather—"

"That's not true." Franco's restrained voice held a thread of anger. "If anyone here is a liar, it's you."

Her father's gaze narrowed as his face filled with color. "I don't know what your grandfather told you—"

"He didn't have to tell me anything. There's proof. I know for a fact that you cheated."

"Is that what you've been telling my daughter?" Her father stepped toward Franco.

"Stop!" Carla stepped between the two men. There was absolutely no way she was going to let them come to blows.

And quite frankly she wasn't even sure what they were fighting over. It seemed that both men knew something she didn't, and she was so tired of being left out of things. Her mother had done it with her illness. Her father did it with the business. And now Franco had done it with the secret he knew about her father.

Her father continued to glare at Franco. "Then tell your husband to take back his empty accusation—"

"It isn't empty," Franco ground out. "I can prove it."

For the briefest second, surprise lit up her father's eyes. But in a blink, it was gone. It didn't matter. Carla had seen it, and she wondered about this proof.

She stepped up to her father. "Tell me it isn't true. Tell me I haven't been falsely defending you all this time." When her father didn't immediately respond, she said, "Papa, say something."

Her father stepped around her and approached Franco. "I'm telling you that if you hurt my daughter, you'll have to deal directly with me." And then her father turned to her. "And when you're in my office, I expect you to act like a respectable businesswoman."

He didn't say another word as he strode out of the office, leaving her speechless. She felt as though the ground beneath her feet had shifted.

Did he lie to me?

All this time she'd just taken it for granted that her father was an honorable man, who always spoke the truth. She'd have defended him until her final breath. But had she been wrong about him?

No. That is not possible.

But she'd caught a glimpse of worry in his eyes before he'd moved to confront her husband. She didn't know what to believe.

She wanted to go after him and have it out, but she resisted. She vividly remembered the doctor's stern warning about avoiding undo stress.

Hurt and angry, she turned to Franco with an accusing glare. "How dare you speak to him like that?"

"Me?" He pressed a hand to his chest. "What about him? He's the one throwing around insults."

She crossed her arms and frowned at him. "And you're the one that kept egging him on."

"Why are you mad at me? He's the one that barged into your office—an office that had the door closed, I might remind you—and yet you're attacking me."

"Because you're strong and healthy. He's not." With each word uttered, her emotions rose, as did her voice. "He needs to be taken care of. He doesn't need you yelling at him—"

"I didn't raise my voice, but if he'd kept it up—"

"You'd what?"

Franco huffed out a breath as he raked his fingers through his hair. "Nothing."

"Oh, it was something, all right." She tapped her foot. "And I want to know what you were going to do if he hadn't left."

His intense glare met hers. If he thought she was going to back down, he had another thought coming. Because as fiery as their passion could be, it appeared their tempers ran just as high. "I wasn't going to just

stand by quietly while he insulted me, my family...
and most especially you. I had to speak the truth. I'm
sorry you ended up getting hurt. That was never my
intention."

"Is that why you kept this secret all this time? Why
did you let me make a fool of myself defending him?"

He glanced downward. "I know what it's like to have
a distant relationship with my father. I didn't want to say
anything to cause trouble between you and your father."

She paused as she took in his words. And suddenly
the fire went out of her temper. But she refused to get
swept off her feet by his chivalry. Still, she wanted to
be sure she heard him correctly. "You were coming to
my defense?"

He glanced away as he shrugged. "Yeah. Sure. I
guess. Now can we move on?"

It wasn't the strong affirmation that she'd been hoping for, but it definitely wasn't a denial. "You were lying
when you told my father there was proof, weren't you?"

She really needed him to say yes. Because if he said
something else, that would mean what she believed
about her father—being an honest, loyal and respectable
man—wasn't true. And...and that just couldn't be so.

Franco turned his back to her as he bent down to start
gathering the evidence of their moment of reckless passion. That exquisite moment seemed so long ago now.
If her father had set out to drive a wedge between her
and Franco, he'd succeeded.

"Franco, answer me." Her voice wavered ever so
slightly with emotion. "Do you have proof?"

He didn't answer her as he continued to pick up papers and pens from the floor. Once everything was
placed on the side of the desk, he straightened. And

then he turned to her. "We should drop the subject. I shouldn't have said anything to your father. I'm sorry. It's just that he got to me."

"My father is good at pressing people's buttons. But that still doesn't answer my question."

"Does it matter?"

"It matters very much."

Franco blew out a deep sigh. "There's a video of your father cheating at a high-stakes poker game."

Her gaze searched his. Nothing in his demeanor said he was lying or in any way out to get her. Instead, sympathy reflected in his eyes.

She pressed a hand to her mouth as she gasped. It was true. Her father had cheated at cards and then publicly shamed Franco's grandfather by calling him a liar to friends and business associates alike.

Her vision blurred. How could he have done such a thing? The man that she'd looked up to her whole life—the man that she'd given up her dreams for—had lied to her. He had told her that her sweet, kind husband was a liar—he'd insisted on it—and all along he was the liar, the cheat.

Her heart ached. Her father hadn't respected her enough to tell her the truth. Did he think she'd stop loving him? That would never happen. But she was hurt and disappointed. A tear splashed onto her cheek.

The next thing she knew, Franco was drawing her into his embrace. He held her and stroked her hair. "It's okay. It was a long time ago."

Her tears spilled onto Franco's blue dress shirt. It was only then that she realized she was crying. She hated to cry. She wasn't this weepy person. She was strong.

But hearing that about the one person in her life whom

she thought she could trust thoroughly had broken something within her. Maybe it was the childhood belief that her father could do no wrong. Maybe it was losing her mother so quickly and far too soon that had her putting her father up on a pedestal. Whatever it was, she'd never look at him quite the same way again.

Drawing on the strength she knew lurked deep down inside her, she pulled back from Franco. She swiped at her eyes that must be a smear of mascara by now. "I'm sorry about that."

"Don't be." His voice was soft and warm like a giant hug. "I'll take any excuse to hold you in my arms."

Her gaze dipped to his lips. And then, throwing caution to the wind, she leaned forward, pressing her mouth to his. At first, he didn't move, as though he was totally caught off guard by her boldness.

As his mouth began to move over hers, she felt careless, reckless. It was as if by finding out her father wasn't the man she thought him to be that she no longer had to hold herself back and play by the rules.

"Hold that thought," she said. And then she lifted her phone and dialed her assistant. She sent her home early. Then she locked her office door.

When she turned back to Franco, his eyes lit up with interest. "Should I be worried?"

She kicked off her heels and slowly approached him. "That depends. What are you worried about?"

A smiled toyed at the corners of his mouth. "With the way you're eyeing me up, I have a feeling you're about to take advantage of me."

She felt freer than she'd felt in a very long time, which was funny because she was married and not free at all. And in this moment, being married to Franco was all right with her. "Do you want to be taken advantage of?"

When she came to a stop in front of him, he gazed deep into her eyes. "Oh yes, I do."

That's all she needed to hear. She once again tugged at his tie, loosening it. And then her fingers fumbled with the shirt buttons. This time there were no reservations, no doubts about her actions.

In this particular moment, all she wanted was Franco—all of him. She loosened two buttons before he swept her up into his strong arms and carried her to the couch. He laid her down and then joined her.

His lips pressed to hers. It was like a balm upon her broken heart. As the kiss intensified, she momentarily forgot about the lies, the pain and the disappointment. In this moment, she felt wanted and cared about. She didn't want this moment to end.

CHAPTER TWELVE

CARLA WASN'T GOING to be outdone.

Three weeks of working practically nonstop and they were making great strides. With all the pressing matters to be resolved, she hadn't had time to visit her father. She still phoned each day, but their conversations were short and stilted. However, she made sure to send over updates on this new venture with Marchello Spices out of courtesy.

Oh, who was she kidding? She'd purposely been avoiding seeing him or having any meaningful conversation. She knew the subject of the infamous poker game would inevitably come up, and she wasn't ready for what he would say.

Because even though she'd denied the truth as long as she could, she knew the one man she'd trusted most in this world had lied to her. But hearing him admit it... it would change their relationship forever.

When he called, she always rushed off the phone. And when he'd invite her over for dinner, she said she had work to do on her big project. She noticed that he was going out of his way to be nice to her, but she wasn't ready. Not yet.

She knew she couldn't avoid him or the subject forever. But she told herself that she'd deal with it when the time was right. She just wasn't certain when that might be.

Right now, she had other matters on her mind. In exchange for putting Marchello Spices in all of the Falco restaurants, Franco was advertising their restaurants on their website and print ads, as well as adding a "Now featured in Falco Fresco Ristorantes" to their spice labels.

Their joint staff had pushed for promoting their marriage as a marrying of the restaurants and the line of spices. And under normal circumstances it would be an ideal PR campaign with the two heirs marrying, but they both knew this marriage would soon end, and they didn't want their divorce to tarnish all their hard work.

The staff had been disappointed, as they'd already brainstormed all the ways their marriage could be used to promote their family businesses. Carla and Franco explained away their reluctance to make the campaign personal because the businesses involved more people than just themselves.

Monday morning, Carla had been up before the sun—in fact, she'd been up before Franco—and out the door. At every meeting so far, it felt as though he was always a step ahead of her. And that wasn't good.

This deal had been her brainchild. She should be the one leading the way through this new collaboration. As such, she'd called an upper management meeting. She'd told them she didn't care if it took overtime, she wanted new material for this collaboration from additional product placement to innovative advertising targeted at the young crowd. She wanted everyone to know that this wasn't just their grandparents' and parents' place to eat but a destination for first dates and engagements.

She didn't care what part of this venture it was, she wanted fresh ideas. And lately she'd found herself quite distracted between her sexy new husband—erm, her partner, and worrying about her father, who in turn was worried about her.

Carla glanced at the time on her computer monitor. Less than an hour and Franco would show up. He liked to show up early, looking all prepared, while she was scrambling to put out fires before pulling together her latest developments on the project. She seemed to think that people who showed up early didn't have enough work to do. She definitely had enough work to do and then some.

Knock. Knock.

She glanced up at her open office door to find Stu Phillips, the head of publicity, standing there. The man was in his sixties. His white hair was trimmed short. His black-rimmed reading glasses sat low on his bulbous nose. His gray eyes peered at her over the rims. He still wore his dark suit and tie, even though a few years back she'd talked her father into implementing a business-casual policy.

In his hands were a stack of papers. *Oh, good. This is just what I need.*

Carla waved him inside the office. "I was hoping to have something to present at our meeting today. What do you have for me?"

"We've worked on some new labels for the spices." Stu was polite, but he wasn't overly enthused that she was now in charge. He was part of the old guard, personally hired by her father. "I honestly don't know why we have to change all our labels just because we're going to add a couple of spices from that Marchello company."

This wasn't the first time he'd voiced his complaint. He must have thought that repeating himself would make her agree with him. He was wrong. "You're doing this because I told you to."

"But when your father comes back—"

"My father will back my plans." Her unwavering gaze met his. "But in the meantime, I'm here and I'm the boss. So we're going to do this my way."

Redesigning the in-house labels perhaps wasn't where she would have started. She'd have probably worked on the macro vision for this project and then worked her way down to the micro images. But she wasn't one to tell people how to do their jobs, so long as they got good results. "Let's see what you have."

She held out her hands for the printouts. He glared at her, and she mentally dared him to continue to argue with her. She wasn't in the mood to take any flak. She had more important things on her mind.

He wisely chose to hand over the papers quietly.

She glanced over the new labels, taking in the choice of words, the font used and the colors selected. None of it was what they'd discussed. They greatly resembled their current labels.

She set the pages on the desk and lifted her gaze to meet his. "Were you in the same meeting as I was when we discussed the new look?"

"Yes, but—"

"No buts. This is not what I want. None of this is going to work. Go back and do better."

His gray brows drew together as storm clouds gathered in his eyes. He hesitated to move as though he was ready to tell her that he knew better. He didn't. The truth of the matter was that he was costing her time—time she didn't have.

"You know what," she said, "I'm going to accompany you back to your department. We're going to review what I expect so there are no further misunderstandings. And definitely no more delays."

Not waiting for Stu to disagree, she got up from her chair and headed for the hallway. She didn't have much time before Franco showed up, but this was critically important to the launch of their plan. Franco would understand if she wasn't sitting here waiting for him. At least she hoped so.

He was early.

Franco liked to make it a habit to be early to meetings. He supposed that it was a bit of his grandfather coming out in him. He had been taught that a person who took his work seriously made time for it and didn't use excuses to explain being unprepared.

Promptness showed a person's character. He liked to think that his early arrivals showed everyone around him that he was very serious about his business and that there wasn't anything more important to him.

He moved with long strides down the hallway until he came to the outer area of Carla's office. They'd planned to meet privately before the committee meeting in the conference room. The inner door to Carla's office was open, but she wasn't inside. When he turned his attention to her assistant, she was on the phone. Rosa held up a finger, indicating that it'd just be a moment.

He backtracked into the hallway, not wanting to lurk

about and overhear her conversation. He was hoping to catch sight of Carla. They'd missed each other that morning.

What had her up and out of the penthouse so early? He couldn't help but feel that it had something to do with their collaboration. Right now, it was the main focus for both of them, because they were both working within shorter time constraints. And lately they'd been hitting one stumbling block after another.

"*Signor,*" Rosa called out to him.

He stepped into the office. "Sorry to bother you. I was supposed to meet with Carla."

Rosa nodded in understanding. "She said you would be stopping by. She had to step out of her office for a moment. She said you could wait inside for her. She shouldn't be long."

"*Grazie.*" He smiled at the woman before stepping into the office.

He sat down in one of the black leather chairs facing her desk. He lifted his briefcase to his lap and pulled out some papers he'd brought to show her.

Carla's desk was filled with binders and folders, so he stood and walked around to place the printouts in the center of her desk where she could see them right away. As he turned away, he noticed the image of a spice container.

He recalled her mentioning that they were going to work on the product labels. He picked up the papers and looked over it, finding that it said nothing about the Marchello brand. If it weren't for the name of the blend, he would think this was an old printout, but Harvest Zest was a name for a blend that had been developed at Marchello. He and Carla had discussed that particular blend at length.

And yet as he flipped through the pages of images, they all had the Falco name in large letters at the top as though the spices were theirs. Franco's jaw tightened. This couldn't be happening.

Had he trusted Carla too much? Had she found a loophole in their contract? Was she planning to take their ideas and run with them on her own?

He'd trusted Rose in the beginning, and she'd stared straight at him as she lied about her supposed pregnancy. Unease churned in his gut. Had Carla just done that with their business arrangement?

His back teeth ground together. This couldn't be happening. And he had no one to blame but himself, because his grandfather had warned him that the Falcos were cheaters. Foolishly, Franco had thought it was just Carla's father that couldn't be trusted, but now he had to wonder about her, too.

Knock. Knock.

Rosa stood in the doorway. "Excuse me. Carla just called and asked if you'd meet her in the conference room."

Franco placed the papers back on her desk just as he'd found them. "Thank you. I'll do that. I just need to place a quick phone call."

"I'll leave you to it." Rosa closed the door, giving him some privacy.

He quickly dialed his legal team. He alerted them to his concern that Carla might try to write Marchello Spices out of the deal. He didn't like to think he'd married someone who would turn on him, but he couldn't afford to take anything for granted.

He still didn't trust Carla, even though his legal team had assured him there was no way she could cut him out of this deal. He wanted to believe them—believe in his wife. But he knew firsthand that the people you were supposed to trust the most were the ones that could let you down the most.

If it hadn't been for his grandfather always pushing for everyone around him to do better, would his father still be here? Still be a part of his life?

As a child, he hadn't understood why his parents had left. He'd decided way back then to focus fully on being the best CEO possible when he grew up. And his goal never wavered—until he met Carla. Now he wondered what it'd be like to share his life with someone he loved and trusted. Could Carla be that person?

His heart said yes, but his mind kept throwing up caution signs. He had no choice but to confront her about the redesigned labels he'd seen on her desk. He didn't want her to think he'd been spying on her, but he didn't see how he had any other choice.

He disconnected the call and set off down the hallway. The door to the conference room was ajar, and Carla was the only one inside.

She glanced up from her laptop. "Looks like we're the first ones here."

"We need to talk." He closed the door, giving them some privacy.

She shut her laptop. "It sounds serious."

"It is."

He cleared his throat. "How are the labels for the spices coming?"

She glanced down to straighten some papers. "They aren't ready yet."

He was waiting for her to explain the reason her company's name was on the label instead of his. "Anything I can help with?"

She shook her head. "I've got it. I've been working on it personally."

That just made it worse. Any thoughts of pursuing some alone time with Carla just fizzled away. If he couldn't trust her, he just couldn't let her get close to him.

He cleared his throat. "Why isn't the Marchello name on the in-house labels?"

Her gaze met his. Worry reflected in her eyes. "What are you talking about?"

"I saw the mockups on your desk. They look a lot like your current labels."

She sat up straight. "You weren't meant to see those."

"Because you're planning to cut me out of this deal and run with all of our ideas on your own?"

Her mouth opened as though she was appalled by his accusation, but he noticed she didn't immediately deny the allegation. Then her glossy lips pressed into a firm line as her eyes darkened with anger. "Is that really what you think of me?"

"You wouldn't be the first person in my life to put your personal interests ahead of your obligation to me."

All of a sudden, the flames of anger were doused and she looked upon him with sympathy. "Are you talking about your parents?"

He shrugged. "It doesn't matter. I just need to know that you're going to keep your word."

"I am. I promise."

He wanted to believe her. But could he? His heart said yes. But his mind said to be cautious.

CHAPTER THIRTEEN

"WHERE ARE WE GOING? There's work to be done."

The following week, Franco smiled at Carla's complaint. He guided his dark sedan along the roadway toward the northern Lake Como region. He had just seen the new in-house labels with the Marchello name prominently displayed. Carla had kept her word.

And now he'd planned a special field trip for them. They'd been working night and day ironing out the details of this collaboration. At times, it'd been intense. At other times, they'd played off each other's inspiration.

This venture was going to be so much more than he'd ever hoped for—bigger than any PR campaign that Marchello Spices had ever participated in throughout the history of the company. And he couldn't wait to reveal it all to his grandfather. It would prove to him once and for all that he was the rightful successor.

"Franco, you missed the turnoff to the lake."

"I know. We have a stop to make before we go to the villa."

"But I thought you said this was going to be a working weekend."

"It is, but today is so warm and sunny that I thought

we'd work outdoors." He smiled as he thought of the special plan he'd put together.

"Outdoors? I don't think so. Now isn't the time to lose focus. We are so close to having this plan all mapped out. Then we just have to put all the pieces into action."

They already had quite a few projects in the works. Both of their companies had come into this agreement with plans already underway. Carla's company had the facelifts planned and in motion with the restaurants, while his company had worked on new spice combinations as well as recipes to highlight those spices.

But there was still one area where the two of them just couldn't come together—the advertisements for this new venture. Carla wanted to go with the tried-and-true ad segments with young people enjoying food in a Falco restaurant. She was eager to draw in the young crowd who would turn into lifelong patrons.

He, on the other hand, wanted to do something totally new to show the viewers, both young and old alike, that even though it was still their favorite reliable restaurant, there was something new lurking beyond its doors. They'd even had numerous PR teams pitch ad campaign after ad campaign. While they liked bits and pieces of the various ads, none were the full image they'd been hoping for.

But Franco had something in mind, and he was willing to gamble a day of work to play it out and see if he and Carla could agree upon one vision that they could take back to their teams.

"Just relax." He easily guided the car along the narrow, winding road.

She didn't say anything as she leaned her head back

against the seat and stared out the window at the passing greenery. He hoped the crew he'd put in charge of this surprise wouldn't let him down. He'd given them very precise instructions.

Finally, their destination came into sight. Franco slowed the car and pulled off to the side of the desolate road near a white panel truck with the Marchello Spices slogan emblazed on the side.

"Where are we?" Carla sat up and looked all around at the empty field.

"This property belongs to a friend of mine."

Just then the men climbed into the white truck and with a wave pulled away, allowing a view of a table with a red-and-white tablecloth in the middle of the green field with the mountain range in the background.

"What is this?" Carla asked.

"It's my surprise. Come on." He climbed out of the car.

She joined him. Then he took her hand and led her to the table. He pulled out a chair for her. And then he sat across from her. In the center of the table stood a candle and some flowers. There was a slight breeze, so the candle remained unlit.

"This is—" she glanced around "—definitely different. But I don't understand what we're doing here."

That's when Franco reached into the insulated box next to him and removed two covered plates as well as wrapped utensils. "We talked about new dishes for the menu that utilize the Marchello Spices blends."

"Oh." She lifted the lid from the small china plate and found an arrangement of pasta and a side of a vegetable medley. "This is very impressive."

He smiled. "I hope you like the taste as much as the appearance."

"I hope so, too."

He poured them each a glass of sparkling water. And then they started sampling the food. There were numerous plates all done up with specifically chosen dishes as well as garnishments.

They ate and then compared notes. Some were pretty good. Some dishes were not so good, but a few were exceptional.

When they'd finished eating, Carla said, "I think we've found our menu items. Of course, we'll have to run them by our focus group, but I can't see how they won't love them."

"Good. I'm glad to hear it. My group has been perfecting these recipes since before we started working together."

Carla took a sip of water. She glanced toward the road as a couple of cars slowed to stare before passing. "It looks like we're getting some strange looks."

"They're just jealous and wish they could have a picnic lunch like ours."

She turned to him. "Why did you pick this place? Why not eat at the villa?"

"Because I thought this might inspire thoughts for the ad campaign."

She looked all around. "You want to feature a field for the backdrop for eating our new dishes?"

"It's not just any field. It's picturesque, with the Alps in the background." He wasn't doing a good job of explaining his concept to her.

"I think I know what you mean," Carla said. "The food can transport you to a different place. By eating

Falco Fresco with Marchello Spices, it can take you from enjoying the ordinary to experiencing something extraordinary."

He pulled out his phone and started making notes.

"What are you doing?"

"Well, it seems I'm not the only one good at thinking up slogans. I wanted to write it down before I forget."

"It's not that good."

"I think with your words and my vision, the ad campaign will be a big success."

She smiled at him, warming that spot in his chest. "I think we make a great team."

"I do, too." And he truly meant it.

"It's a good thing I thought of it." She sent him a teasing grin.

Carla got to her feet and pulled out her phone. She started taking photos of their surroundings. "I do like the idea of a table in the middle of a green field."

Franco cleared the table, placing their dishes back in the cooler. Then he texted his team to come back and pick up everything. His job here was done. Well, almost...

"Do you think our families will be impressed?"

"How could they not be?" She smiled at him. "You mentioned seeing your parents from time to time. Will either of them attend the reveal party?"

He shook his head. "My father never attends public functions, especially if they're about the family business. And my mother, well, I have no idea what she's doing these days."

Carla reached out, placing her hand over his. "I'm sorry. I shouldn't have mentioned it."

He didn't like her looking at him like he was weak

and not as good as everyone else—the way he felt in school when there was a special event for his parents to attend and instead he either skipped it or brought his grandparents. And it didn't go unnoticed by his classmates, who'd make snide comments. He pushed the painful memories to the back of his mind.

Instead of speaking of his past, he asked, "You lost your mother, too. Is that why you let your father get away with so much?"

She glanced away and then nodded. "I'd been away at school when my mother got sick. She insisted they wait to tell me about her prognosis until I came home for the holidays. What neither of my parents anticipated was how quickly her disease would progress."

"So they lied to you?"

"They did. When I saw my mother again, she was so weak and sick." Carla swiped at the tears on her cheeks.

He'd thought he'd had a rough childhood, but at least no one had lied to him. No one ever said his parents would come back for him and his brother. No one was that good of a liar.

He glanced down where their hands were still joined. This time, he was the one to give her a reassuring squeeze.

"I'm so sorry," he said.

"I feel like if I had known, I could have done things differently, which is silly, because nothing I could have done would have saved her. But I wasn't ready to lose her. There were so many things I wanted to say to her, things I wanted to ask and things I wanted us to do together."

"Like plan your wedding?" When she nodded, he said, "When you get married for real, your father will be happy for you, and your mother will be smiling down upon you."

The thing was, he'd started feeling that this marriage was the real deal. When he had business dinners, Carla was the first person he called and profusely apologized to for not being able to dine with her. The truth was he'd lost his interest in wooing new clients. He'd rather be eating on the couch while watching some comedy rerun Carla had picked out.

It was only then that he realized in the short amount of time they'd been married, they'd settled into a routine—a comfortable routine. Perhaps too comfortable. Definitely too comfortable. Because what would happen when Carla left? And she would leave.

"Enough about us." Carla's voice interrupted his thoughts. "We should get back to work. When we get to the villa, we need to go over the final party details for our grand announcement." She got to her feet and then turned back to him. "Are you coming?"

"I, uh, sure."

She smiled at him.

"What's that for?"

"You just surprise me. I thought your whole life was about work, but it's not."

"It's not?"

She continued to smile as she shook her head. "This is a prime example."

"It is?" He wasn't sure he was comfortable where she was going with this, because his work was what was most important to him. It was what he could count on—what he could control.

"You could have given me a presentation on all this." She waved her hands around at the serene field and the picturesque mountains. "But instead you brought me out here for a leisurely picnic."

He'd thought he was making a strong pitch—one she couldn't resist. But would he have gone to such lengths for any other business associate? The answer was a resounding no.

And that worried him. Carla had him acting out of character. And worse yet, he liked doing all these things with her. But he didn't do commitments.

CHAPTER FOURTEEN

IT WAS LATE, and she was tired.

There were pressing matters on her desk. But nothing that couldn't wait for another day.

However, there was one thing that had been nagging at Carla. The way her stomach constantly felt as though it was on a roller coaster. For the past couple of weeks, she'd been so busy putting the final touches on this big reveal party that she hadn't had time to stop.

And dinner, well, dinner usually came from a takeaway container. Even though she'd been pleasantly surprised to learn that Franco was an excellent cook, neither of them had been home long enough to visit the kitchen for anything other than a coffee to go. And so for the past several days, she'd blamed her uneasy stomach and consumption of antacids on her poor diet.

Moments ago, she'd heard a couple of women in the break room talking about one being pregnant. She momentarily wondered if that was her problem. She quickly dismissed the idea. There was no way.

And just as quickly the memory of their wedding night came back to her. Oh yes, it was possible. In her flurry of nervous activity, she'd missed taking her birth control one day. One measly day. Was that all it took?

Carla rushed to her desk and picked up her calendar. Yes, it was a paper calendar because phones were great and all, but sometimes she needed to see things in print. Her crazy schedule was one that she wanted laid out in front of her.

And on her calendar, she kept some personal notes. She religiously marked the first day of her period with a little star in the bottom corner of that appropriate day. Now she just had to locate the little star. Surely it couldn't be that long ago.

There was no way she was pregnant with Franco's baby. No way at all. Because that would definitely complicate things in so many ways.

She'd just flipped a page in her weekly planner when there was a knock on her open door. Why in the world had she left the door open? Now was not the time for interruptions.

"Hi." Gianna stuck her head inside the doorway. "Can I come in?"

Carla pushed away her day planner and waved her cousin into the office. She sent her a weary smile. "I'm surprised to see you."

As Gianna stepped into the office, Carla couldn't help but notice how her pregnancy was already starting to show. Carla's hand instinctively moved to her still-flat abdomen. Would she look like her cousin soon—all round with a baby?

When she realized what she'd done, she glanced down, grateful that the desk had shielded her action. She didn't need Gianna asking any questions, because she had absolutely no answers. She didn't even know what questions needed to be asked.

The only question that came to mind at the moment was…was she pregnant?

"I wasn't sure you'd still be around." Gianna's voice focused Carla's thoughts on their conversation instead of the frantic, rambling thoughts floating around in her mind.

"I had some last-minute things to do." Her gaze moved to her open day planner. There were no stars on the exposed page. But her search would have to wait for a couple more agonizing moments.

Gianna arched a brow. "Is everything ready to go for tomorrow?"

Carla nodded. Though internally she felt everything was anything but good. In fact, if her suspicions were right, everything was so very wrong. "We're all set for the big announcement."

"And how's your father taking all this?"

"So far he hasn't acknowledged my husband. All he can think about is how I married the enemy. But he's intrigued by the changes to the restaurants."

Sympathy radiated from Gianna's eyes. "I'm sorry. Is there anything I can do?"

Carla shook her head. "It'll all work out in the end. My father may be stubborn, but even he can't argue when presented with profits."

"I'm just so glad this is going to work out for you and Franco. You two make a good couple. Not only do you get along at home, but you also work well together at the office."

Did they work well together both in and out of the office? As she thought back over the last several weeks, she realized that in the beginning things had been a bit rough, but as time went by, they'd learned to complement each other. Where one was focused on the cost, the other was focused on the creative end of things. Together, they balanced each other out.

But if she was pregnant, would that balance shift? Would the alliance they'd formed shatter? Or would Franco surprise her and be eager to be her partner through this, too?

"Carla?" Gianna waved her hand in front of her face. "Where did you go?"

"Sorry. I was just distracted...wondering if everything had been taken care of for tomorrow."

"Then I should leave you to get back to your work. I just wanted you to know that I have delivered the last of the prints."

They'd hired Gianna to photograph not only the face-lift at the flagship restaurant but also the meal in the field just as Franco had imagined it. And Gianna's work was stunning. No wonder she was an award-winning photographer.

"Your work is awesome!" Carla stepped out from behind her desk. "Thank you. You did a wonderful job making the colors pop. It's almost like you could step into the photos. And you really brought Franco's image to life with the mountains in the background. He was so pleased when he saw the proofs. I'm sure he'll tell you when you see him."

"I kind of thought he'd be here with you."

"He had a last-minute business meeting. It seems the word is out about our collaboration, and his company is picking up a lot of new distributors."

"That's great!" Gianna smiled. "Well, I'll see you tomorrow."

"Yes. I'll see you then. Thanks again." They hugged.

And then Carla was once again alone in the office with her thoughts—her ominous thoughts. She closed the door before rushing back to her desk. She couldn't bear any further interruptions right now. She felt as though the world she knew was about to explode.

She had absolutely no idea how she felt about the idea of a baby. At this stage in her life, she hadn't even considered whether she was going to have a family or not. Instead she'd been focused on her career and taking care of her father.

She drew the day planner closer. Her gaze scanned the page again for the elusive star that appeared to be missing from page after page. *Where is it?*

Was it possible she'd forgotten to make the notation? Yes, that was possible. Right now, she was willing to grasp any reasonable explanation, but at the same time she knew the missing star hadn't been a clerical error on her part, because she didn't recall having her period in a quite some time.

She groaned. *This is not good, not good at all.*

She flipped through too many pages for her comfort. And then she came to the week of her wedding. She noticed now that she'd doodled on it with wedding bells. She kept going. And then two weeks before the wedding, she found the little star.

She groaned again.

This can't be happening. Not to me. Not now.

There was only one way to tell. She grabbed her purse and headed for the door. She had a pregnancy test to pick up on her way home.

Please say it isn't so.

* * *

The pregnancy tests were in her hand.

All four boxes.

Luckily Carla had taken her oversized purse to work that day. She stuffed the tests inside the bag. They barely fit. But there was no way she was leaving something this big up to one measly test. Whatever the outcome, she had to be sure. She had to be absolutely positive she wasn't pregnant. Though the more she evaluated her symptoms and the amount of time since her monthly, she was more and more certain she was carrying a little Franco or a little Carla. She inwardly groaned.

All she could hope was that Franco's dinner meeting ran late.

What was she going to do if Franco was home when she got there? She probably should have called him to see what time he expected his meeting to end, but she was worried he'd detect the worry in her voice. And then the questions would come one after the other. She just needed a little time to herself. A chance to take the test alone. Because if her instinct was right, she'd be in shock. A baby was not in her plans. Not now. Not ever with Franco.

As she pulled into a parking spot, she groaned when she saw Franco's car. What was he doing home so soon? Usually his business meetings dragged on and on. But then she realized he might have left his car at home and gotten a ride to dinner. That thought bolstered her mood a tiny bit.

She headed inside and took the elevator to the top floor. She slipped her key in the lock and let herself inside. She paused and listened.

She didn't hear anything. *Thank goodness.* She

unbuttoned her coat. It was such a relief to be home alone—

"There you are."

Carla jumped. Her heart lodged in her throat.

Franco stepped into the hallway and smiled at her. "I was surprised to beat you home."

"You...you're here?"

"Of course I'm here." He arched a dark brow. "I live here. Remember?"

"I... I know." Heat swirled in her chest and rushed to her cheeks. *Act natural. Don't let him suspect anything.* "I'm just surprised."

She slipped off her coat and flung it over the bulging purse. The last thing she needed was for it to spill open.

Because there was no way she was mentioning any of this to Franco. If she ended up not being pregnant, he'd get worked up for no reason at all. And right before the biggest day of their careers just wouldn't be fair to him.

And if she was pregnant? Her stomach took a nervous lurch. Well, she'd deal with that hurdle when she got to it.

"Carla, are you all right?"

"Sure. Fine." She plastered a smile on her face. "Why wouldn't I be? Tomorrow is our big day."

"It's just that you look a little gray."

"Gray? Boy. No wonder you don't have a girlfriend with compliments like that."

"Excuse me. But I can't have a girlfriend because we're married." He sent her a flirtatious smile. "Remember? Or should I remind you?"

"No. No. I remember." She ducked around him, hoping to escape to her room.

"Carla, have I done something to upset you?"

She paused and turned to him. His concern for her feelings would have normally made her heart flutter, but not tonight. Right now, all she could think about were the tests in her purse.

"Not at all," she said, "I'm just wiped out. I'm calling it a night." She headed for her bedroom. "I'll see you in the morning."

"But—"

She kept going. She just couldn't keep pretending that everything was all right. And she was scared that he was going to figure out what was going on with her. Though the logical part of her mind said there was no way that he could guess. But Franco knew her better than any other man ever had.

Finally she closed the door behind her. She didn't have time to stop. She needed to get this over with—just like removing a bandage, it needed to be done quickly. She took one of the tests and headed for the bathroom.

And then the waiting began. She checked the timer on her phone. Barely thirty seconds had gone by. Not able to sit still, she paced back and forth in front of her king-size bed.

Her phone buzzed. She checked her messages to find a text from her assistant. It would have to wait. She couldn't concentrate on business right now. She couldn't think about anything but the test result. It had to be negative. It had to be—

Knock. Knock.

No. No. No. Not now.

"I'm busy," she called out.

"Sorry. I just wanted you to know I brought home some food for you. It can be reheated."

"Thanks. I'll be out later."

She could hear his retreating footsteps. That was thoughtful of him. Franco was a really good guy, but she distinctly remembered him telling her he didn't want to be a father.

She resumed her pacing.

Five minutes later, the timer on her phone dinged. The moment of truth had arrived.

She rushed into the bathroom, picked up the test and found it was negative. A big whoosh of air escaped her lips. It was over. She'd been worried about nothing.

She picked up the box to throw it away when a folded piece of paper slipped out of the box and fell to the floor. It was the instructions to the test. She probably should have read it before she took the test, but she'd been so anxious. And she had read the instructions on the back of the box. But this slip of paper had so much more information printed on it.

Her curiosity prompted her to unfold the paper. She started reading. A negative test result could not be guaranteed to be truly negative. A future test could be positive as the pregnancy progresses. But a positive test was a hundred percent accurate. Carla frowned.

She continued reading and found the test was most accurate first thing in the morning. She sighed. There was more waiting. But if this test was negative, she told herself the next one would be negative, too. She was worried about nothing.

CHAPTER FIFTEEN

TODAY WAS A big deal. A great big huge deal.

This was the day they'd been working night and day toward for six very long weeks.

Franco smiled. All the worry, all the stress and all the sleepless nights crouched over his laptop had been worth it. Because he'd done something even his own grandfather hadn't been able to accomplish—he'd gotten Marchello Spices back into the Falco restaurants.

There was no bigger restaurant chain in all of Italy. And as their chain expanded beyond the Italian border, Marchello Spices would go along for the ride, expanding their demographics into other locations. The sky was the limit as far as Franco was concerned.

A smile pulled at his lips as he buttoned the collar of his crisp white dress shirt. The only thing that could make this better was if Carla was right here next to him. And yet she'd withdrawn from him last night.

After how far they'd come from being adversaries to learning to be friends to something he wasn't quite ready to name—now she was shutting him out. Was it because the hard work was over? Their plan was in motion. Was she afraid he was going to bail on their marriage now that they were revealing the first stage of their plan?

Nothing could be further from the truth. Because he'd signed onto this agreement for six full months and that's exactly what he was going to do. This wasn't the end, this was just the beginning of their successful alliance—business and personal.

Because as good as they were in the office, they were even better at home. In fact, these days he now looked forward to coming home to her. Carla made him smile and laugh. She was great company, even when they were just sitting on the couch together watching one of her romantic comedies that he'd previously avoided at all costs. Now he actually didn't mind the lighthearted movies or the way Carla sighed at the end when the hero proclaimed his love and kissed the heroine.

Carla had shown him a marriage that was centered around a friendly companionship. She'd shown him that someone could offer a friendly gesture without expecting anything in return. And he'd found himself eager to get up in the morning to see her smiling face. Because he'd come to trust her—to know that she wasn't going to run away when things got tough.

But he also knew he couldn't judge what they had now like it was a real marriage. Because there was no expectation of forever. No one had laid their heart on the line. There were no entanglements to keep them trapped in this marriage.

They were both free to walk away. Just the thought of having a choice to stay or go made him feel lighter. Maybe this marriage contract hadn't been so bad.

He stared in the full-length mirror as he straightened his blue tie. Blue for victory. Today was a victorious day.

He walked out his bedroom door and headed over to

Carla's bedroom. He rapped his knuckles on the door. "Carla?"

No response.

He knocked again. "Carla, are you ready?"

Still no response.

Maybe she was in the shower. He headed for the kitchen for his cup of coffee, not that he needed the jolt of caffeine today. Adrenaline pumped through his veins. He'd been dreaming about this day for a long, long time.

When he stepped in the kitchen, he found Carla standing in front of the sink. "Good morning."

"Morning." Her voice lacked enthusiasm.

"It's going to be a great day. Are you ready?" It was then that he noticed she was still in her pale pink robe that gave a teasing glimpse of her toned thighs. His gaze lowered down the length of her long legs to her bare feet.

She turned a worried gaze his way. "Are you sure your grandfather won't be at the party?"

"Positive. He said he wouldn't celebrate anything that involved your father—"

"Because if they ran into each other—" her voice wavered with emotion "—it wouldn't be good. It'd be very bad. And with my father's health condition—"

"Shh…" Franco pulled her into his embrace. As her head came to rest on his shoulder, he said, "I know you're exhausted. You worked so hard for this moment, but trust me when I say this evening will be amazing. The hard work is done. Now it's time to enjoy our accomplishment. Tomorrow we'll worry about what comes next."

Her arms snaked around his sides, pulling him close. The weight of her body leaned into him. And in that moment, everything felt right in his world. Maybe they didn't have to rush out the door quite so soon—

Before he could put his plan in motion, Carla untangled herself from his arms. She smiled up at him. "You're right. Everything is going to be fine."

"You know, we don't have to rush off to the office right now—"

"Yes, we do. We've worked too hard not to see to every last detail. I'm running a bit late, but you go ahead."

Disappointed that he was being chased away, he said, "It's no problem. I can wait."

She shook her head again. "You should go ahead without me. I'll be a while. I need my hair and makeup to be just right."

He approached her. "Carla, what's the matter?"

She turned to him and flashed him a big smile, but he noticed how it didn't quite reach her eyes. "Why would anything be wrong? This is the day we've been working toward."

He also noticed that she was a bit pale. "Are you feeling all right?"

She glanced away. "I didn't realize I looked so bad."

"No. It's not that. You're always beautiful." It was the truth. With her long hair clipped up with some loose curls framing her face that lacked any makeup, he thought she was striking. But it was the lack of color in her cheeks that had him worried. "It's just that you look a little pale."

She shrugged off his concern. "It's no big deal. I didn't sleep well last night. A little makeup and I'll be good as new."

He glanced down at her hands. He'd expected to find her drinking coffee to give herself a boost of energy after a night of tossing and turning, but instead he found her drinking milk. "Are you sure you're feeling all right? Because if not we'll have to figure out somehow to explain your absence from today's events—"

"I'm fine. Stop worrying. Now if you'll get going, I'll be able to get ready in peace."

He hesitated. He had this feeling there was something she wasn't telling him, but maybe that was just a bit of his old insecurities surfacing, because over the process of putting together this large and complex project, he'd learned that he could trust what Carla told him. Why should today be any different?

"Okay. Do you need anything before I go?"

She shook her head. "I'm good. I'll see you soon."

And with that he walked away. The door clicked shut behind him. Though there was a part of him saying that he should have stayed just to make sure everything was fine with her, the other part of him said to trust her.

He was right.

Everything was going to be all right.

Carla had taken comfort in his words. She really needed to believe that everything would be all right. She wanted to believe all the worry over her father's health and then taking part in this fake marriage was what had her body all out of sorts.

And now that she thought it over in the light of day, it sounded quite plausible. After all, last night's pregnancy test was negative. Today's test would be negative as well. She was all worked up for nothing.

She dumped out the remainder of her glass and placed it in the sink to deal with later. Right now, she had other matters on her mind—matters that had kept her awake most of the night. She had to know for certain one way or the other.

She rushed to her room and once again went through the process. This time she took three tests at once. She wanted an actual reliable result—something she could count on.

Carla lined the three tests up on the countertop and then set the timer on her phone. She'd never known that five minutes could last so long.

She had a lot of things she needed to do that morning. She didn't have time to waste. She should be choosing her wardrobe from her work attire to her little black dress for the big cocktail party, but instead she paced back and forth just as she'd done the night before.

Her phone rang. She let it go to voice mail.

Her phone chimed with a new text message. She ignored it.

A minute or so later, her phone rang again. She also let it go directly to voice mail. Work could wait. This could not. She felt as though life as she knew it was on the line. And once she got the results, positive or negative, life would not go back to the carefree way that it had once been with Franco. She felt as though their relationship had been altered, even if he didn't know it. This marriage was more than business—much more. But what did she want from it?

Ding. Ding. Ding.

It was her time of reckoning. She silenced the timer and then rushed to the bathroom. The breath caught in her lungs as her heart pounded. She picked up the first test.

Positive.

What? No. No. No.

She picked up the second test. Positive. Her heart was beating so hard it echoed in her ears. Her breaths came faster and faster. *This can't be happening.*

One last test. She picked it up. Positive.

By now her breathing consisted of short, rapid gasps. She felt dizzy and sick to her stomach. She sank down on the white tile floor. She put her head between her knees to try and keep the world from spinning madly around her.

She was pregnant with Franco's baby. How was she going to tell him?

CHAPTER SIXTEEN

THIS DAY WAS GREAT.

Carla was amazing!

And Franco couldn't stop smiling. The day had been a whirlwind of interviews and photo ops celebrating the new Falco-Marchello project. Carla's office had handled setting up all the PR, and they'd done a fabulous job. The conference room had been filled with eager reporters and plentiful cameras.

When he'd first had the idea of getting Marchello Spices back in the Falco restaurants, he'd just thought about getting a couple of spices back on the tables. But with Carla's help and vision, they'd gone so far from his basic vision to something with momentum.

This project had taken on a life of its own from general spices to carefully blended combinations exclusive to the Falco restaurants. To new menu items that utilized Marchello Spices. And finally to the new ads featuring that special place Franco had taken Carla for that very special lunch. Every time he caught a glimpse of Gianna's prints, he couldn't help but smile.

They did great work together. And his grandfather was wrong when he said that working with a Falco was a mistake. Carla had proven time and again that he could trust her. And though he'd been leery of the marriage in the beginning—okay, more like downright opposed to it—it'd worked out. They hadn't gotten too caught up in it. At least nothing that couldn't be undone without destroying either of them.

And he was going to see if Carla wanted to continue seeing him after the divorce. Because he just couldn't imagine his life without her in it. Every time he thought of her, he got this warm feeling in his chest. He refused to put a name to it.

Maybe she wanted the same thing—maybe that's why she'd tried a couple of times that day to draw him away for a private word. But each time she'd approached him, right behind her was a member of the press. They'd latched onto this story because it had a lot of history— most families in Italy had at one time or another eaten a memorable meal in the Falco restaurants, and the red, white and green Marchello Spices shakers had at one point been a staple in most households. So their reunion was something that touched many lives. There was a lot of excitement.

But now as evening rolled around and they were about to head into the cocktail party, he didn't see Carla anywhere. He was eager to find out if she'd had the same thing on her mind about them giving in to their rising desires. He really hoped so.

With a plan to seek out Carla, he started to move around the room. His progress was hampered by business associates. He pasted on a smile and shook hands, but all the while his gaze darted around the room, searching for Carla. Where could she be?

And then he reassured himself that there was nothing to worry about, as she probably wanted to make a spectacular entrance. That was something his stunningly beautiful wife could do without even trying.

When his gaze strayed to the door, he came to an abrupt stop. The breath caught in his lungs. He didn't so much as blink as his mind rushed to make sense of what he was seeing.

It was his grandparents. They'd shown up at the party. Sure, they'd been invited—it'd been a matter of formality—but his grandfather had blustered on about not stepping foot in a Falco building or celebrating this ill-advised venture. Was his grandfather finally willing to admit that he'd done something even his grandfather hadn't been able to do—make Marchello Spices relevant once more?

Once the initial shock had passed, Franco moved toward his grandparents. "Hello."

His grandmother beamed at him. "I'm so proud of you. You're finally living the life I'd always hoped for you—a sweet wife and making your mark upon the company."

"Thank you." He wasn't so sure what else to say. His grandmother didn't usually speak to him in this manner.

And then she did something so out of character for her—she stepped forward and hugged him. The simple gesture had a profound effect on him. Franco hugged his grandmother back. He blinked repeatedly—all the flowers in the room must be making his allergies act up.

When they parted, he turned to his grandfather, wondering if he felt the same way. His grandfather wore a noncommittal expression. "I still can't believe you're not only married to a Falco but also doing business with one. I told you they can't be trusted."

"And how many times do I have to tell you that Carla

is different? She's not like her father. She's up front and honest. She'd never take advantage of anyone."

"Don't be too trusting." Just then his grandmother elbowed his grandfather, and not subtly, either. His grandfather cleared his throat. "But you've done a great job with the business."

His grandfather did something that Franco hadn't been expecting at all—he held his hand out to him. When Franco gripped his grandfather's hand, he gave him a firm handshake.

Then the most amazing thing of all, he saw pride reflected in his grandfather's eyes. He hadn't known how much he'd been craving that until this moment.

He walked his grandparents around the room, introducing them to some associates from the Falco group. They stopped at the buffet table. The spread was all finger foods with Marchello Spices being prominently displayed as well as utilized.

While his grandparents perused the table, Franco's thoughts turned to Carla. He couldn't wait to share his grandparents' reactions to this joint venture. She was never going to believe it. Because the success of this venture would be a hollow victory without Carla to share it with him.

She was a mess of emotions.

And she was scared. Her world was imploding.

And worst of all, she still had to tell Franco. Carla had tried repeatedly that day to draw him aside, but there had been one interruption after another. She felt as though she was sitting on a powder keg that was about to explode at any given moment.

She was hoping by telling Franco sooner rather than

later that he would take the news better. After all, how could he blame her when it definitely took two of them to get into this predicament?

And so she'd skipped out on a few media events that day, letting her trusted staff and Franco handle the countless questions, including the one about why the two brands had ceased working together years ago. No one wanted to answer that question, but the more they evaded, the more insistent the media became.

Instead she'd spent time closed up in her office, finishing up some final details. It was all she could do to focus. Her insides were twisted in a nervous knot. She had to do something to calm down, because she couldn't show up at the party all frazzled. Everyone would know something was wrong—especially Franco.

She needed something familiar—something to ground her. As a matter of instinct, she grabbed her keys and headed out the door. It was time to go home.

Because when all was said and done, it was the place where she'd been raised, and her father was there. She might be upset with him right now, but it didn't mean she loved him any less.

When she entered her father's living room, she found him on the couch. His brows lifted in surprise. "I didn't expect to see you today."

"I…" She searched for a plausible excuse. "I needed to take a break before the party."

"Everything's all right?" His concerned gaze probed her.

She nodded. "The project is running ahead of schedule."

"Maybe then you'll be able to slow down and eat a meal with your father."

"We'll do that real soon."

It was on the tip of her tongue to ask if that invitation included her husband, but she stopped herself. She didn't think she could keep her emotions at bay if she started talking about Franco.

"You must be excited about tonight. I've gone over all the information about this joint venture. I know I was totally opposed to it in the beginning, but now I think you've done a great job. And I couldn't be prouder of you."

His kind words broke the dam around her rising emotions. She blinked repeatedly, but a tear escaped and landed on her cheek.

Her father stepped up to her. "Carla, what's the matter?"

She shook her head. "Nothing."

"You don't cry for no reason. Tell me what it is."

She swiped away the tear and forced a smile to her lips. "You've just never said anything like that to me before."

"Said what? That I'm proud of you?" When she nodded, he continued. "I've always been proud of you. And that's why I'm going to the party tonight."

"You are?" This was the first she'd heard of it.

"Of course I'm going." He moved to the hallway. "I already have my suit picked out." He motioned for her to follow him. "I just need help choosing a tie."

This was new. Her father never relied on her to make decisions for him—not about his wardrobe or any other part of his life. She didn't know what to make of it.

Still, she walked with him and then chose a wine-colored tie. "Are you sure about this?" Her phone rang, but she ignored it. "It's going to be a big evening, and I don't want you wearing yourself out."

"Do you need to get that?"

She shook her head. "I have staff to take care of any problems that might crop up. Right now, I'm more concerned about you overdoing it. Remember what the doctor said about you slowing down and taking it easy."

"I'm not an invalid. Just because you have taken over the company doesn't mean I'm going to languish at home."

She nodded in understanding. "That's not what I meant. I'm just worried about you."

He paused and looked at her. "Now you know how it feels to worry about someone and want to protect them when they don't want to be coddled."

Carla opened her mouth to say something, but the words faded. She wordlessly pressed her lips together. What was her father saying? That everything he'd done—from trying to stop her from taking over the CEO's position to his matchmaking—it had all been his attempt to protect her?

This was too important for her just to let slide by. "Are you saying you never wanted me to run the company because you were trying to protect me from something?"

He sighed as he sat down on a bench at the end of his bed. "I never wanted you to repeat my mistakes."

Maybe with him calm this was the right moment to broach the subject of him lying to her. "Are you admitting that you cheated at the poker game?"

With a deep, resigned sigh, he lowered his head. "Yes."

The one word was like a dagger in her heart. Her

wonderful, amazing father whom she'd held up on a pedestal all these years fell back to earth with a re-sounding thud.

She struggled to speak as emotions clogged her throat. "But why?"

Her father ran a hand over his jaw. "It was a bad time in my life."

"Bad enough to cheat and then lie about it—lie to me?" She didn't know what he could say to make any of that all right.

"It wasn't that long after we lost your mother. I was struggling."

He was? "You never let on to me."

"I couldn't. I'd promised your mother that I'd make sure you were all right. But when you weren't around, I was drinking a lot. The more I drank, the more I gambled. For a while, it was okay. I was on a winning streak. But then the tide turned and every hand was a loser. I drank more and gambled even more, trying to win back what I'd lost."

Carla sat down next to her father. "Oh, Papa, if I'd known—"

"I didn't want you to know. I knew how hard it was on you losing your mother. It got to the point where I'd lost all my money. I had to get it back. I only had one thing left that was worth enough money—the business." His voice wavered with emotion as he stared straight ahead as though lost in his thoughts. "I was certain that my luck would change. It had to, but I wasn't taking any chances. I'd slipped an ace up my sleeve. I didn't think I'd need it."

As her father revealed the whole sordid tale, Carla struggled to keep her mouth from gaping. Her strong, proud father seemed to shrink in front of her eyes. She didn't know how to react. She was a ball of emotions: anger at being lied to, disillusioned that her larger-than-life father was fallible like the rest of us and sympathy for him that he'd suffered in silence.

"In the end, being accused of cheating was the best thing that could have happened to me. I just didn't see it that way until now."

"Why?" Her voice was barely more than a whisper. She wasn't sure she wanted to hear the answer.

He blew out an unsteady breath. "Because accusations were thrown about and Marchello had no choice but to walk away—without my company."

"And yet you called him a liar?"

Her father's head lowered. "It wasn't my finest hour. I was so full of anger, and he became my target. It wasn't right, and I regret it."

"Then why haven't you apologized?"

There was a drawn-out pause. "It's not that easy. What would he think of me?"

"But Franco's grandfather already knows the truth, and there's a video—"

"There is?" When she nodded, he asked, "But then why did he just walk away? He could have taken everything from me."

"Not everything. You will always have me." She leaned her head against his shoulder and hugged him. "Maybe Franco's grandfather was a better friend to you than you ever knew."

Her father was silent for a moment as he considered her observation. And then he cleared his throat. "That was the moment I started to get my act together. But you have to understand that I made mistakes before the drinking and gambling."

"Everyone makes mistakes." She should know—she was carrying Franco's baby.

"Before all that I made the business the center of the world. I always thought there would be time for other things—like taking your mother to see the world. It had been her fondest wish, but then she got sick and there was no more time."

"I... I didn't know." Her mother had wanted to travel. And here she'd always thought her mother had been content to stay at home and look after her. She hadn't realized her mother had other aspirations. She wondered what else she'd never known about her mother.

"Your mother didn't feel a need to talk about it. She knew that eventually there would be time to follow her dreams. None of us expected her to get so sick so quickly."

The pain of her mother's sudden loss could still be felt after all these years. "And so you wanted me to get married and have a family because you wanted me to be like my mother."

"No. Though would that have been so bad?"

She thought of the baby she was carrying now—with every passing moment, the idea of being a mother was becoming more attractive. "No, it's not bad. But why did it have to be one or the other? Business or a family?"

"Because your mother told me from the time you were little that you were so much like me. I, of course, didn't believe her. I saw her in you from your dark curls to your caring heart. But your mother was known for seeing things that I was blind to. And then without your mother around to watch over us both, I feared that her

prediction was right—you'd turn out just like me—
make my same mistakes."

She'd never known any of this. Her father had never
opened up to her. He had always been the one to keep
things close to his chest. But it appeared that his recent
heart attacks had had a profound affect not only on her
but on him as well.

Buzz. Buzz. Buzz.

Who kept calling her? She pulled her phone from her
purse and saw Franco's name on the caller ID. He was
probably calling to remind her that they were to have
some press photos taken with some prominent people
at the party, but it was just going to have to wait. This
conversation with her father was too important to walk
away from now.

She placed the phone back in her purse. "What mistakes?"

His tired gaze met hers. "I made the mistake of
thinking that if I built a successful business, it would
keep my family safe. I was so driven to make sure my
family wanted for nothing financially that I missed the
fact that I was no longer an active part of your or your
mother's lives. I was absent for too many birthday parties and anniversaries." His gruff voice hitched with
emotion. "I... I didn't want that for you. So I thought if
you married and had children, you would see that there
was more to life than just work."

"I never knew." Her mind rewound back to all the
arguments they'd had over her marrying. They could
have been avoided if he would have explained this to
her. "Why didn't you say anything?"

"Because I knew you'd ignore my warnings. Your
mother was right—you are stubborn, just like me."

Carla wanted to argue with him. She wanted to tell him that his worries were wrong—that she wouldn't have put her career ahead of everything else. Instead she bit back her denial, because ever since Matteo had hurt her in the worst way, she'd closed off her heart—she'd closed it off to Franco, too.

Instead of letting herself be put in a position of being loved, she'd focused on her career. It was something she could control. It had been the safe choice.

And now that all three pregnancy tests showed positive, she felt more vulnerable than she'd ever been in her life. How was Franco going to react to the news? Would he blame her?

She shoved aside the troubling thoughts so as not to get emotional again and have her father ask questions—questions like what was she going to do next? She didn't have any answers. It was all so new—so shocking.

She changed the subject. "Thank you for being honest with me. You don't have to worry. I promise to have a life and a career."

He reached out and squeezed her hand. "I just want you to be happy."

"I will be." She just wasn't so sure about her happiness in the near future. "I have to go get ready for the party. Are you sure you won't consider staying home?"

"Absolutely not. I need to go brag about what my amazing daughter has accomplished."

At least Franco's grandparents wouldn't be there. He had been quite certain his grandfather would be too stubborn to go to a party and acknowledge Franco's accomplishment.

She hugged her father. "I'll see you later. And if you

change your mind and decide to stay home, I won't be upset. Just call me. I'll keep my phone on me."

"Stop worrying. I'll be fine."

And then Carla was gone. As she checked the time, she realized she'd spent more time with her father than she'd intended. And now she was late for the party.

As for telling Franco the news about the baby, well… it'd waited all day, so it could wait until tomorrow. Because the party was no place to tell him the news. And looking back on earlier today, it hadn't been the time to tell him, either. It's just that she'd been in shock and her first thought was to tell Franco.

But waiting until the morning wasn't going to change the test results. As the instruction sheet had told her, a positive result was definitely positive. What was Franco going to say now that their fake marriage had become very real, with real consequences?

CHAPTER SEVENTEEN

WHERE WAS SHE?

Franco had slowly worked his way around the room, twice over, and there was still no sign of Carla. He'd even tried her phone a couple of times. Every time, it had gone directly to voice mail. What was up with that?

Was she avoiding him? He didn't think so. It's not like they'd had a fight or anything. Sure, she'd been a bit more distant in the last day or so, but that was probably just due to exhaustion.

But none of that explained why he hadn't found her yet. He'd stopped to ask her assistant, Rosa, but she hadn't heard from her in the past hour or so, since she'd left the office. He recalled Carla's pale complexion that morning. Perhaps she was sick. He was about to leave and go to the apartment to see if she was right.

As he headed for the door, Carla entered the room. He took long strides toward her. "Where have you been?"

She didn't look at him as she smiled at the passing guests. "I had to check on my father."

"Is something wrong?"

"No. I just wanted him to know that I would be fine if he stayed home."

He was relieved to hear that nothing was wrong with Carlo. Not that he had any warm feelings toward the man who had lied about him and his family all these years, but Carla loved him dearly and what was important to her was important to him—

Wait. Had he just thought that? While Carla paused to say hello to the CEO of an up-and-coming tech company, Franco realized just how important Carla had become to him.

When Carla was free again, he knew this was his opportunity to draw her aside. He placed a hand on her upper arm to gain her attention. When she paused and looked up at him, he asked, "Can we speak now?"

Her gaze met his, but her emotions were closed off to him. "Not now. It's a party."

"I know something is bothering you. Does it have to do with the launch?"

She shook her head. "Everything is on track."

"Then if it's not business, it has to be something to do with me." As someone passed closely by them, he quieted down and forced a smile to his face. "What have I done?"

Carla turned a smile in his direction—a smile that didn't reach her eyes. "This isn't the place."

Just then a flash went off in their faces. He'd forgotten about the media photographers covering the party. Franco wished they'd give them some privacy.

When Carla set off again, he fell in step with her. "But you were the one that insisted we speak earlier. I'm ready now."

She came to an abrupt halt and turned to him. This time there was anger reflected in her eyes. In a hushed voice, she said, "And I'm supposed to drop everything because suddenly you've got time in your schedule for me? I don't think so."

He stifled a frustrated groan. "You took that out of context. I'm sorry I was busy earlier. You know how fast everything is moving."

Just then a reporter approached them. The woman's face was perfectly made up, and not a hair was out of place. "Do you have time for a few questions?"

"We were just about to go take care of something," Franco said.

"But it can wait a moment or two." Carla flashed the reporter her fake smile. "What would you like to ask?"

"Would you mind if I record this?" She held up her phone. "I just want to make sure I get my facts right when I go to write up the story."

Carla nodded. "Of course."

"You two have made quite the stir this year. First your sudden marriage. Where was it that you tied the knot?"

Carla spoke up first. "It was at Franco's country estate in Lake Como."

"That must have been so romantic. You know, to be swept off your feet and a secret wedding and all."

"It was sudden, but we both knew what we wanted." Carla elbowed him. "Isn't that right, Franco?"

He was still pondering what Carla had on her mind. Whatever it was, it wasn't good. Worry seeped into his bones as he pasted on a fake smile to match Carla's. But whatever was wrong, he would fix it.

He slipped an arm around her waist and pulled her closer, just like happy newlyweds would do. "We just couldn't wait to be husband and wife."

"You two always look so happy, so in love. So what's it like to work with your spouse?"

"It's been great," Carla said. "Franco is great at coming up with solutions for tricky problems."

"And Carla is great with concepts and tie-ins."

The reporter smiled and nodded. "This sounds like the beginning of many successful collaborations."

"I don't know," Franco said with hesitancy.

"What he means is that we haven't gotten that far. We're just on the eve of launching this new campaign in all the Falco restaurants."

The reporter nodded in understanding. "And what about on a personal front? Will there soon be any additions to your family?"

Franco didn't hesitate to answer. "No. We're happy just the way we are."

When Carla didn't echo his sentiments, he glanced at her. Her face filled with color. "We haven't discussed having children."

It was true. They'd never once talked of having their own children. Still, her answer was definitely not an affirmation of his words. It was not the answer he'd been expecting. And now there was this agonizing suspicion swirling around in is mind.

The breath caught in his throat. Was she pregnant?

For a moment, it felt as though the floor had gone out from under his feet and he was hanging over an abyss. This couldn't be happening. Not to him. He'd always been so cautious—so very careful—until Carla.

Why had he instinctively trusted her? It wasn't like this was his first go-around with an unplanned pregnancy. At least the first time with Rose it'd all been a ruse to get him to marry her. But Carla wasn't like Rose. She wouldn't intentionally get pregnant. Would she?

"I appreciate you both taking a moment to speak

with me." The reporter's voice jarred him from his frantic thoughts. "Our readers will be anxiously waiting for word of a little Falco-Marchello to carry on such a delicious merger. Now I'll let you get to your other guests."

When the reporter moved on, Carla tried to slip away, too. But Franco was hot on her trail. He leaned over and whispered in her ear, "We need to talk now."

Just then Carla's assistant, Rosa, approached them. Franco groaned inwardly. Why did they have to be at a party, of all places? Trying to find just a moment alone was virtually impossible.

This was his fault. He should have insisted on making time to speak with Carla earlier in the day—when they could have had this conversation in private, without worry of being interrupted.

Because what he was thinking right now just couldn't possibly be true. There was no way Carla could be pregnant. But he also knew she could be pregnant. It wasn't like they hadn't enjoyed their marital benefits.

But in the beginning, Carla had insisted she took care of birth control. He'd believed her. Had he been too quick to believe her? Was it possible she'd lied to him? For what purpose? Was she that anxious to have a family that she'd do it at any cost?

With every outlandish thought that came to mind, his heart beat faster. His blood pressure had to be creeping into the red zone.

Desperate for a moment alone with Carla, he turned to her assistant. "Rosa, could you cover for us for a moment?"

"Um…sure." Worry reflected in her eyes. "You aren't leaving, are you?"

"No," Carla said firmly. "There's not a chance we'd miss out on this big night."

"Something came up and I need to discuss it with Carla. No big deal."

Rosa nodded in understanding. "I'll see to things."

"We'll just be in the hallway." Carla pointed to where they'd be.

And then Franco slipped his arm around his wife's slim waist as they made their way toward the doorway that led to the back entrance to the building. He hoped it would give them the privacy they needed. Because he needed to hear Carla say that she wasn't pregnant. She just couldn't be pregnant.

What were the chances of that happening? The odds have to be minuscule. Right?

Once in the vacant hallway with the door closed behind them, Carla turned on him. "What are you doing?"

"What am I doing? What are you doing telling a reporter that we might have children?"

Her face was devoid of color. "That's not what I said. I said—"

"I know what you said. What you didn't say was that we aren't having children, not now, not ever." He paused, waiting for her to agree. Instead an ominous silence filled the void. "Carla?"

Her gaze was cast downward. "We should get back to the party."

"Not before we clear this up." His gut knotted as bile inched up his throat. "Carla, what did you try to tell me earlier today?"

"It can wait."

"No, I don't think it can." It seemed as though she

couldn't work up the courage to say it, so he would have to do it for her. "Carla, are you pregnant?"

Her gaze met his. There was a whole host of emotions reflected in her eyes, from fear to anger. She didn't say a word. She didn't have to. It was written all over her pale face.

And then she wordlessly nodded.

His heart fell. His head started to spin. *This can't be happening.* This was never supposed to happen. And yet it had happened, and he had no idea what to do about it.

No wonder she hadn't wanted to tell him. She knew he never wanted a family. But with Carla, it seemed like one thing always led to another. They'd started out as in-laws, which led to chemistry on the dance floor at his brother's wedding. That had led to a business dinner. From there she'd proposed a deal that he just couldn't turn down. A fake marriage had led to a very real wedding night. That night had led to him seeing her not as one of those Falcos—the ones that had lied—no, instead he found her to be a caring, loving and generous woman. And now he didn't know what to think about any of this. He couldn't even formulate any words—

The door burst open. Rosa rushed up to Carla. "Carla, you have to come quick."

"What is it?" Carla's voice echoed her concern.

"It's your father—" and then Rosa looked at him "—and your grandfather. They've gotten into a very loud and contentious argument in the middle of the party. It's a disaster."

"Oh no!" Carla turned an accusing stare at him. "You promised your grandfather wouldn't be here."

She didn't wait for him to explain as she rushed in the door. He'd meant to tell her about his grandparents' unexpected appearance, but when he'd grown worried about her unexplained absence, it'd slipped his mind.

Franco was right behind her. This night was supposed to be so perfect, so amazing, but it was turning into a disaster.

The sound of angry male voices boomed through the room. It was the first time the two men had confronted each other since the cheating episode. It appeared that time had not lessened their anger toward the other.

Carla worked her way through the thickening crowd as a number of people pulled out their phones to film the devolving event. Franco's own personal nightmare was going to have to be put on hold until they separated the men.

"Liar!"

"Cheat!"

At last, Carla stepped inside the circle. "Papa, stop."

"I…" Carlo Falco stopped speaking. "I…" Then he clutched his chest before collapsing to the floor.

A horrified cry erupted from Carla's throat. She knelt by her father's side. Franco grabbed his phone and called for an ambulance. It seemed like forever until he'd answered all the operator's questions. Yes, Carlo was still breathing. No, he wasn't conscious.

Franco knelt next to Carla. Time moved slowly. He'd never felt so helpless in his life. Carla held her father's hand as she pleaded with him to hold on. The desperation rang out in her voice.

And when Carla finally turned her big brown eyes to Franco as the unleashed tears streamed down her cheeks, he felt as though his heart had been torn in half. He would do anything to fix this for her, but he didn't know how.

"He's going to be okay." Franco didn't know that, but he certainly wanted to believe it.

Before Carla could say anything, the crowd parted and the paramedics rolled a gurney into the room. They stepped back, giving them room to work. It took a few minutes to take his vitals and hook him up to oxygen.

Franco reached out to wrap his arm around Carla's waist, giving her his shoulder to lean on, but she wordlessly pushed his arm away. He didn't like it, but he understood that she needed to focus all her thoughts and energy on her father.

When they lifted the stretcher with her father, Franco said, "I'll get my car and drive you to the hospital."

"No." Carla turned to him with more anger than he'd even known she was capable of feeling, and it was all aimed at him. "You stay here. You aren't welcome at the hospital. This is all your fault. You and me, we're over. My attorney will send over the papers."

Each of her words were like arrows slamming into his chest. His fault? What? How?

By the time he was able to translate his thoughts into words, she was gone. And he'd never felt more alone in his entire life.

How had things been so right, so promising one moment and then so wrong the next? Now what was he going to do? His wife didn't want him in her life, and they had a baby on the way. It felt as though he was reliving his parents' nightmare.

They'd both married for the wrong reasons, and then they'd both complicated matters with an unexpected pregnancy. He raked his fingers through his hair. What was he supposed to do now?

CHAPTER EIGHTEEN

SHE'D NEVER BEEN so scared.

Carla couldn't remember exactly what had happened between her admitting to Franco that she was pregnant until she watched her father being loaded into the back of an ambulance. She vaguely recalled being furious with Franco but not her exact words.

She paced back and forth in the hospital waiting area. What was taking the doctors so long? She'd begged them to let her stay, but they'd insisted it was protocol for her to stay in the waiting area until they'd done their initial workup.

Please let him be okay. Please let him be okay.

She kept repeating the silent prayer over and over in her mind. With her head down, she kept moving. She couldn't sit still. She was filled with pent-up anxiety.

A hand touched her shoulder.

She came to an abrupt stop and turned. She expected to find the doctor in his white coat, but instead it was her cousin. Gianna's face reflected her own worry.

They wordlessly hugged each other. Part of her wished that it was Franco holding her, but she had too many conflicting emotions where he was concerned.

And she couldn't deal with him right now. It was just too much.

When they pulled apart, Carla swiped at her eyes. Gianna guided her over to one of the orange chairs. "Sit down. You look exhausted."

"I'm fine." She didn't feel fine. She felt as though her life was being pulled apart at the seams.

"Have you heard anything?"

Carla shook her head. "They threw me out and told me to wait here."

Gianna reached for her phone. "Do you want me to call Franco?"

"No."

Gianna slipped the phone back in her purse. "Okay. What's going on?"

"This whole thing is my fault. I know I blamed Franco, but I shouldn't have. This whole marriage and business venture was my idea. I knew about the bad blood between my father and Franco's grandfather, but did that stop me? No. I'm the one who should be blamed. If anything happens to my father, it's all on me."

"Whoa. Slow down. Start at the beginning."

And so Carla did exactly that. Her father's matchmaking, her plan to take care of him and then the marriage contract—it all came tumbling out. She even briefly mentioned their wedding night and now its complications.

"You're pregnant?" Gianna's excited voice came out loudly.

"Shh…" Carla glanced around to make sure there was no one around to overhear. "Yes, but it's the very last thing Franco wants."

"You told him?"

Carla nodded. "Right before my father collapsed."

"And he said that he didn't want the baby?"

"No. But he'd previously told me about his childhood and how he never planned to marry or have a family. He doesn't want to repeat his parents' mistakes."

"When did he tell you this?"

"A while ago."

"Maybe things have changed since then. He said he didn't want to marry, but he sure looks happy these days. Even Dario mentioned that he'd never seen his brother happier."

This was all news to Carla. "I don't know. He's probably just happy about our business venture coming together."

"No. I've seen the way he looks at you. It isn't the way a platonic business associate looks at the other. He looks at you like you're a double chocolate cupcake that he can't wait to devour."

Heat filled Carla's cheeks. "He does not."

"Oh, but he does. And I've seen the way you look at him when you think no one notices. You are crazy for him. It's the reason I never questioned your quickie wedding. I figured it was love at first sight. Or maybe second sight."

Was that true? Did he love her? And if he did, did it change things between them? Would he still love her even if she was carrying the baby he never wanted?

That evening couldn't have gone any worse.

Franco took one look at his grandfather's pale, drawn face and knew he was in no condition to drive. Franco and his brother had helped their grandparents into their car. His grandmother never did like to drive, so he drove them home. Dario followed them in his car.

As he drove out of the city, he just couldn't help but think about how things had looked so promising one moment and then in the next his world had come crashing in around him.

A baby.

He was going to be a father.

In that moment, he promised himself that he wouldn't be like his father, who was constantly avoiding his responsibilities. If it wasn't for his grandfather, he might not know what it was to have a father—how to be a father. Franco was going to be there for his child in every way possible. No one would drive him away.

When holidays and birthdays rolled around, he'd be there with an armful of gifts and a big smile. He would let his child know how much they meant to him.

He would do for his child everything that he'd wanted his parents to do for him, but instead they'd been too wrapped up in their own world—in their own problems—to see that their two little boys had been utterly and totally forgotten.

"Franco." His grandmother's concerned voice interrupted his thoughts. "Franco, you missed the turn."

He blinked. His gaze took in his surroundings, and he realized his grandmother was right. "I'll just circle back around. No big deal."

"Something is on your mind. It's your grandfather, isn't it?"

His grandfather was sitting quietly in the back seat for the first time since Franco had known him. A glance in the rearview mirror showed his grandfather with his arms crossed over his chest as he stared out the window. Franco thought for sure he'd have a few disparaging words to say about Franco missing the turn, but he continued to be mute.

Returning his gaze to the road, Franco thought about his grandmother's question. "Actually, I was thinking about my father."

"Oh." She didn't like to talk about her son. The pain was always evident in her eyes when his name was brought up, and so Franco had learned to avoid the subject all together.

But today was different. All the skeletons in the closet and the ghosts that had been swept under the rug were going to be aired out—the light shined on them. Maybe that was the problem with their family. Maybe they avoided the tough subjects too often. Instead of the silence helping, it was hurting them.

Now that both he and Dario were about to be fathers, they didn't have the luxury of ignoring the past. They had to learn from it if they hoped to do better by their children.

He eased the car into the drive and parked in front of the massive villa. This subject could wait until they were inside.

He jumped out and opened both car doors for his grandparents. As they got to their feet, he noticed that they both looked as though they'd aged considerably since the confrontation at the party.

Once inside, Dario joined them. "Well, that's certainly going to be in the news tomorrow. I'm guessing that's not the headline you were hoping for."

Franco paced back and forth, raking his fingers through his hair. Then he stopped and faced his grandfather. "Why did you have to pick today of all days to change your mind and show up?"

"It's my company." His voice boomed in the large foyer.

"It was your company," Franco corrected him. "Remember, you're retiring."

"He's right," Nonna agreed. "You can't keep running the company forever. It's time you let Franco take over."

His grandfather's lips pressed into a firm line as a muscle in his cheek spasmed.

"I know that you never thought I lived up to this image you had of me." Franco's voice shook with frustration. "I've tried and tried to make you proud of me, but I'm done. I just can't do it anymore. You can keep the company. I quit."

"What...what?" For the first time ever, his grandfather looked to be at a loss for words. "But you can't."

"Oh, I can and I am." As he swung around to walk out the door, he caught the grin on his brother's face.

It seemed like not so long ago that Dario had had a similar conversation with their grandfather—then, Franco hadn't been able to understand how he could just walk away from his legacy. It'd taken a bit, but now he finally understood.

"Wait," Nonna called out. When he turned to his grandmother, she said, "Don't go." Then she turned to his grandfather. "I've been quiet for too long. I thought you knew what you were doing where the boys were concerned, but you've gone too far now. Don't let him walk away. Not like this."

Nonno shook his head. "Let him go."

"No." His grandmother's voice brooked no argument.

"Fix this. I won't lose yet another member of this family. I let you drive away our son."

"He wasn't strong," Nonno said. "He wouldn't stand up for himself. He always wanted to take the easy way out of everything."

"Maybe if you hadn't pushed him so hard, he'd have figured it all out."

"You blame me for him leaving?"

"I do. And I won't stand for it. Not again. Franco belongs at the helm of the company. He has earned the right to continue running it the way he sees fit." Nonna glared at his grandfather. "And if you don't step aside, don't bother coming to bed tonight or any other night." She turned and stormed away.

His grandmother had stolen all of Franco's thunder. She'd left him utterly speechless. He'd never seen her so angry. When he gathered himself to lift his sagging jaw, he glanced over at his grandfather, who appeared to have lost his ability to speak as well.

Franco had always taken his grandmother's silence to mean that she agreed with everything his grandfather said and did. It appeared that wasn't the case. He was relieved that she'd finally spoken up, but he couldn't help but wish that she'd done it much sooner.

Franco hesitated, waiting to see if his grandfather would say anything. The silence stretched on. It went on too long. Franco continued toward the door.

"Wait," Dario said.

Franco didn't want to wait. Turning his back on his grandfather wasn't easy. Even if the man wasn't the easiest person to care about, he still loved him. But he couldn't just walk out on his brother, who'd always had his back. Through everything, they'd been there for each other.

Franco smothered a frustrated sigh and turned back. "It's not going to work," he said to his brother. "He's too stubborn to listen to anyone—"

"That's not true." Nonno's voice wavered, as though he wasn't quite certain.

Both brothers turned to their grandfather. His shoulders were slightly slumped as worry lines bracketed his face. It was though he'd aged right before him. Franco had never seen his grandfather anything but strong and assured. He didn't look like either of those things right now.

"You don't understand," their grandfather began. "You didn't know your father—"

"Let's sit down and talk." Dario moved toward the living room and glanced over his shoulder to make sure both men were following him.

Their grandfather fell in step behind Dario. Franco still hadn't moved from his spot near the door. He wasn't so sure there was anything his grandfather could say at this stage to change his mind about remaining a part of this family.

But then his gaze connected with his brother's. Dario nodded toward the living room. He could see in his younger brother's eyes that he was pleading with him not to walk away. It was so funny how things had flip-flopped between them.

Not so long ago, it was he who had coerced his brother into attending the family's Sunday dinner after he'd broken up with his now wife. And Franco couldn't help but wonder if he hadn't somehow been instrumental in getting those two back together—but as soon as the thought came to him, he dismissed it. Because it was perfectly obvious to anyone who saw Dario and Gianna that they belonged together. Even without him, they would have found their way back to each other.

But this talk didn't have anything to do with romance. It was about something much deeper—the fracture of his family. He'd always told himself that it was all in the past and to keep looking forward. But if it was all in the past, why was he so hesitant to make a commitment to the most amazing woman in the world? Maybe it wasn't all in the past like he'd thought.

With great reluctance, he followed the two men to the living room to hear whatever it was his grandfather had to say to them.

His brother sat on one couch. His grandfather sat on the other couch. Franco crossed his arms and propped himself up against the doorjamb. When Dario nodded for him to join them, Franco shook his head. There was only so far he was willing to go.

Nonno leaned back on the couch. He rubbed a hand over his clean-shaven chin. "I tried to do my best. I tried to raise your father to shoulder his responsibilities, but he resisted me every step of the way. He thought because we had money that he shouldn't have to work for things. I wanted to show him what it took to accumulate that money. Perhaps I pushed too hard." He hesitated as though his thoughts had drifted back in time. "No, that isn't right. I did push him too hard. I'd only meant to help him, but I went too far."

Franco stood perfectly still, afraid that if he moved his grandfather would be jarred out of the moment. And it was only then that he realized just how desperately he wanted to understand his father so he could better understand himself.

He had never heard his grandfather talk this way— never heard him admit to his own weaknesses. And yet he was acknowledging how he'd made mistakes raising their father.

"I didn't want your father to rely on others to take care of him. I wanted him to stand on his own two feet. I gave him every opportunity to find his way in the family business."

"Maybe he didn't have a mind for business," Dario offered. "I know that's not where my interest lies."

Nonno's gazed downward as he nodded in agreement. "I'd have to agree with you, but I couldn't see it at the time."

"But you just let him walk away." Franco's voice boomed with an anger he'd kept hidden for a lifetime— even from himself. He wasn't willing to let this subject go so easily. He needed to understand how he and his brother had been forgotten by the one person who was supposed to love them most of all. "You didn't try to stop him when he dumped his wife and two small children."

His grandfather's eyes reflected his deep regret. "I tried to reason with him. I ordered him not to go. When that didn't work, I begged him. And when he wouldn't listen to anything I had to say, I tried to bribe him. He… he took the money and left…left you, your mother, the business, his mother…and me." He lowered his face to his hands.

"But I don't understand," Dario said. "Every now and then, without warning, he shows up in our lives.

He never stays long. He's like a distant uncle who just passes by and says hi."

Nonno lifted his head and met Dario's gaze. "That is something I never wanted you to know about."

"You've told us a lot already," Franco said, "so you might as well tell us the rest. It's not like we're kids anymore."

Nonno drew in an uneven breath and then blew it out. "Your father comes around when he needs money."

"And you give it to him?" Dario's voice thundered with anger.

Nonno's gaze once more lowered as he nodded. "I knew that way he'd keep coming back. I thought... I'd hoped he'd see what he was missing by not being in your life."

"So he never once came around just because he wanted to see us?" Dario wasn't going to let this go. Because they'd both hoped all these years that somewhere deep down their father loved them in his own way.

Nonno kept his head down as he shook his head. "I... I thought I could shield you from him—from his lack of caring."

His father didn't love him.

His father had never loved him. No wonder he'd walked away.

Franco was glad he had the wall to hold himself up. He'd had absolutely no idea that all this time he'd been blaming his grandfather for driving away his father, when in fact his grandfather had done everything he could think of to make his father stay.

Whatever his father's problems were, they appeared to be all his. Though his grandfather put on a tough exterior, he really did have a heart beneath it all. Maybe now they'd see a bit more of it.

But one thing was clear. Even if his grandfather hadn't loved them quite the way they'd wanted, he did truly love them. And that meant the world to Franco.

This revelation also told Franco that his assumption that his father had loved them and still let them down had been false. He hadn't loved them, and he didn't care about letting them down.

But the fact was that Franco cared a great deal about Carla—dare he say it, he loved her. It was the first time he'd had the courage to admit it to himself. And now that he had said it to himself, it wasn't so scary after all. In fact, admitting that he loved his wife was freeing. He felt as though he no longer had to deny all the joy and happiness that she brought into his life.

And he found himself admitting to loving their little baby. He couldn't imagine abandoning them. Even if Carla still wanted to dissolve their marriage, he wouldn't be far away. He'd be a part of her life as much as she'd allow him. And his son or daughter would become the center of his world.

Because his father had given him something else besides life. He'd shown him what not to do to those people you loved. Franco could do better. He would do better.

CHAPTER NINETEEN

AT LAST SHE could see her father.

A nurse showed Carla to the hospital room where they'd moved her father. The room was darkened except for a light above his bed. His eyes were closed as though he were sleeping. Her gaze moved to take in all the wires attached to him. Next to the bed was a monitor with his blood pressure and heart rate. She blinked away the unwanted tears. She would keep it all together for his sake.

Still, she couldn't ignore the significance of the situation. This was a scene she'd experienced more than once in the past several months. Each time it scared her.

Her fingers tightened around her purse strap. She just couldn't lose her father. She wasn't ready, especially now that she understood him so much better. This was a time for a new beginning for them.

She perched on the edge of a chair placed next to the bed. When she glanced over at her father, his eyes were now open.

"There you are." He smiled at her. "I'm sorry for the scare."

"So you're all right?" She wanted to ask if he'd had

another heart attack, but she just couldn't form the words.

"I'm fine. My heart is fine. They said I got a little too worked up."

"I'm sorry about that. I didn't think Franco's grandparents were going to show up or I would have warned you to stay away."

"It's my fault. I went to apologize to Giuseppe, but he thought I was there to argue about the past and things quickly escalated." His eyes reflected his remorse. "I apologize for ruining your big evening."

"It's okay. And you won't have to deal with the Marchellos any longer."

Her father pressed the button on his bed so he could sit up straighter. "What happened? Don't tell me that Franco walked out on you. Because if he did, I'll be having a word with him."

"No. I'm the one who sent him away." The memory of the pain reflected in Franco's eyes cut into her heart. She consoled herself with the knowledge that he would be happier if she set him free—free just the way he wanted.

"I don't understand. Why would you tell him to leave? Did he hurt you?" Concern reflected in her father's eyes.

"No. He didn't do anything wrong." And then the truth about the marriage contract came spilling out. "And now...now I'm pregnant."

"Pregnant?" Her father's eyes widened. A moment later, as the information sank in, he smiled. "That's wonderful." When she didn't smile, he asked, "Are you happy about the baby?"

"I'm still in shock, but yes, I'm happy about it. However, I don't think Franco is. He never wanted any of this—a wife or a baby. After his traumatic childhood, I can't blame him. And now…now I can't tie him down with a family he doesn't want. I know Franco, and I know he'd stay out of obligation. That's not right for him, for me or for the baby. We all deserve more than that."

"Are you sure about all this?"

"Of course I am. Do you think I'd have told him things were over if I wasn't sure?"

"And Franco told you that he didn't want the baby?"

"Well, no. But he told me before about his broken family and how he never wanted to do that to his own children."

"That was just his fears talking, when he thought he'd never be a father. But he is now. Are you sure his feelings haven't changed?" Her father's gaze searched hers.

"Why would they have changed?" A spark of hope burned in her heart. Was her father just saying what he thought she wanted to hear? Or did he have a specific reason for his suspicion?

"I've seen the way Franco looks at you. He's a man in love."

"But the baby—"

"Have you asked him how he feels about the baby now that it is very real?"

"No."

"Then what are you doing here? Go find your husband and talk to him—really talk to him."

She went to stand but then turned back to him. "But I can't leave you."

"Of course you can. I've had a big day. I just need

some rest, and tomorrow morning, if you want, you and your husband can give me a ride home."

Her eyes widened in surprise at his willingness to have Franco's company. Maybe there was hope for change. "Are you sure?"

He smiled and nodded. "Go fix things. I'll be fine."

She leaned over and kissed his cheek. "I love you."

"Love you, too. Now go."

She smiled. "Okay. I'm going. Be good while I'm gone."

And then she was out the door and headed for the elevator. She had to find Franco. She had to apologize for being so abrupt and pushing him out of her life. Was it possible her father was right? Was it possible this marriage had evolved into the real thing with genuine love going both ways?

He'd tried her phone. Numerous times.

Each time his call went to voice mail.

Franco wondered if she was ignoring him or if she was still at the hospital with her father. How was her father doing? Franco berated himself for letting her go alone. He should have been there with her, whether she wanted him nearby or not. But then he recalled the anger and pain reflected in her eyes right before she left with the ambulance. Maybe she did need some time away from him. That acknowledgment hurt him.

His first stop was the hospital. Even though it was getting late in the evening, he was hoping he'd be able to check on Carlo. At that hour, he didn't have a problem finding a close-by parking spot. He rushed to the front entrance of the hospital.

Franco yanked the door open and came to an abrupt halt. Carla was in front of him. Talk about good timing.

"Hi." He didn't smile. He didn't want her to think he wasn't taking everything that happened that day seriously.

"Hi." She didn't smile, either.

He backed up, letting her step outside. All his thoughts and practiced words became all jumbled up in his mind.

He drew in a deep breath, hoping it would calm his racing heart. "How's your father?"

"He's good. They said it was a panic attack."

"So no heart attack?"

"No. Thank goodness. They're going to monitor him tonight, and then he'll be released in the morning."

He shifted his weight from one foot to the other. "That's really good news. I'm happy for both of you. Do you need to go back now and see him?"

"No. He said he was tired and told me to leave."

Franco at last smiled. "It sounds like he's back to being his old self."

"Well, not quite."

The smile fell from his face. Just then another couple exited the hospital. They stepped off to the side to let them pass.

Once they were alone again, he asked, "What's the matter? What aren't you telling me?"

"Could we take a walk?"

It was a cool evening but it wasn't frigid out. And it wouldn't matter if it were snowing. He would have agreed to whatever activity that allowed him to spend more time with his wife.

They walked quietly beneath the streetlights. He let

her lead the way because he only wanted to be wherever she was.

When they reached a small park, she turned to him. "Can we sit down?"

"Sure." He didn't know if he should be worried or not, but he sensed she had something on her mind. Maybe he needed to speak up first.

"I'm sorry," they said in unison.

They looked at each other in surprise. Then they smiled.

"You go ahead," she said.

It seemed like the gentlemanly thing to let her go first. He'd waited this long—he could wait a little longer. "No, you say what you have on your mind."

"My father and I talked before the party." She went on to explain about his confession to cheating and how he'd meant to apologize to Franco's grandfather. She also told Franco about her father's driving need to see her married and that it had nothing to do with his doubts about her ability to run the restaurant business.

"That's great news." He was truly happy for her.

When she lifted her chin and gazed into his eyes, the moonlight twinkled in her eyes. It was as though a spell had been cast over him. His gaze lowered over her high cheekbones and pert nose to her glossy lips. They were so tempting—so ready to be kissed.

He gave himself a mental jerk. They were a long way from kissing. In fact at this point, he was pretty certain if he tried it, he'd get slapped down, and rightly so. He had things to say to her—important things.

"You aren't the only one to have a meaningful talk. I just left my grandparents' house. My grandfather explained a lot about my past—about my father. He answered questions I didn't even know I had." Franco leaned back and went on to explain that his grandfather hadn't chased away his father—that his father had walked out on his own family of his own accord.

"I'm sorry." She placed a hand on his arm and squeezed. "That must be so hard for you."

He shook his head. "It's more like a relief. I know that my grandfather truly loves my brother and me. He tried to keep our father in our lives. My father's actions were all on him and no one else. I really needed to understand my past, especially now that you're pregnant."

"I know I totally mishandled the situation with my pregnancy. I was so sure that you wouldn't want a family, and I didn't want to force you into a situation that would make you miserable—a family you don't want."

He turned to her. He stared deep into her eyes. "That's the realization I came to."

"That you don't want this? Us?"

CHAPTER TWENTY

HER HEART TUMBLED.

The backs of her eyes stung.

Carla blinked repeatedly. She sucked down her rising emotions. She'd promised herself that if this didn't work out the way she'd hoped, she wouldn't fall apart.

But when her gaze met his, her heart leaped into her throat. *Please don't say you want out. Please don't disappear from my life.* The words hovered at the back of her throat.

It wasn't fair of her to ask him to do something that went against what was in his heart. The worst thing she could do was force him to relive his past. She loved him too much to cause him any pain.

Franco shook his head. "No. That came out wrong."

"No, you don't want us? No, you do want us?"

His gaze met hers. "Before I met you, I was so certain what I wanted in life—I wanted to take over Marchello Spices and expand it."

"And now what do you want?"

His gaze searched hers. "You don't know?"

Her heart pounded so loud that it echoed in her ears. "No."

"I want you." His hand moved to her abdomen. "And I want this little guy or girl."

Tears of joy splashed onto her cheeks. "You do?"

"I do. I love you. I think I fell in love with you at our wedding, when we were dancing and you stepped on my toes—"

"I did not." She smiled. "You stepped on mine."

"Did not." He returned her smile.

"Did, too."

"Either way, I knew in that moment that my life would never be the same. But the question is, what do you want?"

She couldn't believe he was saying everything she wanted to hear. "I want you, too. I think I fell for you back at Gianna and Dario's wedding, but I was too stubborn to acknowledge it to myself or anyone."

"Ah, see…it was my dance moves." He smiled proudly. "They won you over."

She let out a little laugh. "Is that what you call what you do on the dance floor?"

"Hey, be nice." He continued to smile at her.

Her laughter bubbled over into a full belly laugh with happy tears in her eyes. It wasn't the thought of him dancing, but rather a release of her pent-up worries. Her father had been right—Franco loved her. Her heart swelled with joy.

Then Franco moved to kneel down on one knee. He took her hand in his.

"Franco, what are you doing?" Heat warmed in her chest and rushed to her cheeks.

"Something that I should have done months ago. I'm properly proposing to you."

"Oh." Her heart fluttered in her chest as her lips bowed in a smile.

"Carla Falco Marchello, I fell for you the first time we met in Lake Como. Your bright smile and sparkling eyes drew me in. But it was your caring heart and generous spirit that completely put me under your spell. I couldn't imagine living my life without you. You are my sunshine in the morning and my twinkling star at night. Please say that you'll marry me."

"But...but we are married."

"Will you marry me again?"

She knelt down in front of him and threw her arms around his neck. "Of course I will. I'll marry you over and over again. I love you."

"I love you, too." He leaned forward and claimed her lips with a kiss that promised love forever.

EPILOGUE

Five months later,
a small chapel in Lake Como

IT WAS A wedding do-over.

Carla never would have imagined that six months after saying *I do* to Franco, she'd be saying those words again and meaning them. This time it all felt right. Her father was there to walk her down the aisle, and she felt her mother's love shining down upon her.

Carla's hand moved to her expanding midsection. "I love you, little one. And so does your daddy—"

Knock. Knock.

"Unless you're Franco, you can come in." Carla turned back to the mirror.

She turned this way and that way in the same wedding gown. It had to be let out a little bit for her baby bump. There was something missing, but she couldn't put her finger on what it was.

Gianna poked her head inside the door. "It's just me. Is it all right if I come in?"

"Of course it is. You're my matron of honor." She glanced past her cousin. "Where's your husband?"

"He's changing Georgia's diaper."

"Wow. Impressive." She couldn't help but wonder if Franco would be that involved with their baby. If his current actions of attending all her doctors' appointment and helping to decorate the nursery in their new house were any indication, he was going to be an amazing father.

"I'm so happy for you." Gianna hugged her.

When they parted, Carla swiped at the tears of joy tracking down her freshly made-up face. "Everything is working out for the both of us. We've both found the men of our dreams. And we're sisters-in-law, cousins and best friends."

Gianna smiled brightly. "I don't think we could be closer if we were sisters."

"You are like a sister to me."

They hugged again. But Gianna quickly pulled back. "As much as I want to stand here celebrating all that is good in our lives, you have an anxious bridegroom waiting for you. We better get you down that aisle."

"I'm ready." She'd been ready for a while now. She'd been so anxious to say *I do* again and this time mean it with all her heart.

Gianna frowned at her.

"What did I forget? I keep feeling like I've forgotten something."

"First, we have to fix your makeup. Have a seat."

Carla did as told and Gianna set to work covering the trail of her happy tears, but Carla was quite certain there would be many more of those happy tears spilled today. A little cover-up and powder fixed things.

Gianna stepped back to admire her work. "You're frowning. Don't you like what I did?"

"It's not that. You did a great job. I just can't shake the feeling I'm forgetting something important."

"Oh, that reminds me. Your father gave me something to pass on to you." Gianna rushed over to the chair where she'd placed her beaded purse. When she turned around, she had a string of pearls in her hand. "Your father said you wanted something of your mother's to wear when you walked down the aisle. He said your mother wore this necklace on their wedding day."

Again the tears rushed to her eyes. Carla blinked and fanned her face, trying to keep her emotions under control so she didn't mess up her makeup again.

"Can you put them on me?" Carla turned around. After her cousin hooked the clasp, Carla fingered the pearls as her heart filled with love for those who'd passed through her life, those who were in it and, as her hand lowered to her slightly round abdomen, those who would soon enter her life. "Now I'm ready."

With her father at her side, they set off down the aisle. Whereas the first time Carla had married Franco, her knees had felt like gelatin, this time her legs felt sturdy and she had to restrain herself from rushing down the aisle.

This time when she met Franco's steady gaze, she smiled—a big, sunny, full-of-love smile. This time they were getting married for all the right reasons.

And their families were with them. His grandfather and her father were in the chapel without any arguments. Miracles really did happen.

And though their respective businesses were both important to them, they were no longer the center of their world. Their love and their growing family would be their focus. The rest of it would fall into place.

And when she finally stopped next to Franco, she

turned to her father, who kissed her cheek. And then she turned back to Franco.

She couldn't help herself. She whispered, "I love you."

He whispered back, "I love you, too. Let's get married. Again."

* * * * *

COMING SOON!

We really hope you enjoyed reading this book.
If you're looking for more romance, be sure to
head to the shops when new books are
available on

Thursday 2nd
September

To see which titles are coming soon, please visit

millsandboon.co.uk/nextmonth

MILLS & BOON

Coming next month

RECLAIMING THE PRINCE'S HEART
Rebecca Winters

Rini was hooked up to an IV and one of the nursing staff was checking his vital signs. After a while Luna could tell he was coming to because he moved his strong legs and turned his head to the other side of the pillow.

She moved to the other side of his bed to be close to him. Without thinking, she whispered, "Jeu carezel tei, Rini," in her native language. It meant I love you.

Suddenly he opened those translucent gray eyes she'd thought she'd never see again. They stared at her without recognition. She assumed it was because he was still sedated. "Ti discurras rumantch?"

Her heart turned over because he'd heard her outpouring of love and understood. He'd just asked her if she spoke Romansh. That was the strange language no one understood?

"Gea." Yes, yes, yes.

"How come no one else can communicate? Where am I? I've been going insane that no one understands me. But you do. Why? Do you know me?"

His questions were fired one after another. The last question shocked her, but now was not the time to try and understand what was going on.

"I know you very well." Her voice shook. "Your name is Rini and I'm your wife, Luna."

An incredulous expression entered his intelligent eyes. "Impossible! I've never been married."

Help. Something was terribly wrong. Don't panic, Luna. "Thank heaven you're alive and that I've found you. You're in a hospital in Rezana, Slovenia. I'm going to take you home. A helicopter is on the way."

At that moment Carlo appeared at the door. He motioned her to come out in the hall. Her gaze shot back to her precious husband who was so disoriented, she realized he was still under the effects of the anesthetic. "I have to leave you for a few minutes."

"You can't go. No one else understands me." He sounded utterly frantic. It wrenched her heart.

"I promise I'll see you in a few minutes. Trust me."

Continue reading
RECLAIMING THE PRINCE'S HEART
Rebecca Winters

Available next month
www.millsandboon.co.uk